# The Way Back

Jeff Turner

PAGE PUBLISHING, INC.
New York, NY

First originally published by Page Publishing, Inc. 2013

ISBN 978-1-62838-143-6 (pbk)
ISBN 978-1-62838-144-3 (digital)

Printed in the United States of America

Cover design by Zachary Turner and Julianna Cameron

# *One*

I never caught my wife in the sack with her lover. She was never spotted with a mysterious stranger by anyone from the neighborhood or work. She never allowed any unexplained credit card charges to show up on the monthly bills. Instead, she unwittingly left a trail for a furry little creature to discover, which eventually exposed her deception and unleashed dark forces into our lives.

A mouse told me my wife was having an affair.

I know this sounds ridiculous but it's true. If a mouse hadn't set into motion a chain of disturbing events, I might've never discovered her betrayal. She skillfully covered her tracks so that the often telltale signs of infidelity never met anyone's eye.

This tale must be told from the very beginning, a cold and windy Saturday evening in mid-October. While we were having dinner, my wife Claire and I thought we heard scratching coming from the attic above. Actually our 14 year-old son Nathan thought he heard sounds even before we sat down, but figured it was the wind causing tree branches to scrape against the roof. At one point we stopped eating and became still, listening for a few moments. The scratching stopped but then returned in earnest, this time accompanied by a pitter-pattering across the length of the ceiling.

Mice ... and from the sounds of it, quite a few. No one likes to hear mice scurrying through their house, but we weren't surprised given the time of year and the fact that nights were getting colder in Connecticut. My first reaction was to grab a flashlight after dinner and go up for a quick look, but decided it made more sense to pick up some mouse poison the next day and do my scouting then.

So on a Sunday afternoon, there I stood in the attic—the big game hunter—hot on the trail of any tell-tale signs of mouse droppings or nests. I was alone in the house, Claire and Nathan had left earlier to do some shopping at the retail outlets in nearby Clinton and Westbrook. Armed with several packages of poison gel cubes and my flashlight, I scanned the length of the joists, as well as the surrounding eaves in the area just above the dining room. It had been a while since anyone had been in this portion of the attic; a layer of dust coated the plywood pathway and surface of the insulation. Nothing looked disturbed and no fresh prints of any kind were evident. I didn't see anything out of the ordinary.

Slipping the packages of poison into my breast pocket, I decided to pull up sections of insulation and inspect the bare plasterboard underneath. I moved along the joists on all fours. The first three attempts yielded nothing but clouds of dust and fiberglass particles. The fourth upturned section revealed what I was looking for: piles of rod shaped droppings and small pieces of shredded insulation, cardboard, and what appeared to be furniture stuffing. The scattered debris ran the length of a joist, which likely accounted for the back and forth scurrying we'd heard last night. While I couldn't see a nest or any actual mice, it was obvious I had found one of their main passageways and some building materials.

I broke open one of packets of poison and placed gel cubes at intervals along the joist. I was about to put the insulation back when I noticed what appeared to be shredded pieces of red foil Christmas paper at the far end of the joist. I thought it strange to find Christmas paper here, and went over to the opposite side of the attic to inspect the cardboard boxes holding our holiday decorations. When I tipped one of the boxes on its side, I discovered that the mice had gnawed through the bottom. Apparently they'd feasted on a couple of old candy canes that somehow had been left in the bottom of the box, and chewed everything in their search for more. Because the long rolls of wrapping paper inside the box were ruined from clawing and nibbling, I began removing them and setting them aside for the trash.

I stopped when I saw some chewed edges of white paper extending from inside the red foil roll. Holding the roll up to the light and peering through it like a telescope, I could see some papers that had been wedged inside. I had no idea what the papers were or what they were doing there. I pulled the nibbled pages out and began unrolling them, finding three sheets in all. They were copies of email correspondences.

I was both puzzled and curious, but needed my reading glasses to make out the small email print. I brought the pages downstairs with me and spread them out on the dining room table, unfurling the edges and pressing the torn pieces together. Then I put on my glasses and looked at what I found.

And so it was that I discovered Claire's secret hiding place, as well as her love letters to another man.

At first, I didn't know what they were. I suppose I was thrown off by the idea that Claire, always clever, would keep something so private and incriminating, but then, who would possibly go looking for, much less stumble upon, something wedged inside a roll of Christmas wrapping paper?

As the realization of what I'd just found washed over me, my heart began racing and my eyes darted from paragraph to paragraph like I was on speed. I tried to control my breathing. The words blurred together and nothing made sense.

I told myself there was no way this could be true, that there had to be some mistake on my part and that a logical explanation from Claire would immediately clear things up. I was jumping to conclusions and overreacting. I was absolutely certain that Claire would never get involved with another man, nor could she. She was married, had a teenage son and a demanding career. How could she possibly fit in an affair around all this? She didn't have any exclusive male friends in her life, or so I thought. Besides, we didn't keep secrets.

But the emails spoke to the contrary, and as I looked them over nothing seemed to fit or make sense. I felt I was in a fog, shuttling back and forth between anger and disbelief. I let out a deep breath and had to will myself to calm down.

It took me a minute or two to follow the flow of email exchanges. He did not use his name, nor did Claire. There were eight emails in all, four from Claire and four from him. The best I could tell, the emails were exchanged about a year ago, although two of the dates had been nibbled away by the mice.

Claire used her AOL screen name, *Clairell*, and his was *Strap95* from Earthlink. There were no greetings or closings by name, just text. I got a pen and piece of paper from the kitchen and wrote down his screen name for later reference, sticking the paper in the back pocket of my jeans.

I started at the very beginning, slowly reading one paragraph at a time and absorbing what had been written. The first email was initiated by Claire and was apparently an early evening follow-up to a daytime rendezvous:

*I wanted you to know that I got home safely. I was in the door well before J and he does not suspect a thing, so please don't worry. I had a wonderful time with you this afternoon, although it is getting harder and harder for me to say goodbye. I am still tingling all over. When we're together nothing else seems to matter, it's as if the whole world stops when I'm with you. I can't wait to see you again. Write me if you can when you get home.*

Talk about jumping right into the fire. Obviously this wasn't the first time Claire had seen this guy, which immediately made me wonder how long this had been going on. My eyes fixed on, 'tingling all over.' "You've got to be kidding me," I said aloud. This did not look good, not good at all. I closed my eyes and tried to imagine my wife screwing another man, my groin momentarily stirring. I drummed my fingertips on the table and could feel the muscles tensing throughout my body.

Later that same evening, Claire's lover wrote back:

*When I saw that I had mail waiting from you, I became excited and couldn't stop smiling. Talk about feeling like a teenager again! Thank you for getting free today and seeing me. You looked so beautiful and sexy, as usual. I carried your scent home with me in the car and it made me relive the entire afternoon. I miss you already.*

Now my thoughts centered on the mysterious stranger, and my mind flooded with questions. Who was this guy? Did I know him? Did he live around here? Was he married? Was he young or old? My eyes were glued to, 'I carried your scent home with me,' and felt anger bubbling up like hot lava inside of me. This can't be happening, I thought. I swallowed and stared down at the table. How could I have missed what was going on with this kind of involvement? Was I *that* oblivious to my wife and our marriage?

The next email was written at night a few days later.

*Thank you for yesterday. It was so nice to spend a few hours sitting by the water. We have such a lovely spot. You make me feel so warm and appreciated. I feel as if I rambled on yesterday, especially about the accident, but I guess I needed to say the things I shared. So now you know. Thank you for your kind words and gentle understanding. I wish you were around back then, but I'm so glad you're here now. I don't feel so alone anymore.*

This email bothered me more than Claire's first, and I went from angry to sad. I was upset that Claire had shared our private lives, namely the tragedy that rocked us as a family. Claire had reached out to another guy who apparently provided what I hadn't. This was obviously not your casual affair, the old one night stand. Nope, this had escalated into something much more involved and serious, the words hitting me between the eyes like a mallet. I stared out the window trying to make sense out of this, massaging my temples with my fingertips. It seemed I could handle the sexual element better than the emotional bond, or at least I thought. I was clearly threatened by what they shared and the depth of their involvement.

I felt psychologically violated and betrayed, which stoked my fire even more. How could she have done this? What we went through was no one's business but ours. I wondered if Claire told this guy about our therapy sessions or the drinking problem I had when we hit rock bottom. My mind was spinning, a million thoughts racing through it. I felt like I'd entered another world.

A day passed before her lover wrote back:

*Sorry I couldn't get back to you sooner, but things got a bit crazy. I really enjoyed our time together, too. I thought a lot about what you shared, and can only imagine how dreadful it must have been for you and especially Nathan. I want you to know that I feel your pain, and will always be there to listen if you feel like sharing more. I am looking forward to next week. If I don't hear from you I will meet you Wednesday at noon. You know where. Hugs to you.*

I seethed when I read the reference to Nathan. She had no business dragging his problems into this. How could this guy possibly know anything about the pain my son endured, let alone my family? He didn't know us. I slouched back in the chair and ran my hands through my hair, then clasped them behind my head. This is bad, I thought, far worse than I could have ever imagined. Screwing my wife was one thing, nosing around my kid was another. I was getting angrier by the moment.

The next exchanges had been badly damaged by the mice, and portions were missing. I could not tell when Claire sent hers, but in it she wrote:

*... touched by the gift. You make me feel so special and the gift is so symbolic, something to be treasured forever. I would never have thought of something like this. I will be home alone all day tomorrow, so call me if you can. Thank you again for your thoughtfulness, for being you.*

So now we're into gift giving. I was curious as to what the 'symbolic' gift was. A photograph, perhaps, or a special book or article of clothing? I didn't know what the unfaithful gave each other nowadays. Maybe there was a shop in the mall that specialized in gifts for that special cheater or fraud in your life. Was the gift hidden like these letters or did Claire flaunt it right under my nose? Would I even notice if she wore something different or placed something special on her bureau or bedside stand? Probably not, but you could bet that I was going to start sniffing around. I winced when I reread the swipe at me, 'I would never have thought of something like this.'

Parts of his reply were also missing, including the date. He wrote:

*... making you happy. You looked so thrilled when you saw the gift. You deserved something special because you are so special. Have you looked into getting away for the day and going to Newport? We could meet at our spot in the morning, leave your car somewhere and ...*

The end of that sentence was chewed apart but the email finished with:

*... place we can stay. Tomorrow can't come soon enough. I can't wait to see you again.*

I wondered what words were missing, although it was obvious that this bastard had a getaway day in the works, including checking in somewhere and drilling my wife in the sack. This guy could obviously lay it on thick, a smooth operator. I wondered what he did for a living. It was hard for me to believe that Claire had fallen for this chump and his corny psychobabble.

I heard a car outside and froze, thinking Claire and Nathan had returned home early from their shopping. I did not want them walking in on me like this. I hurriedly gathered up the pages, but relaxed when I saw that it was just a car from the neighborhood driving slowly around the block. I didn't want to get caught with these emails, at least not now. I knew I needed some kind of plan on how I was going to handle this, time to think things through.

I looked at the last exchanges, dated November 9. They were undamaged:

*I am counting the hours until we go away tomorrow. I've told people at work that I'm doing a site visitation at the other end of the state and will be gone for the entire day. N is going to his friend's house after school and has been invited to dinner—I'll pick him up on the way home. J will be at the college working late and won't know the difference anyway. I'll meet you at 7:30. Sweet dreams.*

It takes two to tango, I thought, and Claire had obviously helped plan this and cover her flank. I got the paper I'd stuck in my jeans and jotted down November 10. I would later get a calendar to see if I could reconstruct what we were doing that day. I felt queasy. My wife had used deception and dishonesty to run around and knock boots with another man. In the process, she lied to her employer, the people she worked with, her husband and her son.

The final email in the chain was sent by Claire's lover a few hours later that same evening. He wrote:

*That was me who called a little while ago and hung up. I didn't know Jack was home. I'm sorry. Anyway, it sounds like you have all your bases covered for tomorrow—so do I. It took a little more juggling than I thought, but it will be worth it. No one will know or suspect a thing. Getting away and spending a whole day with you will be like a dream come true. We've talked about it for so long, and now we're actually doing it. Can't wait! I will meet you in the morning where we planned and we'll go in the Saab.*

And that was it. I stared at the last page, hoping to learn more but knowing I wouldn't, at least not now. The two lovers had planned their day, manipulated and tricked those who stood in the way, and I could only surmise pulled it off without a hitch. I didn't know if there were any more email exchanges after this, or before, but I would comb the house when I had more time and knew I had the place to myself.

I got up and got a beer from the refrigerator and sat down in the living room. My head was throbbing and I pressed the cold can against my forehead for some relief. The emails had hit me like a hammer blow, and I was really shaken, waves of anger and hostility pulsating through me. I knew that I had to get myself back under control.

I sat there and tried to figure out what I was going to do. I closed my eyes, willing my mind to work, trying to think of how to best approach this. After a few moments, I got up and gathered the emails. I made copies of them in the study, where we had a small copier. Once I did this, I hid the copies as well as the notes I'd taken in a zippered divider in my briefcase. I would put them in a safer, more secure location later. Then I went back up to the attic and put the original pages back into the red foil tube the way I found them, then returned all the rolls of wrapping paper back into the cardboard box. I restored the box to its original location, positioning it the way I found it.

I went over to where I found the mouse droppings and picked up all the red foil scraps, but left the insulation pulled back. I retrieved the gel cubes I had placed along the joist, put them back in the packet, and slipped it back in my pocket. I descended the staircase and as I reached down to refold it, I hesitated and thought for a moment. I decided to leave the staircase down and kept the light on in the attic.

I went into the kitchen and finished my beer, tossed it in the garbage and got another. Claire and Nathan were sure to arrive shortly, and I didn't want to be here. Too much was swirling around in my head, and I knew I was a powder keg just waiting to explode. I needed to get out of the house and be alone for a while. Perhaps a drive in the car would give me more time to see things more clearly. I jotted a quick note, saying that I needed to get some more mouse poison and run a few other errands, and left it in plain view on the kitchen counter.

I drove around aimlessly under a dull and heavy sky for a few hours while trying to sort things out. Passages from the emails replayed in my head, an endless loop of sadness and dismay. I told myself over and over that all I had read were words, that nothing on paper had been confirmed or proven as factual. This was not solid ground for confrontation. Claire could deny every accusation I made, and the burden of proof would then rest squarely on my shoulders. At this point I had none, except for a few dated, nibbled emails. I did not know who her lover was, how many times they saw each other or even if they were still seeing each other. Obviously the picture I had was incomplete and fuzzy.

The last thing I wanted, was to go off half-cocked and do something I'd later regret. I knew that cooler heads had to prevail. Claire could listen to what I had to say and then choose to leave me, and I didn't want that. We'd been through too much already. The fact that all this had implications for Nathan added to my caution. He had been through one devastating crisis in his young life and didn't need another.

I decided the smartest thing to do right now was sit tight and not make any decisions in the middle of turmoil. I needed to lay low and begin paying more attention to what was going on around me, especially Claire's comings and goings. The emails were a warning shot across the bow and I vowed not to get caught sleeping again. More snooping was definitely on the horizon.

As I headed home, I sorted out what I knew and what I didn't. Assuming the emails were factual, the exchanges took place about a year ago, although I had no idea when the relationship began or how long it had continued. Whether or not Claire was still seeing this guy was the one piece really rankling me.

I pulled into the garage and just sat there for a moment or two. As frustrating and annoying as this had become, I was not in the dark. On the contrary, I'd learned some things that would hopefully lead to a trail. For instance, I had the guy's email address and knew my wife and he had talked by phone. I knew at one time he drove a Saab. He had also given her a 'symbolic' gift, something Claire vowed to treasure forever. I'd also learned they planned a day trip to Newport, and I had the date for that. They sometimes met at a certain location before going anywhere, and finally, they sometimes liked to sit and talk by the water.

I realized that I had more information than I first thought, and more than a few things to mull over. It was a beginning. I couldn't help but wonder what kind of journey this would take me on, what I would find along the way.

When I walked through the house, I realized that Claire and Nathan were downstairs in the family room eating pizza and watching television. I announced that I'd join them after setting down more mouse poison in the attic. The staircase was still down and the attic light on. Once I got up there, I placed the gel cubes along the joists, then returned the insulation to its original location. Before I left I went over to the box of Christmas wrapping paper and found the red foil roll. I pulled it from the box and held it up again to the light, eye balling one end then the other.

Claire's emails had disappeared, as I had suspected they would.

# *Two*

I suppose I slept that night, though I'd be hard pressed to say when I finally drifted off. I'd gone to bed around eleven, knowing I needed sleep after such an emotionally rugged day, but lay awake for hours. I finally got up around midnight, having had my fill of pillow pounding, thrashing around and checking the clock. I poured myself a stiff drink to help me relax and fell asleep on the living room couch only to awaken with a start around two o'clock, one of those stupors in which you don't really know where you are or how you got there. I stumbled my way back to bed, where sleep eventually overtook me deep into the night.

I blinked my eyes to the gray morning light and realized I'd slept later than usual. When I went to the kitchen to get some coffee, I found Claire and Nathan caught up in their morning routines and in their own worlds, which suited me just fine. I remembered from a conversation last night that Claire was dropping Nathan off at school today, and that because he was staying after school to work on a history project, I would be picking him up. The three of us talked on the fly as I tried to act as normal as possible, chiming in with the right words and postures. I'd done the same thing with Claire last night, bridling my emotions while acting polite and civil. No smoldering anger, no cold words. Judging from Claire's behavior, I had no reason to believe that she sensed anything was wrong or out of the ordinary.

A light rain began falling as I left the house and headed to work. I'm an associate professor of humanities at Guilford College, a small private college located on the Connecticut shoreline, about halfway between New London and New Haven. I've been here for six years and before that I briefly taught at the University of Massachusetts at Amherst. At Guilford I teach courses in both composition and literature, usually one course in the fall and two in the spring.

The commute to Guilford from Spencer Plain takes me about 20 minutes and this morning I found myself with time to spare. I picked up a coffee at a drive-thru just outside the campus and still got to the classroom about 10 minutes before any of my students. Although I was dragging, I was glad to be teaching. I needed to have my attention diverted from the crap rattling around in my head, at least for a little while.

That morning's class was a course in creative writing. I began putting the desks in a circle, a seating arrangement I prefer when I teach. Over the years, I've found that a circular design enables students to talk face to face rather than at obstructed or awkward angles. I staked off my turf by placing my briefcase next to one of the chairs and my coffee on the desktop.

I was moving the last of the desks into place when students began filing in. Lois Winslow and Rachel Pond were among the first to arrive. They were in the midst of a lively conversation, both talking animatedly with their hands and giggling. Rachel wore a lime green rain poncho and carried an umbrella under her arm, her cheeks rosy from the cold weather. As she shook the umbrella dry, she looked over at me and smiled, wrinkling her nose.

The two of them were among my brightest writers and thinkers. They were best friends and added a special dimension to this particular class. I have a soft spot for nontraditional students, probably because of their gritty determination to push forward with their education while balancing job and household demands. Neither was afraid to ask questions or speak out in class, and both had learned to ignore the whispered titters behind them that sometimes came from their younger counterparts.

Sam Chiang strolled in next, a diminutive, floppy-haired kid. In the classroom he liked to park in a seat near me, and preferred to be called Chiang, not Sam. He was a shy one when the semester started, someone who tended to avoid eye contact and didn't give off many signals. All I knew about him in the beginning was that he was Chinese-American, had family in Boston, and was graduating from Guilford the following year. As the weeks went by, though, he came out of his shell and warmed up to me and the other students, especially Lois and Rachel. He began asking questions in class, and contributing his ideas and thoughts to discussions. Before long he was hanging around after class and even made it a point to drop by my office to shoot the breeze. Chiang had enormous potential as a writer: he was well read, had an impressive command of the English language, and laid claim to an inquiring, imaginative mind.

I wished that I could say the same about Barry Crider, who as usual was the last to arrive and frowned the minute he saw the desks arranged in a circle. While most students seemed to enjoy the classroom set up this way, unprepared or unmotivated buffoons like Crider invariably didn't, a circle hardly being the setting to hide or catch a few winks. As far as I was concerned, this was just another example of his lousy attitude about the course in general and me in particular.

Crider was a big guy, wide and beefy, who wore his dirty blonde hair in dread locks and had a scraggly goatee, which combined to give him a skuzzy appearance. He was a cocky know-it-all type who had really gotten under my skin this semester. Every so often I'd get a student like this, a collegiate blowhard bent on usurping my authority and challenging everything under the sun. Whenever I voiced an opinion during classroom discussions, this guy would give me a pained, anguished expression—not unlike the facial strain accompanying constipation—and disagree.

Crider had carried on like this since the beginning of the semester, acting as if he were some kind of self-proclaimed expert in creative writing, gracing the class with a steady stream of boneheaded prattle. I often wondered how Crider got this far in his studies at Guilford College, and whether he'd pulled the same crap with other professors. I'd tolerated his classroom antics so far without any major bloodshed, although my patience was wearing thin. During the past few weeks, I'd had to sit on him a few times for inappropriate language and rudeness to other students. Crider's classmates usually rolled their eyes when he opened his mouth, and I think most of them regarded him as a bully, as well as a bore. I regarded him as a social misfit and certified block head.

He looked as arrogant as ever as he strutted over to a chair and pulled it a few feet away from the circle—a statement I suppose—and glanced my way to see if I was watching. I pretended I wasn't as I slipped off my sports jacket and draped it over my chair. Maybe his other teachers bowed to his insolence or buckled under his intimidation, but there was no way in hell that I was going to give him the benefit of a reaction or prance around his shenanigans.

He finally sat down next to Anthony Slocum, his bosom buddy. Someone told me the two of them were tight, taking many of the same classes and partying the weekends away. Slocum was supposed to be a top scholarship baseball player at Guilford, which didn't impress me in the least. All I knew was that the two of them were burrs under my saddle. In addition to being unmotivated, both were unimaginative, lousy writers. In class Crider manufactured nothing but rhetorical slag, while Slocum had mastered the fine art of sleeping while sitting up, robbing the class of precious oxygen. Two developmentally delayed chumps.

I walked over and closed the classroom door, taking my seat in the circle next to Chiang.

I opened a file folder containing my lecture notes. "Last week we discussed the concept of moral positioning in our writing and various ways to achieve it. It's important for writers to have some sort of moral philosophy, a belief system that transmits your values and teaches the reader something about life."

I pried the lid off my coffee, blew on it and took a sip. "Good writers are caring, sensitive people. They feel. They're compassionate."

I stopped when I realized that my voice was competing with a conversation to my left. I wasn't surprised to see that Crider was the culprit, talking to Slocum. Talking in class when I'm speaking–or anyone else for that matter–is a sore spot for me, and this wasn't the first time I'd spoken to either one of them about it. This morning, it was obvious that Crider could have cared less that the class had begun. He was sharing something juicy, cupping his hand over his mouth and leaning closer to Slocum, who was nodding his head and chuckling.

"Gentlemen." I raised my voice to get their attention.

Crider took his sweet time finishing whatever he was saying to Slocum, then turned to me. I stared at him with iron in my eyes and measured my words. "Whenever you're ready to join the rest of us, Mr. Crider." Slocum shifted in his chair.

Crider shook his head like I was the bad guy, then put two fingers to his brow and directed a mock salute my way. "Yes sir," he smirked, his voice laced with sarcasm. He reached into his back pack and pulled out a book, opening it on his desk. No apology, no remorse.

It took some doing to return to the group. "Let's try this again," I said. "All of us are on a moral journey. Think about your own journey, especially when you were younger. Think about the values that have become important to you, the things in life that truly matter or mean something. As children you learned the difference between right and wrong and the importance of such traits as responsibility, honesty and forgiveness. The words and actions of your characters will reflect what you've learned, what hurts and what feels good."

I leaned forward on my elbows. "This is what makes the moral of the story so important, so interesting. Plot lines involving good guys and bad guys invariably require a moral compass, one that illuminates what you regard to be the right or proper thing to do. Of course, only you can decide who holds the moral high ground in your writings. You're the gatekeeper. For many writers, this is the stuff heroes are made of, and various techniques can be used to capture the struggle between good and evil. The showdown that unfolds serves to illuminate this struggle and in so doing, becomes the moral fiber of what you're writing."

I paused for a few moments. "Morality and values walk hand in hand. The characters you create reflect what you consider important and care about in life, values like kindness or loyalty. Similarly, your dark characters can be a vehicle for what you find distasteful or disdain, like the strong arm tactics of a schoolyard bully or the dishonesty of an unfaithful spouse."

Images of Claire and the emails I found crept into my mind. I looked down at the floor.

It took me a few seconds to refocus. I continued: "Keep in mind that the most believable and interesting characters are those with depth, especially the heroes. The reader must be able to truly see the world through their eyes, to understand their words and deeds. We need to appreciate what they feel, why they care, how they bleed."

Across from me, Rachel Pond nodded. She waited until I finished and said, "Like a Henry Fleming." Last week the class analyzed the writing style of Stephen Crane in *The Red Badge of Courage*.

Rachel and I looked at each other. She was married, in her late thirties and quite attractive, blond hair complementing high cheekbones and a pair of striking, pale blue eyes.

"Exactly," I said. "Like a Henry Fleming. Crane hooks us because we can see the horrors of war through a soldier's eyes, especially Fleming's inner turmoil readying for battle."

I looked around at the class. "How did Crane achieve this?"

The wind picked up outside, driving a heavier rain against the window.

A few seats away, Willie Fraser shifted in his chair. I looked his way and saw that he wanted to speak. I raised my eyebrows and nodded slightly, coaxing him.

Willie was a nontraditional student, probably in his mid-fifties. He had graying hair and oversized glasses, always wore an easy smile. Willie was a member of the Mohegan Native American tribe, which owned the enormously successful Mohegan Sun resort and casino, located about 45 minutes away in the town of Uncasville. Because he was a tribal member, Willie received free tuition and other incentives to finish his college degree. While he had labored through some of his course work at Guilford, he never gave up and was now one semester away from getting his diploma. A semiskilled worker most of his life, Willie told me that never in his wildest imagination did he think he would ever attend college, let alone graduate. This was of course before the tribe struck gold and spread wealth among its people. I had him in a literature course last spring and was impressed with his love for books, and this semester he was developing into a decent writer. I liked him a lot.

Willie pushed his thick glasses up against the bridge of his nose with his forefinger. "He made Fleming ordinary, like one of us. He was just a soldier, a youngster facing the unknown. He'd joined the army against the wishes of his mother and wanted to be a hero. But he panicked and ran away from battle and was afraid he'd do it again. He was ashamed of himself. He didn't want to be a coward."

"That's right," I said, approval in my voice. "None of us do. Fleming felt the crossfire of emotions that any one of us would have felt in similar circumstances, especially the smell of fear, which is what makes this character so compelling, so believable."

My eyes roamed the room. I went on: "Henry Fleming is a human being at odds with himself–embattled on the inside, with troubling emotions and torn about how he should act. Crane shows how we can rise above our failures and shortcomings and achieve heroic qualities like a Henry Fleming. When Fleming returns to his unit and goes into battle again, he simultaneously wages an inner war against fear and cowardice. As we know, he chooses to charge the moral high ground, in the process discovering the bravery of heroism and the meaning of courage."

Lois Winslow broke into the discussion. "So perfection isn't a necessary character trait of heroism?"

I shook my head. "Oh, no. No one is perfect—remember even Superman's cape gets wrinkled. Instead of perfection the central character has faults or faces internal struggles, which have to be overcome to successfully meet the challenge." I paused. "In Fleming's case, he had to first wrestle with fear before he experienced bravery or courage."

I looked down at the coffee container cradled in my hands. "We must also keep in mind that not all literary heroes are victorious. The good guy doesn't always ride off triumphantly into the sunset. Some characters have heroic potential but fail in the end."

I picked up the pace. "Take Malamud's character of Roy Hobbs in *The Natural*. Malamud creates a baseball hero of mythological proportion, a fresh-faced farm boy blessed with natural talent. He is given his Arthurian Excalibur–a baseball bat forged by the gods–and ends up playing for a team called the Knights. How fitting. Along the way, though, Hobbs chooses to spurn his natural gifts in favor of women, fame and fortune. In short, the knight errant chooses pleasure over principle, in the process falling from grace and having to pay a terrible price for his flaws. Even his entrusted Excalibur deserts him in his moment of trial. He is proven an unworthy hero."

To my left, Crider stirred. He'd been text messaging ever since the class began, no doubt reading and sending a steady stream of blather and trash. I don't allow electronic entertainment devices in my class, and virtually all of my students honor my wishes. I see texting in class as disrespectful, disruptive and irritating to both teachers and students. But despite repeated warnings, Crider snuck his in anyway, just so at his whim or fancy he could text message his muddleheaded friends during class time.

Anyway, Crider heard my last comment about Roy Hobbs and jerked his head upwards, stiffening his shoulders. He interrupted: "That's bogus, man. You don't know what you're talking about. Hobbs was a freakin' hero, he won the game with a home run. Everyone knows that."

His voice was loud and biting, a scathing rebuke to let everyone know I hadn't gotten the story straight. Crider looked around at the class, lifting his head like an ostrich, and smiled triumphantly with a lopsided, moronic grin.

Next to him, Slocum nodded his head in animated agreement, acting as if his mentor had just solved the mystery of the Bermuda Triangle or developed a plan to put an end to global warming. Slocum wore a baseball cap with the bill turned sideways at one of those foolish angles, the hat extra-large so that he could stick his ears inside. He wore an oversized NY Jets football jersey and baggy gym shorts that hung below his knees, unlaced high topped sneakers and no socks. I'm sure he wanted to look like some kind of bad-ass from the streets, but instead he looked like a jug head from the streets of Mayberry.

I didn't respond right away, instead turned my head and looked out the window. The sky was dark purple with thick rolling storm clouds, sheets of hard rain sweeping the grounds. I could hear the faint rumble of thunder in the distance.

I waited some more. In my mind, Robert Redford was circling the bases under a shower of sparks from the shattered stadium lights.

Finally I looked over at Crider. "A game winning homer?" I said, arching my eyebrows in mock surprise. "Really? Is that how the novel ends?"

I would have bet my eyetooth that neither of these MTV nincompoops had read the book, nor even knew that one had been written. I waited patiently for an answer but didn't get one. Instead, Crider looked around, no doubt hoping for someone to get him off the hook. He had a snowball's chance in hell of being rescued, which amused me to no end.

I couldn't resist pushing the knife in a little deeper. I suppose in retrospect I should have let all of this go, but I was still smoldering about the earlier rudeness and all the crap these two derelicts had shoveled in my stall since the semester began. I also knew I had a short fuse and was on edge because of Claire. The previous night was catching up to me, and I was drained from too little sleep and too much raw emotion.

I leaned back in my chair, clasped my hands behind my head. "Of course, you read the book, right?"

Crider froze up and looked at the floor.

I repeated myself, "Right?"

He gave a little snort and shook his head, slouching in the chair. His face had gone ghastly white, no doubt the result of a hot air leak from his punctured, oversized ego. The classroom was silent except for muffled voices and footsteps out in the hallway.

Meanwhile, Slocum had turned sideways in his chair and was trying his hardest to somehow disappear into thin air. However, I wasn't about to leave him unscathed. "Surely you can do better than that, Mr. Slocum, I mean, after all you did agree with him. Why don't you pony up and enlighten us, show everyone your 'A' game." I flashed him a grin. "Come on, bail your buddy out and tell us what happens at the end of the novel."

Slocum looked at me and coughed nervously. His cheeks flushed and his eyes darted back and forth. He lowered his head, decided to study his fingers. Another moment of silence.

I happened to look over at Rachel, who brought her hand up to her face to suppress the slightest touch of a smile. Our eyes briefly linked.

I cleared my throat and scanned the class. "Surely someone can tell me how the novel ends, and I don't mean from a Hollywood screenplay."

I heard some whispering and soft laughter. After a few moments, Chiang raised his hand.

"You've read the book?" I asked. "Care to share?"

Chiang nodded and said, "I read it a while ago, but I think this is pretty much what happened. The Knights had rallied but were down to their last out. Hobbs came to the plate with a chance to be the hero. The pitcher takes one look at Hobbs and I believe faints right on the mound."

Chiang paused and looked at me. I nodded for him to continue.

He said: "The other team brings a rookie relief pitcher in from the bullpen. He was young and cocky and very fast. Hobbs hits a ball out of the park foul but breaks Wonderboy, his special bat. He gets another bat but the magic is gone. The pitcher rears back and Hobbs strikes out. The Knights lose and Hobbs never plays again."

"End of game, end of story?" I asked.

Chiang tilted his head. "What do you mean?"

"That's it? I mean, isn't there more to the book than this?"

"Well sure, if you read into it."

I scratched my chin and decided to turn up the thermostat. "Why don't you do that, Chiang. Enlighten us."

He thought for a moment. "Well, I think the young relief pitcher did to Hobbs what Hobbs did to the 'Whammer' in the beginning of the book. Both Hobbs and the 'Whammer' were spoiled and hung up on themselves, but in the end they both got defeated and humbled. I suppose you could even say disgraced. Everything went full circle."

He looked at me. "That's my take, anyway."

"Dead-on," I said, nodding approval.

Chiang returned the nod, pleased with himself.

The kid was sharp, no doubt about it. Several students nodded their heads, impressed with Chiang's interpretation. Slocum looked at Crider and mumbled something under his breath.

I looked around at the class and said, "Hobbs is the prototype of the fallen hero. He never realizes or appreciates the heroic qualities he's been given because he's not willing to self-sacrifice, to place his needs secondary to those of others. You might recall Hobbs saying that he wanted to be remembered as the greatest baseball player ever. This is a telling statement about the man's sense of purpose in life. We have to ask, is that all he wants out of life? His self-absorbed thirst for fame and fortune is his undoing and derails his journey, reducing him to ordinary status."

We spent the next few minutes kicking around larger than life fictional heroes, characters who walked taller than mere mortals and accomplished great deeds. Then we switched gears and discussed everyday heroes, average people who have gone out of their way to do something extraordinary, like saving lives, going beyond the call of duty or taking a stand on something deemed important. I remarked that in the aftermath of the World Trade Center attack and the spread of terrorism, we hunger for evidence of heroic qualities in humans, people who we can look up to and not have to question, people who make a difference in someone's life forever.

Across from me, Rachel nudged Lois in the arm and both giggled softly.

"What?" I asked, looking their way.

"Oh, nothing," Rachel said, smiling.

"Come on," I prodded. "What's up?"

Rachel gestured toward Lois and said, "We have a hero right here in this class, but you'd never know it because Lois doesn't like to gloat. She even made the newspaper, picture and all."

I looked at Lois. "Is that right? A true, live hero? Now you definitely have to tell us."

Rachel nudged Lois in the arm again. "Come on Lo, tell the class. I mean, it's not as if the story doesn't relate to what we've been talking about."

Lois was touching a heart-shape pendant on a gold necklace, sliding it back and forth. She let go of it and said, "Okay."

Lois was a plus-sized, middle aged woman on the quiet and bashful side, someone who had really blossomed since the course began. She was as sensitive as she was perceptive, and held great promise as a writer. She often bared her soul in our various writing assignments, such as sharing her religious convictions as well as how she's struggled with weight her entire life. We've swapped quite a few ideas about writing, and from all indications she's thrived on the constructive criticism received.

Lois began: "I was walking home one day from Sound View beach in Old Lyme, which is not too far from where I live. I was alone and there were lots of people walking along the narrow road that leads to the beach. A young boy on roller blades came careening in and out of traffic and lost control, flying head first into the fender of a parked car."

She shook her head a bit, and her expression became serious. She continued: "He wasn't wearing a helmet and sustained a head injury. He began bleeding badly from a deep laceration–the skull bone was visible. He needed help but people just stood there, probably because they didn't know what to do. I'd taken a couple of Red Cross first aid course and just took charge. I managed to control the bleeding and keep the boy from going into shock until the ambulance came."

"Wow," I said, "that's really something. When did this happen?"

"Let's see," Lois said, nibbling her lower lip. "It was just about the time I began a low carb diet, so it must have been four years ago."

In the back, Crider suddenly stirred and cleared his throat, apparently interested in the conversation. He leaned forward in his chair. "So what happened?"

"What happened to the boy?" Lois asked. "Oh, he lived."

"No," Crider said, "what happened to the diet?"

For a brief moment, there was no reaction and the jab hung in the air while Crider stared at Lois. "No, really," he said, "I'm being serious." He added further insult to injury when he said, "How did that diet plan of yours work out?"

More silence. Then, he and Slocum laughed out loud. A few other students smiled and just shook their heads while lowering their eyes. Rachel and those sitting next to Lois sat in stunned disbelief. Next to me, Chiang let out his breath in annoyance.

Lois cast her eyes downward and turned red with embarrassment.

Crider was leering away while scoping the room, no doubt taking an inventory of how funny and clever he perceived himself to be, even at the expense of another student.

I took in the whole scene, anger bubbling inside. The heat in the room spiked.

Crider still had a crooked smile on his face when he finally decided to look over at me. It disappeared when he saw the expression on my face and how ripped I was.

"What?" he asked, dragging the word out like the child who knows he's in trouble.

I looked at him with a bullet-like stare, fighting to maintain my composure. My cheeks were flushed and my ears were burning. Finally I said, "You may leave, Mr. Crider."

Crider's mouth dropped open. "Leave? Me? What do you mean?"

"What I mean is go ... get out of my classroom. What part of that don't you seem to understand?" I could feel my jaw muscles bunched.

"You're kicking me out for that?" Crider recoiled with exaggerated surprise and laughed bitterly, shaking his head. "Come on man, it was a joke, that's all." He gestured toward Lois and said, "She knows that."

Lois didn't respond and kept her eyes downcast.

I wasn't about to engage myself in a discussion of this guy's humor or any other juvenile stalling tactics. Instead I said, "You heard me. Get out."

No one in the class moved, but their tennis match eyes watched every serve. A nervous cough came from somewhere.

"I don't believe this," Crider snapped. "This is such a crock of shit." He slammed shut whatever book he had on his desk, startling several students. Crider tossed the book in the general direction of his book bag on the floor.

He straightened in the chair and stared at me with something like disgust. Then, much to my surprise, he said, "No." He defiantly folded his arms across his chest.

I glared at him sideways, not sure what I'd just heard. "What did you say?"

"You heard me," Crider replied, "I'm not going anywhere, and you can't make me."

The statement took the air out of the room.

Next to him, Slocum's head snapped up, surprise on his face. He got wide eyed and started squirming in his seat, rubbing his hands together like he was about to watch a street fight.

"Showtime," he giggled.

# *Three*

All eyes were upon me and I wasn't sure what to do, although I knew I had to think quickly. I looked at the wall clock and saw that about twenty minutes of the class period remained. Cutting class short and letting everyone go was simply not an option. From my perspective, that would be punishing the good students and rewarding this imbecile.

I got up from my chair and slowly walked over towards Crider's desk. I didn't break eye contact. Once there, I leaned towards him, hands on my knees. I was really in his grill, so close that I could see tiny beads of sweat on his nose and some sleep crust in the corner of one eye. His breath was foul. He was a big kid and took up a lot of space, but I was unfazed. I'd dealt with smart ass bullies like him before, especially as a kid growing up, and refused to back down from the likes of this clown.

There was no mistaking the fact that I had his attention. His face had gone pale and I could have sworn he was holding his breath. I leaned in even closer, a few inches from his left ear, and whispered to him. "You listen to me, Crider, and you listen good. I'm tired of your attitude and I am tired of you. Pick up your crap and get out of my classroom. If you don't, I'll see that your useless ass gets thrown out of the building."

Crider's eyes widened and he looked stunned, like I had just slapped him across the face. Slocum looked mortified and in dire need of some smelling salts. I straightened up and began turning away, pleased that I had taken the tough guy approach with this loser. Clearly, I'd regained the upper hand.

That is, until Crider once again did the unexpected.

"Whoa, whoa, whoa," he blurted. He jerked his head around at the class, his ratty dreadlocks in motion. "Did you just hear that? Elliot just threatened me. I can't believe this shit." His voice was booming and his nostrils flared.

Okay, I thought, so much for the brass knuckled approach to classroom etiquette. This was getting uglier by the minute and I knew that I had to do something fast or things were really going to get out of hand. Right now, I was flying by the seat of my pants and needed to pull something out of the hat. I turned to look at the other students, several of whom had frozen, open-mouthed expressions. I'm sure none of them could believe what was happening.

With my back turned to Crider I said to the class, "Would someone go call campus security? There's a wall phone at the end of this hallway with a direct line to their office." The veins in my temple throbbed, and I fought to keep my voice cool.

For a moment no one moved, which worried me because now I was at the end of my options. I couldn't make the call myself because that would mean leaving the classroom, and I wasn't about to leave this goon alone with the others. He was liable to go off on anyone.

My worries proved unfounded when Chiang sprang from his chair and headed out the door and down the hallway.

I decided to stand over by the door while Crider continued foaming at the mouth, trying desperately to get himself off the hook and turn the class against me. No one paid him much attention except for Slocum, who hung on his every word and joined in tossing insults my way. I chose to completely ignore both of them and look unruffled, even when Crider looked at me and demanded responses. At one point I looked their way and smiled just so, calling them every vulgarity I could think of under my breath.

A campus security officer arrived shortly, which wasn't surprising given our small campus and the fact that bicycle patrols roam the grounds all the time. Chiang accompanied the cop into the classroom, taking his seat back in the circle. Chiang got dirty looks from both Crider and Slocum, anger that would bear watching down the road. I resolved to keep an eye on that.

The officer was a muscular guy, big and strong in the arms and shoulders. He looked to be in his late twenties. He was hatless and wore a standard, blue issue police officer's uniform, including a radio microphone attached to his shirt collar, nightstick and gun belt. His name tag identified him as Oakley.

He offered his hand and I took it, his grip vice like.

"I'm Jack Elliot," I said. "Thank you for coming so quickly."

"No problem," he said. He hooked his thumbs over his holster cowboy style and said, "What can I do to help?"

I looked over at Crider, who had stopped his tirade the minute Oakley walked in. However, there was no way he could wash away his anger and resentment, which hung around him like a storm cloud. He sat glaring at me, face flushed and jaw clenched. He'd extended his arms behind the back of the chair, locking his hands together and looking like a coiled spring.

I pointed at him. "I'd like this student escorted out of my classroom and preferably out of the building. His name is Crider. He's been disrespectful and disruptive and has refused to leave the classroom at my request. I'll stop over to your office after class and fill out the necessary paperwork."

"None of that's true," Crider interrupted. "I'm not lying. I have witnesses."

Oakley would have none of it. He simply looked at Crider and without a moment's hesitation said, "Let's go."

"Come on, man, this isn't fair," Crider snorted, shaking his head.

"I said, let's go," Oakley repeated, louder this time and taking a few steps toward Crider. Oakley glared at him. "I won't ask again," he said.

"Okay, okay," Crider said, spreading his hands wide, a portrait of innocence. He rose from the chair, picked up his book bag. The two of them began walking toward the door and Crider muttered, "Fuck this place." He pointed an accusing finger at me and said, "You haven't heard the end of this."

"That's right, brother" Slocum said, smacking fists macho style with Crider as he brushed by. Slocum looked my way, smirking and shaking his head. He pulled out a pair of sunglasses from his pocket and put them on, wearing one of those, 'How fucking cool am I?' expressions. Just as I looked away, I could've sworn he blew me a kiss. My anger bubbled once more.

Oakley and Crider were at the door when I said, "Just a minute." I pointed at Slocum and said, "While you're at it, take Mr. Showtime here with you. His name is Slocum."

Slocum went white as a sheet, as if he'd seen a ghost. He removed the sunglasses, blinking his eyes wildly. I suppose he thought he was innocent and beyond reproach, but I was sick and tired of his dumb and dumber routine with Crider. He'd been an accessory to all this and needed to be held accountable. He attempted to speak, but his mouth proved uncooperative, sputtering only "Wha...wha...wha?" These were easily the most intelligent sounds he'd made all semester.

"Same complaint?" Oakley asked, meeting my eye.

"I'll think of something. Right now, he's a nuisance and I can't stand the sight of him. Just get him out of here."

A smirk creased Oakley's face, and I thought I detected a look of enjoyment. He turned to look at Slocum and gestured with his thumb toward the door. Slocum got up and joined them, his head and shoulders sagging like the wind had been punched out of his sails. After the three of them left I closed the door, much to the dismay of a few gawkers milling around in the hallway.

I returned to my seat. I'd be dishonest if I said I wasn't disturbed or upset. My emotions were turned upside down. No one likes confrontation, especially when it turns ugly like this. Strangely, I didn't feel nervous or jumpy when everything happened. Now though, I sensed a sheen of perspiration on my forehead and my breathing was labored. One of my hands was shaking a little, so I stuck it in my pocket and hoped no one would notice.

I could feel the tension and apprehension in the room. I tried to smile, but it flickered and died on my face. The students were watching me closely, waiting for my next move. Several were wide-eyed, a little shell-shocked perhaps. I suppose some were simply unable to believe what had just taken place. Who knows, maybe some were afraid of me in the aftermath of this mess. Whatever the reason, silence enveloped the classroom like a blanket.

I gathered my wits and took in a deep breath. I tried to use a tone of authority, one of control. "I'm sorry you had to see that, especially something so disruptive right in the middle of a class. I apologize if what you saw was upsetting. That certainly wasn't my intent and I take full responsibility for how I handled things."

I wove my fingers together. "I will deal with these students later, on my terms, but you need to know now I will not tolerate behavior like his. I have a short fuse when it comes to rudeness or disrespect, and I won't allow anyone to ridicule other people, not for a punch line or anything else."

Around me, several students nodded their heads in agreement, including Rachel. Her eyes were big and she was watching me closely.

I looked over at Lois and said, "I'm sorry for this, Lois, I truly am." Our eyes met, and I could tell she was bothered by what happened. She nodded, then looked away. I decided to not say anything else, at least not here.

The class seemed to have relaxed a bit, which made me feel better.

"Everyone okay?" I asked.

Most nodded their heads, several offering reassuring smiles.

Willie Fraser furrowed his brow behind his glasses and asked, "How 'bout you, Doc?" Willie was a kind soul, and there was nothing patronizing about his question or his intent.

"How about me what?" I asked.

"You okay?"

"I'm okay." I downed what was left of my coffee.

Willie gave me one of his easy smiles.

I waited a few more moments just in case anyone else wanted to say something, but no one took the bait. While a few still looked skittish and uneasy, for the most part classroom stability had been restored.

"Well then," I said, getting up from my chair, "why don't we call it a day."

# *Four*

I was in no mood for sticking around the classroom. I packed up my briefcase and headed for the door, the students giving me a wide berth. Other classes had been dismissed so there were lots of students in the hallway. I got more than a few looks and even some finger pointing as I snaked by. I heard words and snatches of conversation. Juicy news spreads like wildfire on college campuses, Guilford being no exception.

Once I got to the outside door to the building I tried calling Claire on my cell, but got her answering service and chose not to leave a message. The rain had stopped and the sun was beginning to peek through the clouds, so I decided to walk over to the campus security building and fill out an incident report. It was a standard form, one that essentially asked why I had summoned security and whether or not I was going to pursue the matter with the Student Affairs office. I didn't complete this last part, instead writing a note saying that I wished to think this part through and would get back to them. From there I walked over to the student union and got a bite to eat, choosing to eat alone rather than in the faculty lounge. When I was done, I went to check my mail at the campus post office.

I'd gotten several textbooks in the mail and was juggling the packages in my arms when I exited the building. I decided to drop the packages off in my car in the nearby faculty parking when I heard someone calling my name. I turned and saw that it was Chiang, although I almost didn't recognize him. He was wearing a knit cap pulled down over his ears, one piece industrial coveralls, and construction boots. He'd just turned off a gas powered weed trimmer, which he carried by his side. A cigarette dangled from his lips.

I squinted. "That you, Chiang?"

"It's me," he replied, taking a drag on the cigarette and blowing a plume of gray smoke from the corner of his mouth. "Outfit threw you, right?"

"That it did," I replied.

He pulled up next to me, bent down and put the weed trimmer on the pavement.

"I didn't know you worked for the college," I said.

"Work study," he replied, pulling off a pair of worn leather work gloves and sticking them in a side pocket. "When I'm done with your class I clock in for the rest of the day."

"How long you been doing it?"

"Since I got here." He rubbed the back of his neck and moved his head from side to side, as if working out a crick. He rolled his shoulders. "Helps pay the bills."

"Always worked for the maintenance department?" I caught a whiff of gasoline from his coveralls.

"I started in the library when I was a freshman then got switched to the bookstore, but neither job did much for me. This clicked because I like being outside and doing physical work."

I looked at him and nodded, although I would have guessed the opposite.

Without asking he reached over for the book packages I was carrying and tucked them under his arm. "Let me help you with those. Where you heading, Boss?"

"Just over to the faculty parking lot. I was going to throw this stuff in my car before I headed back to my office."

We both fell in step.

"Listen," I said, "I'm glad I ran into you. I wanted to thank you for this morning, for stepping up when I needed help. I would have been high and dry if you hadn't called campus security."

He nodded, then took a handkerchief out of his back pocket to wipe perspiration from his face. "My brother always told me that too many people in the world stand around and do nothing when the proper thing to do is staring them right in the face."

"Your brother taught you well." I remembered that Chiang wrote about his older brother Ray several times for class assignments. I recalled that Ray died unexpectedly for reasons unknown to me, but obviously imparted many life lessons to his younger brother. Based on what I read, the two had been close.

Chiang took the cigarette from his mouth, flicking it away on the pavement. Just as quickly he removed a pack of cigarettes from inside his coveralls and pulled out another. He offered me one, but I declined. "You know," he said, "all of us were getting sick and tired of that Crider dude…" All he does is talk smack. You don't deserve that kind of disrespect, no teacher does."

He took a drag on the cigarette, let the smoke pour out of his nostrils. "For what it's worth, I'm glad today happened. That guy needed a wake-up call."

We entered the faculty parking lot and I fished the keys out of my pocket. We walked over to my car, a new Volvo C90 purchased just a month or so ago. Its silver metallic exterior still had a showroom luster, making it stand out from the others in the faculty lot. I unlocked the doors with my remote and the tail lights winked at us.

Sam whistled softly through his teeth. "Sweet wheels, Doc. New?"

I looked over at him and nodded. "Yeah, one of my play toys." With a delivery price that nearly gagged me, I thought.

"Gonna let me road test this bad boy out on the highway, you know, so I can see what it's got under the hood?" Chiang asked.

I smiled and shook my head. "Keep dreaming," I said, delivering a playful elbow to his ribs.

Chiang laughed.

I opened the back seat door, and took the book packages from Chiang, stacking them on the seat. Once I closed the door, I turned and thanked him for the help. We talked for a few more minutes, then he said he had to get back to work. I took his hand and we shook. His hand was quite small, almost childlike.

I WENT BACK TO MY OFFICE AND STARED AT THE YAWNING mouth of my computer, its darkness taunting me to write something productive, anything, but I hadn't even touched the mouse. I was supposed to be working on a new course proposal, but images of this morning's freak show kept getting in the way. As hard as I tried to not think about what happened, I couldn't. I mentally replayed everything, even reconstructing a script of who said what to whom, one of those 'I said,' then 'he said' memory loops. No matter how I rehashed what happened, it spelled disaster.

I tipped my chair back and put my feet on the desk, clasping my hands behind my head. I thought about how I was going to handle Crider, what I was going to say to him. I realized that I would also have to deal with Slocum. Although he wasn't the instigator, from my point of view he exacerbated the situation and I wasn't about to ignore that. Since the class didn't meet again until next week, I was thankful I had time to think through some options.

A soft knock on the half open door interrupted my thoughts. I looked up as the door slowly opened and saw Rachel Pond framed there, smiling. She looked like sunshine on a stormy day. She had a raincoat draped over her arm, a cardboard tray with two coffees in her hand.

"Busy?" she asked.

Rachel had taken me by surprise. "No," I said, "please come in." As she did, I quickly slid my feet off the desk and stood up.

She took one of the coffee containers from the tray and handed it to me. "This is for you. Regular, right?"

"Yes, regular," I replied, flattered by the gesture. "How nice."

"After that scene this morning you looked like you could use some relief."

I gestured toward one of the chairs and said, "Can you stay?"

"Just for a bit," she said, sitting down and perching herself on the edge, almost sideways. Her eyes roamed the office, taking everything in. Even though we'd talked after class several times, Rachel had never stopped by my office. It seemed like we always conducted our business in the hallway, in between classes or on the fly.

She studied me for a moment. "You okay?'

She was wearing a white turtleneck tucked into beltless, faded blue jeans that hugged her legs, chocolate suede mocs, and white ribbed athletic socks. Her blonde hair was worn up in some kind of soft curl - her usual style - with the exception of some loose wisps on the sides, which softened her face.

"I'm fine," I replied, taking a sip of coffee. It tasted good. "Why wouldn't I be?"

"Because I think I know you better." She raised her chin and said, "Now tell me how you're really doing."

I smiled and scratched the back of my head. Ordinarily I avoided discussing any student with their peers, but felt this was an exception. Rachel was older, someone I felt I could trust. Plus, she had seen the entire episode as well as everything that had led up to it during the semester. Besides, I needed to vent.

"You really want to know?" I asked.

"I wouldn't be here if I didn't." Her expression was serious.

The fact that she had gone out of her way to check in on me meant a great deal. I liked Rachel, both as a student and a person, and admired her drive to better herself. I always looked forward to seeing her in class, and enjoyed reading her writing because she put so much effort into it.

I looked at her and shrugged. "To be honest, I've been second guessing myself since it happened. I shouldn't have let things get to a boiling point, I mean between Crider and me." I looked down and shook my head a little. "I let him get away with way too much all semester, let too many things build up. Same with Slocum."

She sat there listening, hands wrapped around her coffee.

I let out a breath. "This morning's class was a disaster. I wish I could get it back, start all over. I could've handled things better, should have handled things better. I shouldn't have fenced with him or Slocum about *The Natural*. Maybe I shouldn't have even called campus security." I set my coffee down on the desk. "I lost my cool, Rachel, plain and simple."

She stayed quiet, appraising me.

We sat in silence for a little while. "I suppose I'm being too hard on myself," I said, "but that's the way I am. I tend to beat myself up pretty good."

Rachel thought about this for a while. "You sound more like a masochist than a faculty member. I mean, aren't all professors supposed to be narcissists?"

I had to laugh at that one.

She settled back in the chair. "So tell me, how would you have handled things differently? I'm curious." She had a soft, pleasing voice.

I thought for a minute. "Oh, I don't know. I suppose I should have tossed him sooner."

"This morning or sooner in the semester?"

"Both."

Rachel leaned forward, putting her coffee container by the side of her chair. She leaned forward in the chair, rested her chin on her hand. "Let me tell you something. He wouldn't have gone either time. Obviously he's defiant and has a problem with authority. I mean, look at how he pushed your buttons this morning."

I nodded. She was right. He had a chip on his shoulder the minute he saw the circular seating arrangement and was rude several times during class, even before he turned on Lois.

She continued: "You don't hear half the stuff that comes out of his mouth. He loves putting other people down, putting the school down. He takes pride in the fact that he's been caught drinking on campus, been placed on social probation several times. I mean this guy is crude as well as a bully. Believe me, I've seen him in action."

I raised my eyebrows.

She shifted in the chair. "He's in another class I'm taking this fall. He walks around thinking he can do or say anything he pleases, whenever he wants."

"His teacher lets him get away with it?" I asked.

"I think Crider intimidates his professors, although I doubt you'd get any of them to admit to it. I've seen my other professor tell this guy one thing, like stop talking in class, and then watch as Crider continues doing whatever he was doing, usually with some kind of attitude for the teacher."

She reached down and got her coffee, then sat back and crossed her legs. "When I started classes I couldn't believe what he got away with and wondered what kind of place this was to allow behavior like that." Rachel had taken courses from other area schools, including Wesleyan and Connecticut College.

She took a swallow of coffee then looked up at me with her light blue eyes, their hue reminding me of pale aquamarine stones. They were offset by high, prominent cheekbones.

"We're not all like that," I said.

She nodded. "I know you aren't anyway. You hold your students accountable, at least from what I've seen."

I shook my head slowly. "More than once I've asked myself how this guy could have gotten this far in school. I mean, the kid's a senior and I'm told he's been here all four years."

"It does make you wonder," she agreed. "I'll bet most of his teachers just want to avoid a confrontation."

She went on. "I remember the first two or three weeks of classes. My other professor got annoyed with Crider and a couple of his buddies because they took turns getting up in the middle of class to go use the bathroom. They would do this whenever they wished, swaggering as they walked back and forth, sometimes banging the door behind them."

I tried imagining the kind of distractions these guys created. It was hard enough getting a class focused on the material at hand without crap like this going on. At least Crider hadn't pulled that one on me, not yet anyway.

Rachel coughed quietly into her hand. "Crider had a routine where he would arrive to class late, then within five or ten minutes he'd get right back up and head for the bathroom. It used to drive me crazy. I mean, he's late and causes one distraction, then creates another within minutes."

"The teacher did nothing?" I asked.

"After a while, you could tell it was getting to him. So one day the professor makes this big announcement about how no one would be allowed to make trips to the bathroom during class. He said that if anyone's bladder couldn't function properly for the duration of the class period he would give them time off to go see a urologist, which got a big laugh."

"Did that take care of the problem?"

"For one class period, anyway. Well, I shouldn't say that. The other guys stopped, but Crider was back to his old tricks within the week. He still gets up pretty much as he pleases, although not in the beginning of class. When he does, he often looks right at the teacher with that attitude of his, daring him to say something, which of course isn't going to happen."

She tugged at the sleeves of her turtleneck and pulled them half way up her forearms. She had attractive hands and nicely manicured nails. A gold bracelet dangled from her left wrist.

We were both silent for a moment.

"Have you ever had students like this?" Rachel asked.

I had to think about it for a moment. "Not here, maybe a couple up at UMass. I think most professors get some sooner or later. You know, blowhards who think they know everything or egotists who like to hog discussions or put other students down. But never to this extreme. Guys like this haven't appeared on my radar."

I had some more coffee and shifted the conversation. "How's Lois doing? Is she all right?"

Rachel smiled. "She'll be fine. She was upset at first but we talked and she was much better afterwards. Trust me, Lois is a woman comfortable in her own skin. She's sensitive but knows Crider is a zero, a real head case. She appreciates what you did, believe me. We all do."

"The two of you are tight," I observed.

"Yes," Rachel replied, "we've known each other for years. She's a special person in my life. Trust me, she's a strong woman and has no doubt put all of this behind her. "

I nodded.

We sat there looking at each other for a long moment. She used the side of her hand to brush back a wisp or two of her hair. I wondered what she looked like with her hair down, if it was straight or had some curl, how long it was, or if she brushed it at night.

She said, "I admire a person who stands up for what he believes in and doesn't back down. If I remember correctly from one of my classes, it has something to do with character."

We both giggled. She was a sly one, this Rachel Pond.

"So tell me, did you really threaten Crider like he claimed?"

I frowned, or maybe it was more of a grimace.

"What do you think? I asked.

She pursed her lips, tilted her head. "I don't think you went over there to invite him out for a few brews. Judging from his reaction as well as the face made by 'that thing' next to him, I'd lay odds that you came on pretty strong. A lot of testosterone was sprayed back there."

I told her what I said to Crider when I leaned over and spoke in his ear.

Rachel widened her eyes, then nodded. "He deserved it," she said flatly.

The office phone rang. It was Nathan, calling me from school and reminding me that I needed to pick him up on my way home and asking if I could also take his best friend Forrest Poole home. Forrest lived about a mile away from us in Spencer Plain.

While I was talking Rachel got up and looked around the office. I watched while she gazed at pictures on the wall and various books on my shelves. She looked at a ceiling mobile of silver seagulls, setting it in motion with her fingertips. She picked up a knick-knack or two from a table, including a mahogany cube inscribed with the words, 'writer's block.' She ran her fingers over its smooth surface and smiled. Claire had given the cube to me one Christmas and it never failed to catch someone's eye.

When I finished with Nathan, she returned to her chair and sat back down in that sideways roost of hers.

"I really should be going," she said.

I nodded my head, although I didn't want her to leave. I looked away with a distant smile.

She cocked her head. "What's that smile all about?"

"Oh, I don't know, something stupid I suppose."

"Tell me," she implored.

I thought for a moment. "I've wondered for a while now what it would be like to talk with you alone, you know, away from the classroom, without distractions or interruptions, without people listening in. Thought about what we would say if we ever bumped into each other at the mall or around town, that kind of thing."

"Talking with me alone? Really?" A sudden brightness moved into Rachel's eyes, and she looked genuinely flattered.

"Really."

"That's so sweet." She tilted her head and said, "Well, how'd we do?"

"I think we did just fine."

"I agree," she said, getting up from her chair and reaching for her rain poncho. She turned to face me as she put it on. "You're going to be okay, right?" she asked.

"Yes. I'm good."

She took a slight bow. "Rachel Anne Pond at your service."

She had her poncho on but was fumbling for the hood, which had somehow gotten stuck inside. She lifted both of her arms up and back at the same time to pull it free, looking over her shoulder. As she did, her full breasts strained against her turtleneck, in the process untucking it and revealing a part of her flat, bare belly.

I was caught totally off guard and simultaneously mesmerized. I was staring at her exposed flesh when I realized she was looking at me. I glanced up and our eyes met. She gave me a look of playful admonishment, one that said she'd just caught me being a bad boy. I got red faced and flustered, my eyes darting away like an embarrassed choir boy.

"A penny for your thoughts, professor," she said, zipping her poncho and heading out the door. A smile flirted across her mouth.

And just like that, Rachel Pond was gone.

# *Five*

I left my office and drove to the high school to get Nathan, the goings-on of the last two days pounding away in my head. Disturbing thoughts of Claire and her lover were joined by today's classroom debacle orchestrated by Crider and Slocum, my mind now an endless abyss of distraction and chaos. Little did I know that my life would get even uglier, the other shoe soon to drop.

By the time I got to the high school, the late buses were parked in front and students were either boarding them or milling around. Many wore sweat suits or gym shorts from intramurals, some carried musical instruments, and a few were transporting what appeared to be science projects. Others, like Nathan and his friend Forrest Poole, were carrying books from the library. They were standing alone by the front doors of the school. I honked the horn and waved.

They walked over to the car, a study in contrasts. Nathan wore glasses and was short with a slight build, gangling arms and legs, and a narrow face. His clothes were tidy and trendy, like the Old Navy sweatshirt and jeans he had on, but they hung loosely from his slender frame. Forrest, on the other hand, was taller than Nathan and quite overweight. He had round cheeks sprouting peach fuzz, short arms and pudgy fingers, and a plump belly that strained against dark, nondescript clothes.

The two were best friends. Forrest was the first kid Nathan met when we moved to Spencer Plain, and the two hit it off almost immediately. At the time, Nathan was quite shy and withdrawn, Forrest an outgoing and happy-go-lucky sort. Claire and I often say that Forrest came along at just the right time in Nathan's life and helped him come out of his shell. Before long, they were doing everything together: bicycling, going to summer camps, watching movies, sleeping over, and all the other things teenagers do. The fact that they were both freshmen at the high school and taking many of the same classes drew them even closer. Neither had many other friends.

Nathan greeted me while getting into the front seat and Forrest climbed in back.

"Hi Doc," Forrest said, grunting as he pulled off his book bag and placed in on the space next to him. "Thanks for the lift."

"Not a problem, Forrest."

It was starting to get dark as we pulled away from the curb.

"Did you guys get any work done?" I asked.

Nathan said, "I got some pretty good books." After he spoke, he reached inside his mouth and fingered his lower braces. He was due to have them removed next spring, which couldn't happen fast enough for him.

"What's your topic?" I asked.

"The battle of Thermopylae. You've heard of it, right? Spartans and the Persians?"

"Oh, sure," I answered. "Leonidas takes on Xerxes at the pass. Great topic." How about you, Forrest?" I looked at him in the rearview mirror.

"Well," he began, "I wanted to do it on the Roman Empire, but ol' Barrel Ass told me the topic was too broad. She told me to narrow it down." Forrest thought about this for a moment, then added, "She's the one who should narrow it down, you know. She's got way too much junk in the trunk."

Both of them broke into fits of giggling.

"Come on now, fellas," I said, "be nice. Remember, she's your teacher."

I had difficulty keeping a straight face. 'Barrel Ass' was a reference to Edith Beckwith, who has taught Western Civilization at Spencer Plain high school for the past 40 years. She knows her stuff and plays a prominent role in the local historical society. She is also a stern disciplinarian who doesn't put up with nonsense from her students. Her iron fist approach to the classroom is legendary, but so too is her nickname. She is quite broad in the stern, so to speak, made even more prominent over the years by the hunched over, plodding way that she walks. I'm told the nickname has been around forever.

In recent years Ms. Beckwith has added to her notoriety by accidentally passing gas while bending over in one of her classrooms. Apparently the sound was audible even to those dozing in the back row, and she exacerbated the situation by attempting the old cough and conceal maneuver, which only served to increase her turgidity and create a truly memorable tuba concerto. Rumor has it that she had to cancel the class because she couldn't get the students to stop laughing, many of whom were literally crying and pounding their desktops in hysterics.

I could hear Forrest opening up his backpack behind me. He pulled out a package of candy, which didn't surprise me because he always seemed to have a stash of goodies somewhere. He never ate in front of anyone, instead choosing to share whatever he'd brought along. Forrest didn't get much nutrition supervision at home, and both his mother and younger sister were overweight.

"Red Hots anyone?" he asked, the prototype of civility. I declined but Nathan angled his hand back for a few.

"Hey Nate," Forrest said, "did you hear that Billy Halliday got busted today?"

"No, what happened?"

"He got caught stealing some of Kyle Sinclair's baseball cards. I guess they went into his locker this afternoon and found some other stolen stuff."

"Really? Like what?" Nathan turned sideways so that he could see Forrest. He began twitching his fingers together, a nervous childhood habit he never outgrew.

Forrest shifted his Red Hot to the other side of his mouth. "I heard some CDs and a leather jacket. The leather jacket had a cell phone in one of the pockets."

"What's going to happen to him?" Nathan asked.

"Someone said he might get kicked out of school," Forrest replied.

I asked, "Is that Sean Halliday's son, from the jeep dealership?"

"Yeah, that's his father."

We bought Claire's jeep from Halliday a few years ago. He was a manager or some kind of big shot at the local dealership, a rangy guy who talked a lot and was pushy, which wasn't surprising given his line of work. I recalled that Halliday snapped his gum a lot, sucked his teeth, and sported a rather prominent drinker's gut. When he met us out on the lot, we made it clear from the beginning that the jeep was for Claire. However, much like other car salesmen, Halliday directed his sales pitch and energy toward me, which I knew irritated my wife. She knows just as much about cars as I do and can hold her own in any sales transaction. When Halliday eventually caught on and stopped being a sexist asshole, he succeeded in selling Claire a new vehicle at a fair price. I've bumped into him a few times since, mostly when Claire's jeep was being serviced. He always asks how the 'little woman' or 'princess' is doing.

I said, "Well, Mr. Halliday isn't going to be a happy camper."

Forrest said, "I don't think he'll even care. Billy brags about all the things he gets away with. He even steals from his father. Talk about stupid." Forrest touched Nathan's arm and said, "Remember the credit card story Nate?"

Nathan nodded his head.

"What's the credit card story?" I asked.

Forrest leaned in my direction. He said, "Get this. When Billy needs some quick cash he takes his father's gas card when the old man isn't looking. He then tells one of his friends who needs gas to meet him down at the Mobil station. Billy uses the credit card to fill up the kid's tank, then charges twenty dollars cash. Billy makes out because he's got twenty bucks and his buddy gets a tank of gas that would have cost a lot more."

"But what about Billy's father?" I asked. "Hasn't he picked up on this? I mean, doesn't he look at his credit card charges at the end of the month?" Right after I said this I realized that I couldn't remember the last time I double checked mine.

"Nope," answered Forrest. "Billy puts the credit card back in his father's wallet when he gets home and nobody knows the difference. I heard he only does it a couple of times a month and so far he hasn't been caught." Forrest shifted the Red Hot around in his mouth again and dropped back in his seat.

This was a new one on me, the scenario playing out in my head. A teenager steals from his father, lures a friend into the scam and pockets cold cash, all right under the father's nose. Good Lord, talk about some crooked turns. Who do you blame here, the kid for ripping off his father, or the old man for totally missing the boat?

We drove in silence for a few moments. I turned my head and spoke evenly, matter-of-factly. "I want the two of you to stay away from this kid. Sounds like he's bad news."

"We see him almost every day, Dad. He's in our algebra class," Nathan said. "He flunked it last year and has to repeat it."

I eased off the gas pedal, as we approached an intersection. "Does he pick on you guys?"

"He picks on everyone. He likes giving people a hard time," Forrest replied.

I looked over at Nathan. "Just stay clear of him." I turned my head toward the back seat. "You too, Forrest."

"We will," Forrest responded.

We pulled up in front of Forrest's house, a raised ranch just past our road. It wasn't an old house, but one that had fallen into disrepair. The paint was faded and a section of the front gutter sagged. The shrubs were overgrown and the lawn often needed mowing during the summer months. An oversized mailbox was rusting and leaning to one side.

No lights were on inside the house, so I waited until Forrest got safely inside before we turned around and headed home.

CLAIRE'S RED JEEP was in the garage when we arrived. When we walked in, she was in the kitchen transferring Chinese food out of white cartons onto serving plates. The sight of Claire brought back a wave of anger from yesterday. I knew I had to keep my hostility in check and mask it with outward composure, at least until I got my facts straight. I kept telling myself there had to be a reasonable explanation for what I'd uncovered.

I walked over and gave her a quick hug and peck on the cheek. "Chinese food," I said, "nice treat."

She had her shoulder length brown hair pulled back with a clip and was wearing a maroon cable knit sweater and blue oxford shirt, and light chinos. She said: "We got done earlier than planned at Cromwell and on the way home I thought Chinese would taste good. I stopped at Jimmy Wong's and picked up some shrimp lo mein for us and General Tsao's chicken for Nathan." Jimmy Wong owned the *Mein Event*, one of our favorite take-out places in nearby Old Saybrook.

Claire was a landscape architect and finishing up a major project in Cromwell, a town located in central Connecticut, a tad southwest of Hartford. She worked for a landscape firm in Old Lyme and was personally responsible for landing a contract for an industrial park, the biggest ever undertaken by the firm. It involved the extensive location of roads, walkways, outdoor lighting, decorative fountains, and such landscaping touches as vegetation, sod, trees and shrubs. The Cromwell Pointe project was her baby from the get-go and she'd spent the better part of the past year supervising its completion.

I helped set the plates on the dining room table and got some napkins and silverware. I noticed that Claire had already gotten a glass of wine for herself so I grabbed a can of beer from the refrigerator and poured Nathan a large glass of milk before sitting down.

We dug in and enjoyed the food in front of us. After a few forkfuls and a swallow of beer I looked at Claire. "Everything coming together at Cromwell?" I asked.

She looked at me, straightening a bit in the chair. "We got good news all around today. The site supervisor brought me up-to-date and everything has fallen into place." She speared a shrimp with her fork. "I got a tour of the park and things look great. We'll cut the ribbon this week as planned."

"Good for you," I said. "Congratulations."

She smiled when she looked at me, and I briefly met her eye before looking away.

Nathan said, "Good goin', Mom."

"Why thank you, gentlemen," she said, taking a bite of the shrimp. "Now what kind of day did the two of you have? Did you get the books you needed, Nathan?"

Nathan was in the kitchen getting a second helping of food. "Yeah, I stayed after and found some pretty good ones. Dad picked Forrest and me up at school and brought us home."

Nathan sat back down in his chair and slumped over his food, his face a few inches from the plate. At one point he took a break from shoveling and guzzled some milk, smacking his lips when finished then breaking the stillness with a resounding burp. He looked our way and apologized, using the back of his hand to wipe away a white mustache. I've never doubted that adolescence is linked to lower life forms.

Claire wiped the corners of her mouth with a napkin and looked my way. "Thanks for getting Nathan, Jack." She finished her wine and set the empty glass down on the table.

I studied her for a moment or two. Her complexion was glowing, probably the result of all the outdoor air and exercise she got at the Cromwell work site today. She looked good, I thought, very relaxed and upbeat. But after yesterday I could no longer be sure why Claire looked the way she did, nor believe what she said or did. In the blink of an eye I had grown suspicious and mistrustful of my partner of 18 years. I was suddenly cautious and uneasy, having no idea what would emerge from these murky waters.

After a bit Nathan finished his meal and excused himself from the table, while Claire and I sat and talked a little more about the Cromwell Pointe project. At one point she looked at me and said, "So, professor, how's life at

Guilford?"

I have to admit, I flinched a little at the question. I went to the refrigerator and got myself another beer and chose to lean against an adjacent breakfast nook rather than return to the table. I popped the tab and took a long swallow. "Bad day at Black Rock," I said, slowly shaking my head.

"Why?" she asked, immediately sensing my mood. She turned in her chair to face me.

I didn't answer right away, instead mentally replaying snatches of what happened in my classroom today. When I did share, I realized I was giving Claire a condensed version of what took place with Crider and Slocum and while the details were accurate, they were also diluted. I had no desire to tell her all that happened, and never mentioned the visit from Rachel Pond. All of this bothered me and made me realize, again, the distance that had been literally created overnight. Claire and I had always shared our lives and were never afraid to disclose, never fearful of rejection or abandonment. It was strange now finding myself being cautious and tentative about reaching out. I wondered how long I would choose to be tight-lipped or want to hide in unreachable places.

To her credit, Claire listened to me and absorbed the few details I shared. She looked at me and crossed her arms, the two of us exchanging a glance. She was obviously upset about what happened, her face reflecting a mixture of disbelief and anger.

"You did the right thing," she said, her eyebrows pinched together. "Both of those creeps should be ashamed of themselves." She paused for a moment thinking, then added, "How are you going to handle them?"

I raised my eyebrows. "I don't know, that's the tough part. I need to give it some thought, maybe talk to some people before I decide on anything." Since the class didn't meet again until next Monday, I had some time to think things through.

She nodded thoughtfully. "Are you thinking about talking with Cy?" she asked.

"Yes," I replied. "I'm going to try and see him tomorrow." Cyrus Rollins was one of my closest friends, a fellow professor at Guilford who was Chair of the life science department. He and I attended graduate school at the University of Massachusetts and he was one of the principle reasons I came to Guilford six years ago. I trusted him and knew I could count on him for advice.

Claire started getting up from the table and I pushed away from the counter. I decided to change the subject and switched to the Billy Halliday story as we cleared the table.

She remembered Sean Halliday immediately. "The sexist jeep guy, right?"

"That's him," I said.

She shook her head when she heard about the credit card scam.

"Incredible," she said, staring at me. "I've never heard that one before."

"Me neither," I said, finishing my beer. "It's pretty clever when you think about it."

Claire loaded the knives and forks into the dishwasher, then stood there with her hands on her hips. "Are you going to say anything to the Hallidays?"

I let out a long breath. "I wasn't planning on doing anything," I admitted. "I don't know the kid and I barely know the father." I paused and looked at her. "I mean, it's really none of our business, Claire."

Until now, I hadn't even considered this angle. Clearly the kid was in the wrong, but who was I to drop something like this in the parents' lap? Was there a moral obligation here? If the situation were reversed, would I want a relative stranger sticking his nose in our business? I needed to think this through.

"Well, I suppose sooner or later the kid will get caught," Claire said. "Hopefully it will be by his parents and not the police. Sounds like it's only a matter of time before Billy finds bigger fish to fry."

I put the leftovers in the refrigerator while Claire swiped the counters with a sponge.

She added, "I wonder if this is the kind of stuff we'll be facing with Nathan. I thought all we had to worry about were tattoos, tongue studs and social networking."

I walked over to her and said, "Whatever happened to drugs, sex, and rock and roll?"

Claire tilted her head. "Get with it, Elliot. Haven't you heard? Woodstock's come and gone."

"It has?" I screwed up my face. "Bummer."

Claire left the kitchen to get some work done in the study and I watched a little television and did some light reading. It was about ten o'clock when I said goodnight to Nathan, who was in bed and had just finished watching one of those reality shows on television. He was pretty good about keeping his ten o'clock bedtime, although he gave us a run for our money about all the house rules a few years ago. We talked for a few minutes, a night time ritual I try to do as often as I can. With his glasses removed, braces, and the covers pulled up under his chin, he looked like a child instead of the teenager he had become. The days of kissing him goodnight had ended, so I tousled his hair and gave his hand a squeeze instead.

When I got to our bedroom, I discovered that Claire had fallen asleep. Her reading light was still on and a book lay opened on the bed beside her. I closed the book and switched off the light. I quietly got undressed and used the bathroom, then padded to the bed and slipped between the covers. She stirred and rolled on to her side facing away.

I lay there listening to her breathing, her body lifting and falling very quietly. I stared at the ceiling, exhausted and on edge. I closed my eyes and tried to take it all in, this incredible mess that had unfolded over the past few days. The classroom altercation still replayed in my mind and I had no idea how I was going to handle matters. Of course, this had been heaped on Claire's infidelity, which rocked the very foundation of my life. I was clueless as to why my wife would wander away and put herself in such a compromising position, why she'd want to live a smoke and mirrors existence. For that matter, I didn't know why she'd allow herself to fall so easily from grace, to turn her back on her family in order to be with someone else.

Nothing made sense, except that I knew I was in a bad place.

## *Six*

The next day I had the house to myself and no classes, circumstances that couldn't have come at a better time. With no one underfoot, I had things I wanted to do and later on, people I needed to see. The shock of finding Claire's emails had somewhat lessened, replaced by a strong need to start making sense of what happened. I refused to believe Claire's secret ended in the attic, especially since she took the bait yesterday and retrieved her emails from the roll of Christmas paper. This might have brought her some peace of mind, namely that her secret was safe, but in my eyes further pitted her credibility.

Once Claire and Nathan left the house, I poured myself a heaping mug of coffee and went into the study to get the email copies from my briefcase. Our study is one of the largest rooms in the house and was designed a few years ago to support three workstations. Mine is a corner desk that has two surfaces, one occupied by a top of the line desktop computer. The rig cost me a small fortune but has all the bells and whistles I needed for research and writing, including top of the line processors and graphics, high performance peripherals, a multi-track task pad, multiport availability, and an oversized flat screen. A writer's true dream machine. It is my workhorse and no one uses it but me. An L-shaped table butts against the far adjoining wall, a state of the art printer, copier, scanner, and fax on its top surface along with boxes of mailing envelopes, unassembled shipping boxes, sealing tape, and reams copy paper below.

Claire's area is situated along another wall and consists of an adjustable drafting table that doubles as her computer workstation. A large folding table is set up nearby and contains materials from her various projects, like working drawings, models and photographs. Resting on a small table nearby is a docking unit for her laptop as well as a cell phone charger. A two drawer filing cabinet and a bookcase for work related materials sit next to the drafting table.

The family workstation consists of an antique cherry desk with an oversized writing surface. Here we do everything from opening and sorting mail to paying our monthly bills. Nathan often does his homework here, although he has a desk set in his bedroom. Our family computer and telephone answering machine sit on opposite corners of the desk. We own a fairly recent desktop computer, although it's nowhere near as fancy as mine. However, it has all the applications we need, including email and entertainment capabilities. Next to the desk are filing and storage units containing the paper trails found in most homes, from canceled checks and credit records to insurance policies and warranties.

I sat down at the family desk and saw that the computer had been left on by Claire, who usually checks her email before heading off to work. I brought the monitor to life hoping that she'd forgotten to sign off, but had no such luck. She had switched from her screen name, *Clairell*, back to my screen name, *Jackel*, which was also the master screen name and without password protection. The third screen name was Nathan's *Offthehook*. He thought using parts of our first and last name as screen names was as bogus as it was corny and coined his own.

I put on my reading glasses and looked at the email copies, wondering if Claire had sent any of them from here. Of course, I recognized that she could access her AOL address from her wireless laptop anywhere or from the server available at *Original Dimensions*. Curious, I got a pencil from a holder on the desk and circled the hours when she'd opened the stranger's email and sent hers. With the exception of one from him, all of the emails were exchanged during evening hours.

This came as a surprise. While Claire occasionally worked late at the agency she was more apt to use her laptop right here in the study, where she had access to all of her job stuff. I could count on one hand the number of times I've seen her using her laptop in other locations of the house, and then hardly ever at night. She was more likely in front of the family computer at night, checking her emails just like she does each morning.

This meant that in all probability she was passing love notes back and forth to her boyfriend right underneath my nose.

How could I have been so blind? I pressed the pencil against my lower lip, trying to take this in. Had I been that immersed in my own world to have missed what was going on around me? In my own defense, I didn't think so, mainly because Claire hadn't done anything to arouse my suspicion. She never made an effort to conceal what she was doing, like frantic mouse clicking or turning off the monitor if I happened to walk in. If she was interrupted while online, she never reacted with anger or defensiveness. She didn't stay online at night after I went to bed, nor had she ever changed her screen name or created additional ones. Claire and I have had the same screen names for the past five years.

I switched the computer over to Claire's screen name, staring at the AOL prompt for her password. Until yesterday, I never questioned her decision to keep her password secret, just like I never questioned her possessiveness of her briefcase and cell phone. She always kept her cell phone in the briefcase and the briefcase locked. This was clearly her turf and I respected her privacy, just like she respected mine. Furthermore, she had every right to safeguard them, particularly with electronic crimes running so rampant these days. I knew that her computer files contained important client files in addition to costly landscape design programs and mapping systems.

I drummed my fingers on the surface of the desk, reading glasses perched on my head. To snoop or not to snoop, I thought, to hack or not to hack. My temptation to pry ran counter to Claire's right of privacy, placing me smack in the middle of an approach-avoidance conflict. Do I start taking steps to understand what the hell was going on, or turn a cheek? I reminded myself that I was the victim in all this, that I'd been blind-sided. I'd earned the right to pry, to be just as sly and secretive. Claire's retrieval of her emails yesterday was added incentive to push forward, to somehow start connecting the dots.

I suppose my decision to snoop was also spurred by the kinds of information I could potentially access in the computer. If successful, I could see her email, address book, buddy list, and maybe even her filing cabinets. I could also take a peek at her history trail, cache and downloaded folders.

I stared at the password prompt, then began typing in possibilities. I experimented with variations of her full name and maiden name. I tried all of our family names, her parents' names, nicknames and pet names. I tried them all backwards. I attempted her astrological sign and birth stone. I switched to numbers and plugged in birth dates, graduation dates, street numbers and phone numbers. I tried number sequences and then a combination of words and numbers. I entered letters, abbreviations, exclamation marks and an assortment of other characters.

I got nowhere and realized that I was doing little more than twiddling my thumbs. I could spend days doing this and have zero to show for my efforts. I was about to give up when I suddenly remembered another possible access route, one I'd learned about not too long ago from a parent having trouble with her teenage son's online activities. She described how this access route enables you to read email from all screen names within an AOL account without having to enter a password, although the messages are fragmented and a bit hard to decipher.

I had to stop and think for a moment about the access directions she gave. I switched over to my screen name and went to the 'C' drive, clicking on 'My Computer.' I opened the 'AOL Online Folder' and clicked on the 'Organize' folder. Once there, I easily found our screen name files. There were three files under my screen name, two under Claire's, and one under Nathan's. I clicked on one of mine, wanting to give the system a dry run before opening hers. I was greeted by a prompt asking me to identify which operating program I wanted to use. Before I made a selection, I placed a check mark in 'Select the program from a list.' I then scrolled down the options and double clicked 'WordPad.' The monitor then filled with a dizzying array of symbols and characters, not unlike hieroglyphics. I remembered the mother telling me not to feel overwhelmed by these configurations, to just keep slowly scrolling.

Sure enough, pieces of my emails began to appear, first words and then sentence fragments. It was time consuming and tedious to ignore the symbols and piece everything together, but after a while I got the hang of it. I had no idea that this hidden, password free cache existed and wondered how many AOL users knew about it. In certain instances I discovered that only parts of my emails existed. At the very least, though, the cache contained the screen names of those who had written to me as well as the destinations of mine, including dates.

I left my cache, buoyed that learning more about Claire's email correspondences was just a few clicks away. I went back to the 'Organize' folder, selected one of Claire's files, and opened it with the 'WordPad' program. Similar hieroglyphics appeared and I scrolled down, waiting patiently for the words to appear.

When they did, my spirits sagged almost immediately. Unlike the sizable number of emails I found stockpiled in my cache, hers contained only a few dozen, all exchanged within the past month or so. I thought I'd done something wrong, so I went back and repeated the steps. The same small cache appeared. Thinking another program might be the answer, I tried 'Notepad,' but got the same results. I tried all of the remaining programs from the options list, but none were able to handle this function. When I opened her second screen name file, I got the same results.

I read through the few emails I found in Claire's files. There were no surprises, just the standard email fare of short notes to family and friends, a few internet jokes, and a bunch of work-related correspondences. I scanned through the emails twice to see if Claire had exchanged anything with the mysterious *Strap95* from Earthlink. Nothing. In fact, no unfamiliar addresses appeared anywhere.

I stared at the monitor, tapping a finger against my chin. I was seeing a stealthy side to Claire I didn't recognize. First the emails, then her retrieval of them, and now recently emptied caches. It was becoming increasingly obvious that Claire was trying to keep some ghosts from leaving her closet. She kept looking back over her shoulder.

My eyes ached from reading the encrypted emails and I rubbed them with the heels of my palms. I'd reached a dead end here and saw no sense wasting any more time. I printed a copy of the files I found and closed the program.

I attacked the house file cabinets. Claire handles the bulk of the monthly bills and has a good filing system of cancelled checks, monthly bills, credit card receipts, cash advances, and the like. Our records go back for the last few years, the rest stored in the attic.

I looked at the phone bills first. We get three separate monthly statements, one for the house and one each for the separate cell accounts we have with the same company. As I organized the bills, I thought about Claire's phone manners around me. Much like her computer behavior, she hadn't done anything to arouse my suspicion. She wasn't secretive about her calls, never rushed to answer the phone, nor was one of those types who constantly checked her cell for messages.

I leafed through the bills to see if any monthly statements were missing, perhaps kept hidden from my eyes. They were all there. I got a pad of paper and pen and sifted through the house bills, jotting down any long distance numbers that seemed out of place, like unfamiliar locations or repeated numbers that I didn't recognize.

Since neither one of us gets itemized billing, the cell phone statements didn't give me much to go on, just the minutes used and the monthly service charges. From what I could see, nothing seemed out of line. Of course, it was what I couldn't see that bothered me, like her received call log, last-call return or saved messages. I needed to get my hands on her cell for that, which would prove tricky. She almost always kept it locked in her briefcase or within arm's reach.

I turned my attention to our credit card bills and bank statements. Similar to the phone bills, no monthly statements were missing. I flipped through charge slips and store receipts, paying attention to Claire's purchases last fall, including those made at gift shops. Nothing seemed out of place. The gas cards also seemed to be in order, with no unusual fill ups or strange gas station locations. She'd gotten a lot of fill ups in Cromwell during the past year, but I knew they were connected to her project. Finally, Claire had put a number of lunches on charge cards over the past year, not unusual since business lunches were part of the agency lifestyle. Cromwell again appeared as a repeated location. I recorded all of the restaurants she'd frequented and how much she'd charged.

I looked at the ATM withdrawal slips and canceled checks. Having an affair undoubtedly involved expenses and Claire was the kind of woman who always insisted on paying her own way, even back to when we were dating. It stood to reason that she'd need pocket money, especially if she went away last November. There had to be a cookie jar somewhere. My eyes flicked back and forth on the withdrawal slips looking for unusual times, places and amounts. Nothing jumped out at me. Finally, I rifled through the canceled checks, looking for amounts made out to cash. Nothing out of the ordinary.

I put all the files back where I found them and stood up, rubbing my arms to restore circulation. I went into the kitchen and poured another mug of coffee, then walked over and stared out the window into the backward. Our back yard is spacious, several perennial rock gardens offsetting a rolling lawn, a gazebo, and lots of shade trees. I sipped my coffee as I watched two squirrels scamper across the roof of the gazebo and down two dogwoods Claire had planted last fall. She'd landscaped the gazebo area when I was away for a weekend, surprising me with her efforts when I returned.

I came back to the study and decided to poke around to see if I could discover hiding spots, places where Claire might keep cards, money and even gifts. I looked through all of her file cabinets, especially the spaces in the back, and behind her desk. I fanned through pages of her books and manuals, examined all of her storage containers. Nothing.

I ran my hand along the wall molding and trim, looking for loose pieces, and pulled at the corners of the carpeting for hiding flaps. I pounded along the walls listening and feeling for dead spots or hidden spaces. I went inside the study's double closet and searched through everything on the shelves, including hard to reach spots up top. I looked for openings in the unfinished wallboard inside the closet. More nothing.

I continued searching in the bedroom. I searched all of the bureau drawers, including my own, checking behind and underneath each. I pulled the bureau out from the wall and looked behind it, felt underneath it. I went behind the bedroom television set, inside baskets and ornamental boxes, and behind pictures. I looked under the mattress and the bed. Nothing there. I again pulled on molding and carpeting, pounded on the walls. I went into the walk-in closet and patted down the jackets, blouses and dresses hanging in a row. I got down on one knee and pushed the clothing out of the way, checking the bottom of the closet. Nothing. I slid my hand under folded sweaters and turtlenecks on the closet's top shelf. Nothing there either.

I straightened the room and stood there, hands on hips. I'd reached the end of my rope for the morning and didn't know what else I could accomplish. While I found no evidence suggesting any ongoing involvement with her lover, any relief was thinly veiled. Claire's deletion of her AOL cache as recently as a month ago nagged at me, as did her retrieval of the emails yesterday. I needed to discover why she was restless and still covering her tracks.

I knew I'd barely scratched the surface in the last 24 hours, hardly enough to see things clearly and certainly not enough for any kind of confrontation. I told myself that I had to be patient as well as persistent. I was convinced that what I learned today would lead to another piece of the puzzle, then another. Sooner or later, enough of the puzzle would come into focus and make sense. Then, and only then, would I drop it in Claire's lap.

In the meantime I would keep sniffing and watch her closely, especially when she was out of the house. It wouldn't hurt to follow her a few times, I thought, maybe verify her supposed destinations and whereabouts. Also, I needed access to her computer and cell phone accounts, but was a total novice. Maybe I'd talk with someone about surveillance devices. I'd heard there were software programs that recorded all online activities as well as phone call-display monitors that could be plugged into hidden jacks. She had proven tricky and elusive, and I needed any advantage I could muster.

My trump card, of course, was that she had no clue I was on to her.

I SHOWERED AND DROVE TO THE COLLEGE, hoping to catch Cy Rollins during one of his afternoon office hours. I traveled south on the old Boston

Post Road and picked up Connecticut Interstate 95, a totally unimaginative stretch of highway distinguished only by its bottle neck traffic jams and ongoing road work, projects that have succeeded in accomplishing little except backing traffic up for miles.

Thoughts of Claire steamrollered through my mind during the drive to Guilford. I was still very much in a daze, and my head felt large and fuzzy. A roller coaster of emotions rushed through me, and I felt wrung out. My brain was fried. The past few days seemed unreal, and I was hoping that I'd wake up at any moment and discover that everything had been just a bad dream.

I thought of where we were a year ago as a family, when Claire supposedly had her affair. I had just finished my fourth year at Guilford College, and Claire had been at the landscape firm in Old Lyme, *Original Dimensions*, for a few years. Nathan was thirteen. I thought Claire and I were happy with each other and satisfied with our careers, successfully juggling the chores and responsibilities that go along with dual earner households. Our family was financially stable and free of medical illness or disease. Although we lived through a tragic, freak accident when we lived in Hadley, Massachusetts, I thought our lives were on an even keel.

I racked my brain trying to think of any marital friction that might have gotten in our way last year, but could think of absolutely nothing. Claire's behavior was not unusual or out of the ordinary. She was not distant or cold, nor did she ever seem preoccupied or distant. Claire was responsible and accountable as both a partner and parent, and she was always where she was supposed to be, almost to a fault. While all couples have marital spats, I couldn't recall any earth shattering miscommunication or problems we couldn't or didn't resolve.

Our sex life has always been great, which made it difficult for me to believe that Claire had jumped into the sack with another guy just for some action. We both enjoyed sex on a regular basis, and it never felt like a chore. I always thought that our lovemaking was passionate and had that special spark. I could not recall Claire ever complaining about sex or avoiding it because she was disinterested or turned off. She was an exciting sex partner—wild and uninhibited when the mood pleased her—and sometimes just thinking about her in the bedroom gets me wired.

It came as no surprise that another guy was attracted to Claire, because she has that kind of effect on men. Over the years, many have commented on her charm, intelligence and physical beauty. She is a complete package and I have often been told how lucky I am to have landed her. No argument there.

Claire is the sort of woman who commands attention when she walks into a room. She radiates a healthy, youthful vibrancy and has a great complexion and smile, gorgeous green eyes flecked with gold, and a lean, well-defined body. She carries herself with poise and confidence and has always kept in shape, especially after Nathan's pregnancy. She's a dedicated jogger, plays tennis on a regular basis and is an active member of the local health club.

She dated quite heavily before we met, and I know more than a few guys have come on to her after we tied the knot. However, she's always deflected such advances with graceful assertiveness, calling them both harmless and misguided, or at least that's what she's told me all along. I don't consider myself a jealous man, nor am I possessive. I have never felt threatened or insecure by any of the attention she's received.

Until now, anyway.

I PULLED MY CAR INTO THE FACULTY parking lot and made my way to Cy's office. He was sitting at his desk in a white lab coat talking to two male students when I knocked on his partly opened door. He beamed when he saw me and started to get up from his chair, but I waved him off and reached for his hand.

I looked over at the two students and said, "Sorry to barge in, guys."

Cy was about my height and age. He had sandy hair brushed to one side, large brown eyes that sparkled and a smile that radiated boyish charm. Cy was Chair of the life sciences department and a popular professor among the students. He was intelligent, knew his stuff, and was well respected at the college.

Cy looked over at the two students, gestured toward me. "Gentlemen, allow me to introduce Dr. Jack Elliot, campus wordsmith and Guilford's most fluent and prolific writer."

I smiled and we exchanged handshakes all around.

Cy said, "Jack, I was just sharing with these young men the virtues of academic honesty and integrity."

The two students shifted in their chairs and looked a mite uncomfortable. One of them had a shaved head and was wearing a Guilford hooded sweatshirt. He sat there jiggling his feet while nervously licking his lips. The other was acne scarred and looked dazed, like he had lost contact with the mother ship. He had a long neck accentuated with a protruding Adam's Apple.

I realized that I had walked in on a serious conversation and cursed myself for not calling earlier to see if Cy was going to be tied up. "Listen, I'm sorry to interrupt," I said. "I didn't mean to catch you at a bad time." I reached behind me for the door.

"No, no, stick around for just a minute more. I want you to hear this... it's a terrific little story."

Cy turned to the two students. "You see fellas, there was this professor who was convinced two students had cheated on his examination, so he called them into his office for a little chat. The professor told them that out of 50 multiple choice items, their answers on 49 of them were identical. This was statistically impossible, the professor said, unless one student deliberately copied from the other. The two swore up and down that they didn't cheat, that they studied together for weeks, which explained why their answers were identical. So the professor looked at them and said, 'what you're telling me, then, is that you guys didn't cheat?' 'Absolutely,' chimed the students. 'Okay,' the professor said, 'then maybe you could explain this,' as he pulled their two answer sheets out of his desk. They were identical except for question 50, next to which each student left a handwritten note. One student had written on his exam sheet, 'This is the hardest question on the whole test!' The other student wrote on his, 'I agree!'"

Cy can deliver a punch line with the best of them and he howled with laughter at his own material.

I had to admit the joke brought a smile to my face, even though I'd heard it before. I could tell by the faces of the two students, though, that they didn't know what to make of the whole scene. It was clear these guys were on the hot seat and it was really time for me to disappear.

"Good stuff, Cy, but I should go," I said, turning for the door.

Cy got out of his chair and said to me, "Hold on, Jack, I'll walk you to the stairs."

When we got out of earshot, he leaned in low with a devilish grin and said, "Those little fuckers, I caught them dead to right cheating on my midterm and now they're both sitting in there denying it. I'll break the bastards down, especially chrome dome. He'll crack first. You watch, I'll have him chirping like a fucking canary before the afternoon is over and he'll end up ratting on his buddy. Guaranteed."

Deep down, I think Cy took fiendish delight in unleashing his linguistic repertoire in the company of others, especially the timid and uninitiated. I believe he liked being seen as the campus rogue and used salty language every so often to instill shock or underscore his presence or position. Whatever the reason, Cy Rollins was Guilford's undisputed crowned prince of the life sciences and the reigning monarch of vulgarity and impropriety. I must add that whenever Cy blisters the air with cuss words, I often find it impossible to keep a straight face.

I let a moment or two pass. "Cy," I said, looking around to make sure no one was around, then turning my head toward him. I lowered my voice, scratched my chin. "I stopped by to see you because I need a little help, some advice really."

Cy immediately picked up on my mood change and looked at me with concern. He started to say something, then stopped. "Of course, Jack. What's up?"

I swallowed, my mouth a little dry. "I had a classroom altercation yesterday, and I'm not sure if I handled it properly or where I should go from here." I hesitated a bit but then described the incident, starting with Crider's outburst and the eventual escorting of he and Slocum from the classroom. I tried not to leave anything out.

Cy watched me closely as I talked, his eyes widening when I got to the confrontation with Crider. I could see his personality shifting gears as he went from his usual jovial self to an angry, protective friend.

When I was done, Cy took a deep breath and straightened. He looked at the floor for a bit then spat, "Those bastards." He was quiet for a few moments and the color rose in his cheeks. He looked up at me and said, "Give me their names, Jack, and I'll take care of this."

"No, no," I sputtered, stepping in front of him, lightly pressing my fingers into his chest. "Listen to me Cy, that's not why I'm here. The names are unimportant—I can handle all of this on my own."

He angled his head and shot me a puzzled glance, not at all sure where I was going or what I was asking.

I repeated myself. "Really, Cy, I'm okay."

He shook his head slowly. He looked to the left, down the hallway, then returned his gaze to me.

I scratched my chin again and said slowly, "I did make a few wrong moves, though. I need your advice."

His eyebrows arched, an invitation to continue.

"I guess my biggest regret is that I lost my cool. I used profanity when I talked with the student, although no one else could hear what I said." I let out a long breath. "I let my anger get the best of me." I looked back at him and my voice got quieter. "I actually threatened the kid."

His face got taut. "You threatened him? You? That's a little hard to believe, Jack."

"Well, I did." I told Cy what I said to Crider.

Cy paused for a moment, then leaned towards me. "Listen, Jack, we all say things in the heat of battle that we later think twice about. What you did was regrettable, but understandable. Your motivation to protect your students intensified what you were feeling. Sounds like this guy needed a good wake-up call anyway."

He shifted gears. "Did anyone hear you threaten him?"

"I don't think so, although his buddy was sitting next to him." I described how I walked over to Crider's chair to get his attention. "I was pretty much whispering in his ear when I said it."

He shrugged. "Then let it go. When the kid comes back, set up some time with him and apologize—disarm the whole thing—if that's what you think you want to do."

Cy got a faraway look in his eyes, then laughed quietly. "Personally, I think the worthless moron got what he deserved. Maybe now he'll think twice about opening his mouth and abusing people who can't fight back."

I slowly nodded my head.

Cy put his hand on my shoulder. "Jack, let it go—it's over. You can't get back what you did. None of this will amount to a hill of beans—no one will make an issue over this." He took a look at his wrist watch and I knew I was keeping him from the students in his office.

Cy scratched the top of his head and said, "With all this said, I think you have two pieces of unfinished business left. The first is deciding what you're going to do with these two good-for-nothing rejects when they return to class. You need to give that some careful thought. The second is the damage control you've got to do with the rest of the class."

I told him that I wasn't sure what I was going to do with Crider and Slocum. I had several ideas in mind but wanted to give each more thought. I wasn't sure about his second suggestion, though. "What do you mean by damage control with the rest of the class?"

"The ship, Jack, you need to right the ship. If I were you, I would think about what you're going to say to the rest of the class when you meet again. If you're asking for advice, I'd suggest going in and having a little heart to heart, even though you already had one at the end of the freak show yesterday. You need to regroup the troops. Tell them that what they witnessed was an unfortunate classroom incident and that you'd be happy to address any questions or concerns. Even if you did this the day it happened, do it again. Emphasize that you want to keep everyone's best interests at the forefront, ensure that everyone completes the course on a good note. Make it a point to say that your door is open to anyone who wishes to discuss the matter privately."

I nodded and zippered my jacket, appreciative of the advice. It was time for me to shove off.

I thanked him and gestured with my chin toward his office. "You catch those guys today?" I asked.

"Yeah, last period. The nerve of those losers. I caught the pencil-necked geek with a cheat sheet, but I know he and cue ball were sharing it. Their exams are almost identical." He rubbed his hands together in fiendish delight. "I'm going to get two wankers for the price of one today, Jackie, I can feel it in my bones."

"Well, don't be too hard on them," I said. "We've all been caught with a hand in the cookie jar, you and me included."

Cy stuck his hands inside his lab coat. "I know, I know. But these guys have to face the music." He gave me a grudging smile. "Choices, Jack. It's all about choices and living with those we make."

He was right, of course. Little did I know how often I'd be turning those words over in my mind in the days and months to come.

## *Seven*

The weekend rolled around and Claire and I were getting ready to attend a special agency dinner. It was in recognition of this week's ribbon cutting at Cromwell Pointe, an event owner Hal Morris felt worthy of celebration and cheer. He was footing the dinner bill for the agency staff, as well as invited guests, including yours truly. Claire had been excited about the event the past few days, and rightfully so given the time and energy she'd devoted to the project over the past year.

I was getting dressed in front of the bedroom bureau mirror, having selected a dark green herringbone sports jacket to go along with a blue oxford button down, black wool slacks and dress loafers. Claire was heading for the shower and suggested a tie, which I wasn't going to wear, but deferred to her judgment since she was seldom wrong about these kinds of things. I knotted a burgundy regimental stripe tie.

We'd imported Forrest to keep Nathan company tonight because it looked like we'd be getting home later than we normally do. While Nathan had outgrown babysitters a while ago, we were still a bit uncomfortable leaving him alone and liked the idea of having someone around for him, especially at night. Forrest was always a ready and willing houseguest, usually jumping at the chance to hang with Nathan.

As Claire showered and got ready, I got in the car to pick up pizzas for the guys, pepperoni and plain. When I returned, I found Nathan and Forrest outside shooting baskets in the driveway, which surprised me. I'd erected a basketball goal off to the side of the driveway when we first moved in, even attaching spotlights to the garage for night play. But Nathan never took to the game, just like he never returned to the baseball diamond after the tragedy at Hadley. This used to nag at me when he was younger, probably because I was an athlete and knew the benefits sports could bring. But, I've since come to terms with the reasons and his decisions. I suppose part of coming to grips with midlife was recognizing that my kid was never going to be the next Ted Williams or Larry Bird, or for that matter enjoy sports as much as the old man.

I stopped the Volvo in front of the garage, turning in my seat to watch the two 14 year-olds for a few moments. They were playing a clumsy game of one-on-one, both of them uncoordinated and unskilled, stumbling and bumbling. Nathan double dribbled whenever he handled the ball, sometimes using two hands at once, and hacked Forrest mercilessly on defense. They shoved and pushed each other out of the way, sometimes by lowering their heads and barreling into each other. While Nathan tossed up brick after brick, Forrest was lucky to hit the backboard when he let loose with a barrage of two-handed set shots, the kind most kids abandon in grade school. Nathan's glasses kept fogging and Forrest had to keep hitching up his sweat pants every other minute because of his bulging belly.

They were indeed two lost souls on the court, the sad sacks you felt sorry for out on the playground. Fat and skinny, geek and nerd, blimp and wimp, spastic and oddball, take your pick. They were the kids destined to be the last picks on any team, or even worse, the ones unclaimed simply because nobody wanted them. They were the guys most likely to be ridiculed and laughed at, the ones who got the wedgies in the locker room or their asses flicked with wet towels. They were the kids who became mascots or team managers out of desperation to fit in somewhere, the ones who steered clear of jocks for the rest of their schooling, or the ones who became loners and withdrew, simply because it was safer that way.

I watched Nathan travel with the ball, taking five extra steps after the dribble and throwing up a ball that hit the bottom of the rim and caromed out of bounds off his head. I felt a wave of sadness, wondering if he'd already been singled out, bullied by thugs like Crider and Slocum, who roamed the hallways like vultures menacing the weak and different. I thought about how hard Claire and I have tried to protect him since we left Hadley, constantly thinking about the things he would have to learn about in the world and hoping to ward off any more turns for the worse. I'd see Nathan goofing around with Forrest or doing normal kid stuff and I'd start to relax, telling myself that I was worrying for nothing and being overprotective, that he was going to be fine, that he was just quiet and different. But then I'd see him other times with his head down or walking alone and I'd go into a funk thinking about what was going through his mind. He had a way of looking so burdened, so frail.

I was jolted back to the present by Claire's knuckles rapping against my window. I hadn't seen her come out of the house because I'd mentally drifted away. I smiled up at her and slid the window down, handing her the pizzas for the guys. They came over to the car sweaty and hot, red cheeked and starved. Claire told them everything was set up in the kitchen and gave them marching orders for the night. They shouted thank yous and goodbyes and were off in a blur.

Claire walked around the front of the car and began pulling on an overcoat. She wore a long, dark cranberry knit dress with a scoop neck, and black pumps. She had her hair down and was wearing makeup, which she only put on for special occasions, tonight being one of them. She looked lovely.

When she got in I backed the car out of the driveway, both of us fastening our seat belts. I kept the window down for a little while to get rid of the interior's pizza scent.

She looked over at me. "What was that all about?"

I raised a brow.

"Back there, at the house, with the boys. You were watching them and you were miles away, off in another world."

"Oh that," I said, turning her way, shaking my head and smiling a little. "Nothing, really."

We drove in silence for a little while. We didn't have too far to go, just the downtown borough of Spencer Plain.

She nudged my right thigh with her fingers. "You okay, Jack? Something on your mind?"

Take your pick, I thought. "I'm fine, Claire, really." I lied, sticking to my plan of avoiding conflicts and sidestepping tension. For the time being, I was determined to keep my mouth shut and eyes open.

"You still upset by what happened in class?"

Good topic, I thought, much safer. "Yeah," I said, "I've tried not to think about it, but it keeps coming back like a bad dream. Still too many loose ends, I suppose."

Although I held back on Monday, I ended up sharing everything about my classroom debacle with Claire this week, spending hours venting my frustration and anger. In true Claire fashion she wanted to know every single detail, making me retrace my steps to get a complete picture, and asking lots of questions. She'd always been a great listener, truly one of her strengths, and ended up giving me valuable feedback and advice.

"Have you thought any more about your options?" she asked, reaching over to the instrument panel and putting the heater on low. It was a crisp fall night.

I tapped my fingers along the bottom of the steering wheel. "I have."

We'd talked about different ways I could handle the situation. One alternative would be to follow up on the incident report and request that Student Affairs handle the situation, letting the chips fall where they may for Crider and Slocum. Another approach would be to avoid disciplinary action from Student Affairs and handle the situation myself, in my office and on my terms. We both agreed that getting Cy's input on this would be important. A third approach would be to take no further action, letting the humiliation of being tossed out of class and escorted out of the building serve as the punishment, as well as fair warning that I meant business. I suppose a fourth would be to take a tire iron to their kneecaps.

"And?" she asked, tilting her head.

I thought for a few moments. "I've decided that I'm going to call them into my office and handle things myself. I'm going to give them a break for reasons I'm unsure about, especially with Crider, and give them the no bullshit approach—you know, 'my way or the highway.' If they don't agree to what I propose then I'm going to turn the whole thing over to Student Affairs."

"Sounds like a plan," Claire said. "What are you going to propose? I assume an apology to you is one of the conditions, right?"

I turned left and descended down Main Street, old fashioned street lights splashing the sidewalks with golden orbs. With stores open until nine o'clock on Saturday, lots of shoppers were moving up and down the sidewalks. Up above, a harvest moon peeked out from behind a blanket of clouds. Claire and I pointed it out at the same time.

"Oh God, yes. I expect an apology from the two of them as well as assurances that something like this will never happen again. Zero tolerance, no second chances. That's the easy part. We can do that in my office, keep it between the three of us."

"What's the hard part?"

I pulled into the restaurant parking lot, nosing the Volvo into a spot not too far away from the main entrance.

I kept the engine running. "I expect Crider to apologize to Lois in front of the class. She deserves that. No person should have to endure the kind of humiliation he dished out."

Claire considered all of this carefully. "What if he wants to apologize to her in person instead?"

"That's not good enough," I said firmly. "He chose to degrade someone and be a smart ass in front of everyone. It's only fitting the class hears the apology, too."

"What about Slocum?" she asked.

"Once Crider apologizes to Lois, I expect Slocum and Crider to apologize to the entire class for their rudeness and the disruption they created."

I turned off the engine and pulled the key from the ignition. "Those are the conditions. I will accept nothing less."

A moment or two of silence passed. "Well, what do you think?"

She unfastened her seatbelt. "I think it's a break for both of them. If you let Student Affairs handle this they'd be screwed, Crider more than Slocum. The administration of any college would never tolerate this kind of faculty or student abuse. You're cutting them a deal, but you're certainly not letting them off the hook or giving them an easy way out. Making them publicly apologize will be a humbling experience, something they're not likely to forget."

Claire took my hand in hers. "I think you're being fair and reasonable and teaching them a valuable lesson. I like the plan." She leaned over and kissed me on the cheek. "Now do it and put the whole business behind you."

In hindsight, I wish it could have been that simple and easy.

THE DINNER WAS AT THE HEMPSTEAD INN, ONE OF Spencer Plain's largest and most recognized buildings, located directly across from the town hall. It's a rambling, three story wooden building constructed in the late 1700s, one that has remained structurally unchanged since it was built. The food is pricey but excellent, and the ambiance of the place is enhanced with an impressive collection of antiques and period furniture. There is an old fashioned bar next to the dining room, complete with a large fieldstone fireplace, where patrons can order food and drink and listen to nightly Dixieland entertainment.

We arrived early and were directed to a room just off the main lobby where private functions are held. The room was quite large and beautifully decorated. It had a number of circular dining tables underneath a ceiling crystal chandelier, thick gold carpeting and large, multi-paned windows, each with a decorative candle on the sill. Oil paintings hung from the walls, which were covered with ornate velvet paper and enameled wainscoting. A marble fireplace and a gleaming piano added a further touch of sophistication.

Many people were already there, some standing and postured in conversation, others sitting next to one another on elegant, plush chairs arranged throughout the room. It was a posh setting, soft background music and the scent of freshly cut flowers greeting the senses. The people were relaxed and upbeat, most smiling away and sipping cocktails while sampling the hors d'oeuvres being circulated. All were well dressed, some decked out more than others, and I was immediately glad that I took Claire's advice and wore a tie.

We met another couple as soon as we walked in the entrance, and struck up a conversation. We chatted for a while before others came over and joined us, Claire handling the introductions and making me feel at ease with the group. Right from the start I could tell Claire was in her element and enjoying herself, being playful, light-hearted and spontaneous.

I was determined to put forth a good effort for Claire and keep up appearances, but also looked at this as an opportunity to start paying closer attention to her life outside of the house. As I watched her interact, I looked for any differences in her mannerisms or mood with the other men in the room, something different about her eye contact or voice perhaps. At the same time, I took mental stock of the men, looking them over and trying to picture them with Claire, wondering if any could be the intruder.

At one point Claire branched off and was talking business with several members of the office staff, while I stood listening to a guy named Callahan entertaining a group of us with a steady diet of jokes. I use the word diet quite loosely because he was on the short side but must have tipped the scales at 300 pounds. He'd removed his sports jacket and rolled up his cuffs, a rumpled, moss green tie hanging at half-mast. He'd pounced on every tray of appetizers that came his way, having eaten enough to feed a small army and clutching enough used toothpicks to start a dangerous forest fire. While he talked he sweated profusely from every pore, especially his brow, which he kept mopping with a handkerchief soiled with what appeared to be mustard and guacamole dip. I reasoned that if he didn't sweat he'd likely explode.

Callahan was in the middle of a joke when he spied a fresh tray of appetizers coming his way. He stopped midsentence and literally licked his chops while flagging the waitress down, looking like he was hailing a taxi in Manhattan. His eyes rolled back when he saw that the tray contained fresh gulf shrimp, an audible gasp escaping his mouth. He turned to stake his claim, painstakingly dipping each shrimp several times in mounds of cocktail sauce. He then refocused his attention on the group, demonstrating the lost art of devouring three shrimp at the same time, simultaneously extricating the toothpicks from his frothing mouth with a graceful sweep of the hand. People just stared wide-eyed, captivated by the magical talents of this extraordinary man.

I felt like a drink and excused myself from Callahan's antics, strolling Claire's way to see if she wanted anything from the bar. When I got there, I could see that she already had a glass of wine in her hand, courtesy of one of her coworkers. I should have expected that since Claire was the star of the show and people had been bowing at her feet ever since we arrived. With the choice of listening to Claire talk shop with her friends or watching Callahan sweat cocktail sauce from his pores, my feet found their way to the bar.

# *Eight*

The bar at the Hempstead Inn was one of the most popular watering holes in Spencer Plain, and the place was busy. Lots of people sat at the bar drinking and chatting, others were eating at small tables nearby. I managed to get the bartender's attention and ordered a Rolling Rock long neck, no glass. I stood drinking at the bar taking everything in, checking out people and catching glimpses of a college football game being broadcast on an overhead television. The crowd was a mixed bag with a variety of neighborhood folks, trendy up and comers, and college kids all hanging out together. Very friendly place, very cozy.

The bar room was unpretentious and countrified: dark wood paneling, a hand-stamped tin ceiling and weathered floorboards. Empty peanut shells covered the floor, along with scattered sawdust. An old fashioned movie-style popcorn machine stood in the corner, next to a few antique wooden kegs and an old chopping block. Lots of antiques hung from rough exposed beams, and a fire blazed in the fireplace, every so often crackling and shooting sparks up the chimney.

The first beer went down to my toes and relaxed me so I ordered another. While wetting my snout I caught an inviting glance from a woman at the other end of the bar, a cute blond in a tight cocktail dress, thirty-something. I wondered if she was alone, or if her partner had just left her unattended for a few moments. I figured if Claire could look, so could I. Hell, she'd done far more than take a look at someone else. I took a swig and shot the woman a glance, but she looked away. However, she coyly looked back to re-engage eye contact. She smiled and flipped her hair.

Any further flirting was interrupted by a booming voice behind me and a hand planted firmly on my shoulder.

"Jack Elliot!"

I didn't even have to turn around to know that it was Hal Morris, Claire's boss and owner of the architectural firm *Original Dimensions*. When I did, he had one hand extended and the other wrapped around the last of a giant martini. I must have missed him in the other room or maybe he arrived late, but here he was bigger than life, if only in his own eyes.

"Hello Hal," I said, trying to muster enthusiasm in my voice. I shook his hand, wondering for a moment if he saw me sending smoke signals to blondie. I quickly dismissed that thought as I caught him admiring his profile in the bar's long rectangular mirror.

Morris and I never clicked and although we get along, our relationship will always be surface level. We don't have much in common and I don't run with his crowd, a collection of bow-tied, egocentric, Ivy League snobs. They like to stand around with their trophy wives conversing in clipped tones and furrowed brows, updating each other about the yacht club, exotic time shares, cricket and other completely useless crap. I've tried fitting in and listening politely to their puckered and pouting conversations, but their self-absorbed preening and crowing literally makes my skin crawl.

Morris was in his late fifties, tall and narrow-faced with thin lips and a pointed chin. His eyes were set close together and he had a long, skinny neck, all of which combined to give Morris the look of a rodent. Looks notwithstanding, he was quite the clothes horse and tonight looked especially dapper in an exquisitely tailored charcoal suit, a brilliant white shirt offset by a dark maroon silk tie and matching handkerchief in the jacket's breast pocket. His shoes were an Italian design and probably cost more than the refrigerator Claire and I replaced in our kitchen last month.

Wardrobe aside, as far as I was concerned Morris was also an aristocratic blowhard with a broomstick planted firmly up his ass. He'll show up at parties decked out in tweeds and cashmeres, holding his head back in a superior sneer. When he chooses to speak with you, he'll purse his lips as if he smells something rancid. Morris is one of those pompous losers who constantly looks past you while talking, undoubtedly on the prowl for better pickings to come along.

Claire once confided that while Morris likes me, he thinks I'm a bit of a social maverick with some rough edges. He claims I can come on a little too strong, blunt even. The nerve of that swaggering and pompous bottom feeder.

Morris fancies the sauce and I've seen him pasted on more than a few occasions. I could see that tonight he was already a little tipsy, a mite roasty toasty from knocking back a few. His smile was phony and he was a little too happy to see me. I was about to congratulate him on the Cromwell Pointe project, but he held up a finger imploring me to stop while he gulped the last of his martini, smacking his lips together for emphasis and promptly requesting another from the bartender.

He turned to me and said, "Jack, do tell, how art thou?" Not waiting for an answer, he surveyed the bar crowd instead, his radar taking everyone in, including the hottie down at the end. He flashed her his best toothy grin, but she looked away almost immediately and rolled her eyes at me, one of those 'lucky you' expressions.

"I'm just peachy, Hal," I said, taking a long swallow of beer. Morris stared at the long neck, probably wondering from his high brow brain how anyone in their right mind would want to drink from a bottle in a public establishment. Amused, I took another pull and smacked my lips for effect. He completely missed the slight, being the supreme doofus that he was.

When the bartender delivered his martini, Morris immediately tossed a third of it down the chute. As I watched him, I wondered if Morris might be the outsider in Claire's life. It didn't take long to throw that possibility out the window. Hal Morris? No way. He was simply not her type. Lots of money and power, but too stiff and glitzy, too egocentric. Besides, he was too old, having maybe twelve or fifteen years on Claire. He probably needed a six pack or two of Viagra to boink his wife, an old hag I've had to endure at previous agency parties. Nope, Claire was safe around Morris, I was sure of that.

Morris leaned in and said, "You must come along, Jack. Claire has reported you missing in action and sent me out on a scouting party." He reached over to straighten my tie as if we were school chums getting ready for a dance. When he was done he turned the tie over, inspecting the manufacturer's label.

He pursed his lips and gave me one of his superior sneers. "Lands End neckwear. Very nice, Jack."

"Thanks, Hal," I replied, "coming from you that's a real compliment." What a classless chump, I thought, wondering if tie turning was something he and his yacht club cronies did for kicks, maybe after a grueling round of afternoon croquet. He once told me that a Brooks Brothers tie I was wearing didn't count as the real deal because it was a retail outlet purchase, even having the gall to point out the label's retail code.

Morris patted down my tie and put a patronizing hand on my shoulder, guiding me toward the door. "Off we go," he said, winking. "Mingling time, very important you know."

So was tripping time, I thought, imagining what this fool would look like taking a belly flop on the dingy bar room floor, courtesy of my outstretched foot.

Morris led the way out of the bar, but not before I shot a glance over my shoulder at blondie, who still sat alone. She caught my eye and raised her drink to her mouth, a single outstretched finger waving goodbye.

Many more people had come into the dining room since I left, the group now nearing about forty people. I found Claire standing by a circular table and talking with many of the guys from the Cromwell Pointe project, most of whom I knew by name. We chatted a bit and when dinner was announced, Claire invited them to sit with us.

The food was good and the wine flowed freely, as did the table conversation. I stayed on the quiet side, preferring again to discretely watch the interaction of Claire and the men around her, seeing if I could pick up on something, maybe a nervous glance here or a secret smile there. But I sensed nothing as the conversation flowed around me, leading me to believe that Claire's lover was not connected to her work, at least not among those here.

Toward the end of dinner, just as coffee and dessert were being served, Morris got up from his table on the other side of the room and walked to the front. He brought his drink with him, taking a hit before putting it down on an empty table. He swayed a bit and I was hoping he'd miss the table with the glass and send it crashing to the floor, or better yet send himself crashing but neither happened.

The room silenced as he stood there, the proud peacock in front of his troops. He stood straight and tall, hands clasped behind his back, a distinguished image with his tailored suit and graying temples. Too bad this image contrasted sharply with a schnozola brighter than Rudolph's on a stormy night. I could have sworn his rodent nose blinked once or twice.

His eyes roamed the room. "Welcome everyone and thank you for coming to our special dinner this evening. I'd like to begin by sharing a story."

He thoughtfully scratched his temple and began pacing, looking at the floor. I suppose he was having trouble retrieving whatever hogwash was to come from his pickled brain.

He cleared his throat and cocked his head. "A crow sat perched on the limb of a tree, staring idly off into space and doing nothing. A rabbit came hopping along and looked up at the crow. The rabbit asked, 'Can I be like you and sit around and do nothing all day long?' The crow replied, 'Of course you can, anyone can.' So the rabbit found a spot on the ground and sat. Suddenly, a fox ran out of the woods, pounced on the rabbit and ate it."

Morris paused for effect and slyly looked around the room, no doubt thinking he had cast some kind of a magical spell and put everyone on the edge of their seat. I was indeed captivated, although it wasn't because of his cornball story. Rather, it was because his tongue had gotten tangled several times and at one point spittle had come flying out of his mouth, most of it nailing an innocent woman sitting in front. I was hungry for more.

He finally said, "Of course, there's a moral to the story." He cocked an eyebrow, hiking it up and down a few times. "To be sitting and doing nothing, you must be sitting very, very high up."

Morris delivered the punch line and leaned back laughing, his knees bending. I thought he came dangerously close to toppling over and was again hopeful, but somehow he straightened and then clapped his hands a few times to honor himself. He stood there rocking on his heels and grinning, acting like he'd just pulled off the caper of the year, tricking everyone with his incredible wit and superior intelligence.

He did get some laughs from a few people, including a guy at our table, who got carried away and mixed it up with some snorting while catching his breath. I didn't think the joke was that funny but broke out into fits of laughter over the barnyard sounds coming out of this character. Claire knew what I was up to and kicked me under the table.

Waiting for the room to get quiet, Morris switched gears and tried to get serious. "I suppose I sit high up, but I don't just sit there and do nothing. I get a good look at what's going on around me. I see the people who just come to work and punch the clock and I see those who have distinguished themselves as valuable team players."

Morris demonstrated his prowess as a golden orator and master of timing with a strategically released hiccup—or quite possibly a combination hiccup and burp—it was hard to tell which. He paused for a moment and put his hand to his mouth with one of those 'oh my' expressions, the captain of the ship trying to get his stomach convulsions under control. This was turning into quite the sideshow.

He continued in a composed manner. "I see the ones who complain and goof off, and I see those who know how to roll up their sleeves and set the bar at the next level."

Morris looked over at Claire, squinting because by now he was likely seeing the world in triplicate. "The Cromwell Pointe project is clearly that next level, thanks to the work of Claire Elliot. Claire," Morris said, looking a little cross-eyed, "I'd like you to come up here and join me for a moment."

Claire rose from her chair and went to the front of the room, standing alongside her boss. She shot a smile over at me and I smiled back.

Morris looked out at the group: "As you know, Claire was responsible for landing the Cromwell Pointe project, one of the biggest contracts this agency has ever landed. This was Claire's first major project with us and we gave her full reign, soup to nuts."

Morris stuck his hands in his suit pockets and leaned forward as he spoke. "This was no easy project, let me tell you. We hit some major bumps in the road and there were some, shall we say, creative design differences from within. But Claire stayed cool under pressure and when all was said and done, she produced a masterpiece of landscape architecture. Those of you at the ribbon cutting this week saw our agency sparkle because of the person standing next to me."

Morris turned to look at her. "Claire, I want you to know how pleased and proud we are of you."

Applause began to fill the room, scattered at first and then louder and sustained. Claire blushed and shifted a bit on her feet, not quite knowing how to deal with the obvious support and adoration from her colleagues. Morris gave her a hug, then walked over to a table and picked up a wrapped gift. He also picked up the martini he'd set down earlier and finished what was left. On the way back he had the nerve to hand the empty glass to the woman victimized by his saliva blitzkrieg.

He stood next to Claire. "Claire, anytime you get nostalgic and need to see your work on display, all you have to do is visit Cromwell Pointe. I suspect that jeep of yours knows the route to Cromwell by heart."

A few of the guys at our table chuckled, knowing that Claire practically lived at Cromwell during certain phases of the project.

Morris paused and took a handkerchief from his pocket to pat his glistening brow, alcohol sweats telling him to get to a refueling station immediately. He put the handkerchief back in his pocket and said, "But we thought you might want to look at something a little closer to home."

With that, he handed Claire the gift. She unwrapped it and looked inside the box for a few moments, removed some tissue paper, then got wide eyed and smiled. She removed a pewter, ornamental plate from the box. She studied it and got a little misty eyed.

Morris tried coming to her rescue and took the plate, holding it up for everyone to see, but not before first letting it slip from his grasp. Somehow he managed to catch it in midair, and then made a big show of cleaning it off with his handkerchief and blowing some imaginary dust away. I prayed that Morris's boozy breath wouldn't reach the candles at the nearest table and ignite the joint.

He went on: "We decided that Claire needed something for her trophy case. It has Cromwell Pointe written across the top, and Claire's name and the agency at the bottom, along with the completion date. If you come up afterwards and take a closer look, you'll see an etching of Claire's landscape design in the background." He paused and looked at her. "Congratulations from all of us, Claire."

Claire received another round of applause, this time accompanied by someone shouting "Speech!" from the back. If I wasn't mistaken, it was Callahan, his energy undoubtedly replenished by a square meal and the prospects of a dessert tray heading his way.

Morris gave one of his patented liver-lips grins and extended his arm towards Claire. "Would you like to say a few words?"

Claire thought about it for a moment, then nodded. She stood there holding the plate in front of her, looking like a school girl on graduation day. She paused, searching for the right words, looking a little embarrassed. "As you can see, I'm not very good at this."

She laughed a little, a tension releaser.

"The engraved plate is beautiful," Claire said. "I thank Hal and everyone else for such thoughtfulness and kindness. It will always be special."

She looked around the room for a moment or two. "We had our work cut out at Cromwell," she said, "and really had to pull together as a team."

At one point in the early going, Claire told me about chronic internal bickering over methods of construction and materials. Some disagreements led to heated exchanges. They were worse than old hens, I remembered her saying, someone's feathers always getting ruffled.

Claire looked toward her team, sitting at our table. "To my colleagues," she said, "thank you for your hard work. Each of us will remember a project that was challenging and at times frustrating, but rewarding."

She continued looking our way and smiled. "I'll remember all of you.

I'll remember those who were stubborn and irritating, and believe it or not, those who actually agreed with me. In the end, we managed to minimize our differences and maximize our talents. We set out to do a job, and we did it right."

Heads nodded at our table.

Claire hesitated, just a beat, and stood straighter. "It was my honor to be your supervisor."

The room filled with applause. Claire briefly bowed and smiled, clutching the pewter plate against her chest. I clapped along with everyone else, watched a steady flow of well wishers get up from their seats and congratulate her with hugs and kisses. I took it all in at a distance, watching this woman of talent and poise, this woman of beauty and grace.

This wife of great mystery.

## *Nine*

Nathan and Forrest were still up when we got home, sprawled out on the floor and watching the tail end of a DVD Forrest had brought along. Forrest needed to be taken home, but the two of them wanted to see the ending of the movie. I mean, who could blame them with the fate of the world resting on the broad shoulders of Vin Diesel? Heaven forbid if he happened to be our last option, I thought. It was late but I relented, agreeing to play taxi when it concluded. I shooed Claire off to bed, who looked like she could barely keep her eyes open.

I watched a little bit of the video with the guys, then went into the bedroom to hang up my sports jacket and tie. Claire was in the bathroom brushing her teeth, barefoot and wearing a black camisole and undies.

I waited for her to finish and went over to her, wiping a smidgen of toothpaste from the corner of her mouth with my thumb, giving her a big hug.

"You were wonderful tonight," I said. "I'm proud of you and the work you do. You deserved every bit of praise you got."

I really meant it, too. She'd obviously given her heart and soul to this project, in the process turning heads in upper level management and sweetening company profits. She was climbing, and fast.

She hugged me back and looked up at me, combing her fingers through my rumpled hair, straightening it.

"Thank you, Jack. Your support means a lot, especially tonight." She rose on her tiptoes and kissed me on the lips, then rested her head on my chest for a few moments.

"Hal Morris was quite the show," I said. "Very entertaining."

Claire sighed. "I know, he loves to throw parties and then gets tipsy."

"Drunk as a skunk is more accurate. He needs to learn when to put the plug in the jug," I replied.

"I agree, but he means well," she said.

We stayed that way for a few more moments before Claire looked back up at me, cocking her head. "You sure you're okay?"

I hesitated, but only for the briefest of moments. "I'm fine, really."

"You'd tell me if you weren't?"

"Of course."

She held on to me for a little longer, then I felt her body relax. I kissed the top of her head and said, "You're exhausted. Get to bed."

Claire didn't argue. She stretched and said, "Drive carefully, mister," making no effort to stifle a big yawn.

I CAME TO BED A SHORT TIME LATER, HAVING gotten Forrest home safely and Nathan tucked in for the night. Claire was sound asleep when I crawled between the flannel sheets. I read for a little while, from time to time hearing Claire snore softly. After a while my lids got heavy and I switched off the reading light. I was asleep within minutes.

During the night I heard Claire get up to use the bathroom. I rolled over on my back and pulled the covers up, extending one arm over to her side of the bed. When Claire got back she snuggled close, which she often does, resting her head on my shoulder and wrapping an arm around me. I slid back into the night.

Some time later I felt Claire nudge me awake and whisper my name. I was groggy from sleep but felt her hand inside my tee shirt, gently stroking my stomach with her fingernails. She began softly kissing my neck and ear while slipping her hand inside my underwear. Claire raised herself up on an elbow and lightly kissed my lips, her warm breath an erotic mixture of alcohol and sleep, her hair seductively brushing against my face.

Claire licked and nibbled my lips, parting them with her tongue and sliding inside my mouth. She ran her tongue along the length of mine and encircled it ever so slowly, then hungrily sucked it and drew it into her mouth.

It didn't take me long to become fully awake, not with that kind of stimulation. Claire and I rarely made love in the middle of the night, which made we wonder if her sexual cravings were connected to her lover. Whatever the motivation, I was aroused and didn't resist.

Claire was wearing her black camisole but had removed her undies, probably when she had gotten up earlier. She drew her leg up and over my thigh, pressing her wetness against me. I reached to touch her, and could feel the heat from her body.

She raised her body and moved her head downward, stopping at one point to swirl her tongue inside my navel. She removed my underwear and tossed it aside, spreading my legs with her hands. I got up on my elbows to move toward her, but she pushed me back down. She was as ravenous as she was greedy, and obviously wanted full control.

She then took my penis into her mouth, encircling its ridge with her tongue while slowly moving her hand up and down the shaft. Her tongue was warm and soft, and she gradually swallowed more of me until it all but disappeared into her hungry mouth. Several times she removed my penis from her mouth and stroked it, her fingers gliding over its wet sheathing, then resumed licking and sucking.

After a while Claire rose and swung one leg over my hips, straddling me. Given her mood, I knew she wanted to keep me pinned down and take me from above. She then proceeded to slowly impale herself, easing her weight down until she had all of me deep inside. Claire then began moving up and down, slowly at first and then with more intensity, moaning with pleasure. Several times she bent forward and plunged her tongue deep into my open mouth. Our mixed sexual scent began to fill the bedroom.

At one point Claire leaned back for more penetration, the movement pulling at her camisole and partially exposing one of her breasts. She then proceeded to reach down and touch herself, making small circular motions with her fingers against her clitoral hood without disrupting our pelvic rhythm. A sheen of perspiration coated her face and she was breathing heavily through her mouth, panting almost. Her closed eyes and tousled hair gave her a sultry look, her breasts straining against her skimpy silk top, straps seductively dangling to the sides. She was somewhere else, a woman in sexual ecstasy riding the crest of a wave, driven by desire.

Our rhythm picked up and I could no longer hold back. I placed my hands around her waist and pushed her hips down hard on to mine, guided her up and then back down repeatedly, my fingers digging into her flesh. I shuddered as I climaxed, spurting inside her while my body convulsed in forceful spasms. Claire continued for a few more moments until a wave of orgasm hit her, causing her to draw a sharp intake of breath and softly cry out. Her rhythm slowed but did not stop, and I felt her body shuddering. She lowered her face into my chest and sagged against me.

We finished in a tangled heap, satisfied and exhausted. Claire eventually went to the bathroom to freshen up, returning to cuddle under the covers as she'd been before we ravaged each other. As I watched her fall asleep, I thought about her sexual urgency as well as my own arousal and excitement. It dawned on me that neither of us had spoken during our lovemaking, but then again words probably would've gotten in the way. We were both in our own worlds, the bedroom darkness heightening our erotic passion and enabling lustful fantasies to play out. Even now, the fantasies lingered, holding her and being held.

Claire in the arms of her lover, Rachel Pond in mine.

## *Ten*

The next morning came fast, and a pounding headache told me that I had too much to drink last night. I cracked my eyelids to face the day, disoriented for a few moments. I reached over for Claire, but her side of the bed was empty. I'd forgotten she had a doubles tennis match this morning at the local health club. An early riser, she was likely long gone by now.

I rolled over on my back and rubbed the sleep from my eyes. I stayed that way for a while, enjoying the stillness of the morning and knowing that I didn't have to teach at the college. My mind seemed to have wings this morning, and I let it float and drift to where it wanted, including the sexual interlude with Claire last night. As I was trying to mentally untangle that whole scene, my thoughts for some reason took a sudden turn and brought me back to Hadley. Images began spilling into my consciousness, none more pronounced than the family tragedy we experienced.

How long ago was the accident? Six, seven years? God, it didn't seem that long. Claire and I settled in Amherst shortly after getting married and lived there for 10 years. Amherst is a college town located in western Massachusetts, about 25 miles from Springfield. It is a community brimming with cultural richness from the five colleges within its borders: the University of Massachusetts, Amherst College, Hampshire College, Smith and Mount Holyoke. I met Claire while finishing my doctoral degree at the University of Massachusetts. She was there completing a masters degree in landscape architecture.

We met at a place called *Fiddlers*, a college pub in downtown Hadley known for its live bands, Mexican food and oversized margaritas. The conversation flowed easily and we stayed until the place closed, exchanging phone numbers in the parking lot. We had our first date the following weekend and we've been together ever since.

After graduation I taught at UMass. Claire landed a job as a landscape architect in the nearby town of Northampton. Five years on we decided to start a family, and nine months later – with us both in our late twenties - Nathan Fitzpatrick Elliot entered our world. Claire stayed at home for Nathan's first few years, then went back to work, part-time at first. This was something we could afford to do because I'd become a successful published author. When I couldn't find a book that fit my classroom needs I decided to write my own, a college level textbook on creative writing.

And the gods smiled.

In its first year, my book bolted out of the gates and never looked back, outselling many of the established textbooks and leaving competing publishers scratching their heads, wondering who the hell was Jack Elliot. More titles would follow.

My professional life skyrocketed. Positive textbook reviews appeared in all the major research journals and within two years the book was translated into Japanese, French and Polish. And I was banking royalty checks that at the end of a couple of years added up to six figures. All of a sudden we were able to put aside a big chunk of change for Nathan's college education and purchase a new home. We moved into a spacious split level in Hadley, a dream house complete with a large swimming pool and fifteen acres of land.

I felt like I was riding the crest of a wave and I guess I was—we all were—until a tsunami arrived and nearly washed us away.

I DECIDED TO GET OUT OF BED AND START the day, even though it was the weekend. I let loose a mighty yawn and walked into the bathroom. I ran my fingers through my uncombed hair and walked to my end of the double sink. I splashed cold water on my face and as I toweled off, the reflection in the mirror wasn't kind. I had a tired, socket-eyed expression, the left side of my face creased with sleep. Too much booze, too much stress.

I threw on a flannel shirt and jeans, found my slippers and checked on Nathan. He was still sound asleep, dead to the teenage world. I closed his door quietly and went into the kitchen to make some coffee. While it brewed I went out to the mailbox and got the morning newspaper. When I got back, I poured myself a cup of coffee and sat down in the living room. I put the newspaper aside and my thoughts returned to Hadley.

It was supposed to be a celebration pool party. Nathan had finished his first year of organized baseball, and his team went undefeated and won the Hadley Little League championship. We offered to host a celebration party at our house in late July and everyone showed up—players, parents and coaches.

Our backyard was filled with nonstop action. It was interesting to watch Nathan and the younger players in total awe of their older teammates, following them around like devoted puppies. The twelve year-olds constantly barked orders and led the way in splash competitions in the pool, games of basketball and volleyball, and a karaoke contest that proved to be the highlight of the party and left everyone in stitches. Some of the bolder parents tried their hand at karaoke but were booed mercilessly by the team, including Claire's spirited but ill fated rendition of 'Material Girl.'

When it was time for the party to end, a number of parents cleaned up, some collecting trash in garbage bags and straightening furniture while others parading leftovers into the house. Nathan and one of the boys whose ride hadn't yet arrived remained in the pool, while the rest of the kids dried off and began leaving with their parents. The backyard emptied quickly and I stayed there to keep an eye on the pool. Between the sun beating down on me all afternoon and a few beers along the way, I was tired. It had been a great party, but I was more than ready to call it quits.

My mind often replays what happened next, and many versions of it still exist in my head. Sometimes the flashbacks are in slow motion, other times they race through my mind at breakneck speed. Sometimes they come out of nowhere and hit me without warning, other times they visit me as nightmares when I sleep. Sometimes they are in color, other times in black and white. Sometimes they contain just a snippet of what happened, other times they include every excruciating detail.

Nathan had just gotten out of the pool and was drying himself off with a large beach towel. He'd gotten a can of soda from a cooler someone had forgotten to bring in the house and sat down to watch the diving antics of Charlie Ledger, a rambunctious 12 year-old. I barely knew Charlie and for unknown reasons neither of his parents had attended the party. They were late in picking Charlie up from the party.

Charlie was putting on quite a show, repeatedly jumping off the board every which way and making facial contortions to create maximum laughter and splash. After staying underwater for as long as possible, he would explode out of the pool and then head back to the board, egged on by Nathan's cheering. As Nathan watched, he fiddled with the pull tab to the soda, working it back and forth. As I scraped the grill and looked up now and then, I had to admit Charlie was quite entertaining. I was outside the pool fence, about 20 feet away.

As Charlie ran past Nathan for his final performance, he grabbed Nathan's soda can and despite Nathan's objections, raced to the diving board. Nathan continued shouting words that I couldn't quite hear, but to no avail. Charlie proceeded to do a running cannonball off the board while gulping a mouthful of soda in midair before hitting the water. This brought more shouting from Nathan, who got up from his chair to get a better look at Charlie's underwater show.

We don't allow those kinds of antics in the pool and I sternly told Nathan that it was time to close the pool. A few moments later I was bent over turning off the grill's propane tank when I heard Nathan screaming my name. It was one of those high pitched, blood-curdling shrieks from a child that creates immediate parental panic and fear. I raced for the pool and saw Nathan scrambling back and forth by the deep end pointing excitedly into the water, then kneeling down and looking into the pool. He had panic in his eyes.

Charlie was at the bottom of the pool, a pinkish cloud of blood spreading in the water. God, I thought, please don't let this be a head injury. Without breaking stride I dove into the water fully clothed. He was floating face down, his arms spreading slightly from his body. I grabbed his long hair to lift his head and realized that the cloud of blood was coming from his mouth. His eyes were opened wide and unblinking, a mixture of total surprise and shock on his face.

I hooked my arm around Charlie's chest and hauled him upwards. When we broke the surface we were still in the deep end and I struggled to tread water and keep Charlie's head above the surface. His eyes and mouth remained open and with the exception of a single, slight sound right after we surfaced—kind of like a soft hiccup—he made no noise. He was heavy and limp.

As I struggled, Nathan was standing nearby on the concrete, horrified by what he was seeing. I shouted for him to get his mother, and he broke for the house.

I had to get Charlie to the shallow end of the pool, but as I turned in the water to use an armpit tow, I lost my grip and he started sinking back to the bottom. I dove below and got my arms under his, my face inches from his. His dilated pupils created blackened, lifeless eyes and his long hair swirled eerily, giving me the creeps. I hauled him back to the surface.

I remembered thinking I'd screwed up big-time.

I got Charlie over to the shallow end. I carried him up the pool steps like a fireman and laid him on his back. I was panting and out of breath. Blood was trickling from the corner of his open mouth and streaks of it were on both of us. I turned him on his side and looked for a wound but couldn't find one. I didn't know where the blood was coming from. The kid's eyes were still wide open and unmoving. I put my hand on his chest and realized he wasn't breathing, nor could I find a neck pulse. His lips were blue, his tongue somewhat distended. I still didn't know what had happened. I was scared.

I tilted his head backwards and forced open his mouth in an effort to clear his airway. I tried using my fingers to explore the inside of his mouth, but his tongue had swollen and prevented me from getting a good look or feel. I knew drowning victims died when the lungs fill with water, depriving the respiratory system of oxygen. But it seemed like something was blocking his air supply, choking him.

The Heimlich maneuver flashed through my mind, although I had never been trained in it and had only seen it on television. I scurried behind Charlie with my legs spread and lifted his upper torso so that it was up against my chest. I reached around his chest, clasped my hands together and pressed upwards on his diaphragm. Nothing. I waited five seconds and did it again. Still nothing. I knew I was running out of time and put him flat on his back. I remembered thinking where the hell was Claire? Where were the paramedics?

Charlie's mouth was still open and his tongue still looked distended and larger than normal. I'd lost track of time, didn't know how much had gone by. I had to get oxygen into his lungs, had to breathe for him. I tilted his head backwards again to open his airway. I pinched his nostrils closed with my fingers, hooked my thumb over his bottom teeth to keep his mouth open and breathed twice into his bloody mouth. His blue lips contrasted with his white face, and his mouth had a disturbing odor of mucous, chlorine and copper. I'd never forget that smell.

I could feel my breaths meeting with some kind of resistance. I placed my hands in the center of his chest and pushed down fifteen times. I saw no movement in his chest and when I put my head next to his, couldn't hear or feel any air being exhaled from his mouth and nose. I repeated the procedure five more times but got the same unsuccessful results. After each repetition I prayed that my efforts would be rewarded with a sputter of water and gradual thrashing movements from Charlie, but I got nothing.

I was frightened and had to try something else. I covered his mouth with my right hand and breathed directly into his nostrils, followed by more chest compressions. Nothing. I repeated this five more times without any response. No chest rise, no inhales or exhales, no neck pulse. Just those open eyes and immense, unmoving pupils. I felt like he was staring right through me.

I was physically exhausted. My arms were trembling and my legs were weak. I was out of breath, literally panting. My lungs hurt and my chest was hammering with an adrenaline rush. My knees and elbows were scraped raw from the concrete.

I was losing it and screamed for my wife. I didn't know what else to do, couldn't think straight. I didn't know how much time had gone by since I pulled him out of the water, or for that matter how long he'd been underwater or choking, if that's what he'd been doing. I didn't know anything except that I was alone and terrified, and that a boy I hardly knew was probably dying despite everything I was doing to save his life.

I was angry that I was too late and nothing worked, and that no one was there to help me. I cried as I pounded my fist on his chest, slapped his cheeks, and shook his entire body, not knowing why I did any of these things. I finally just gathered his limp body in my arms, cradled his wet head against my chest and rocked.

And that was how Claire found me.

CLAIRE WOULD LATER TELL ME THAT when I sent Nathan for help, he panicked and started crying. He couldn't find her and frantically searched the house several times over. He didn't know that Claire had walked the last family from the party to its car and was out of earshot. When he finally located her, she raced to the phone and dialed 911, then was with me when the paramedics and police arrived minutes later. Claire instructed Nathan to remain in the house, but he watched the activity from the edge of the nearby deck. I was thankful he hadn't seen me working on Charlie.

The paramedics tried placing a breathing tube into Charlie's throat as well as injecting him with a stimulant, but met with failure. I think they knew right away that he wasn't going to make it. I filled them in as much as I could about what happened, including the unexplained bleeding, as well as my resuscitation attempts. Claire clung to my arm the whole time, nervously kneading my forearm, fingernails digging into my skin. Every so often she brought her hands up to her mouth and took a deep shuddering breath. I remember feeling the tension in her whole body.

It was Nathan who remembered the soda can, and when we looked for it, found it floating in the pool just under the diving board. The can would shed much light on the actual circumstances, including the blood coming from Charlie's mouth, and the autopsy would supply the details. When Charlie guzzled soda while jumping off the diving board, the pull tab of the can had somehow broken off and lodged in his throat. He was underwater when he began choking violently, the sharp edge of the tab apparently getting caught in his windpipe and causing bleeding. The autopsy would state that Charlie died from a lethal combination of choking and water in his lungs.

I GOT UP AND POURED MYSELF another cup of coffee. I checked on Nathan and saw that he was still asleep. I sat back down and let my mind drift some more.

The year following Charlie's death was a difficult one, a black cloud hovering over each of us. While we weren't mourning the loss of a son, we were simply unprepared for the amount of negative energy brought into our lives. We were victims of circumstance left standing, but reeling. A few people called or stopped by to see how we were doing, but for the most part we suffered alone.

The pool was a daily reminder of Charlie's death, and once the police and detectives finished their investigation, we covered it up and put the patio furniture away, months earlier than we normally did. Parts of the cement where Charlie died were stained with blood and although I got most of it out with wire brush scrubbings, a few faint spots remained. We barely ventured into the backyard for the rest of the summer or fall.

We saw a family therapist a few times in an effort to regroup and help find our way. After years of smooth sailing and obviously protected lives, we discovered the hard way that life can be unfair and that bad things can and do happen to good people. Charlie taught us how fragile we are, how lives can change in an eye blink.

It seemed like we couldn't shake the depression that had wrapped itself around us. Our peaceful and comfortable lifestyle had been shattered and replaced by annoying and destructive friction. We were on edge and our tempers flared, often without warning and over things that weren't important. When we weren't snapping at each other, we were avoiding each other. It seemed that whatever conversations took place were robotic. We talked but didn't really say anything, listened but didn't really hear.

Our biggest problem, of course, was the guilt that each of us felt and the crosses we chose to carry. We were told in therapy that this was a common reaction among those connected to tragedy–survivor's guilt–and that we each needed to find the strength to overcome self-blame. However, this was much easier said than done. Nathan felt responsible because he waited too long to shout for help when Charlie was underwater, and because he wasted precious minutes searching an empty house for his mother. Claire blamed herself for not telling us she was walking party guests to their cars and being so far out of earshot. I felt guilty because I couldn't rescue Charlie Ledger. I failed when I was needed the most.

When school began in the fall, we still carried our emotional luggage. I went back to the university preoccupied and cranky, and not surprisingly, developed a case of writer's block that sidetracked my creativity and sabotaged my publishing deadlines. I tried to soldier on but was drinking too much to rid my mind of horrible nightmares and flashbacks. Nathan began to retreat into his own world and pulled away from his school friends, his once happy go lucky disposition replaced with dark, distant moods. His grades began to drop and he lost interest in sports. Claire internalized her pain while trying to present a united front to the family, avoidance behaviors that in the long run only deepened her despair. She was in constant turmoil worrying about Nathan.

All of this went on for some time before we finally sat down as a family and said 'enough.' We obviously weren't happy and recognized that we had to take control if we wanted our lives back. Luckily, the financial security I'd established through writing gave us some options and alternatives. We put the house up for sale because we refused to share any more time with the backyard ghosts. I took a leave of absence from the university to hopefully gather my wits and discover where in hell's orchard I'd hidden my creative writing. Claire left her landscape job so that she could be home for Nathan full-time, which made both of them feel more secure and stable. Claire had every intention of returning to her career, but only after things settled down for all of us.

While the house was on the market I learned of the teaching vacancy at Guilford College and after mulling it over with Claire, decided to apply. I talked about the job a few times with Cy Rollins, who taught there and spoke highly of the college and its faculty. When I was offered the position, Connecticut beckoned with an opportunity for us to start a new chapter in our lives and leave behind our troubling past. There was little hesitancy to move on Claire's part and Nathan surprised us both with his enthusiasm and eagerness to relocate. The academic dean at UMass initially frowned upon the move, but once she learned of my summer circumstances, relented and approved with regret. I accepted the position and we moved to Spencer Plain in July, about one year after the death of Charlie Ledger.

I GOT UP AND DECIDED TO SHOWER. Nothing is more refreshing for me than a cascade of hot water, and I felt my muscles relaxing as steam billowed around me. I could feel my body waking up, blood flowing again and the grogginess from last night being washed away.

As I toweled off, I thought of Cy Rollins and broken bones. For some reason–I think because I'd once injured myself in a pickup basketball game–I asked Cy if a broken bone could mend itself if not properly set. As a biologist, Cy was a good, free source of medical information. He replied that an unset bone would mend, but would do so imperfectly–crooked or gnarled were the expressions he'd used–and it would likely cause impairment, unless of course it was rebroken and set correctly.

I thought of Claire's emails and questioned again if what happened in Hadley had anything to do with her infidelity. While we left behind a nightmare six years ago, I wondered if something had resurrected and surfaced in a different form. Did we heal crooked or gnarled because we hadn't confronted all the demons at our door? Had Charlie's death started an uncoupling process that slowly pushed Claire and I apart, one that got masked by the sweeping changes made in our lives?

I didn't have any answers.

# *Eleven*

On Monday morning I saw the red message light on my office answering machine blinking in the dark as I fumbled for the light switch on the wall. Once I got the lights and shrugged off my overcoat, I entered my password and found three messages waiting. Bruce Whitbourne, the humanities department chair, called to see what I was going to do with Crider and Slocum. I spoke with Whitbourne last week shortly after the classroom incident since he was my direct supervisor and needed to be kept in the loop.

I deleted Whitbourne's message and made a mental note to contact him later in the day. I also reminded myself that I had to stop at the campus security office and complete the incident report, informing college officials that I would handle the situation myself. I was increasingly comfortable with the decision I made and planned on talking with both Crider and Slocum after class tomorrow. Claire was right, it was time to go forward and leave this mess behind.

The second message was a total surprise and brought a smile to my face. It was from Rachel Pond, who called to check up on me, her voice bright and full of energy. She said there was no need to return the call, that she'd touch base with me later in class. I replayed the message, picking up on what appeared to be a nervous pause or two, maybe even the hint of a giggle. Cute, very cute. I jotted down her number on a post-it and stuck it in my pocket.

The last message was also a surprise, but for entirely different reasons. It was from Evelyn Chadwick, Vice President of Academic Affairs at Guilford. When I heard her voice, strong and measured, any further thoughts of Rachel Pond quickly vanished.

"Good morning Jack, Evelyn Chadwick over in Academic Affairs. Kindly give me a call when you get this message. We need to set up some time to talk about your classroom incident last week. Let's do this as soon as possible, shall we?"

There's something a bit unsettling about blind phone messages left by bigwig college administrators, especially when the intended parties are low profile faculty members like me. While I certainly knew Evelyn Chadwick, I didn't have much contact with her: I'd served with her on a couple of college committees, she'd sat in on one of my performance evaluations with my department chair, and I'd watched her from a distance as she presided over faculty meetings. While our professional relationship was courteous and respectful, it was safe to say that I didn't know her very well. What I did know was that she didn't call to chitchat with little old me.

Evelyn Chadwick was a trim woman, I'd guess around fifty, short black hair offsetting rather hawkish facial features. She was reasonably attractive but often walked around with a pinched and combative expression, a facial grimace frozen somewhere between a scowl and a frown. She tended to go heavy on the makeup, overdoing the blusher and wearing dark lipstick, which made her mouth look like a black slash when she got riled. When she tilted her head and jutted her mouth out just so, it reminded me of Popeye's before he'd toss a can of spinach down the hatch.

Chadwick worked hard and seemed driven by accomplishment and achievement, having worked her way up from the faculty ranks. I was told she was often the first to arrive to work at the college and the last to leave at night. She was an excellent writer and articulate speaker, and had a number of prestigious fellowships and sizable grants under her belt. Rumor had it she was jockeying for a shot at our college presidency, which would become vacant at the end of next year. Our current president was on the last leg of a three year contract and would be leaving Guilford for a similar position overseas.

From my vantage point, I thought Chadwick was a competent administrator, but felt she was wound a little too tight and frayed around the edges. The few times we talked I got the impression that she had other things racing through her mind, and she always seemed to leave in a rush to get somewhere else. She struck me as the sort who never learned how to unwind, even on vacations. I'd bet my bottom dollar her cell phone and bulging briefcase followed her everyone.

Chadwick conducted faculty meetings with surgical precision and professional dispatch, whipping through agenda items with whirlwind speed. She had zero tolerance for faculty whiners and cry babies, and wasn't afraid to crack the whip or rattle cages. If you were stupid enough to disagree or tangle with Chadwick at faculty meetings, she had a way of zipping lips by tilting her head just so, drumming her fingers on the podium and staring intently beneath furrowed black brows, vaporizing you on the spot. I learned early on at Guilford that Chadwick was a force not to be crossed, a warning contributing to her nickname "Ice Maiden," spoken in whispers behind her back, of course.

It was no small wonder that my stomach was doing a few flips as I replayed Chadwick's voice mail. Why did she want to see me? I'd reported the incident to my department chair, following the college's established chain of command, and had every intention of keeping Whitbourne fully informed. I was puzzled as to why Chadwick had chosen to intercede on an incident well on its way toward successful resolution. Surely she had better things to do.

I was surprised that Chadwick's office even knew about the Crider incident, leading me to believe that something had transpired since I reported the incident. Perhaps campus security had communicated the matter to her office, or maybe Whitbourne had touched base with her following our discussion last week.

I pressed Chadwick's extension and reached Livinia Dawson, her administrative assistant. She picked up on the first ring.

"Good morning Liv," I said, "Jack Elliot here."

"Hi there Jack," she replied. "How're you doing?" Liv had a surprisingly deep voice, bordering on sultry.

Liv was a tall and willowy African American woman, the senior administrative assistant at the college and the front line for Chadwick. While I didn't have extensive contact with Chadwick, I did speak fairly often with Liv over the phone, usually about student absenteeism, grades, travel expenses, and the like. She was a friendly and upbeat person, an outgoing sort who always had time for my calls and questions.

I often wondered how the two of them clicked, Liv with her sunny disposition and Chadwick with her imperial frostiness, an odd pair if I ever saw one. But they did, and I'm told had done so for years. Liv was also unflinchingly loyal to her boss. She was worth a king's ransom to Chadwick because she knew how to schmooze with the faculty, stay cool under fire and put out brush fires without having to sound the alarm. She was especially gifted in directing office traffic, keeping the pushy at bay and the unwanted away, creating an impenetrable wall around the Ice Maiden. The truth be known, Liv ran the command center and literally held the keys to Guilford's academic fortress.

"I'm doing fine, Liv," I said, "but need to arrange some time with Evelyn. She called this morning and would like to meet as soon as possible." I kept my tone as casual as possible, like I was arranging a tee off time at the local country club or something.

"Oh yes," Liv said, "she told me you'd be calling. Hold a sec, Jack." She put the phone down, and I could hear papers rustling on her desk.

A moment later she was back. "Let's see, Evelyn is booked solid today and then she'll be away at a conference in Princeton for the rest of the week." She made soft humming sounds as she scanned her appointment book. "How about first thing Tuesday morning–let's say 8:30?"

Liv paused for a moment then cleared her throat, one of those 'by the way' attention grabbers. She said in a hushed tone, "Jack, you should know that Dr. Whitbourne has also been asked to attend. He can make Tuesday at 8:30."

This was getting more interesting by the minute, and it wasn't taking me long to do the math. Chadwick had already contacted Whitbourne and I was likely the last to be added to the dance card. The fact that Whitbourne was coming meant something was definitely brewing. I wasn't about to be blind sided by any of this, so I decided to track Whitbourne down and frisk him for details as soon as I hung up the phone.

Meanwhile, it didn't look like I was going to be seeing Chadwick anytime soon, something I'd hoped to do. I should have known that getting face time with her would've been difficult. She was a major player at the college and undoubtedly had bigger fish to fry. I was strictly small potatoes.

"You still there Jack?" Liv asked.

I drifted back. "Sorry, Liv. Eight thirty on Tuesday will work."

I paused for a moment. "Do I need a heads up on this, Liv?" I didn't think a little sniffing around would hurt.

"Meaning what?" she asked, a coy smile crinkling her mouth on the other end of the line. I was certain she had the complete scoop but was sworn to secrecy.

"I mean, any idea what all this is about?" As I spoke, I wrapped part of the phone cord around my index finger.

"All I know is that Evelyn wants to discuss what happened in your class last week."

That was it. Name, rank and serial number. I'd get no more.

"Dress code?" I asked, resorting to a little levity before signing off. Liv and I had a running gag about my classroom wardrobe, which usually consisted of jeans and casual clothing. She often hoists an eyebrow my way when I dress like this at more formal college gatherings.

"You've got to step up that wardrobe of yours, Jack. Shelve those jeans."

"Any suggestions?"

She paused then said, "Don't be tacky, stick with khaki."

I laughed to myself and said goodbye, jotting the appointment down in my desk calendar.

# *Twelve*

I left my office and walked over to the campus security building, where I finished last week's incident report. I had time before my class so I went to find Whitbourne, who had an office on the first floor of my building. He was slouched over his desk reading a newspaper, munching on the remains of a powdered doughnut and washing it down with some bottled orange juice.

"Got a minute Bruce?" I asked from the doorway. He waved me in with a sweep of his hand while using the other to wipe a few crumbs from his mouth. I sat down in one of his matching leather armchairs and patiently waited for him to finish chewing.

Whitbourne was chair of the humanities department at Guilford, a post he's held ever since I'd been there. He was one of the senior members of the faculty, probably four or five years away from retirement. Whitbourne had a sallow and pock-marked complexion, offset by dark bags under lifeless grey eyes and a rather prominent, hooked beak. He'd lost most of his hair and had buzzed what was left on the sides. In addition to a pot belly, he was narrow in the shoulders and had long arms, a peculiar body made more prominent by lousy posture.

In addition to his department chair responsibilities, Whitbourne was a full professor of American history, with a concentration on the 1800s and the Civil War. He's an authority on the battle of Gettysburg and the exploits of the 20th Maine regiment at Little Round Top, one of the turning points of the three day fight. It was common knowledge on campus that Whitbourne's hero and divine inspiration in life was Colonel Joshua Chamberlain, a college professor who enlisted in the Northern army and eventually commanded the 20th Maine. Chamberlain received the Congressional Medal of Honor for his heroics at Gettysburg and some other battles that followed, and after the war served with distinction as president of Bowdoin College in Maine.

Whitbourne's office offered a pleasant scent of leather and old books. It was filled with enough Civil War books to stock a library, the walls adorned with an impressive collection of paintings, photographs and memorabilia. On a bookcase in the corner sat a burnished walnut display case, lined with red velvet, containing actual bullets, belt buckles and other artifacts found on the battlefield. A brass regimental bugle was positioned sideways in a special display stand. A pair of crossed cavalry sabers encased in their scabbards hung from a wall next to a framed panorama drawing of the Gettysburg battle theater. Draped from the far wall was a replica of the 20th Maine colors, hanging above several photographs of Chamberlain, he of ramrod posture and walrus mustachio fame. The centerpiece of the wall was an engraved plaque with the words spoken to Chamberlain by his superiors that day, 'Now we'll see how professors fight.'

When I first visited Whitbourne's office, I thought it was a shrine and wondered if I should've first removed my shoes and blessed myself with holy water. Stories of his classroom behavior further stirred my curiosity. I was told he'd sometimes show up to class wearing a Union officer's campaign hat and hefting a Civil War field pack. On other occasions he'd darken the classroom and play solemn music whenever he read anything penned by Chamberlain, tears of inspiration welling up his eyes. Once he confided in me that when he first visited Little Round Top at Gettysburg he had an epiphany, a revelation that in another life he'd fought alongside Chamberlain and the 20th Maine. 'The boys stood tall that day,' he said, reverently bowing his head, voice choked with emotion.

As far as I was concerned, Chamberlain was a military hero of great proportion, a man of gallantry and valor. But his legacy was wasted on the likes of Bruce Whitbourne, who in my humble opinion was a mealy mouthed phony. While Whitbourne held Chamberlain's heroic achievements up as divine inspiration for his starry eyed undergraduates, his own character was as sissified as it was diluted. In the years I've been here, I've never seen him take a stand on anything, mainly because he was too busy feathering his own bed or living in fear of his own shadow.

Whitbourne was the faculty's yes man, the academic puppet found in most colleges and universities across the country, the parasite who cozies up to those in power and if need be, turns against his own. Whitbourne was a cardboard cutout of integrity, a glorified errand boy and academic pimp. No one on the faculty trusted him and few wanted anything to do with him. The flamboyant historian and military expert in the classroom was identified by less complimentary expressions among his peers, including a spineless suck-up, a slithering snake in the grass, and a two-faced liar, those being the softer terms of endearment.

Whitbourne aligned himself with the administration, especially Chadwick, who used him as a pipeline to discover faculty scuttlebutt and trade secrets. He became her unqualified henchman, a petrified patsy who sold everyone out whenever she pushed his buttons. When Chadwick needed an advance guard or something pushed through the faculty, her first stop was always Whitbourne, who didn't dare protest or question. He put his stamp of approval on every proposal coming out of the Ice Maiden's office, from budget cuts to hiring freezes, taking it up the keister while spouting back words of gratitude and appreciation.

His behavior at faculty meetings and around Chadwick could turn the strongest stomach. He always made sure that he was sitting in close proximity to the queen bee and hung on her every word, nodding his chrome dome like some kind of indentured servant. A meeting never went by without Whitbourne lavishing her with praise and compliments, enthusiastically volunteering for every harebrained committee assignment to be had, or laughing at something that wasn't even supposed to be funny. Whenever he sensed that the Ice Maiden needed support, he'd chime in with some rambling mumbo jumbo which invariably made no sense to anyone in the room, probably because everyone had tuned him out the minute he started flapping his gums.

As I scanned his military collection, I could only shake my head at this academic bungler and masquerading saphead. If he were at Gettysburg in another life as he claimed he was, I'm certain he would've been given orders worthy of his character, like shoveling horseshit or other boot-licking chores assigned by officers of the regiment. When the first cannon roared, I'm sure Whitbourne would've already turned tail, scrambling for cover halfway up the Maine coastline.

"So what's up Jack?" Whitbourne asked, finishing the last of his powered doughnut and the rest of his juice. When he was done he looked at his fingers and made a face. He put his thumb and forefinger in his mouth and sucked the powder from each, then pulled a round plastic container of baby wipes from his desk drawer and ran one over his face and then his hands.

"I was hoping you'd tell me," leaning forward in my chair, resting my forearms on my thighs. "I understand a meeting has been set up with Evelyn Chadwick for Tuesday. I heard you've been invited."

Whitbourne considered this for a moment or two, as if he needed a search engine to retrieve such data from his extraordinarily gifted brain.

"True," he said, forehead knitted. "I just found out about the meeting this morning." He had a whiny voice, a matter-of-fact demeanor. His grey eyes betrayed nothing at all.

I nodded slightly. Obviously Whitbourne wasn't among my favorites at Guilford, and I'm sure he knew it. So far I'd been able to work with him without any major incident or mishap. He'd left me alone to do my thing, and I'd done the same with him, tolerating his toady image so long as he kept his meat hooks off me.

I think deep down I intimidated Whitbourne, although it wasn't intentional on my part. He knew I was good in the classroom and envied the success of my publications, often questioning me about textbook proposals, contract language and royalties. He was a wannabe college author, a dime a dozen on most campuses, but was never able to muster the right stuff at the right time. He'd written but a single article in his entire professional career, some twenty-five years ago, a wandering and toothless treatise published in a second rate, flea infested research journal. Every year Whitbourne required his students to read the article, his vanity and a fading copyright doubling the undergraduate misery. I read the article out of curiosity several years ago, and found myself yawning for oxygen after the first page. His writing style was as hackneyed as it was hollow, making it easy to see how Whitbourne's writing ambitions, like his career, were on a sunset cruise to nowhere.

I said, "So what's up, or do I have to wait around until Tuesday to find out?" Our eyes met again, trying to feel each other out.

Whitbourne cleared his throat. "You know as much as I do, Jack. I got the same message you probably got. I called down, gave Livinia some times I could meet with Evelyn, and that was about it."

"Chadwick hasn't approached you personally?" I wanted to be careful here, not sounding too pushy. After all, Whitbourne was my direct supervisor. Complicating things was that I was up for tenure this year, and he played a heavy hand in its outcome, as did Chadwick.

"No," he said, shifting in his chair a bit. He briefly looked my way, hesitated, then raised both hands into the air. "Honest, Jack," he said, "that's all I know."

I suppose I believed that much. However, the fact that Chadwick was involved in this whole thing nagged at me.

I tossed him a quizzical look. "Bruce, why is Chadwick even sticking her nose into this? I reported the incident to you last week like I was supposed to." Whitbourne nodded. "Since then, I've devised a plan that I think works in everyone's best interests."

He clasped his hands behind his head and thought about this for a minute. "I suppose Evelyn just wants to hear what happened directly from you." He reached over and capped the empty juice bottle, swiveling in his chair and dropping it in a nearby recycling container. He swung back my way and said, "Let's face it, Jack, it isn't very often that a professor calls campus security to have students escorted from class. You were a hot news item last week." He smiled a smirk.

I ignored the dig and thought about Chadwick. It made sense, I guess. Chadwick was the chief academic officer at Guilford and had every right to know what was going on in all of the classrooms, especially when campus security was involved. The meeting on Tuesday was more than likely just her way of covering all the bases, including the invitation extended to Whitbourne.

Approaching footsteps echoed in the hallway and stopped at the door. I looked up and was surprised to see Cy Rollins. Rollins nodded curtly to Whitbourne then saw me, breaking out in one of his trademark grins. He waltzed into the office uninvited, gave me a friendly pat on my shoulder on the way by, and sat down in the leather chair next to mine.

"Jack Elliot, you campus desperado," Cy said, "I've been hunting you down this morning like the dog you are." His sandy hair was wet and slicked back, probably from a shower at the campus fitness and health center. Cy was in top shape and hit the weight room and exercise machines on a regular basis. He looked ruggedly handsome this morning in black turtleneck and cords, a down insulated vest for outerwear.

"Mornin' Cy," I said. "I was going to call you later this morning." I eased back in the chair, glad to see him.

"I went upstairs to your office, then took a chance that you'd be down here." He unzipped his vest and made himself comfortable, all the while ignoring Whitbourne. "After our talk yesterday I wanted to find out what you're gonna do." He swiped at his mouth with the back of his hand and dropped his voice into a John Wayne impersonation. "So how're you gonna handle those two outlaws, pilgrim?" He pointed two pistol fingers at me, firing one then the other.

I smiled and looked over at Whitbourne, who sat poker faced, arms folded across his chest. I said, "We were just in the middle of discussing it."

Whitbourne shifted in his chair, looking at Cy. "Maybe Jack would like a little privacy on this matter, a closed door alone perhaps."

"Really?" Cy acted surprised, looking at the door and then over at me. "You want me out of here?"

"No, you're fine," I said. "Stay, please. I was going to tell you about this anyway."

"Good," Cy said, "because I wasn't going to leave anyway." He laughed out loud and looked at Whitbourne. Whitbourne shook his head slowly, irritated. He and Rollins were on equal footing as department chairs, but it was plain to see their relationship was an uneasy one.

Whitbourne looked my way. "So what is it you're going to do, Jack?" he asked, jutting his chin out and scratching it. He looked at me with his dead gray eyes.

"I've decided to handle the situation myself rather than filing a formal complaint." I laid out my plan in detail, especially when I got to my expectations for Crider and Slocum.

When I finished Cy said, "Sounds good," nodding his head encouragingly. "I like it. I'd probably do the same thing myself."

"You're comfortable with this?" Whitbourne asked in a dubious tone.

"I am," I replied, "although I'll be breathing a little easier after I see them."

Whitbourne looked my way for a few moments then shook his head slightly, as if in doubt. I shifted in my chair. An uncomfortable silence crept into the office.

I let a few moments pass, looked at Whitbourne. "What's wrong?" I asked.

Whitbourne picked up a pencil and began tapping it on the desktop. "I just wish it hadn't come to this." He paused, looked around the office. "This whole deal could've been handled better."

I just sat there for a long minute staring at him, not believing what I'd heard. I shifted in my seat, felt my mouth twitch. "What's that suppose to mean?"

His smile stayed in place. "I just wish something like this didn't have to involve the security office. I mean, this a college campus and we're supposed to be a bit more civilized than the rest of the world, aren't we? After all, we're the humanities. It all seems a bit extreme to me."

I was totally miffed. When I saw Whitbourne and told him about the situation right after it happened, he seemed to be completely on my side. I thought we were speaking the same language, but could see now the tides had changed.

I blew out a shaky breath and said: "I'm not sure where you're going with this. I told you last week I did everything I could to maintain control of this guy."

I was going to say more, but Cy's voice cut through the air. "Jesus H. Christ, Whitbourne, what do you mean, 'it all seems a bit extreme to me.' How can you say that? Put yourself in Jack's place. He was out of options with this fucking kid." He was agitated, his voice climbing the ladder.

Whitbourne got up from his desk and went over to close the door.

When he got back to his chair, I looked at him with a penetrating gaze. I was getting angry and knew I had to watch my step. "Bruce, I was between a rock and a hard place, you know that. We talked about that." I thought for a moment and frowned. "Am I missing something here? Are you telling me now that I should've tried something else?"

Whitbourne shrugged his narrow shoulders. "I don't know," he said slowly, "maybe it would have been better just to have ignored the whole thing."

I arched my eyebrows in his direction. I tried to hold his gaze but he glanced away.

He paused and inspected his fingernails, picking at one of the cuticles. "If it were me," he said, carefully choosing his words, "I wouldn't have paid attention to Crider and maybe would have let things calm down on their own. I would've focused my attention on the other students in the class."

Whitbourne looked at me with one of those vinegary expressions, the kind used by intellectual stiffs to show how superior they think they are. It registered somewhere between sarcasm and amusement, which made me want to knock him into the middle of next week.

"And you wouldn't have tossed Crider for his mouth or his attitude," I realized, frowning.

"No, I wouldn't have." He paused again, staring dully at me. He smirked, "I wouldn't have let it come to that," a thinly disguised putdown.

I slumped back in the chair and rubbed my hands over my face, then let out a long breath.

Cy could sense my displeasure and charged in again, eyes widened. "Oh, that's just great Whitbourne. Let things calm down on their own. What terrific advice. What do you think we're dealing with here, a bunch of second graders? You've got an oversized moron who shouldn't even be enrolled in this college terrorizing and humiliating students, including women, insulting the professor, and refusing to leave the classroom when he's told. He's been warned about his smart ass and foul mouth attitude all semester. And here you are telling Jack that he should have ignored the situation. That's brilliant, man, fucking brilliant. What's your next pearl, letting this insolent cocksucker take over teaching the class?"

Whitbourne looked like he'd been slapped and sat there glowering, jaw clamped. He didn't move for several moments. He then reached over and picked up a cell phone on the desk, staring at it as if an incoming call would somehow rescue him from further attack. Cy took the opportunity to look over at me, tapping a finger to the side of his head and mouthing the word 'Asshole.'

I looked down and massaged my temples with my fingertips.

After a minute, Whitbourne put the cell back down on the desk. He mumbled something unintelligible then regained his composure, looking over at Cy. "It was just a thought," he mumbled, eyes narrowed. "Why don't you chill and relax, Rollins."

I almost laughed out loud. I suppose Whitbourne had to save face by saying something, feeble as it was.

Cy, though, beat no retreat. Instead he knit his eyebrows together and leaned forward in his chair. "I'll chill and relax," he said, pointing his finger in Whitbourne's direction, "when I know you've supported Jack and how he's chosen to handle these worthless losers. He did what he had to do last week, and there's nothing wrong with his follow-up. He offered assistance to a woman in distress when no one else would and fought the good fight. Now stop your drooling and blubbering. It's time to fix bayonets and stand tall in front of your faculty. For once in your life show some goddamn teeth."

This obviously registered inside Whitbourne's muddled head and he bristled, the admonished soldier and war hero. His lip twitched as he sat quietly for a moment, dog-faced, then looked at his watch and the door. "I've got a class," he announced abruptly. It was clearly a dismissal and I pushed myself up from the chair and started to leave. Both Cy and I also had a class and he followed my lead, veering around me and heading out the door.

On my way by his desk, Whitbourne held up a finger and said, "Jack, do what you've planned with the students. Let me know if there's a problem, otherwise I'll see you Tuesday morning with Evelyn. I promise to keep you in the loop if I hear anything." He avoided eye contact and after giving me a vague flick of his hand, began shuffling papers on his desk.

I left Whitbourne's office without saying goodbye, catching up with Cy. We walked down a hallway rapidly filling with students. We got outside the building, took a few steps and stopped.

I turned to face Cy. "Listen, I appreciate you being there and speaking up the way you did."

Cy squinted in the morning sun, then flipped his hand in a dismissive gesture. "No problem, Jack."

"Man, you were really amped in there. You were more upset than I was."

He smirked. "Someone's got to keep that melon head in line. Besides, I can get away with that kind of talk, you can't."

I was up for tenure this year and had to be on my best behavior. "I know," I said. "I'm trying to put my best foot forward, especially around him."

Cy shook his head and looked back at the building. "Is he a prize or what?" Cy pursed his lips and imitated Whitbourne's tinny voice, "Why don't you *chill* and *relax*, Rollins." We both started laughing. Cy dropped his head and his shoulders shook.

When our smiles faded Cy said, "So what's this meeting with Chadwick all about?"

"I don't know. Whitbourne and I just found out that she wants to talk with both of us about the incident."

"Why?"

"I don't know that either. That's why I was in Whitbourne's office to begin with."

Cy arched an eyebrow. "She wants to see both of you?"

I nodded, sticking my cold hands in the flapped pockets of my sports jacket. My overcoat and gloves were in my office.

"Together?"

"Yep."

Several students walked by engaged in conversation, voices loud and full of energy. Another in a worn denim jacket zipped around them on a skateboard and stopped just short of the classroom building. When he stepped off, he kicked the skateboard up and caught it with one hand while using the other to open the main classroom door.

"What do you think?" I asked, tilting my head.

"It's probably nothing. Go in, answer her questions, speak your piece and leave."

I nodded, then looked up at the cloudless, morning sky where two ospreys were circling high above. Guilford College, like Spencer Plain, was located along the Connecticut shoreline and ospreys were common. I followed their flight as they swooped out of sight, then studied the sky for a moment or two.

Cy stood there watching me, then reached over and touched my forearm. "Jackie, what's going on?"

"What do you mean?"

"You know what I mean. What the hell is going on with you? You haven't been yourself these last few days. Jesus, you're tighter than a mosquito's ass on a lemon wedge."

I looked at him and did a double take, wondering how he could see through me this easily. Obviously Claire was weighing heavily on me, but I thought I'd done a pretty good job keeping things to myself. I hadn't expected anyone to pick up on anything.

I didn't know what to say and tossed him a puzzled expression instead.

"You've been acting preoccupied, man." He studied me for a few moments. "Is it this classroom shit? You're not rattled by all this, are you?"

The other night I debated confiding in Cy about Claire with the hope of gaining some objectivity and guidance, but decided against it. Cy was someone I could trust, but I just didn't feel comfortable dropping this in his lap. I suppose most of my reluctance was a pride thing, sprinkled with lots of shame. No husband wants to admit that his wife was running around with another man.

Similar to my conversation with Claire the other night, I welcomed the chance to switch gears. I took a deep breath and exhaled annoyance. "Irritated is more accurate. I mean, who needs these kinds of headaches? It's like you were saying the other day, life is full of choices and we have to live with the ones we make. I'm sorry now I even reported this." A moment of silence passed. "I'll deal with it, though."

Cy nodded. "Of course you will. I can't blame you for what you're feeling, especially with that lamebrain involved." He gestured in the direction of Whitbourne's office. "He's probably in that Boy Scout museum of his right now, speed dialing the Ice Maiden and telling her how he kept us roughnecks in line."

He ran his fingers through his hair. "When are you seeing Grader and his sidekick?"

"Crider," I replied. "His name's Crider, not Grader. Barry Crider."

Cy tilted his head and scowled. "Jack, who the fuck cares what his name is. When are you seeing the two assholes?"

I shook my head as I listened to his colorful language and the way he casually worked it into conversations. "I have them in class right now."

"How about if I walk in with you? Might not be a bad idea to have another faculty member around when you first see them."

"Thanks, but I'll be fine. I'm going to keep this as low key as possible, behind closed doors."

"Well, if you change your mind and need some muscle, call me. You can reach me toll free at *1-800-bitchslap*."

I had to laugh again at Cy.

The ten o'clock chimes from the chapel drifted our way. Cy looked at his watch and said, "We've gotta rock and roll amigo, and we're both late. We've got to educate the minds of tomorrow today."

He grinned and slapped me on the back before making a mad dash for his classroom, tossing me a wave before he disappeared.

# *Thirteen*

I arrived to class literally out of breath. After I left Cy I had to go back to my office and get my briefcase and notes, then took the stairs two at a time. I walked to the front of the classroom, muttering an apology while trying to get myself organized. High among my priorities was forgetting about Whitbourne.

The class was a bit rambunctious, probably because my tardiness ticked precariously close to fifteen minutes, at which point students had the right to get up and leave. A playful groan greeted my ears along with a, 'You're late,' from somewhere in the back row. I tossed a scowl that way before flashing a smile and shaking my head, amused. Undergraduates can be such adorable but predictable simpletons.

I tugged a fistful of corrected assignments from my briefcase and began distributing them, knowing that a heaping spoonful of red ink was a powerful elixir for wayward minds and happy feet. As I called out names while roaming the aisles, I spied the empty chairs of Crider and Slocum mocking me from the back row. I bristled with annoyance, my plans for dealing with them today as well as the rest of the class obviously tossed out the window. The fact that their crap would drag on rankled me to no end, and I cursed them under my breath.

I gave the students a few moments to read their corrected papers. As a whole, they'd done a pretty good job with the assignment and I was pleased with what they submitted. Many had shown significant progress since the beginning of the semester, especially those on the brink of doing a swan dive in the course. Many grades were on the upswing, and I could detect a positive shift in attitude, including visits to my office for extra help. Of course, Crider and Slocum hadn't even bothered submitting the assignment, adding another chapter to their excellent pinhead adventure.

While I waited, I stuck my hands in my pockets and leaned against the wall. I saw that Chiang had already zipped through his paper and tucked it in his backpack. When our eyes met he squared his shoulders and tossed me one of his crisp nods, which I imitated and returned, bringing the trace of a smile to his face. Chiang had truly discovered his element in this class, and even though I admittedly put his work under a microscope and created higher expectations, he never failed to deliver. I was convinced this kid was writing his future.

I looked over at Rachel Pond, who was sitting as usual next to Lois Winslow. She sat reading her paper, elbows resting on the desk, chin in hand. She raised her head at one point and caught my stare, smiling briefly before returning to her paper. I looked away but my eyes wandered back to her. I couldn't help it. She'd been on my mind quite a bit since last week, and I'd been looking forward to seeing her.

Rachel looked both graceful and delicate in her simplicity. She wore a white Polo button down and indigo jeans, no belt, making me think of her flat belly. Her high cheekbones were heightened by a ruddy blush, giving her face a healthy glow. Her soft blonde hair was pulled up and away from her face, and she wore a pair of gold hoop earrings.

I walked to the other side of the room, pulling a roll of peppermint lifesavers from my jacket pocket and popped one into my mouth. One by one, the heads lifted and I got everyone's attention back. I made some comments about their papers and answered a few questions about how the class did. The class seemed upbeat and relaxed, back to normal. After the fracas last week, I honestly didn't know what to expect from them in terms of mood or reaction. With the exception of Rachel and Chiang, I hadn't run into any of them all week, making any predictions about their behavior even trickier. But they seemed fine and any residual worries I had quickly evaporated. And although it could've been my imagination, I sensed a certain warmth and added respect being sent my way.

I'd later learn that it wasn't my imagination. Apparently my name had been tossed around on campus and the news had spread about what had happened in class. Whitbourne was right, Jack Elliot had become a hot news item. I was the professor who wasn't afraid to mix it up with the campus bully, the teacher who stood up to the tough guy who'd pushed people around for four years, all to defend a woman's honor no less. I got a good chuckle over this. I wondered if I should start wearing a white hat and strapping on a pair of six-shooters while I walked the streets and protected the frightened townsfolk of Guilford. While I was at it, maybe I needed a western nickname to toughen my image, something like Cactus Jack Elliot, the bookish, gun totin' death machine.

That morning I began a new topic, dreams and creativity, one of my favorites. Not every professor includes a discussion of dreams in a creative writing course, but I've always considered the topic worthwhile and important. From my standpoint, to sleep is to dream, and to dream is to wonder. I'd written a chapter on dreams and creativity in my own book and over the years it has gotten rave reviews among students as well as professors. In the classroom, the topic has always proven to be a goldmine for discussion and inquiry.

I spent the first part of the period easing into the nature of dreams, asking students to think about their own. I'm not trained in psychology but threw out some standard information on sleep cycles, especially REM sleep, the so-called sleep of dreamers. I told them it was from REM sleep that we enter our own private worlds of mystery and wonder, dreamscapes that defy logic as well as scientific explanation. Our dreams may make us young or old, happy or sad, courageous or terrified. Dreams may reunite us with those who've gone away, resurrect long lost landmarks or transport us to worlds we've never before experienced. It is in this way, I said, that creativity and mystery live with each of us and visit us regularly when we close our eyes and drift away.

I began pacing in front of the class, immersed in the topic. I could tell the class was getting into the subject matter too and I played off its positive energy. I told them to think of dreams as a magical darkness from which imagination and fantasy spring forth. To help them see the possibilities, I drew reference to Edgar Allen Poe, who frequently used dreams as the basis of his stories, and Charles Dickens, whose characters were sometimes created from his. I also shared how many of Shakespeare's plays had dream themes running through them. To make the lecture material come alive, I read excerpts from each of the writers I cited, pausing to discuss key points and field questions from the class. A lively give and take unfolded.

I told them the story of Robert Lewis Stevenson's *Dr. Jekyll and Mr. Hyde*, one of my personal favorites. I shared how Stevenson struggled with writing the tale for some time, and had met with continual frustration trying to develop a decent story line. He was rewarded one night when he dreamed the now famous split scene in which Hyde, pursued for a crime, took the magical potion and underwent the change in the presence of his pursuers. The dream proved to be pivotal in the development of the plot and the rest of the story soon followed, as did Stevenson's fame and fortune.

At one point I turned the tables on the class, asking the students to think of literary or artistic creations shaped by dreams. Almost immediately, Lewis Carroll's *Alice in Wonderland* was brought up, quickly followed by Frank Baum's *Wizard of Oz*. Stephen King was mentioned several times, including how a recurring childhood nightmare set the plot for *Salem's Lot*. Several song writers were also identified, including Paul McCartney, who supposedly dreamed the music to the best-selling Beatles' hit *Yesterday*.

I spent the last portion of the lecture describing ways to harness the creative potential of dreams. Unfortunately, I said, most of us tend to see dreams play out then forget them, which means we must act quickly if they are to be remembered. I recommended keeping a notebook or journal by the bedside and immediately writing down images or scenes, even if it's in the middle of the night. In fact, I suggested setting an alarm clock at odd hours during the night to try and catch a dream unfolding. Also, I told them that waking up a half hour early and then falling back to sleep might aid dream recall. Whatever technique is used, I stressed the importance of trying to capture as much of the dream sequence as possible. I emphasized working fast and not puzzling over small details, since this will take valuable time away from reconstructing the whole pattern.

I ended the class with the story of how Salvador Dali, the surrealist painter, remembered his dreams. Dali used to doze off in a chair or couch with a spoon in his hand and a metal bowl on the floor directly underneath. Once he fell into a sleeping state, his grip on the spoon would slip and it would clatter into the bowl, awakening him. He'd bolt upright and rush immediately to the canvas and paint whatever he last saw in his mind. In this fashion, Dali's bizarre and often nightmarish dream images, whether it be melting clocks or burning giraffes, provided the raw material for his creative energies.

I dismissed the students. The class had been a good one and I was pleased with the start we made on a new topic. After last week's disaster, it was easy to see that we'd gotten back on track. Crider and Slocum seemed like a distant memory, and while their absence initially irritated me it turned out to be a blessing in disguise, helping to chase away any remaining storm clouds. Class participation was never better.

The students began filing out of the room, some stragglers milling around. A few seats to my right Rachel and Lois sat talking while Chiang and Willie Fraser looked as though they were comparing a homework assignment for another class. I was packing up my belongings when a student named Malcolm Taylor approached my desk. Malcolm was African American, a student I'd had in one other class last year, someone I didn't know very well. He seemed to be a nice enough kid but wasn't about to set the world on fire with his academic talent.

I greeted him with a nod and a smile.

"Dr. Elliot," he said, "I called you about missing the last test because I had to go home. You left me a phone message to come see you when I got back."

I remembered the message I left. When I called him I had to endure one of those lengthy greetings of hip hop music followed by sheer mastery of the English language, you know the kind: 'Yo, dude, whazzup? I ain't here right now, but leave me a trail, dawg.'

Malcolm was a handsome kid, but a little goofy bordering on the nerdish side. He wore his hair short and had on a pair of oversized tortoise shell, non-prescription eyeglasses, the kind designed not for vision but rather to capture that cool intellectual look. He wore a dark cable-knit sweater with no shirt, a rumpled corduroy sports jacket and faded jeans.

Malcolm never showed up anywhere without a puzzled expression on his face and an attaché case in tow, the square, molded kind with keyed locks. I remembered the attaché case from last year because it was unusual seeing a student tote one, most preferring book bags or backpacks these days. Also, from what I saw, it was invariably empty, save for a brown bag lunch and a worn edition of Steinbeck's *Sea of Cortez*, which I think he pretended to be reading. Whenever I struck up conversations with Malcolm about the book, he feigned indifference or quickly changed the topic. Between the fake specs, hollow attaché case and literary smoke screen, Malcolm was quite the show.

It took me a moment or two to remember Malcolm's situation, then I recalled he'd been sent home to tend to some kind of family matter and had been granted administrative approval for midterm makeups. I'd left a message on his rap music answering machine.

"Oh yeah," I said, "the *Outkast* guy."

He put the attaché case down and screwed up his face. "The what?"

"The *Outkast* guy. On your answering machine. I listened to the rap music you've got on it. You know, *Outkast*. Big Boi and Andre."

His right hand went to the bow of his fake glasses as if to straighten them, cocking his head to the side. "You're putting me on, right? You've actually heard of those guys?"

Out of the corner of my eye I could see Rachel looking my way. She'd steepled her hands in front of her face, attempting to hide a hint of amusement. We made brief eye contact. The fact that I was in her crosshairs delivered a wicked little tingle.

I looked back at Malcolm. I suppose he was shocked that I knew anything about rap or hip hop. He'd probably dumped me into the category of middle age white professors, a brainy but balding and befuddled collection of pop culture burnouts, totally clueless about the sights and sounds around them.

"Of course I've heard of them," I said, making it sound old hat. "Good music. You might want to mix it up a little more on your machine, though. Maybe throw in some Grandmaster Flash or Eric B. and Rakim." I snapped my fingers. "For that matter, De La Soul might work."

I thought I heard a small laugh escape from Rachel.

Malcolm studied me, removing his Spike Lee eyeglasses and folding his arms across his chest, cocking an elbow while nibbling on one of the bows. He'd obviously mastered some highly intellectual poses to complement his chic image, making me want to whip out my reading glasses and copy a few.

But Malcolm was too quick for me. He slipped the specs back on with one hand while wagging a finger at me with the other, giving me a sly grin. He slowly shook his head in one of those, "Man, you are too much," expressions and swaggered closer to me. He held out his right arm and bumped a closed fist against mine, the old knuckle tap, detached and so wickedly hip.

He stepped back before I could reciprocate and showcase some of my smoother soul brother moves. I was thinking of delivering a few low fives, some fist stacks, maybe a forearm smash or two and some good old fashioned chest bumping. Malcolm could probably see all of this coming, which would of course tarnish his sleek image and accounted for his backpedaling.

Just as well, since I needed to get serious and talk turkey. I looked at Malcolm. "How about if we schedule a makeup right after class next week. That work for you?"

Malcolm immediately picked up his attaché case and placed it on a nearby desk, unsnapping the tabs like a business executive and removing a large weekly planner. My curiosity got the better of me and I stole a peek inside the briefcase, spying the same Steinbeck book and what appeared to be a peanut butter and jelly sandwich in a zip lock bag. Still packing light, I mused. Malcolm leafed through mostly blank pages of his weekly planner and got to the proper date, scrutinizing its wide open spaces as if he forgot to write down an important commitment, like heart transplant surgery or a flight to Rio. He finally looked at me from over the top of his fake eyeglasses and announced that he was available, taking great pains to write it down with a fancy Cross pen.

"Good!" I proclaimed, overjoyed that he'd somehow managed to fit me in on a day he'd be here anyway.

Malcolm put the planner back inside the attaché case and snapped it shut. He turned to leave, but hesitated as if he'd forgotten something. He whirled around.

He did another of his head tilts, this time throwing in some pretty impressive squinting. "Is this going to be a hard test?"

I managed a weak smile and sighed. "No, Malcolm, not if you study. I'll probably ask you some questions from the book, then give you something creative to think and write about. Maybe I'll have you explain whether the earth is round or flat."

He chewed on this for a moment, rubbing his chin. "That's easy enough."

"Not if I want it explained both ways," I dead panned.

Malcolm's face gradually went blank and slack, not sure whether I was joking or not. He looked around the room, eyes darting back and forth, frozen. He frowned and scratched his head, trying to figure out how to respond, what to say.

I realized I'd made a mistake and Malcolm wasn't going to answer the bell. "Malcolm," I said in a gentle and reassuring tone, "that was a joke. Round earth, flat earth. Creative writers can make it happen either way because they're imaginative. Get it?"

Malcolm nodded slowly, tapping a finger against his chin. I could almost see the gears turning in his skull, in all probability weighing the joke's multidimensional qualities on some sort of intellectual scale. A moment later he chuckled, tentatively at first and then with more gusto. I returned the chuckle, wanting to maintain a light tone, throwing in a fist stack for good measure. I knew I could somehow mix in one of my bad boy moves.

We talked a little while more, mostly about the textbook chapters the examination would cover, then Malcolm announced that he had to dash off to an appointment, most likely with the peanut butter and jelly sandwich he had tucked away. He left at a brisk pace, the harried and overwrought executive.

I walked over to where Rachel and Lois were sitting and put my leather briefcase and overcoat on a desktop.

Rachel looked at me with a sly grin. "Do tell, professor, is the earth round or flat?"

I returned the grin and shrugged my shoulders. "Depends on who you ask. Talk to a creative writer and you get limitless possibility." I pulled up a chair and sat next to Lois, Chiang and Willie joining us a few moments later.

I said to Rachel, "Reminds me of that old gag about the writing professor and the chair."

"Haven't heard it," she said.

"Well, this professor was teaching a creative writing class and one day told his students to write about the chair that wasn't really there. The students thought about it for a few moments then plowed into the assignment, writing page after page of description. The next day when the papers were returned, only one student got an A. No one in the class could understand how this was possible because only two words had been written."

I paused.

"What were the two words?" asked Rachel.

I replied, "What chair?"

The joke was lame and older than the hills, and it got the pitiful ripple of laughter it deserved. I was glad I hadn't thrown it Malcolm's way. Given his reaction time, he'd need the rest of the semester to make sense of it.

After a moment Lois looked at me and said, "Today's class was really interesting." She was finishing a container of hot chocolate she'd brought to class. When she was done she patted the lid back on and dabbed the corners of her mouth with a napkin.

"Thanks," I replied. "Dreams always generate good discussion. They have that universal fascination."

Rachel said, "I knew a few of the stories you told, but hadn't heard the ones about Paul McCartney or Robert Lewis Stevenson. I really enjoyed the Salvador Dali story."

I said: "Everyone likes that one, especially when you think of those weird melting clocks. The one draped over the tree branch always caught my eye. Makes you want to try spoon holding when you go to bed."

Willie Fraser said, "I've got a question for you, Doc." He sat up in his chair and leaned forward on his elbows. "What about people who don't dream?"

I raised my eyebrows, worked my hand like a spindle. "You?" I asked.

He nodded. "Yeah, I sleep like a baby but never remember any dreams. My wife says it's because there's nothing in my noodle, that I've used them all up." He released one of those nervous, "Heh!" laughs, which got me chuckling.

After a while I said, "The shrinks say everyone dreams, Willie. It's just that you can't remember yours. You can't use them up, same goes for creativity. The more you use, the more you have."

Chiang cleared his throat and we looked over at him. He shifted uncomfortably in his chair, as if bothered by something.

"It was strange talking about dreams this morning," he said a bit tentatively. "I had a really bad one last night." He lowered his head.

"I'm sorry to hear that," I said. "Want to talk about it?"

He hesitated. "It's kind of personal. I just don't want you to think I'm strange or go telling anyone." He looked slowly around at each of us, as if contemplating a blood oath for confidentiality.

Lois gave him a reassuring nod. "It's okay, Chiang," she nudged, "we're your friends, you know that. Go ahead."

Chiang stared straight ahead then blinked his eyes in rapid succession, as if he were awakening from a semiconscious state. He swallowed hard. "Okay, here goes. Last night I dreamed that I was a muffler."

Silence filled the room. Rachel and I exchanged glances.

After a moment Lois said, "Did you say a muffler?"

"Yes, a muffler," Chiang snapped back in a huff. He paused, then said in a loud voice, "And when I woke up this morning I was exhausted."

We collectively laughed then groaned, knowing that we'd fallen hook, line and sinker for his cornball humor. We'd been easy marks for a kid who obviously knew how to tell a joke. He'd established a good setup, drew each of us into the situation, utilized perfect timing, and delivered the wordplay punch line like he'd been doing standup comedy his whole life.

But the funniest part was watching Chiang, who sat there cackling away like a hyena. He threw his whole body into fits of laughter, throwing his hands up in the air and slapping his thighs, all the while shaking his mop of unruly hair and stomping his feet on the floor. We broke into hysterics just watching him. By the time he was done with his convulsions he was literally out of breath, letting out a deep sigh and slumping back in his chair.

I looked at him and just shook my head. I couldn't believe this was the same quiet kid who started the semester in a cocoon, distant and aloof from everyone. Now here he was holding court, quite full of himself. He'd become quite the character.

He also came to my aid in last week's altercation, which I wouldn't soon forget. What he did was difficult for a student, and I remembered the dirty looks he got from Crider and Slocum. Should they harbor a grudge, who knew what the two of them might do to a person half their size. I needed to address that when I saw them.

Chiang looked at me. "Sorry, Dr. Elliot," he said. "I couldn't resist."

I shook my head, still smiling. "You're a funny guy, Chiang. Your brother teach you that too?"

He laughed quietly to himself. "Yeah, as a matter of fact he did." He paused, lost in thought somewhere. "He used to tell me everyone needs a good belly laugh now and then."

Ain't that the truth, I thought. I looked over at Chiang, a slight smile lingering. He still didn't talk much about his brother Ray, but ever so gradually a portrait of his older brother was emerging. Chiang must have really looked up to him.

We were all quiet for a little while.

Finally, Chiang tapped the desktop with a knuckle and got up from the chair, straightening up and pulling on his jacket. He came over and punched me good naturedly in the arm, then shook my hand.

I smiled and held the handshake, looking up at him. "You taking off?"

"Yeah, boss, I gotta work this afternoon," Chiang said, slinging his backpack over one shoulder and heading for the door. "I'm gonna grab some lunch before heading over to the sweat shop."

I'd forgotten for a moment that Chiang was on work study and punched the time clock in the maintenance department several afternoons a week. The fact that he excelled in school while shouldering a job made his academic achievements that much more impressive.

Before he reached the door Chiang gave us a grin and flashed the peace sign. "Nice to have things back to normal around here," he said, then disappeared.

# *Fourteen*

After Chiang left I mentally drifted away for a moment or two, images of the classroom last week flooding my mind: Crider's sneering attitude, campus security being summoned, the astonished and incredulous faces of the students.

I turned in my chair to the others and let out a deep sigh. "He's right. It's nice to have peace restored."

I looked at Lois. She was wearing a dark brown corduroy blazer, a striped broadcloth shirt unbuttoned at the throat, jeans and casual loafers. Her long brown hair had the slightest hint of gray and was worn back and to the side. She was an attractive woman, refined and together.

"Listen Lo," I said, rubbing my brow, "you and I never got a chance to talk about what happened last week." I glanced over at Rachel. "I want to apologize again, and just need to know you're okay. I'm going to be speaking with Crider and Slocum about their behavior, in fact I was hoping to do it today."

She gave me a quick shake of her head. "I'm fine, really Dr. Elliot." She thought for a moment and said, "Thank you for what you did last week."

I nodded. "I got a little hot under the collar, and should apologize for that too." I shook my head slowly and hesitated for a second. "What a nightmare," I muttered.

Lois sighed and put a hand lightly on my arm. "Stop. No more apologies are needed. I'm fine and you will be too. Those two were just trying to be funny. They're immature, that's all, and probably very embarrassed."

I leaned toward her and clasped my hands between my knees. "Lo, they should be. What they did was hurtful and disrespectful. Crider was wrong, and he needs to be held accountable, not only in this class but everywhere else from what I hear. So does Slocum, who didn't help matters by piping up the way he did. They both need a lesson in civility and I intend to give them one."

Willie cleared his throat and shifted in his chair. "That reminds me," he said, reaching inside his jacket. He withdrew a narrow envelope from an inside jacket pocket and directed it my way. "For you, Doc."

I took the envelope. "An academic bribe perhaps, Willie?" I joked. "A way for me to see things your way the rest of the semester?"

Willie released another, "Heh!" He rose from his chair and buttoned a flashy shearling overcoat, then pulled on a tweed driving cap, cocking it fashionably over one eye.

The rest of us took Willie's lead and got up, straightening the arrangement of chairs. Lois excused herself for a few moments to go use the rest room down the hall.

I opened the envelope. Inside were two box seat tickets to a Boston Celtics and New Jersey Nets basketball game, an exhibition match to be played at the Mohegan Sun arena next week. As a tribal member, Willie sometimes received complimentary tickets to the casino's entertainment events and he liked to share them with friends. Willie wasn't much into the sports scene, but knew I was. Last spring he gave me tickets to a few baseball games at Dodd Stadium in Norwich, home of the Connecticut Tigers, a minor league affiliate of the Detroit Tigers. They were fabulous seats, as I'm sure these were.

I went over to Willie and shook his hand. "That's really kind of you, Willie. Thank you."

He smiled. "You're welcome, Doc. I figured you needed some stress reduction in your life. I thought you'd like going to a game, getting your mind off things for a while."

I nodded. My mind could certainly use some relief, not only from last week's classroom fiasco but my ongoing torment about Claire. My meeting with Whitbourne this morning hadn't helped to quiet things down in my life either. The only thing the moral midget had done was spike my blood pressure and create a tighter vise grip on my noggin.

Willie was right, I needed some down time.

"You got someone to take?" he asked.

I looked at him. "How 'bout you?" I asked, tilting the tickets his way. "Want to make it a boys' night out?"

"Not me," he replied shaking his head, "never liked basketball."

Inside, I had to laugh. He gave me the same line about baseball.

"Well, I'll find someone." I pushed a hand through my hair and thought for a moment. Claire barely tolerated sports, although she did play high school softball for a while and was supposedly pretty good. Nathan's interest in athletics came to a standstill in Hadley. Neither would have an interest in going to a basketball game, that was for sure. I thought of Cy, but remembered he would be away all of next week at some kind of biology conference. So much for my short list.

As if reading my mind, Rachel said, "I'm available."

I gave her a sidelong glance. She had her head down, fiddling with the buttons of her dark blue pea coat. She looked up after a moment, pale blue eyes surprising me again. She beamed a smile.

Willie chimed in. "There you go, Doc. See how easy that was?"

Rachel said, "That is, of course, if you can't find anyone else to take." She kept her eyes locked on mine while crossing a long, white cashmere scarf around her neck, tossing one end back over her shoulder.

As I think back I guess I was stunned by the offer, the way it came so totally out of the blue, and from all people, the woman starring in Jack Elliot's forbidden fantasies. She caught me absolutely flatfooted and I didn't know what to say. My cheeks got flushed and my heartbeat accelerated, my mind racing about the prospects of being alone with her. I mumbled something about it being too early to make plans and in a rather pathetic sidestep, opened the flap of my briefcase and began looking for a folder that never existed.

She took it all in while leaning against the wall, smiling bemusedly, hands stuck deep in her coat pockets.

Lo returned and we left the classroom building, Willie leaving in a different direction once we got outside. I thanked him again for the tickets and walked a bit with Rachel and Lois, even though I was running late and due at a curriculum committee meeting in a few minutes. As I was about to branch off, Lois's cell phone rang, sending off some kind of cascading piano sonata. She retrieved it and looked at the number, seeming a bit agitated by what she saw. She excused herself and wandered in the opposite direction, launching herself into a conversation.

The air had bite to it, a brisk wind having dropped the temperature. I put my briefcase down so that I could pull my coat collar up and put on my gloves.

Despite the chill, it was a crystal clear day, the sky filled with puffy white clouds. The wind rippled a nearby duck pond and sent some leaves dancing in the air. Many of the trees dotting the campus were bare, the grounds crew blowing the leaves and hauling them away. The vibrant autumn foliage of a few weeks ago had given way to the dull pewter skies of November.

Rachel turned to face me, books against her chest schoolgirl style. I studied her face, aquamarine eyes sparkling in the sunlight, fine laugh lines bracketing them and lending character. She had some pale freckles across her nose, skin soft and smooth. Very white teeth. Full lips, just a hint of pale lipstick. Attractive and pretty to look at, making me wonder how I'd missed so much.

I cleared my throat and said, "I forgot to thank you for the phone message you left."

She nodded and we kept walking. "You're welcome," she said after a while. You doing better?"

"I am."

"You still seemed wound a little tight back there."

I chewed my bottom lip. "I'm getting there, Rachel. I'll just be glad when all this is over. I was hoping it would be done with today." She didn't know about my encounter with Whitbourne nor my pending appointment with Chadwick.

We moved to the side of the brick walkway as a group of prospective students walked by, an admissions tour guide pointing out various buildings and answering questions. A mother with a stroller and a boy of about five trailed the group, no doubt someone's family. The kid looked thoroughly bored and stuck his tongue out at me when he walked by. I was going to stick mine out in return but was afraid he'd squeal on me to his mother.

I lifted my coat sleeve and looked at my wristwatch. "I've got to run or I'll be late for a meeting."

She tilted her head, squinting in the sunlight. "Jack Elliot, man on the move."

"The one and only," I said with a theatrical sigh. I glanced over at Lo and saw that she was still talking on her cell. I managed to catch her eye and waved goodbye, which she returned with a big smile.

I was turning to leave when Rachel took a step toward me, leaned in a bit. She lowered her voice. "You know, it wouldn't really be a date."

"What do you mean?"

"You know what I mean."

She was right, I did, but I feigned confusion anyway. College professors are quite gifted in looking lost in space.

"We could take separate cars and just meet at the casino, take in the game that way." She shifted the books in her arms. "Provided, of course, you want the company."

I was getting that wicked little tingle again.

Rachel declared, "But I suspect you're uptight just thinking about it, wondering how it might reflect on you." She widened her eyes in mock astonishment. "God forbid, Jack Elliot being seen with a student in public."

"Well, the thought did cross my mind," I said sheepishly.

The wind mussed her hair a bit, and she brushed a wisp to the side.

I added: "Both of us are married and people talk, especially around this place."

She shrugged then pursed her lips.

"What?" I said.

"First of all, it's nobody's business. Second of all, we're talking about watching a basketball game with eight thousand other people, not strolling along a moonlit beach or having dinner by candle light."

I glanced down at the sidewalk, then back at her. "That wouldn't be a problem for your husband?"

"Absolutely not. Besides, my social calendar doesn't need clearance from my husband." She paused for a moment or two. "Does yours?"

"No."

"No what?" she asked.

"No," I said straight faced, "my social calendar doesn't need clearance from your husband."

Rachel shook her head and started giggling, which got me laughing.

"Now you're just being silly," she said. "I meant do you need approval from your wife for something like this?"

I thought about Claire, probably stiffening a bit. My mind flashed with breakneck speed to her emails. I thought of the kinds of things she'd done behind my back, the secrets and indiscretions, the deceptions and lies. And here I was worrying about a basketball game.

"No," I said, "I don't need clearance or approval from my wife."

"Good."

I wondered what she meant by that, but didn't go there. Another minute passed.

"Tell you what," I said, breaking the silence. "I'll think about it and get back to you." I needed to process all of this, get my bearings.

That seemed enough for her.

I started backing away, my meeting beckoning.   "You really into basketball?"

"Very much—played it in high school in fact, starting guard for Daniel Hand High in Madison for four years.  She pumped a fist in the air.  "Go Tigers!"

"Never would have guessed it," I said, shaking my head.

"Really?"

"Really.  You just don't seem the type."

She cooed, "And I never thought in a million years I'd hear the names Big Boi and Andre roll off the silver tongue of the distinguished Dr. Jack Elliot."

I grinned and shrugged.  "The things you learn these days."

"We make quite the pair," she said.

"That we do," I replied.

# *Fifteen*

The following night I sat in my parked car in a mall across from Claire's agency in Old Lyme. I was sandwiched between two cars and hidden from view, the front of my Volvo nudged out just far enough to allow a view of the agency's entrance. I kept one eye on the building and the other on Claire's jeep, sipping from a steaming cup of coffee I'd picked up down the road. It was just after five o'clock and darkness had fallen.

I was there on a whim. I had been leaving the college when Claire called and informed me she'd be working late at the office. At one time, I wouldn't have raised an eyebrow or thought twice about something so trivial, but these sentiments changed with my discovery of her emails. Almost overnight I'd become a suspicious and mistrusting spouse, directing a wary eye toward Claire's comings and goings and vowing never to get caught napping again. Her working late anywhere no longer translated into a portrait of innocence; on the contrary, Claire's call set off alarms in my head.

I was exiting the interstate and trying to figure out what to do when Nathan called and unwittingly provided some direction. He and Forrest had stayed after school to work on their history projects and then decided to watch the remainder of a late afternoon freshman football game. Forrest's mother was taking them home and feeding them along the way, an added bonus. I was off the hook, not only for taxi duty but dinner preparations as well. Better yet, a chance to snoop on Claire had fallen squarely in my lap.

Claire's agency was located in a modern professional complex next to the Lieutenant River, which snaked in and around Old Lyme. *Original Dimensions* was a fairly large building located next to a walk-in medical center, nail salon, sandwich shop and convenience store. I was parked across the street in the town's shopping center, next to a post office and in front of a country boutique shop.

Even though Claire's jeep was in the parking lot, I called her office phone as soon as I pulled in, wanting to make sure she was in the building and hadn't left with anyone. She answered on the first ring and seemed surprised by my call, but I had the perfect alibi with Nathan's change of plans. She seemed relieved with the sudden windfall of time, and I encouraged her to take full advantage of it and not rush home. I told her I'd pick up a bite to eat and then work at the college for a while, not concerned a bit about lying. We chatted some more before I said goodbye and pressed the button to end the call. I put my cell away and waited.

Since my earlier search of the house, I'd come up empty handed. I turned every room and closet upside down, as well as the attic, garage and basement. I didn't find anything, not even the emails Claire had removed from the attic. I found no evidence of the supposedly symbolic gift she received from her lover, nor any kind of trail connected to November 10, the day the two of them went to Newport. I was striking out everywhere.

When Claire wasn't around for a few hours the other day I seized the opportunity to search her jeep. I sifted through whatever papers I could find and looking under seats, under carpeting and in storage bins, glove compartment and even the tire well. My search produced nothing, no questionable receipts or ticket stubs, phone cards, hidden gifts or cards, or even unfamiliar CDs. Claire continued to cover her tracks on all fronts, which I suppose didn't surprise me anymore.

I felt like I was chasing smoke.

The computer remained unyielding of its secrets, and while I had her lover's screen name from back then–*Strap95*–a search of Earthlink's member directory provided no additional information. One night, fortified by several belts of scotch, I created a new screen name on AOL and sent a blank email to *Strap95*, just to see if the address still existed. It did, but since I wasn't sure how to proceed at that point, I deleted the AOL screen name. I didn't want to leave a trail, playing my own version of cat and mouse.

I'd also met with steady frustration trying to access Claire's cell phone and the numbers she called. The cell was in her name, as was mine, making any efforts to track her calls next to impossible. She continued to keep it close to her person or locked in her briefcase. If Claire was still involved with this guy, I was convinced her cell would reveal some kind of trail. I remained hopeful that someday I could sneak it away for a few minutes, just long enough to eyeball her call log and jot down some numbers. Her call log held up to twenty numbers, including the date and time of each. It would be interesting to see who she called first in the morning after she left for work and last at night before arriving home.

Last week I learned what kinds of sophisticated snooping measures were on the market. I'd called Reuben Jumper, an information technology specialist at the college I knew fairly well. I told him I needed to pick his brain about computer surveillance devices, expressing concern over my son's online activities and wondering what my parental monitoring options might be. I didn't want to lie, but felt this was the worst of two evils and I wanted to keep Claire totally out of the picture.

Reuben Jumper was in his late twenties but looked years younger. You could say that he was your classic nerd, from his shyness and pasty complexion to the thick, black-framed glasses that kept sliding down his nose. He once told me with great pride that he liked to cut his own hair, which accounted for its often hacked and lopsided look. The armaments he wore on the job were not for the squeamish or faint of heart, especially an oversized plastic pocket protector stuffed with pencils and pens, and a key ring rivaling the weight of a waffle iron.

There were some who mocked and mimicked Reuben behind his back, but quirks aside I found the guy interesting as well as brilliant in his line of work. It seemed as though there was nothing about computers Reuben didn't know. Bill Gates paved the way for people like Reuben, showing the world that computer geeks are not only smart and cool but sit atop the economic heap. In my mind they also ruled the world, pocket protectors and all.

A number of years ago Reuben bailed me out with his computer savvy. I was in the tech center with another professor bemoaning the fact that one of my students had plagiarized a research paper. I knew in an instant the student hadn't written the paper and was dreading the long hours of investigation necessary to prove my case. Reuben happened to be standing nearby and told me about a software program he'd heard about for suspected cases of plagiarism. Essentially a paragraph or two from the suspected paper is entered, and within minutes the program can tell you whether the material was lifted from another source, and where. I jumped at the chance to try the program, which Reuben ordered for me on the spot. Within days the software arrived, and shortly thereafter the student went belly up, guilty of plagiarizing over 85 percent of her paper. When I told Reuben of my success he became quite excited, becoming before my very eyes an excited and bouncy leprechaun dancing a lively little jig.

Because our business wasn't college related and since Reuben lived in Old Saybrook, we agreed to meet in his neck of the woods one night at a popular bar and pizzeria next to the town's railroad station. I'd never been there before, so I followed Reuben from the college. The place was packed with both young and old, and for good reason. The brick oven pizza had great thin crust and spicy toppings, while the draft beer was as smooth as it was ice cold. Reuben attacked his pizza with particular gusto, sprinkling two pieces at a time with a layer of Parmesan cheese and pepper, then pressing the concoction together like a sandwich and stuffing it down his dough hole.

We eventually got around to talking about computer monitoring. Reuben seemed a bit giddy from the suds or maybe energized about the topic, loosening his hopelessly outdated necktie and unfastening the top button of his plaid shirt. As I expected, he was a fountain of knowledge. Reuben shared that many software programs were on the market, including products like *Desktop Surveillance*, *Cyber Snoop*, and *Stealth Activity Monitor*. His favorite, though, was *Spector*, one of the first software programs manufactured and generally regarded as one of the best. Reuben explained that it could be secretly installed on any computer I wished to monitor. Basically, it operated like a camera, taking snapshots every second or two of whatever appeared on the computer screen. It started recording as soon as the computer was turned on and played back like a slide-show.

Reuben talked animatedly with hands, spouting nonstop about the program's features and capabilities. He emphasized that all online activities could be watched because the software recorded every raw keystroke, even if it was immediately deleted. It could monitor surfing, chat room conversations, instant messages and email exchanges. Reuben leaned close to me and said passwords were even at the mercy of the program. He nudged me in the arm and raised his eyebrows up and down twice, whatever that was supposed to mean.

He described a few other programs and patiently answered the many questions I had. For the most part, I just sat back and listened, thoroughly absorbed in the Big Brother capabilities of new age technology. At one point my concentration was shattered by a train rumbling by, which shook the building to the rafters and even rattled the silverware on our table. I startled in my chair and whirled around, much to the amusement of Reuben and several nearby patrons, obviously seasoned regulars to the place.

When Reuben excused himself to go to the restroom, I just sat there, my mind racing in a hundred different directions. There was little question in my mind that if Claire were still seeing someone and sending emails, this program or one like it would be her undoing, a trap from which there would be no escape. But after hearing Reuben out, I had mixed feelings about going this route. To be honest, the gadgetry left me cold, probably because I saw it as some kind of seedy wiretapping. It was a dirty little secret to expose Claire's dirtier one.

I couldn't deny that I wanted answers, just not this way. Who knows, maybe I viewed it as a kind of desperate, ugly measure to snare a truly despicable partner. While I had every reason to be upset with Claire and what she'd done, I did not regard her as an evil creature nor did I think our marriage was on the ropes or beyond repair. Exactly where things sat, I wasn't so sure.

As we waited for the waitress to bring us a check, Reuben described a few other snooping devices, including video cameras the size of sugar cubes and various bugging devices for phones. By the time he was done, I had a much clearer understanding of the tools available, if, of course I decided to use them. I paid the bill and wrote him out a generous personal check for the consultation, which he resisted at first but eventually pocketed. He was a good guy and I knew he'd gone out of his way to help a friend, sealed lips being part of the deal.

As we parted in the parking lot, Reuben looked up at the bright stars and smiled goofily, announcing that global positioning satellite devices were also available, systems which could pinpoint where a car has been or where it's going. I laughed softly to myself and waved him off, convinced that a sizable chunk of new age technology had passed me by. I was also convinced that Reuben Jumper would have served with great distinction in the Nazi Gestapo.

SO THERE I SAT IN MY VOLVO, A HUSBAND in the dark literally lurking in the dark. Across the street, Claire's agency began emptying, a few people at first and then small groups chatting on the way to their cars. I straightened in the seat and leaned forward for a better look, resting one hand on the steering wheel. I eyeballed them as they headed for their cars, but most were bundled up or moving too fast for me to recognize them. Within minutes, the parking lot had thinned considerably, Claire's jeep among the few that remained.

I settled back in my seat and drank some more coffee, fully expecting to be here for a while. However, I was proven wrong. Claire left the agency and headed for her car within fifteen minutes, hardly what I would call working late at the office. When she left the lot and headed south for the interstate, I followed. Traffic was fairly light and I had no trouble keeping up, staying back a few car lengths.

Instead of picking up the entrance ramp for home, Claire pulled into a commuter's lot almost directly across the street. Since it was crowded and brightly lighted, I had no choice but to drive by and turn around down the road a bit. When I returned, I spotted Claire's jeep next to a pay phone, the metal phone cord snaked through her window. I pulled over to the side, just out of sight, and waited.

I had no idea who she was calling, but found it strange that she hadn't placed this call before leaving the office a few minutes earlier. For that matter, I didn't understand why the call couldn't have waited until she got home. Most puzzling, though, was why she was using a pay phone instead of her cell.

She finished her call within a few short minutes and pulled out of the commuter's lot, picking up the entrance ramp to the interstate. I followed at a safe distance as she crossed the Baldwin Bridge, which spanned the Connecticut River and connected Old Lyme to Old Saybrook. I did a double take as Claire exited for the shoreline instead of continuing on the interstate. She never came home from work this way. This was getting more interesting by the minute.

Claire drove at a moderate speed through the outskirts of Old Saybrook and continued south along the Boston Post Road. While this two lane route would eventually bring her to Spencer Plain, it took much longer than the interstate and crawled through a number of shoreline towns, a scenic drive but a commuter's nightmare.

We traveled a few more miles, passing some open stretches of marshlands and inlets. In between was a succession of restaurants, motels and convenience stores. We passed a few stately homes, widely spaced and well maintained, and then a neighborhood of smaller houses, many close to the road. We drove by a water tower, a white wooden church sitting next to a village square, then a volunteer fire department.

A light mist was in the air, which wasn't surprising since we were hugging the water. I set my wipers to intermittently sweep away the moisture.

I was still several car lengths behind when Claire crossed a trestle bridge spanning a channel of water. She slowed as she passed several marinas and fishing tackle shops, then switched on her right turn signal, pulling into a parking lot of a small seafood restaurant overlooking the water. I drove by, then circled back slowly.

I swung into the restaurant's parking lot from a different entrance and saw her jeep down by the water, not too far from a boat launch area and next to several small boats sitting in dry dock, shrink wrapped for the winter. I inched the Volvo between two parked cars, behind her and to one side, about twenty yards away. I could make out Claire turned in her seat and leaning against the door, talking into her cell. I turned off the engine so that I wouldn't draw attention to myself, and unbuckled my seatbelt.

Twenty minutes passed and she was still talking. I rubbed my eyes and yawned. In addition to being clueless, I was tired and tense. I wondered if *Strap95* was on the other end of the phone, and whether this was a continuation of the call made from the commuter's lot. Maybe she'd driven home this way because she was expecting a return call and wanted privacy, maybe a secluded location away from the busy interstate running parallel to the road she'd taken.

A part of me wanted to walk over there and demand an explanation, but I knew this was neither the time nor place for accusation. Besides, what was I going to accuse her of, talking on a cell phone? She could be talking to anyone. Or, was I going to confront her about carrying on a phone conversation in a parking lot? Anyone who owns a cell phone has pulled off the road one time or another to avoid a dead zone, and the narrowness of this road dictated her finding a safe place to park. And as far as her driving home a different route, maybe she had a rough day and was just taking advantage of the space I'd given her, including a leisurely drive home. I'd done the same on many occasions.

I took a deep breath and slowly exhaled, knowing I couldn't do much right now except sit tight and keep my eyes open. In the meantime, my mind raced in a bunch of other directions. I thought of Crider and Slocum and how the situation was festering instead of recovering. I mentally replayed my frustrations with Bruce Whitbourne, how I got to see his spineless ineptitude up close and personal, making me wonder what was waiting around the bend with the Ice Maiden. I thought about the sturdy character and friendship of Cy Rollins and how he rode to my defense, gritty and unflinching. Images of Rachel Pond also filled my head, her beauty and charm as intriguing as they were erotically appealing. I would be the first to admit I was all over the place.

Of course I also thought about my writing, which had taken a back seat to everything since the storm clouds gathered. Luckily, I could afford to take a step back and not jeopardize my latest project, a new edition of *Creativity in Thought and Action*. I'd completed the manuscript in early October, and it was currently being reviewed by a dozen or so professors from across the country. It would likely be another three or four weeks before I had the reviews in hand, at which time I'd be incorporating their ideas and suggestions into the final manuscript. I thanked my lucky stars that none of my troubles began during the actual writing phase of the project. The distractions and frustrations would've undoubtedly created writer's block, easily rivaling or surpassing the monster I'd battled in Hadley. It would've vaporized the production plan for this textbook and jeopardized my status as a dependable and bankable author.

I flinched when a car pulled into the parking lot directly behind me, bathing the Volvo's interior in bright light. My adrenalin surged and I froze, knowing that if Claire turned around at this moment she could spot me in the glare. But she didn't, and I breathed a sigh of relief when the headlights flicked off. I watched in the rear-view mirror as a family of four poured out of a hulking SUV, loud voices and laughter cutting through the night air. Their footsteps faded away on the crushed gravel lot.

Forty-five minutes later she was still hunched over her phone. Over to the left a dark skinned, wiry kitchen worker lugged some garbage bags to a nearby metal dumpster, flinging them over the top, glass shattering inside. He brushed himself off before hunching over and lighting a cigarette behind cupped hands. He walked away filling his lungs with nicotine, smoke lingering in his wake.

I put the car on auxiliary power and swiped the windshield a few times. I was cold and rubbed my hands together to restore the circulation. My body was stiff and sore, and I really needed to stand and stretch. My coffee had long grown cold and I was hungry. I yawned some more. The smell of fried seafood from the restaurant wafted my way made my stomach rumble.

Finally, I saw movement in Claire's jeep. She straightened in her seat and started the engine, tailpipe smoke and brake lights signaling her departure. She pulled out of her parking space and headed for an exit just to the right of me. I lowered my head when she drove by, pretending to be fidgeting with the radio. She passed without a glance and left the lot, turning south for home. I waited a bit before following.

The rest of the drive home proved uneventful. When Claire turned left on to our road, I stayed on the main drag for a few more miles to kill time and delay my arrival home.

When I eventually pulled into our driveway, the outdoor lights were on and the garage door was open. Claire's jeep was in the garage and she was talking to Marion Poole, Forrest's mother, who had apparently arrived at about the same time and pulled in right behind Claire. I didn't see the boys, and assumed they were in the house.

I parked my car in the garage and walked over to Claire and Marion, catching snatches of a conversation about an upcoming school social event. Claire was standing next to Marion's door, hands in her overcoat. I put on a game face and lightly squeezed Claire's arm, exchanging pleasantries with the two of them before excusing myself and heading inside. On the way, Claire asked that I get Forrest moving so that Marion wouldn't be kept waiting any longer. I flashed a wave of the hand and entered the house.

And there was Claire's cell phone, sitting atop her briefcase smack in the middle of the hallway.

Claire must've been just entering the house when Marion pulled up, prompting her to leave her things inside the door before going outside to talk. Following her phone conversation by the water, she likely forgot to put the cell away or didn't want to fumble around in the dark while driving. Whatever the reason, there it was staring at me, unprotected and unguarded.

I've since thought a lot about that moment. If I didn't chance upon it, none of what followed would've taken place. I'll never know how things might have turned out if I resisted the temptation and walked past it. But the fact of the matter is that I didn't. I snatched it up without the slightest hesitation or guilt. I saw it as my golden opportunity, one that might never present itself again so easily.

I moved quickly, knowing Claire or the boys could appear at any moment. Claire and I owned the same cells, so I knew its features and exactly what I wanted to examine. My hands were trembling as turned on the power. When it came to life, I activated the cell's call log and easily found the last call Claire received, double checking tonight's date and time. Since neither one of us had caller ID, I stared at the unfamiliar number, burning it into my memory.

I eyeballed the other incoming numbers in her log as well as her outgoing calls, looking for matches or anything unusual. Claire's agency number appeared several times, as did calls from my cell and Nathan's. Nothing else registered in my head. Before I switched off the phone I scanned for any text messages Claire might have left. I found nothing.

I set the phone down on the floor and kneeled to open her briefcase, which I correctly anticipated was unlocked. It was minus her computer, which she must have left at work. I flipped through some opened mail and a half dozen file folders, all work related, and fanned through some trade magazines before turning to the briefcase's inner pockets and compartments. I found nothing hidden or suspicious, just a few pens and pencils, a small calculator, a packet of business cards, reading glasses in a quilted case, and some breath fresheners.

I was getting paranoid about getting caught and didn't want to press my luck any further. I closed the briefcase and positioned it the way I found it, placing the cell back on top. I walked through the house trying to regain my composure, the thought of finally finding a clue making my mind jump around. I knew I had to get a grip and take it down a few notches.

I found the guys in Nathan's bedroom in front of a computer game. As distracted as I was, I managed to talk with them for a few minutes before shooing Forrest out of the house. I went into the kitchen and got a beer, downing it in a few long gulps. I took another with me as I changed my clothes and put my things away in the study. The beer smoothed out some of my rough edges.

Nathan had already eaten dinner and was whipped from the outdoor air at the football game. He undressed and had a long hot shower, then barricaded himself in his bedroom in front of the television. Claire wasn't very hungry, so we made soup and sandwiches and sat next to each other at the kitchen's breakfast bar. She was wound tight and rambled on about her day as well as the drudgeries of having to work late at the office. The ease with which dishonesty and deception crept into her narrative was unsettling, and it took everything in my power to look calm and unfazed. I nodded and didn't say much.

The phone number beckoned.

After we finished dinner and tidied up the kitchen, Claire announced that she was going to draw a bath and soak the day away. I watched television in the living room until I heard the tub water stop running, then went into the study to retrieve my cell phone. I was nervous, but my curiosity proved relentless. I knew I wouldn't rest easy until I discovered who picked up at the other end. Unlike the emails, I had no intention of waiting before acting.

Despite my decisiveness, my breathing was labored and the pit of my stomach ached. I had to will myself to lean forward in the chair and press the number. I startled when it was answered on the first ring, a recorded message cutting in:

*'Thank you for calling Simon Trask Properties, proudly serving Connecticut's residential and commercial real estate needs since 1995. Our main office is closed*

*at the present time, so please leave ...'*

I didn't wait for the completion of the message. I instead pressed off and sat there staring at the phone. After a few moments I hit redial and listened to the message again, cutting it off in almost the same spot. I slowly put my cell down and slumped in the chair. I stared out the window into the blackened night, could feel the blood rushing in my ears, the heat rising along my neck up to my cheeks. Simon Trask Properties... 1995. Passages from Claire's emails raced before my eyes.

*Strap95* had a name after all.

I was no longer chasing smoke.

## *Sixteen*

It was late afternoon and I was coming home from the college after a monthly faculty meeting. Our meetings are conducted in a carpeted and plush amphitheater, a setting of comfortable chairs and polished wooden tables arranged in ascending rows. At full steam, about seventy faculty members pack the gallery, full-timers as well as adjuncts. Cy and I usually head for the top row for a bird's eye view of the proceedings, which invariably become boring in a hurry with a steady stream of wandering and useless palaver from administrators, and committee reports often not worth the paper they're printed on. Chadwick conducts the meeting from a slightly elevated podium, her inner troops occupying the first row or two, including lackeys like Whitbourne. His head begins bobbing the minute he parks his useless carcass.

While I'd be the first to admit that I sometimes zone out at these meetings or take the opportunity to correct an examination or two, my offenses pale when compared to the antics of some of my colleagues. For example, while most faculty members are in their seats before the meetings begin, stragglers and no shows are common. Some sit at rapt attention, others are in a slumber mode within minutes. Some dutifully take notes, others doodle and pass notes. Handouts distributed at the meeting are filed by some, left behind by others. Hushed conversations are not uncommon, nor are potshots taken at others. Checking cell phones or sending text messages happens fairly regularly, and laptops have been known to bring instant messages from long lost souls a few rows away. The irony of all this is that these same behaviors are frowned upon, even condemned when exhibited by students. Talk about a double standard.

I was glad the meeting was relatively painless. I was bone tired by the time

I got to Claire's jeep, which I was driving today because my Volvo was being serviced at the dealership. She'd hitched a ride back and forth to work with one of the agency secretaries. I was eager to get home but true to form, the interstate proved uncooperative, courtesy this time of highway construction in Old Lyme and East Lyme rerouting everyone into a single lane. I wondered how many motorists have cursed this wretched stretch of highway, especially in the summer when the traffic reaches a standstill. The bottleneck didn't let up until I exited for Spencer Plain.

My thoughts were drawn to my class that day. Crider and Slocum were no-shows once again, making me wonder about the turn of events since my troubles began. Because of their successive absences this week, my plan to speak with them never materialized, and now I was due to see Chadwick and Whitbourne first thing Tuesday morning. I'd hoped to report on the successful resolution of the situation, but that no longer appeared likely. Who knows, I thought, maybe Crider and Slocum had dropped my course and I wouldn't have to see the likes of them again. Talk about wishful thinking.

While I moved at a snail's pace in the bottleneck of traffic, my thoughts returned to Claire and why she chose to stray. I looked in the rearview mirror and studied myself, wondering why she'd lost interest in me. I had a few miles on me, but didn't think the calendar had been cruel or unkind. I had crow's feet around my eyes along with some frown lines across my forehead. A few wrinkles creased the corners of my mouth. My dark brown hair was beginning to gray at the temples, and my eyebrows had become coarser, or so it seemed.

All in all, I thought I'd held up pretty good. Still had a full head of hair, clear eyes, good teeth. I took care of myself, watched my weight and worked out when I could. I was far from ripped and didn't own a set of bulging pipes, but had good muscle tone. No double chin, no man boobs, no love handles. I wasn't strikingly handsome, but no slouch either. I held my own in the looks department and caught an admiring eye every once in a while. My body had some wear and tear but it wasn't in need of any nips and tucks.

So if I was such a middle age marvel, what was Claire doing bopping another guy? What did she see in him that she didn't see in me? I wondered if he had a bigger crank or performed the four-legged frolic with more passion and gusto. Maybe he was better looking, or younger. Then again, maybe it had nothing to do with sex or physical qualities. Maybe he had big bucks or more toys. Maybe Claire wanted to harpoon a guy who was more sensitive or responsive, maybe even more romantic. His touchy feely emails certainly fit that bill, with enough happy horseshit and wooing to turn anyone's stomach.

I wondered if Claire' affair was some kind of midlife crisis. I knew some people our age who were walking around in a middle age funk, filled with gloom about growing old and pining away for the sweet bird of youth. Some had convinced themselves this was their last chance to kick their heels and grab the brass ring, either that or face regret and despair the rest of their lives. Some were more dramatic with their actions than others, like the local middle aged newspaper editor who got caught doing the backseat mambo with his 23 year-old secretary late at night in the park, or the 45 year-old divorcee across town who quit a plum advertising job, bought a new, shiny red convertible and headed out west in search of an acting career. Talk about the power of wandering eyes and restless feet.

I've never regarded midlife as any big deal. I suppose my acceptance of it was recognizing that I wouldn't achieve all those goals I set for myself in my younger days. I knew I wasn't going to end up with Jennifer Aniston or have the chiseled looks of Brad Pitt. I wasn't going to pen the great American novel or stash my vast riches away in the Cayman Islands. I've accepted the fact that my once lofty ambitions play second fiddle to the realities of everyday life, like picking up the dry cleaning on the way home, trimming the shrubs, or bringing the garbage can out to the curb on Thursdays.

And all that's okay by me. I'm happy and content where I am. I married a wonderful woman and fathered a terrific son. We're not millionaires but we're healthy and enjoy a comfortable lifestyle, better than most. We own a nice home in a fairly affluent neighborhood. I like what I do for a living and have never given a passing thought to a different line of work. Our lifestyle and family routines, although predictable, bring me considerable peace and comfort, security even. We order pizza on the weekends, decorate the Christmas tree together, take turns loading the dishwasher.

Maybe Claire and I no longer shared the same comfort zone. Who knows, maybe she's been bored and unhappy for years, putting on a front but secretly yearning for change. Perhaps years of wiping runny noses, packing lunches and calling the plumber had gotten to her. Maybe she'd found someone who swept her away from all this, recharging her batteries with purpose and passion. Someone to get dressed up for, someone to hold hands with, someone who's shown her that there's more to life than trips to the veterinarian and making grocery lists.

It was difficult not blaming myself for what had happened. I should have opened my eyes and seen what was going on, what she needed. If I paid more attention to Claire, shown more of an interest in her life, maybe none of this would have happened. Maybe I'd been too involved in my writing all these years. I should have been able to pick up on her restlessness, maybe taken steps to rewire our marriage. Engaged her more, asked more questions, listened better.

I felt as though my best friend had turned on me. Over the years we'd stood by each other through thick and thin. I'd always put my faith in Claire, regarded her as someone on whom I could always rely. She was my safety net, my rock. I was in disbelief that she'd violate the friendship we shared and jeopardize the life we'd worked so hard to create.

Maybe that's why all of this was so emotionally devastating. We'd moved from one plateau to another in our relationship, going from friends to lovers, spouses and parents. We'd experienced the joys of dating, anniversaries, new homes and job promotions. We'd shared hopes and dreams, hung on to each other through illness and sorrow, rallied forces against problems and uncertainties.

Or maybe we hadn't. Maybe we were just a house of cards, blown over in the wind.

THE BOTTLENECK OF TRAFFIC CLEARED and I picked up speed, anxious to get home. I had just gotten off our exit and was driving past some wooded areas and open fields when I turned my head a bit to change a CD. Without warning, two white-tail deer bounded out of the forest to my left. Deer are common around here but their movements were so quick, so unexpected, that I was caught daydreaming. They ran right at me, giving me no chance to swerve out of their way or hit the brakes. One turned at the last minute and bolted past the front of the car, but the other crashed headlong into the left front end, making a loud and sickening thump.

Even with my seatbelt on, the impact threw me sideways in my seat, papers and junk scattering through the air. Hoofs and antlers blurred by as I watched the deer catapult over the hood of the car and into a shallow gully on the other side of the road.

I applied pressure to the brakes and fought to maintain control. I slowed down and maneuvered the jeep to the side of the road, the left tire wobbling and metal parts scraping against the road. For a minute, I sat behind the steering wheel, my heart thumping wildly. I had never hit anything before, not even a dog, and I was sweating and shaking. After a few moments, I turned off the ignition and unbuckled the seatbelt. I put on the emergency flashers and checked my rearview mirror. There were no cars coming in either direction.

The door creaked when I tried opening it, and I had to put my shoulder behind it to get out. When I surveyed the damage I was taken back. The door was creased and the quarter panel was cracked and indented against the tire. A portion of the left bumper was twisted and the headlight was broken and dangling from crushed grillwork. The hood had literally curled under itself from the impact. When I looked under the jeep, I could see fluid leaking from the radiator.

Given the damage, I was surprised that I could even pull the jeep to the side of the road. I looked around and knew that I needed to call the police and get a wrecker. I headed back into the jeep to get a cell phone, but stopped when I realized Claire had removed hers when she left this morning. How silly of me to think she'd leave it unguarded twice in the same week. Meanwhile, I'd left mine at home.

I closed the door and was distracted by movement and sounds a short distance away. The injured deer was not in my line of vision because of the gully, but a doe and two fawns were. They stood at the edge of the nearby woods in high meadow grass. The mother held its head erect and carefully watched me. One of the fawns was bleating, a sound similar to the call of a sheep, while the other was sniffing around near the gully.

I walked slowly toward them. It was pretty cold, so I zippered my coat and pulled up the collar. When I got within 20 feet or so, the doe suddenly dashed for the woods and crashed through dense thickets, the fawns following not too far behind.

As I got closer, the buck came into view. He was still alive but lying on his side. He snorted when he heard me and tried to get up, but only succeeded in raising his head and neck. He was big, I'd guess well over 200 pounds, and was watching me with wide, frightened eyes. I kept very still and took slow breaths.

I could see that both of his front legs were broken, one at a grotesque angle, and his antlers had shattered at the base. Blood was flowing freely from a large, gaping chest wound and a widening dark pool spread underneath his body and into the gully. As the buck breathed heavily, his chest rising and falling, a fine red mist sprayed from its nostrils. He was obviously dying. The blood and gore didn't bother me as much as the suffering. No animal should have to die this way.

I was watching the buck struggle and trying to figure out what I should do when a dark sedan approached and slowly drove by. I waved for assistance, but couldn't see inside the car because of its dark window tinting. The car kept going until it reached the jeep, where it stopped for a minute or two, then backed up.

As the car got closer, I could see that it was a larger, luxury model BMW, jet black and buffed to a brilliant shine. When it pulled alongside me, the window slid down. A well dressed, heavyset guy was at the wheel and leaned over toward me, cigarette dangling from his mouth.

"You okay?" he asked, squinting through a cloud of cigarette smoke blown my way.

"Yeah. But I need to call the police."

"Already did," the stranger said, holding up a cell phone. "They should be here any minute." He craned his neck back toward the road and said, "I'll park up the way a bit."

He locked his car and ambled along the side of the road toward me. He was about fifty and big, well over six feet with a rugged build. He wore a tan scarf crisscrossed under an expensive looking charcoal overcoat. His light brown hair was medium length and gelled back, offsetting a squarish face and ruddy complexion. His cologne arrived well before he did.

I stuck out my hand. "I appreciate you stopping. My name's Jack..."

He cut me off, "Elliot. I know who you are."

I did a double take, looking surprised.

"Now don't go getting your dander up," he said. "Spencer Plain ain't no New York City. I sold you your jeep, or should I say your wife, right?"

I nodded. "You've got a good memory. That was a few years ago."

Flashbacks of Sean Halliday hit me as he reached inside his overcoat and pulled out a pack of peppermint gum, offering a stick to me before helping himself. Halliday, the sexist manager of the local jeep dealership and father of Billy, high school crook and credit card thief extraordinaire. I seldom forget fractured family tales, especially one as convoluted as his.

Halliday looked over towards the jeep and said, "I like to remember my customers, plus there are only so many red ones like that one on the road. Wife's name is Claire, right?" I'd find out later that he wasn't as sharp as I first thought. When he passed the accident he stopped and called his dealership, identifying the make and model and connecting the purchase to our family.

He didn't wait for an answer, instead heading toward the gully, working his gum and snapping it as he went. The buck stirred at the approaching footsteps.

"My, my, my," Halliday proclaimed, looking the buck over, "you bagged yourself a dandy, Jack." He sucked his teeth.

I went over and stood next to him, hands in my pockets.

The buck tried lifting his head but was obviously losing strength. He could only raise it a few inches, dropping it to the ground as if it were a great weight. Its breathing had become shallower, and a film had begun coating its eyes. One of the back legs twitched.

"We can't leave him like this," I said.

"I agree," Halliday replied, reaching into his coat pocket and pulling out his cell phone. He tossed it to me laterally like a football and said, "Give that sweet little princess of yours a jingle." He pointed toward his car. "I'll be back in a few minutes."

I turned my back to him and called the house, eyeing the fading sunlight. Neither Claire nor Nathan were home so I left a short message on our answering machine. I didn't mention the accident because I didn't want them to worry, just said that I was running late.

When I turned around, Halliday was walking toward me and much to my surprise, was lugging a pistol. Great Scott, I thought, what's with this guy? He'd gone from car dealer to gunslinger in the blink of a phone call. I don't know much about pistols, but this one was large and menacing.

Halliday saw me staring at the gun when he walked by. "Relax, Jack," he said, "I'm not going to shoot you...at least not until you buy a new jeep from me anyway." He laughed at his own joke, revealing poorly capped front teeth.

He slipped off his overcoat and scarf, then his sports jacket, handing them to me one by one. Everything reeked of cigarettes and whatever cologne he bathed in, Polo I believe. He wore one of those gaudy colored dress shirts, some kind of burgundy, and a loud tie that didn't seem to match anything. He wore rounded gemstone cufflinks, a fat gold watch and three gold rings, one on his pinky, making him look more like a mobster than a car salesman. I noticed the buttons of his shirt were straining against an unrelenting belly.

"Are you going to do what I think you're going to do?" I asked.

He nodded his head as he walked to the backside of the buck. He checked the clip then slapped it in place with the palm of his hand. He was all business, like some kind of bandit or hired gun, which was a bit unnerving.

He said, "The animal's suffering, you can see that. If the police were here, they'd do the same thing."

I couldn't disagree or protest. He was right.

"Listen, get in back of me, Jack. I don't want anyone getting hurt," Halliday said. I walked around him while he chambered a round, causing the dying buck to prick one of its ears. He got within two feet of it, aimed the pistol ramrod straight, and without hesitation fired a round into the back of the buck's head. The sound was loud–more of a crack more than a blast–and rolled in the surrounding woods. The shot thrust the buck's head violently forward, and its entire body seemed to shudder for an instant. It then laid still, head to the side. Over, just like that.

Halliday handed me the pistol to hold while he inspected the front of his clothes. He then put his scarf and other clothes back on, no doubt pleased that he avoided any blood spattering. He took back his pistol and we walked to his car, our footsteps crunching on the gravel along the side of the road. Halliday slid the pistol into a flapped holster and stuck it in his glove compartment, locking it before he closed the passenger door.

Halliday wanted a look at the jeep, and the damage looked worse than I remembered. "You took a direct hit hombre," he said, sucking his teeth again. "You shouldn't be driving with this kind of damage, especially with it getting dark." He looked under the jeep at the puddle of fluid, which had gotten considerably larger. He came up brushing road grit from his hands, shaking his head. "I hope you guys have good insurance," he said, chuckling again at his own material.

I had hoped that I could drive the jeep home, especially since we lived only a few miles away. But Halliday was right. It was getting dark, one of the headlights was smashed and who knows what additional damage I would cause by driving it. This had turned into a nightmare. If things weren't already bad enough in my life, I had to go out and wreck my wife's car, whack Bambi and then watch it get snuffed gangland style.

Within a few minutes a town police cruiser arrived, red and blue roof strobes flashing. A cop got out, hoisted his belt and sauntered toward us. He was some local yokel named Feeney who Halliday recognized from his high school days. After some small talk between them, I described the accident while Halliday chimed in about the shooting. The cop seemed bored with the details, looking about as happy as a clam.

Feeney went over to take a look at the buck, squatting next to it to inspect the bullet wound. He then walked around Claire's jeep looking at the damage. He took my license and insurance papers as well as Halliday's pistol permit, and began filling out an accident report in his cruiser. Halliday excused himself and went inside his car. I leaned against the side of the jeep and waited for them.

The cop returned in about fifteen minutes and handed me my license and registration, along with the accident report, which I signed on the hood of the jeep. He gave me a copy.

"Looks like you've done this a few times," I remarked.

The cop grunted. "Third one this fall."

I nodded and waited for him to continue. He didn't. The police radio squawked from the cruiser.

Halliday got out of his car and joined us.

Feeney handed him his pistol permit. "Hell of a shot, Wyatt," he deadpanned.

Halliday stuck the permit in his pocket while shaking his head, muttering the name 'Wyatt' to himself. He seemed quite amused with Feeney's tag.

Feeney looked at his wristwatch. "That about does it, gentlemen. Any questions?"

"What happens to the deer?" I asked.

"What do you mean?" Feeney countered.

"I mean, do you just leave it here?"

Halliday chortled and clapped me on the back. "You got any better ideas, Jack? What are you gonna do, carry that bad boy home on your back like Daniel fuckin' Boone? You got to remember, your car ain't working too good these days."

Halliday and the cop got a good laugh over that one, two good ol' boys from the backwoods of affluent Connecticut.

I gave them a minute to get over their cackling. I don't like being the ass end of jokes, but bit my tongue and forced a smile.

I said: "That's not what I was asking. I meant will the deer be taken away any time soon? It's not exactly a pretty sight on the side of the road."

The cop gave me a nod and looked over at the buck. "I guarantee you that buck will disappear within the hour. Two guys are already fighting over who gets it."

Halliday added: "When there's fresh kill like this, people around here scramble for the venison, you know, deer meat. Locals will scoop up the carcass and take it to their butcher, get it cut up into steaks and chops and whatnot."

Halliday looked at me and asked, "You ever taste venison, Jack?"

I shook my head. We weren't big meat eaters of any kind.

"Don't know what you're missing," he said. "You ought to try it some day. Healthier than most meats, and better tasting. Had a venison stew just last week that was out of this world."

141

Feeney faked a cough, undoubtedly to hasten his departure and tend to more pressing matters, like blazing a path to the nearest coffee shop. He looked at me. "You okay getting a tow truck and transportation home?"

"We're all set," Halliday said, speaking for me.

I looked over at him, one of those 'Oh, really?' faces.

Halliday said: "I figured you'd be bringing the jeep to us, Jack, so I called ahead and made some arrangements. I've got a tow truck coming from the dealership. Your insurance agent can look the jeep over in our lot whenever he or she gets around to it. I'll drive you over to the dealership now. I've got a loaner waiting for you."

The cop nodded and started walking away. Meanwhile, I stood there miffed by Halliday's boldness, by the fact that he'd gone ahead and made arrangements without even consulting me. I'm not helpless and resent being perceived that way. Maybe I was still smarting from being laughed at a few minutes ago.

Halliday sensed my reaction and said, "This okay with you Jack?"

I paused for a moment or two. Why was I upset? He was right about having the jeep towed to his dealership since we had it serviced there all the time. His dealership had proven to be fair and reliable, so it made perfect sense to have them do the repairs. We would have had to arrange for some kind of rental until the jeep was repaired, so getting a loaner now would be one less headache later. All I had to do now was call my insurance adjuster to come inspect the damage at the dealership, which meant that neither Claire nor I would have to juggle anything.

I really had no right being angry at Halliday. I should have been relieved, not frosted. He hadn't overstepped his boundaries, instead he'd just taken the initiative to help me out. If he hadn't have come along, I'd probably still be hoofing it on the side of the road looking for help in the dark.

I looked at him and blubbered, not quite knowing what to say: "Yes... yeah, I mean, of course that's okay," I said, smiling at him like some kind of jerk. "Thank you. I appreciate all you've done."

"That's settled then," Halliday replied, waving the cop off. He then turned to me and said, "There's no need to wait around for the wrecker, my guy already knows what to do. Get what you need from the little woman's rig and let's saddle up."

# *Seventeen*

After retrieving my briefcase and locking Claire's jeep I got into Halliday's car. The interior was opulent and plush, but the leather seats and deep pile carpets failed to mask the stench of stale cigarette smoke. The ashtray was overflowing with squashed cigarettes of varying lengths, some painted with red lipstick, a snowfall of gray ash on the walnut console below. As we pulled away, Halliday stuck a CD into a state of the arts sound system, flooding the car with classical music. The classical music took me by surprise, Brahms and bullets making strange bedfellows.

We headed south on the Boston Post road. Halliday lit a cigarette with an expensive looking silver lighter, not bothering to ask if smoke bothered me. Between the smoke and his overindulgence in cologne, I wished I'd brought a snorkel. But, I wasn't about to object or complain, not after all this guy had done for me. Anyway, the ride wasn't going to a long one, just the other side of Spencer Plain.

We were small talking when Halliday's cell phone rang. He glanced at the display, then lowered the volume of the CD system with one of those steering wheel remotes. Apparently it was his wife, and Halliday started gabbing with her as he drove with one hand. They were both loud talkers, which made it next to impossible for me not to hear both sides of the conversation. She called to see where he was, and Halliday filled her in on my escapades. They then covered the routine and mundane: how was your day, who did you see, what came in the mail, what's for dinner. Small talk, USA.

Eventually the conversation shifted to Billy, and Halliday's voice perked up. From what I could gather, Billy was in some kind of after school program and earlier in the day Halliday's wife had attended a conference to discuss his progress. Halliday wanted to hear all about it.

As I sat there listening, I was reminded of Billy's credit card scam and the conversation Claire and I had about it. I remembered Claire asking if I was ever going to say something to the Hallidays, which put me in one of those 'to tell or not to tell' dilemmas. At the time I didn't really know Sean Halliday, but here he was sitting right next to me, the Good Samaritan who had ridden to my rescue. It seemed fitting that I return some kind of favor, in this case giving him a simple heads-up, one father to another. This was my chance.

Halliday finished and held the phone away, looking at it and chuckling before he clicked the end button and snapped it shut. "That kid of mine, he's really something. A major piece of work."

"How so?" I asked.

"Oh, Billy got into a scrape at school a little while ago, you know how kids are these days. Hell, you ought to know Jack, you've got one of your own. Anyway, he had to enroll in an after school program. You know, one of those character education things that teach kids respect and anger management and stuff like that."

I nodded at Halliday's soft pedal approach, but broke it down my way: Billy got nailed for possession of stolen goods in his locker, got bounced from school, and the program was a condition for his reinstatement. Bottom line: the kid needed a character transplant.

Halliday eased off the gas a bit and torched another cigarette, blowing the carcinogens my way free of charge. He continued: "So today my wife gets a progress report and the teachers in the program can't stop singing his praises. Here he is—Peck's bad boy—doing his work, helping other kids out and charming everyone. They love him." He shook his head playfully back and forth.

"Sounds like you're amused by all this," I said.

"I am," Halliday replied. "That boy knows how to lay it on thick and throw up the smoke screen when he has too, just like the old man." He was beaming with pride, like the two of them possessed some kind of rare talent that had elevated them to a higher level of being.

I shot him a fake smile.

Halliday didn't miss a beat. "Yeah, he's doing what he has to do, you know, all the right moves in front of all the right people."

"Playing the game."

Halliday took his eyes off the road and looked my way. "Exactly. Playing the fucking game. Billy knows how to wheel and deal, let me tell you. Boy, I could tell you some stories."

With that, the timing seemed right to jump in.

"I'll bet you could. By the way, I heard the credit card story–now that was really something." I scratched my chin. "Where on earth do our kids dream these things up?" I tried to make it sound old hat, like Spencer Plain was a breeding ground for juvenile delinquents and moral degenerates, and that all of us had crooked yarns to spin.

Halliday fell silent and I knew in an instant that he didn't know about the credit card. I got a creeping sensation in my gut.

We pulled up to a stop light and Halliday looked over at me. I knew exactly where he was heading.

"What credit card story was that, Jack?"

I feigned surprise: "You don't know?" I pretended to get distracted by a car passing us. I looked back at him. "I thought you knew all about it."

Halliday said, "Why don't you run it by me anyway."

After a beat I said, "I don't know, it's not really my place. I just overheard some kids talking one day and you know how kids exaggerate." I looked at him and wondered how to best put it.

Halliday pressed. "Come on Jack, stop bullshitting a bullshitter. Tell me what you heard." An edge had crept into his voice, and I could see his facial muscles playing under the skin.

So I went ahead and told him the story. I didn't identify Forrest or Nathan, instead I focused on the credit card and how it was being used. Halliday kept his eyes glued to the road as I spoke. He nodded every once in a while, considering what I was saying. For the most part his expression didn't change, but I could tell he was fuming.

When I was done I felt a wave of relief, glad to finally get it off my chest. I snuck a quick glance over at Halliday then kept my eyes glued to the road. I looked at the glove compartment, thinking now here's a guy who could really shoot the messenger.

Halliday took a deep breath and lighted another cigarette. He took a drag, then asked, "How many people know about this? Is it all over the school?"

"I don't know."

He thought about it for a few seconds. "Do you know if Billy used any other credit cards?"

"I don't know that either."

He hesitated again. "Is there anything else that you can think of about the story? Come on, Jack, help me out here." The guy was obviously rattled.

I shook my head. "I've told you everything I know. Honest."

Halliday sat there behind the wheel, trying to put it all together. I decided to wait him out.

We drove a little bit further and he said, "I appreciate you telling me, I really do." His tone was flat and the words dropped off. He frowned and crushed his cigarette out in the ashtray.

I replied: "You deserved a heads-up." I leaned back in the seat and folded my arms.

We fell into silence the rest of the way. By the time we pulled into the dealership, darkness had completely fallen. The dealership was a multi-tiered building bathed in outdoor lighting, lots of glass and chrome sparkling in the night. On either side of the building were spacious lots filled with new and used vehicles.

Halliday's demeanor changed as we walked through a spacious showroom. He became upbeat and animated, big smiles. The staff all knew Halliday and greeted him by name. The paperwork for the loaner was waiting for us and I just needed to supply some standard information. There was no charge for the loaner.

Halliday walked me outside to the side of the building, where the loaner sat underneath some kind of large sales promotion canopy decorated with multicolored plastic pennants. It was the same jeep model as Claire's, but the most recent version. It was midnight blue and looked brand new.

I raised my eyebrows as Halliday handed me the keys.

He said, "None of our loaners were available, so I substituted a demo. I didn't think this would disappoint the little woman." I cringed at his word choice, images of steam coming out of Claire's ears, but knew he meant well.

"She won't be disappointed," I said.

Halliday said: "Who knows, maybe she'll want to upgrade her rig after she drives this puppy." He gave me a short, piercing laugh. He reached into his jacket pocket, pulled out a business card. "This is how you can reach me if you need me."

I stuck it in my pants pocket and thanked him again for everything. We shook hands.

As I started getting in the jeep, Halliday said, "Jack?"

I turned and faced him.

He looked at the ground and then at me, back and forth, searching for words. "That thing you told me about on the way over. I want you to know I'll take of care it."

I nodded.

He snapped his fingers and pointed at me. "Now you take off and get home where you belong. I'm sure we'll be bumping into each other."

What an understatement that would turn out to be.

# *Eighteen*

Evelyn Chadwick's office was located in McKinney Hall, one of the largest and oldest red brick, Georgian style buildings at Guilford College. It's a stately structure, sitting atop a knoll and surrounded by spreading maples and elms, defined by manicured grounds and wrought iron fencing. Wide marble steps and an ornate balustrade lead to an arched entrance framed by white columns.

Chadwick's office is on the ground floor, which also included the offices of the President, Institutional Advancement, Business and Finance, and Enrollment Management. Everyone knows that Guilford's big hitters hang their hats in McKinney Hall, and I don't get over here very often. When I do, I feel out of place and uncomfortable, like I don't belong. Add the unknown nature of my meeting this morning and it's easy to see why I had a good case of the heebie-jeebies.

Livinia Dawson was not at her desk when I entered the reception area, but I could hear running water and some rustling around in an adjoining kitchenette. She must have heard my footsteps because she leaned out into the doorway, drying her hands on a paper towel.

She wore a big smile. "Morning, Jack. Be with you in a sec, just getting organized for the day." She leaned back into the kitchenette, disappearing before I could respond.

I walked to the far end of the room and looked out a large bay window, taking in an expansive landscaped garden, tidy and dressed for the winter. Everything had been mulched and the perennials and ornamental grasses cut back, some shrubs burlapped for added protection.

I removed my overcoat and looked at my wristwatch, realized I was a little early. I parked myself in a chair.

God, I would be glad when things quieted down in my life. The classroom incident had been bugging me since Chadwick's phone call last week, Whitbourne's waffling and the absences of Crider and Slocum adding uncertainty to the picture. The mysteries swirling around Claire's affair and the deer accident at the end of the week hadn't exactly settled my nerves.

Actually the deer accident proved to be somewhat of a blessing, providing a needed distraction. When I finally got home Friday night, I replayed the accident for Claire and Nathan, who sat mesmerized then pressed me for details, especially about Halliday. Claire was more concerned about my safety than the damage to her jeep, especially lingering injuries I might have incurred. The next day we played phone tag with our insurance agent before filing a claim, then visited the dealership so that Claire could transfer her belongings to the loaner. Both she and Nathan gasped when they saw the extent of the damage to the jeep.

Liv emerged from the kitchenette and slid behind her desk. She was a tall and narrow woman about my age, high strong cheekbones complementing unblemished skin the color of mocha. She was wearing a beige cashmere sweater and a black pleated skirt, some flashy jewelry.

I got to my feet.

"Good morning again," she said, getting settled. She eyeballed my outfit as I approached, and shot me slight nod of approval. I wore a navy wool blazer, a blue-striped button-down, khakis, and dirty bucs.

We small talked a bit before Liv received a phone call and excused herself, angling her body slightly away from me. I took the cue and stuck my hands in my pockets, wandering back over to the window and the bright morning sunlight.

At 8:30 Liv was still on the phone but covered the mouthpiece with her hand. "You ready to go in, Jack?"

I hesitated a moment, looked toward the hallway. "Bruce isn't here yet, Liv."

"Oh, he's already in there," she said in that deep, sultry voice of hers, arching her eyebrows and gesturing toward Chadwick's closed door.

My stomach churned. Not a good sign, I thought.

Liv buzzed me in.

I found Chadwick and Whitbourne huddled over some paperwork at a round conference table in the back of the room. It was a large office, one with lots of expensive pieces of furniture and framed artwork, thick carpeting. Dark wood molding covered the baseboards and cornices, and an imposing, glass-topped executive desk sat next to a wide curtained window. A white, granite fireplace took up most of a side wall.

It was easy getting that uncomfortable, out of place feeling in this building.

Whitbourne rose the minute he saw me, walking over and extending his hand. He wore a rumpled denim shirt and some kind of ratty, tweed sports jacket with wide lapels. His clothes were as out of style as they were ill-fitting, making him Guilford's most famous fashion risk.

"Jack, long time, no see," he bubbled, "thanks for coming over." Cy warned me that Whitbourne pranced around like this in front of the Ice Maiden, trying to create an image of departmental collegiality and affability. His smile dripped with insincerity.

"Not a problem," I muttered. I thought of refusing his outstretched hand but knew tenure was just around the corner and that I had to play the game. I shook his cold and clammy hand, secretly wishing I had a hand buzzer to deliver a jolt to this totally useless jackass.

As Whitbourne moved away and returned to his seat, Chadwick closed a manila file in front of her and stood, stepping my way. She shook my hand with a surprisingly firm grip, dark brown eyes immediately taking hold.

"Good morning, Jack," she said, "good to see you again."

"Hello Evelyn, nice to see you, too."

Chadwick was a striking, compact woman who stood straight, an exquisitely tailored black suit accenting her trim body. She wore her short black hair in a pageboy, no trace of silver. Her dark red lipstick matched her nails. She had on a simple, white silk blouse buttoned at the neck, small diamond ear rings, a few gold rings, and a gold Rolex. Her image was decidedly dominant and influential, and her presence exuded a clear sense of authority and power.

She gestured toward a nearby chair and I took a seat.

Chadwick was fairly attractive, but up close I could see the years at midlife were starting to take their toll. She had a strong brow and cheekbones, but the skin in her neck was beginning to sag. The makeup she favored was undoubtedly used to soften the frown lines across her forehead and wrinkles bracketing the corners of her mouth, creating a downward turn. A few liver spots dotted the back of her hands. Her eyes looked weary.

"What's new in the publishing world, professor?" she asked. This was not a conciliatory gesture on her part. Chadwick had always taken an interest in my writing, and had written several books herself in the field of higher education administration. She knew that authors add research luster to the faculty ranks and represent good public relations for any college.

"Finished a manuscript for a new edition last month," I said modestly. "Just waiting on the reviews."

She screwed up her face. "Ah, the notorious reviewers. Always an adventure, especially that final round when you don't want any surprises or glitches." She had a smudge of lipstick on one of her front teeth.

I chuckled. "Not an exercise for the thin skinned."

"Come on, Jack," she scoffed, "every writer needs to be humbled by a critic's pen now and then. Builds character, doesn't it?"

I thought for a minute, then said flatly, "No, it doesn't."

She laughed out loud, the hardy but phony kind, and got settled in her chair. "Your creativity book has served you well. What edition is this?"

"Fourth."

"No kidding? Not many college textbooks hang around that long. I'm impressed."

She knew the publishing game. Most books nowadays are ready for the scrap heap after the second edition. The competition is fierce and it's easy for a book to go belly up.

Liv entered the office with a full coffee tray and placed it in the center of the table, handing Chadwick a few pink phone messages before she left. Whitbourne got up and poured coffee for Chadwick and himself. I declined.

A few moments passed and the room got quiet. Small talk was over, time to get down to business.

I sat up a bit.

Chadwick cleared her throat. "Jack, first and foremost thank you for coming to see me so quickly."

I nodded politely.

She opened the manila file in front of her and looked down at some handwritten notes. "It has come to my attention that a rather unpleasant situation took place in your classroom last week." She gestured toward Whitbourne. "I know you and Bruce have talked about it several times, but it appears the episode now merits my attention."

Whitbourne's head was already bobbing like a cork.

She flipped through her notes. "Bruce and I talked last week a few times on the phone, and I told him I wanted to hear your take on what happened before it goes any further."

I looked over at Whitbourne but his eyes were evasive and slid away from mine. So the two of them had talked after all. Whitbourne had promised to keep me in the loop but instead had thrown me under the bus.

Chadwick moved her coffee mug to one side and produced a legal size pad. "Do you mind if I take some notes while we talk, Jack? I want this to be informal but I also want to make sure I get my facts straight."

"Not a problem," I said, wanting to come across both willing and cooperative.

She uncapped a pen. "Well then, why don't you fill me in on what happened that day, right from the beginning."

I cleared my throat. I wasn't sure how much detail she wanted, nor what Whitbourne had conveyed, so I just laid out the bare bones. I figured she'd stop me if she wanted more detail. I started with how Crider walked into the classroom and was dissatisfied with the circular seating arrangement, how he pulled his chair away from the group. I told how he disrupted the class by gabbing with Slocum instead of paying attention.

"You spoke to the two of them about their behavior right then and there?" Chadwick asked.

I nodded.

"Do you remember what you said, how you said it?" Chadwick asked. As she spoke she removed a folded, typewritten letter from inside her manila file, and as if on cue, Whitbourne did the same. It looked like the same letter.

"Something general, like 'knock it off, gentlemen.'"

"Nothing rude, nothing sarcastic on your part?"

"No."

She nodded. "Go on," she said, leaning forward and cupping her chin in her hand.

I described how Crider interrupted again when I was discussing *The Natural*, blurting out his interpretation of the book while essentially telling me I didn't know what I was talking about.

She acted surprised, eyes widening a bit. "How did you handle that?"

"I knew his take on *The Natural* was based on a Hollywood movie, not the novel, so I asked him if he'd read the book. I did the same with Slocum, who'd been agreeing with Crider."

Chadwick looked down at the letter, studied its contents. Without lifting her head she asked, "When you questioned Mr. Crider about the book, did you badger him, maybe challenge him to the point of embarrassment?"

Whitbourne was hunched over his copy, chewing on a fingernail.

I looked at the two of them. Suddenly it all made sense, why I was here. Crider had sent a letter of complaint to Chadwick and Whitbourne, Slocum probably signing his name to it.

Those insolent bastards, I thought, no wonder they hadn't been in class since. And here I'd been, totally in the dark, prepared to cut them a deal.

I felt a flush of anger and looked over at Whitbourne, who'd obviously known about the letter and the nature of this meeting all along. He'd been in cahoots with Chadwick from the get go and had sucker-punched me.

Whitbourne returned my look with his lifeless grey eyes, tossing me a smug smile. I felt my stomach flip.

Chadwick broke the silence. "Did you make fun of Mr. Crider?" she asked.

I knew I had to watch myself here, measure my words. Our eyes met. "Crider was disrespectful toward me and disruptive for the second time in less than ten minutes. Besides, he was wrong with what he blurted out. He needed to be corrected and held accountable."

As an afterthought I said, "I don't think asking someone if they've read a book represents badgering or ridiculing."

Chadwick flipped to a new page of her notepad. "Tell me about the incident."

I kept a cool head and shared how Crider played his joke on Lois, then added insult to injury with his out of control laughter. I described how I told Crider to leave, his adamant refusal, and my decision to call campus security. I also spoke of Slocum's involvement and why I had him tossed as well.

Whitbourne stirred, shifted in his chair. He looked down at his hands, rubbed one thumb into the palm of the other. "Jack, do you think the kid was just trying to be funny?"

I gave him an angry stare. "Funny?" I asked.

"Yeah, you know how kids are these days, acting up, speaking out of turn." He picked up his mug of coffee, blew softly on it then took a loud sip, a slurp really.

I regarded him silently for a few moments, no longer surprised at the idiotic comments flying out of his yap trap. He was nothing but a repulsive slug, hands down the most annoying and obnoxious person I'd ever met in my life.

After a while I said, "I'm afraid I don't know how kids are these days, at least the ones in my classes." I shot him a smirk, a cross between disdain and pity. "Maybe someday you can enlighten me, you know, break it all down."

Whitbourne's face got bright red. He was seething and I could've cared less.

Chadwick interrupted with annoyance in her eyes and said, "I urge caution with your tone, professor." She sat there for a moment and just glared at me, a look I'm sure that had made many faculty members buckle.

I looked back at Whitbourne, waited a few moments. "Personally, I don't find humiliating a person in public very funny, do you?"

"Of course not," he snapped, acting gravely insulted. "I'm just trying to figure this guy out, like you."

"I've already figured him out," I said. "He's a royal pain in the ass, a smart-aleck who's as crude as he is spiteful. He likes pushing people around, laughing at them."

I looked at Chadwick. "Of course, he doesn't like it when someone pushes back, which can easily explain that," I said, gesturing to the letter in her hand.

The Ice Maiden frowned again, mouth tightening. "I'm not at liberty to share this, although it's obvious by now that it's a letter of complaint." She shot another scowl at me. "There's an obvious confidentiality issue. It's my responsibility to review the situation, which is why we're here."

I let out a breath of annoyance and looked down. I plucked at a piece of lint from my blazer then smoothed out the crease in my pants.

Chadwick looked at her notes, tapped her pen against the table. "So after Crider's insult you asked him to leave."

"Yes."

"Tell me about that."

I shrugged my shoulders. "There's not much to tell, really. I basically told him to get out."

"How did you say this to him?"

I gave her a puzzled look.

"I mean, what words did you choose? Were you angry, did you raise your voice, shout?"

I thought for a minute. "I don't remember exactly what I said, but it was along the lines of, 'You may leave, Mr. Crider.' I didn't raise my voice, I stayed calm."

Chadwick drummed her fingernails on the table. "And he refused?"

"Yes. He gave me a look of total defiance, a sneer really, and said, 'I'm not going anywhere.'"

She wrote that down. "Was he angry?"

"You could say that," I smirked. "He slammed a book shut and threw it on the floor. Startled some of the kids. Tossed around some profanities."

Chadwick took a deep breath, slowly exhaled. I could tell she was trying to recreate the scene in her mind. "So you've got an abusive and disruptive student refusing to leave your classroom, just defiantly sitting there."

I nodded.

"Did you consider ending the class and letting everyone go, defusing things that way?" she asked.

I shot Whitbourne a steely glare and stuck to my guns. "I thought about it," I said, "but there was too much time left. I wasn't about to reward Crider's insolence and punish those who were there to learn."

She regarded me silently for a few moments, nodded, wrote something down.

After a while she said, "Go on."

I gestured with my hands. "I knew I had to put an end to this. I mean, the class was sitting there hanging on every word, spell bound really. It was ugly, this guy had truly lost his cool." I paused for a moment or two. "So I got out of my chair and walked over to him. I told him I was tired of his little charade and that if he didn't get out, I'd have him removed."

Chadwick and I looked at each other.

"Just like that," she said.

"Just like that," I repeated, not breaking the stare.

She looked down at the letter, hands folded on the desk. "Was your body language threatening or hostile?"

"No. When I got to his desk I leaned over and spoke to him in a firm but controlled voice."

Her eyes returned to the letter. "Did you verbally threaten him?" she asked.

"I laid out the consequences for him if he chose to remain in his seat. The consequences involved being escorted from the building, not verbal or physical harm. I don't consider that threatening someone."

Chadwick thought about this for a moment or two. She picked up the letter. "I'm going to read something to you, and I want you to tell me if it captures what you said." She cleared her throat: "'I'm tired of your attitude, Crider. Pick up your crap and get out of here. If you don't, I'll have your ass thrown from the building.'"

My stomach did another flip. Crider had me dead to right, almost every word. There was no way I could soft pedal this part. I'd reached my limits with him when I said that, knew I'd come on strong.

For a moment I thought about denying it, making it Crider's word against mine. I knew I could probably get away with it. I mean, who would doubt the word of a respected professor against that of an unruly student? Chadwick would never know the difference and would have to support me. Dismissing the case would be a given.

The temptation was enormous.

I opened my mouth but didn't speak. Finally I looked at Chadwick and nodded. "That's the gist of what I said."

Chadwick gave me a hard stare for a few moments, wrote a few more things in her notepad. She sipped some coffee, made a face, sipped some more. Whitbourne said nothing, just sat there enjoying the show he'd helped orchestrate. He smiled confidently at me.

After a while she leaned forward and broke out in another of her trademark scowls, voice thin and tight. "Are you familiar with the concept of academic harassment, professor?"

I nodded slightly, pretending and prepared to stretch the truth. "Somewhat. I know that it refers to the creation of an unpleasant or offensive classroom environment."

"Have you read the Faculty Policy Manual's description of it?"

"I have, but not recently." The truth of the matter was that the manual was gathering dust in some forgotten file cabinet along with other assorted gobbledygook from the administration. The faculty policy manual contained a steady stream of A-Z gibberish that served no useful purpose to humanity, and as far as I was concerned, cut short the lives of too many trees from the Pacific Northwest.

"I suggest you do," Chadwick said coolly, "especially in light of the present situation."

I felt like a teenager, my knuckles having just been rapped with a ruler.

Whitbourne stirred. "You'll find it in section sixteen, Jack," he said solemnly, carefully sliding a copy of the manual from his briefcase and reverently holding it as if it were one of the Dead Sea Scrolls.

I thought to myself, what kind of nitwit walks around with a copy of the Faculty Policy Manual? I just looked at this pathetic lard-ass and slowly shook my head.

Chadwick gestured toward Whitbourne's manual. "Let me see that," more of an order than a request. Instead of sliding it her way across the table, he obediently rose from his chair and hand delivered it to the Ice Maiden. I was surprised when he handed it to her that he didn't bow his head and kneel, or pucker up and kiss one of her rings.

Chadwick rifled through the pages and found the section on academic harassment. She read out loud: "Academic harassment refers to the faculty member's use of intimidating, threatening or insulting language, or behavior that interferes with the ability of students to benefit from the services, activities or privileges provided by Guilford College. We recognize that the type of classroom environment faculty members create transmits a strong message to students, and that a hostile learning environment impedes the academic process. It is our duty to provide a nonthreatening, nondiscriminatory learning environment to everyone."

Chadwick closed the manual and slid it back to Whitbourne. She tapped the letter with her finger. "The implication here is that you created a hostile environment."

I recoiled. "You can't be serious." My eyes darted over to Whitbourne as his raced away.

She said in a strong voice, "The claim is that you taunted Crider as well as ridiculed him, in the process building antagonism and hostility, then threatened him."

I was shocked. What I'd thought was going to be a tidy little follow-up meeting had turned ugly, a witch hunt with yours truly being the main course. I could see next year's contract and tenure at Guilford going up in flames, just like the map of the Ponderosa, Hoss in the saddle laughing at me.

I looked back and forth at the two of them. "You've got things a little convoluted. I didn't create a hostile classroom, I was forced to deal with one. I had an out of control student bent on challenging my authority and humiliating others. Crider was the troublemaker, the one who created this whole mess."

I was getting hot and bothered, trying to digest what had been thrown at me. I looked at Chadwick. "He bullied and offended another student, a woman and mother no less. What's a faculty member to do, sit back and allow roughnecks like this to demean others, hurl insults at will?" I gestured toward the faculty policy manual. "Is that the kind of classroom environment you want your faculty to embrace, the kind of message you want conveyed to our students?"

Chadwick regarded me silently.

After a moment she said, "As I've indicated to you, the incident warrants careful review from my office. It's my job to monitor all of our academic policies and procedures, including something like this."

I sat there stewing, the blood rushing to my head and banging away like a steel drum. Their voices seemed overly loud.

Chadwick added: "Let's not lose sight of the fact that this is the perception of only one student. I'm trying to determine what happened, that's why I asked you to come in first. Obviously I need to dig deeper."

Whitbourne cleared his throat and chimed in. "As long as you're telling us everything, Jack, there's nothing to worry about. None of this is carved in stone." He ran a hand along the top of his shiny, bald head. "Evelyn and I just want a complete picture and not have to fill in any blanks." He gave me one of those reassuring, patronizing nods.

I glared at him and did not respond. I shifted in the chair and crossed my leg, jiggled my foot. It got very quiet. Next door, someone entered the reception room and I could hear muffled voices and some laughter. After a while the person left, footsteps echoing down the hallway.

I finally looked at Chadwick, ignoring Whitbourne. "You know, the irony of all this is that I thought I handled a difficult situation pretty well. I stood up for what I believed in, came to the rescue of a student being harassed. To show you how stupid I am, I even expected some appreciation over here for showing some courage, chivalry even."

Neither spoke.

I slowly shook my head, then spoke in a strangled voice. "I could have ignored Crider and let him have his way, given up control of the classroom. That would have been the easy thing to do. But I didn't. I took the high road." I paused, looked around. "I won't deny talking tough to this guy, and I don't regret standing up to him. He needed a wakeup call. He should be ashamed of himself."

I stopped. There was nothing left to say.

The Ice Maiden shot Whitbourne a glance, took up her pen again. It was so quiet I could hear the pen scratching across the notepad as she wrote.

When Chadwick finished she looked at her gold Rolex and pursed her lips, announcing that she was due shortly at another meeting. I looked at my own watch and was surprised to see that over two hours had passed. I was discovering how fast time flies when you're working your way down the career ladder.

We spent the last few minutes reviewing the incident report filed by the campus security office as well as the paperwork I'd completed with the student affairs office. I read through the documents, although it was hard concentrating. There didn't appear to be any inaccuracies or discrepancies.

Chadwick capped her pen, gathered up her materials and stood. Whitbourne and I followed suit. She looked at me and flashed one of those transparent, polite smiles, thanked me again for coming.

"We'll be meeting again soon," she said.

I stared at her and shook my head, changing the tone. "Not without legal counsel," I replied.

"Oh?" She froze for a moment, eyebrows twitching upward in surprise.

I began putting on my overcoat. "The extent of my participation in meetings like these remains to be seen."

The smile disappeared from her face. "Really?" she asked, tilting her head.

I nodded. "Quite frankly, there are procedural issues I'd like explained and clarified, and I wish to be fully informed of my rights."

I meant it, too. I wasn't going to let these two tag team me again, nor was I about to get picked off alone by Whitbourne, who wasn't a member of the college's faculty federation. I wanted union protection and assurances that everything was on the up and up.

Chadwick stood there for a moment, sizing me up. She looked slightly amused, maybe surprised I'd dug in my heels. I probably overstepped the mark but didn't care.

With an edge in her voice she said, "Personally, I don't think that's necessary. What we're doing is strictly informal, nothing more than trying to piece together what happened. That's why I asked you in, to establish the facts. You'll discover meetings like this are completely legal and within our supervisory rights, professor."

She was starting to really piss me off with the 'professor' line.

I'd later discover she was right about the legalities. I wasn't being reprimanded nor had any charges been filed. Both Chadwick and Whitbourne were exercising their performance review rights. For my own protection, though, I was told to document everything and keep copies of all correspondences. I could also request union representation at any point, which provided some comfort.

That pretty much ended our conversation. Chadwick excused herself and left the room, while Whitbourne escorted me to the door. He walked a bit behind me with his face creased with concern, hand on my shoulder, desperately trying to capture the image of the war weary guardian. He instead captured the image of a total loser, a sorry excuse for an educator let alone a human being.

He reverently said, "I appreciate your cooperation this morning, Jack."

I turned and looked at him. "I appreciate you keeping me in the loop, Bruce," I said, the double entendre immediately lost in the canyons of his hollow head.

Instead, I turned and left, leaving him standing alone in the doorway.

# *Nineteen*

My head was still pounding when I left McKinney Hall. The meeting with Chadwick and Whitbourne had been an unqualified disaster and knocked me for a loop. Whitbourne had kept me in the dark from the word go and ended up feeding me to the lions. In my wildest imagination I never dreamed Crider would go over my head with a letter of complaint, and Chadwick's involvement spelled nothing but trouble.

I decided to walk a roundabout route back to my car, hoping the fresh air would clear my head and help sort things out.

It didn't work. By the time I got behind the wheel the pit of my stomach still ached. Academic harassment was a serious charge and my job had suddenly gotten wobbly, making the home front even gloomier. I had a helpless, sinking feeling, and could feel the world closing in around me.

Next stop, liquor store.

Since discovering Claire's emails and locking horns with Crider and Slocum, I'd been hitting the hard stuff regularly, something I hadn't done since the death of Charlie Ledger. I tipped the bottle back in Hadley for a number of reasons, but mostly to blot out the drowning and deaden the pain, self medication that eventually threw me into a tailspin. While the booze provided a liquid shelter it also created an unhealthy dependence, a habit taking all my energies to kick.

But the vultures had returned and were circling overhead. Maybe they knew I felt alone and powerless, besieged by circumstances moving beyond my grasp. My nerves were frayed and moods sullen. My once peaceful and happy life had become convoluted and murky. I was bewildered, really confused by what was happening, including what had played out this morning in Chadwick's lair.

The old demons were stirring and the temptations of alcohol beckoning. I could feel myself buckling, drinking out of one corner of my mouth while making excuses with the other. I told myself that I wouldn't drink every day and pledged moderation when I did. There would be no heavy-handed pouring, just enough to tweak things here and there, smooth off some roughness. I would be in total control this time and not let alcohol control me.

Spoken like a true drunk.

Who was I trying to kid? The fact of the matter was that I was cruising for a package store before noon, looking for one far enough from the college and away from my neighborhood so that I wouldn't bump into anyone I knew. That should've been the only red flag I needed to heed, but others were fluttering in the breeze. I was shopping alone and would sneak the sauce into the house when no one was around. I planned on taking special precautions to mix the new bottles with the old so that Claire wouldn't be suspicious, maybe hide one in a secret location. I would use cash and toss the receipts so that I wouldn't leave a trail.

No way was alcohol going to get the upper hand on me.

I pulled into a strip mall in Westbrook and found a small package store wedged between a convenience mart and a chain pharmacy. A faded sign on the roof told me the name of the place was *Wilbur's*. In the storefront windows were various beer lights and signs, along with red and blue broad-brush posters announcing the weekly specials. The place looked deserted, which suited me just fine.

I pulled open the door, a buzzer announcing my arrival. A guy standing behind the front counter looked up when I entered. He was short and stocky, fortyish, long hair streaked with grey pulled back in a ponytail that went halfway down his back. He was the only other person in the store.

He nodded a greeting while wrinkling his nose, as if smelling something rancid.

I nodded back, assuming it was Wilbur in the flesh. I don't think I ever knew anyone named Wilbur, in fact the only two I'd ever heard of was Orville's brother and that blockhead on the old TV sitcom with the talking horse in the backyard.

I separated a small shopping cart from a bunch by the front door. Although I'd never set foot in the place, the smell of Wilbur's was like tens of thousands of other package stores: dark and dank with the stale odors of cardboard and dust filling the air, years of leftover cigarette smoke completing the mix. The deodorizing industry somehow missed this corner of the market and would strike pay dirt if it ever formulated the right stuff.

"Help you?" Wilbur asked half-heartedly, giving me a quick up and down before returning his gaze to a television suspended from the ceiling, Dr. Phil spouting his usual happy crappy. Wilbur wore a yellow sweatshirt that read, 'Rehab is for Quitters,' across the front. The sweatshirt as well as its owner had seen better days. He was pasty and cranky looking, a guy under the weather or with a genetic chip on his shoulder.

"I'm fine," I replied.

Good thing since Wilbur had already dismissed me and plunked his useless, fat chowder ass down on a stool behind the counter, eyes glued to the television. It was no wonder the place was empty. I'd have gone somewhere else but problem drinkers have never been known for their consumer smarts.

I scoured the aisles at full throttle, using sonar to spot favorite bottles waiting to be plucked--the green and gold of scotch, the deep blue of vodka, the frosted contours of gin, the purple velvet of whiskey. I loaded one of each into the shopping cart then made my way through the beckoning vineyards, adding various bottles of chardonnay, merlot and burgundy. I topped the loot off with a twenty-four case of Rolling Rock.

Finished. I'd restocked my medicine cabinet in a matter of minutes. I hadn't lost my touch. Translation: You can take the rummy out of the booze store but you can't take the booze store out of the rummy. Or something like that.

I wheeled the cart to the front and hoisted the bottles to the counter, not wanting to hang around any longer than I had to, especially around the likes of Wilbur. I left the case of beer in the cart, tilting the case on its side so that he could easily see the bar code.

Wilbur took his sweet time getting off the stool and made his way to the register, acting like it was a supreme effort to wait on me. He was not a pretty sight up close, sagging eyes and facial stubble complementing a rhubarb beak that sprouted a forest of nostril hairs. He had a fat lower lip that drooped, giving him a hang dog expression. He breathed heavily through his mouth, on the wheezy side.

He looked around for a pair of reading glasses while keeping an eye glued to Dr. Phil, who was interviewing some whining, middle-age bimbo with blond, cotton candy hair. She was complaining that her husband paid too much attention to his hunting dogs and not enough to her. From the looks of it, her husband exercised good judgment.

Wilbur finally found his glasses, a bent pair that angled sharply to the left when he slipped them on. He lined up the bottles on the counter, surveying my purchases as if he were some kind of customs agent. He looked down at the case of beer in the cart then back up at me, tapping the counter with his finger. I felt my cheeks burning, but I obediently lifted the case up and placed it next to the other purchases. I mentally added Wilbur's name to a list of people I intended to poison when I had a free moment, Chadwick and Whitbourne heading the list.

Wilbur stood there looking things over, hands on hips.

"Well now," he huffed, "looks like someone's thirsty." He looked at me with a crooked smile plastered on his face, one in dire need of dental work.

A regular comedian, I thought. I nodded and took the jab in stride, wanting to come across as a good sport. I also wanted to snatch one of the wine bottles off the counter and clout him on the side of his noggin,' giving him something to really wheeze about. Maybe I'd grab that foolish looking ponytail while I was at it and give it a couple of quick tugs, all in good fun of course.

He took forever tallying the amount and counting out my change, dragging his heels I'm sure just to further rankle me. He made a major production of placing each bottle in a separate bag, snapping each open like he was some kind of vaudeville magician. I sighed heavily a few times, hoping he'd take the hint and step up the action, but he ignored me of course.

When he was done bagging Wilbur went into a back room for a moment and returned with an empty box. He began packing the box but stopped halfway, apparently dissatisfied with the arrangement and remaining space. He pulled everything out and started all over. Grade school must have been torture for him. I'd bet a dollar to a doughnut he still mouthed the lyrics to the Star Spangled Banner.

While waiting I inspected the usual countertop clutter found in liquor stores: beer nuts, disposable lighters, breath mints, cork screws, packets of aspirin. A display of nip bottles sat next to the register. I picked up one of the bottles, turned it around in my hand.

"Sell a lot of these?" I asked. I'd never bought nips, even in my old drinking days. I always associated them with skid row bums, seedy types who swigged them on street corners or in public parks, then tossed the empties on the ground. Guys like Wilbur.

He scratched a corner of his mouth and just stared at me, as if I were speaking in another language or was perhaps an IRS agent wanting to see his books.

Finally he said, "Like hotcakes, 'specially the cold ones." He gestured over his shoulder to a tall freezer.

I arched a brow, surprised.

Wilbur stuck the last bottle in the box and slid it my way. He looked over at the display. "Big seller around lunch time or right after work. Spike a soda or some juice, ya know, enjoy a little buzz." Judging from the broken capillaries embroidering his cheeks and honker, this guy had knocked back a few.

I looked at some juice bottles and soda cans in a nearby freezer, then back at the nips. A nearby Budweiser clock in the shape of a keg told me noon time was just around the corner. It had been a hellish morning.

Wilbur got the door for me when I left, a noble gesture obviously spurred by the quick hundred bucks and change I'd just dropped in his lap. I nodded politely on my way out, stepping sideways so that I wouldn't brush up against him. I walked to the car hefting the cardboard box, nip bottles tinkling together like wind chimes.

MY DRINKING GOT OUT OF CONTROL following the death of Charlie Ledger. My mind had become frozen on every aspect of the drowning and I blamed myself for what happened, found fault in everything I did. I'd made a litany of mistakes: I should've been inside the pool fence and not fiddling with the grill, stopped Charlie the minute he started screwing around, been in the water faster.

However, the most troubling part of the drowning was what nobody saw: Charlie slipping from my grasp and going under for a second time. For all I knew, this could have been the thing that killed him. I chose to keep this slip-up to myself, a secret I never shared with Charlie's parents, the police or even my family. For years I thought about why I did this, trying to get a moral handle on it, but never really succeeded. Of course part of the reason was that I regarded myself as a failure, and I'm sure disgrace and shame factored in

165

somewhere. Early on, I thought I might even be blamed for the boy's death.

No fingers were ever pointed at me except my own, which proved cold and unforgiving. In my mind I was responsible for Charlie's death. I never overcame the guilt and by keeping things secret, trapped myself in a vow of silence, one that prevented me from getting a handle on my feelings and moving forward with my life. While I said all the right things in family therapy with Claire and Nathan, the truth of the matter was that I suffered alone, persecuted by my own accusations.

Heavy are such crosses, and I started drinking to steady the soul, and soften the blame. Prior to the tragedy, I considered myself a social drinker, an occasional beer or a glass of wine with Claire. This would change in a hurry, though. Before long I was having a beer or two in the afternoon, then a couple of cocktails with dinner, a nightcap before turning in.

I truly believed booze got my mind off things, and kept the demons away.

At least until the nightmares and panic attacks began.

The first nightmare came a few weeks after the drowning, the details still clear in my head. I'd gone to bed a little tipsy late one night, a combination of too many beers while watching a Red Sox game out on the coast. I remember falling into a bottomless sleep almost immediately and dreaming in disturbing detail.

In the dream I'm diving into the water looking for Charlie, not knowing where he is. I'm searching frantically but my motions are slow, as if I'm fighting some kind of underwater current. The pool in the dream is much larger than the one we owned, considerably deeper. I'm short of breath and know I'm running out of time. My lungs are burning and the water pressure is hurting my ears.

I finally see Charlie, but his position is different from how I discovered him that day. He is floating in an upright position, eyes closed. There is no blood. His arms are at his sides, long hair floating upwards. He looks peaceful, as if he's sleeping. For some reason, tall sea grass is growing under him in the bottom of the pool. It is moving back and forth eerily in the strange current.

I approach him from the front and wrap my arms around his waist, my face inches from his. His skin is ghostly white, body cold and heavy. By now my lungs feel like they're ready to burst. I begin hoisting Charlie upwards.

Suddenly his eyes snap open. They are huge and black as coal, staring right at me. Dead eyes.

I hear screaming. It's Nathan, the blood curdling screams he made that day. I frantically look around for him, but the water has become murky. I can't see him anywhere.

I'm frightened and have to find Nathan. I try pulling away from Charlie but can't. He's holding my arms, fingernails digging into my skin. The long sea grass has wrapped itself around my legs like tendrils, preventing me from swimming away.

I look into Charlie's black eyes.

"You let go," he whispers, like he was sharing a secret only known by the two of us, then releases an evil and wretched giggle that won't stop."

I don't hear the words as underwater garble. Rather, the words and giggling are crystal clear, as if they've been whispered in my ear.

At this point I'm overtaken by a horrible yet familiar stench, a sickening mixture of chlorine, mucous and blood. It was how Charlie smelled when he died in my arms.

The nightmares always stop there. They'd play out many more times during the summer and fall, but never move beyond those last moments of panic and confusion. I'd awaken with a start, often in a sheen of perspiration, my heart beating wildly. I'd find myself short of breath and cold all over, shaking and trembling.

Claire knew I was having flashbacks, although I never shared all the details. She'd turn my way and wrap her arms around me, holding me close to her body. Her warmth enveloped me, protected me. She'd often take my hand and kiss it, hold it against her cheek for a few moments, then kiss it again, press it against her breasts. She'd talk with me in a soft, hypnotic voice, calm and soothing. She was tender and loving, my guardian keeper.

As the nightmares became more familiar, I tried coping with them on my own. While they were still frightening and robbed me of sleep, I chose not to disturb Claire. She and Nathan were also having a difficult time coping with the tragedy and I wanted to protect them from any more upheaval. Furthermore, Claire had returned to work and needed her sleep while I had the rest of the summer off. I made a decision to overcome the fear and horror alone, and keep quiet about the nightmares.

The occurrences of the nightmares were unpredictable, sometimes a few days apart, other times weekly. And while they never moved beyond the putrid odor, variations began to appear. Sometimes I'd get the complete version of the nightmare with the odor, parts of it without the odor, or sometimes just the odor.

Then the odor started tracking me during the day, creating disturbing panic attacks. While the smell lingered for only a few minutes, it produced overwhelming fear. I'd get nauseous as well as dizzy and lightheaded. I felt like I wasn't getting enough air and frozen in place, unable to move. I tried every relaxation response I could think of but nothing worked. I tried distracting myself when I detected the odor, even breathing through my mouth or holding my breath.

The worst part was that the attacks would strike without warning or reason. I could be driving the car, eating a meal or watching television. I could be inside or outside, alone or in a crowd, active or inactive. They'd come out of nowhere, as pervasive as they were unpredictable. Once, I had an attack while lecturing to a class and had to excuse myself and go outside in the hallway to regain control. I didn't know what was worse, the actual attacks or worrying when the next would strike.

I was a man under siege. Nightmares ravaged my sleep and panic attacks paralyzed my days. I constantly replayed the tragedy in my head. Remaining tight lipped about my secret while simultaneously supporting Claire and Nathan further drained my energies. I retreated emotionally, scarred and scared.

I turned to alcohol with a sense of urgency, a means to cope with the terror. Whenever Charlie paid a visit I'd get out of bed and pour myself a stiff drink or two, same thing during the day. I always felt less frightened after a few drinks, more in control. Talk about finding courage in a bottle. Under the influence I could keep Charlie at bay, at least temporarily.

In the beginning, Claire drank with me but it didn't bother me if I drank alone. I was a quiet boozer, never surly and keeping out of everyone's hair. I drank only at home, never going to bars and never driving under the influence. I never got trashed in front of Claire or Nathan. If anything, I used alcohol as a bracer to get through the day, a means to forget and settle my jangling nerves. I admittedly poured with a heavier hand after Claire and Nathan had gone to bed.

It was only a matter of time before my tolerance increased, the curtain of relief demanding a higher price. The bracers during the day became more frequent. The glasses got bigger, trips to the liquor store more frequent. I upgraded proofs for greater potency. I kept a wary eye on the liquor cabinet so that I wouldn't run dry, especially on weekends.

Problem drinking creeps up on people, denial cloaking the damage and concealing the truth. I convinced myself I wasn't a problem drinker and manufactured lie after lie to justify my thirst. I told myself I had every right to drink, that I deserved to imbibe given the trauma I'd experienced. I reasoned the disturbing nightmares and panic attacks demanded a helping hand. I told myself that my drinking was temporary, that I would cut back as soon as things settled down.

These were fairly convincing rationalizations, but my behaviors painted a different portrait, a man clearly in trouble. I became secretive and dishonest, doing whatever was necessary to cover my tracks. I hid empties in the garbage, wrapping them in separate plastic bags or newspapers, sometimes tossing them in public trash bins to avoid detection. I lied to Claire about cash withdrawals from the bank. I blamed hangovers on lingering colds or other imagined illnesses.

Cutting back was easier said than done. I remember one morning being shocked at the amount of vodka I'd consumed the previous night. I told myself I needed to get the upper hand. I refrained from drinking for a little while and began to feel better, confident that I'd taken charge of my life. I'd be brimming with optimism and convinced that I could have a glass of wine or a short cocktail at the end of the day. Of course, this plan failed. I'd have the one and the cycle would start all over.

The summer ended and I returned to the university tired and troubled. I'd hoped a change of scenery would elevate my spirits and restore my groove, but I stumbled right out of the blocks. My lectures wandered and were uninspiring. I graded assignments half-heartedly and grew increasingly impatient with my students. My temper flared with my colleagues.

Yet more reasons to be comforted by the bottle.

Reformed boozers almost always have a story to tell about hitting rock bottom, an incident causing them to slam on the brakes and finally get help. Maybe they made a fool out of themselves in public, or humiliated those around them. Perhaps they regained consciousness in an unknown location, clueless as to how they got there. Maybe they got arrested while driving under the influence and distinguished themselves by making the police log in the morning newspaper.

My moment of truth came at the hands of my son.

Claire was staying overnight at a weekend conference in Cape Cod in November of that year. I was in charge of Nathan and had been looking forward to it for weeks, eager to spend some quality time with my son. He declined inviting any friends, so we made a day of it ourselves. We went to a football game at UMass, enjoyed some pizza at one of Nathan's favorite restaurants, then took in a movie.

We returned home that night happy but exhausted. After Nathan showered and brushed his teeth I tucked him in, perched myself on the edge of the bed talking until his lids got heavy. I remember leaving his bedroom filled with warmth and contentment, pleased with the time we'd shared. A cause for a drink, I thought. I hadn't imbibed all day long and felt a reward was in order. The fact that Claire wasn't home meant I didn't have to tiptoe around.

The next thing I knew someone was patting and pulling on my shoulder, trying to rouse me. It was after two o'clock in the morning and I lay sprawled on the living room couch in an alcoholic haze, trying to regain my senses. I pried my eyelids open and blinked several times, confused.

When I saw it was Nathan, I stiffened.

His eyes were wide and frightened, face flushed and streaked with tears. He sobbed while leaning into me, rubbing one eye with the heel of his hand.

Nathan kept repeating, 'I couldn't find you, I couldn't find you.'

Of course he couldn't find me. I was not where I was supposed to be and had fallen asleep drunk. Passed out probably more accurate.

I sat up and drew him close. He was trembling in my arms, breaths short and fast. I could feel his little fingers opening and closing, bunching the back of my shirt. We stayed woven until his body relaxed and his breathing returned to a slow, steady rhythm.

Nathan swallowed hard and sniffled, told me he'd had a nightmare. He couldn't remember what frightened him, except that he was in the pool alone and didn't want to be there. He'd called out for me from his bedroom and got scared when I didn't come. He didn't know where I was, thought I'd left him alone in the house.

I spoke in hushed tones, did my best to comfort him. I realized I was slurring my words, could smell the booze on my breath.

I got up from the couch and gathered Nathan's hand in mine, led him to my bedroom. I was unsteady on my feet. I covered him up and lay next to him, rubbing his back and gently stroking his hair.

The minutes passed, difficult to say how many. I watched Nathan drift off, his back rising and falling ever so softly, his sleep breath quiet and warm. I reached across the bed and took his hand, held it while he slept. He looked so small, frail and vulnerable.

I had a dull ache in the base of my skull, a heavier one in my heart.

The fact that his nightmare somehow involved the pool was bad enough, but forcing him to deal with it alone in the dark was unforgivable. He would not remember the nightmare in the morning, even when I pressed for details, nor did he ever mention how he found me on the couch.

But I would always remember. I'd let Nathan down and had been incredibly selfish and irresponsible. I'd chosen to tie one on, putting my needs ahead of his and jeopardizing his safety. I hadn't heard him crying or calling out, shuddered to think what might've happened given more extreme circumstances, an illness or accident perhaps, even worse a fire.

I was ashamed of myself.

My son had given me a wake-up call. The thought of placing him at risk was the push I needed to start making changes in my life. I'd crossed that invisible line between social drinking and problem drinking, knew I could no longer deny it. I was in a rut and the booze was doing nothing but making it deeper. It wasn't the answer to my nightmares and panic attacks, or for that matter anything else dragging me down. If fact, it did nothing but make things worse. I'd let it become a cop-out as well as a crutch, and knew I needed help to straighten myself out. Within days, I sought help from a therapist. Along the way, I realized I had to stop blaming myself for what happened to Charlie Ledger. While I'd never forget the drowning, I needed to get off the rack and stop the self-loathing and pity. What happened that day could never be rewritten, the unyielding powers of circumstance and fate having dictated the outcome. I needed to unshackle myself from the guilt and shame and move forward with my life.

I also knew the road to recovery meant sharing what happened in the pool, disclosing the truth to others and setting myself free.

And when all was said and done, the truth was surprisingly simple. I'd done the best I could.

THAT NIGHT I WENT TO BED early, really beat from my morning meeting with Chadwick and Whitbourne. I woke up a little after midnight to use the bathroom, went back to bed but couldn't get back to sleep. I stared at the ceiling thinking about the twists and turns my life had taken, how unsettled things had become.

I padded from the bedroom, careful not to disturb Claire. I went to the liquor cabinet and grabbed the bottle of scotch I'd just purchased, broke the seal and poured myself two fingers worth. I thought of adding ice but didn't want to make any noise. I sat in the darkened living room, sipping and thinking.

The scotch tasted good, the warmth cascading through me and bringing needed comfort and relief. I swirled the scotch in the tumbler, staring at it. I knew I had to be careful, had to keep the beast at bay. I took the last swallow and went to the kitchen, quietly rinsed out the tumbler and placed it back in the cupboard.

I went back to bed and closed my eyes, the booze doing its job and lulling me back into an uneasy sleep.

# *Twenty*

Monday afternoon around two-thirty I was having coffee with Rachel Pond in the student union. It was a spur of the moment invitation from Rachel right after class and I accepted on the spot, not surprising since I wanted an opportunity to ask her to the Mohegan Sun game Thursday night. She was thrilled to be asked and we agreed to meet at the casino in separate cars, neither one of us referring to it as a date.

After a while Lois Winslow joined us, having been at the library doing some research for another class. Somehow the conversation got around to healthy food choices and Lois kept us in stitches with stories about her dietary consultant, a woman Lois affectionately referred to as the 'bitch of spandex.' Lois was bemoaning what she could and couldn't eat, along with recommended vitamins and supplements.

"None of it makes sense," she complained. "I mean, have you ever seen the customers in a health-food store? They're walking skeletons and look like they're ready to croak. Go to a steak house and you'll find the healthiest looking people. They're dying but at least they look good."

She had a point.

"I'm sick of food pyramids, portions and meal points," she said, rolling her eyes. "As far as I'm concerned, the only sensible balanced diet is having the same number of cookies in each hand."

Rachel and I both laughed out loud.

My cell phone rang during a lull.

It was Claire. "Jack, where are you?"

I hesitated for a moment, maybe a little defensive about the question. "I'm at the college," I said slowly. "Why?"

"I just tried calling your office."

I glanced at Rachel, realized she was watching me.

Claire said, "There's been a physical altercation at the high school and somehow Nathan's been involved."

I frowned into the phone. "Physical altercation, as in a fight? Nathan?" Nathan had never been in a fight.

"Yes, I don't have all the details. I just got the call. I'm on my way to the school from a site as we speak. Can you meet me there in twenty minutes?"

I looked at my watch, then at Rachel and Lois. "I'll be there. I'll meet you in the front lot and we'll go in together."

I rang off and stood, taking my cell and sticking it in my jacket pocket.

"Everything okay?" Rachel asked.

I reached for my briefcase. "I'm not sure," I said, "something's going on at the high school with Nathan. I'm heading over there now."

I lingered for a moment before excusing myself. Rachel caught my eye when Lois wasn't looking and winked. I left carrying one of those wicked little tingles.

CLAIRE AND I ARRIVED AT THE school within minutes of each other, Claire throwing me off a bit when she pulled in driving her blue jeep loaner. She wore a cranberry barn jacket and khaki baseball cap, pony tail poking through the back.

She filled me in on what little she knew as we walked toward the school. Apparently there'd been an incident in the hallway involving a group of boys, Nathan included. He'd been injured, nothing serious, but the Dean of Students wanted us notified immediately. School policy, Claire was told.

We signed in at a desk in the main foyer and were directed by a security guard to the Dean's office, located about halfway down a long corridor. When we entered the office, an administrative assistant took our names and asked us to wait while she announced our arrival. She disappeared down a short hallway.

The office was a large one, lots of people coming and going and phones ringing. Over to our right against a wall, a rangy teenager sat alongside a woman who looked to be his mother. When our eyes met, he gave me a rather sullen look then dropped his eyes. He wore a *Sting* tee shirt and sported a nasty looking black eye, the discoloration spreading down and across the cheekbone. The injury appeared to be a few days old, giving me a sense of relief about Nathan, but making me wonder how often fists go flying in the school.

The administrative assistant returned and escorted us to the Dean's office.

Nathan was sitting at a rectangular conference table along with Forrest Poole and his mother Marion. He was holding an ice pack to his lower lip and had blood on his undershirt. The Dean of Students, Janine Rolfe, was over to the side collecting some papers from her desk.

We exchanged quick greetings and checked on Nathan. When he lowered the ice pack, we could see that the side of his lower lip was pretty swollen. A wire in his lower braces had popped loose, puncturing the lip and likely accounting for the blood. The wound was not deep, but was ragged and painful looking. From the looks of it, someone had given him a pretty good pop in the mouth.

Forrest gave me a little wave and seemed okay. He wore a tight fitting Old Navy sweatshirt, one I thought might be Nathan's. I looked at Marion, who mirrored my raised eyebrows. I was puzzled, had no idea what was going on.

Dean Rolfe walked over to where we were standing and formally introduced herself, although we'd met once before during one of the school's orientation programs. She was on the plain side, round cheeks and chin, no makeup, straight black hair.

We sat and Dean Rolfe assured us that Nathan had been examined by the school nurse and was okay. She reported that Nathan's wound had been cleansed and was superficial, although we would obviously have to visit his orthodontist to have the wire reattached.

She cleared her throat and leaned forward a bit. "I asked you here because we had an incident this afternoon involving your sons. As Dean of Students I handle the school's disciplinary situations and it's always been my practice to involve parents or guardians from the very beginning, keep them informed at all stops."

She flipped through the pages of her pad until she got to the section she wanted. "With that said, let me share what happened. These are my notes compiled from students who witnessed what took place, a hall monitor who caught the tail end of the incident, and comments made a short while ago by

Forrest and Nathan. I think I've got a pretty accurate narrative."

I sat up a bit in the chair.

She went on: "Just after the last class this afternoon Forrest and Nathan were in front of Forrest's locker. The hallway was congested at the time. Three students came along, two grabbing Forrest by his arms and forcing him into the nearby boy's restroom. The third student stayed behind and blocked Nathan from following. Once in the restroom, the assailants tore off Forrest's sweatshirt and undershirt. They proceeded to rip the clothing into smaller pieces and flushed them down the toilet."

I looked over at Forrest, who was staring down at the table in front of him. His mother was doing the same.

Dean Rolfe said, "One of the assailants was clearly the leader. He began teasing and taunting Forrest, as well as pinching him primarily in the breast area. This lasted about five minutes. The leader then pushed Forrest out of the restroom and told him to run the length of the hallway. Forrest resisted but was repeatedly shoved forward. Forrest eventually began running."

She paused for a moment and lowered her eyes, bit lightly on her lower lip. This bothered her, no mistaking that.

She resumed and said, "The leader kept shouting, 'Run, Forrest, Run.'"

As in *Forrest Gump*, I thought, my body coiling. I could envision Forrest running bare-chested, reddened with embarrassment. I looked at Claire, could tell she was doing the same slow burn. When she gets angry her cheeks flush, the tendons in her neck become taut.

Bullying infuriates me, especially when it's unleashed against kids like Forrest. His obesity and lack of friends beyond Nathan made him ripe for the pickings. Pick on the fat kid, make fun of him, get a good laugh. Just to make things more amusing, throw in some humiliation. Destroy his clothes, disgrace him in front of others, watch him jiggle.

It was difficult remaining calm.

Dean Rolf flipped to a new page of her notepad. "The rest of the narrative," she said, "originates from the hall monitor. He'd been tending to another matter in a connecting wing and had been summoned by a student."

I shifted in my chair. Outside in the hallway an after school bell rang, voices and laughter penetrating the walls. The strains of marching band practice could be heard from somewhere behind the school.

Dean Rolfe continued: "While running, Forrest apparently tripped and fell to his knees. At this point Nathan broke free from the person restraining him. He helped Forrest to his feet and told the leader to stop, at one point pushing the leader away. Nathan had taken off his sweatshirt for Forrest to wear when the leader started taunting Nathan and shoved him against the lockers, causing the lip injury."

I caught Nathan's eye and felt a swell of pride, the overmatched scrawny kid trying to rescue his best friend, doing whatever he could to prevent further embarrassment. I winked and he flashed a little smile behind the ice pack, his index and forefinger trembling slightly.

Dean Rolfe closed her notepad. "The hall monitor along with a teacher who heard the disturbance intervened and took control of the situation, dispersed the crowd."

We all sat around silently for a few moments, looking at one another.

Dean Rolfe let out a breath, looked at Forrest and Nathan. "It's obvious the two of you were victims of an ugly incident and I'm very sorry it happened. This is especially unfortunate because you're both freshmen and this is not how our students conduct themselves."

She looked our way. "I want you folks to know that my office has zero tolerance for this kind of stuff, anything causing hurt, suffering, or degradation. There's no justification for it and I will not tolerate any form of it. All our students have a right to be educated in a safe environment and protected from bullying. We take incidents like this very seriously."

She picked up a paperclip from the table, began unbending it. "With that said, I'll try and answer any questions you might have."

"I have two," I said, trying to keep my voice steady. "Who's the leader and what provoked this?"

Dean Rolfe started to respond but Forrest interrupted. "It was Billy Halliday. He heard I was telling other students about the credit card scam."

Claire and I exchanged glances, then looked at Dean Rolfe. "Are you aware of the scam?" I asked.

"I just learned about it today."

Forrest added, "Billy was telling people yesterday his old man found out about the credit card stuff and beat the snot out of him over the weekend. That's why he's all banged up." Forrest was nervous, words flying out of his mouth at a pretty good clip.

I raised my eyebrows at Dean Rolfe, gestured with my chin toward the waiting room. "He's the kid out there, the one with the black eye?"

She nodded. "I can't comment on this except to say we're also aware of the eye injury. The school will be looking into this since we have a legal obligation to report such matters."

Suddenly the whole scenario played out before me. I'd tipped Sean Halliday off about Billy and the credit card. The old man stewed about it and decided to clout the kid. Billy somehow finds the leak and comes looking for Forrest and Nathan wanting payback.

Way to go, Jack. So much for taking the moral high ground and giving Halliday a heads-up.

The conversation went on for a little longer, Dean Rolfe answering a few questions from Claire and Marion, as well as collecting a little more information from the boys. Dean Rolfe brought the conversation to a close, announcing she had other parents waiting. She thanked us for coming and promised to keep us in the loop.

When we left the office, Billy and his mother avoided eye contact with any of us. It didn't surprise me that Sean Halliday was nowhere to be found.

WE TALKED IN THE PARKING LOT, MARION having to leave after a few minutes to return to work. She was bothered by the incident, as any parent would be, and we agreed to talk later in the evening. In general, though, we were confident the school would act promptly and take strong measures against Billy Halliday and his followers. Forrest reminded us that Billy was already on thin ice because of the stolen property found in his locker a few weeks ago. He seemed to be the proverbial kid who'd used up all his chances.

Both Claire and I wanted to take Nathan to the orthodontist, so I agreed to transport him in my car and follow her. He was quiet in the car, the detached wire making it difficult for him to speak. When we approached Halliday's dealership along the way, Claire surprised me by slowing down and pulling into a side entrance. She parked the loaner near the service department and got out, scanning the customer lot for her jeep. Once she spotted it, she headed for the service department entrance.

I didn't know what she was doing and went to find out, leaving Nathan in the car.

When I caught up with her she said out of the corner of her mouth, "I have business to take care of, Jack."

I fell in beside her and matched her pace for pace. She went in and approached the counter. A guy with a crew cut and big hands glanced up.

Claire's tone was clipped. "My name's Claire Elliot. I'd like the key to my jeep. It's the damaged red one in the side lot."

He looked down at a large appointment book, trailed his finger along the days with a big finger. "Oh yeah, the deer accident. It's scheduled day after tomorrow." He looked miffed, like me.

"You can cancel that appointment," she said. "I'd like the key."

He shrugged, found the key on a pegboard behind him and handed it to her.

She walked through a door connecting the service department to the showroom. I followed.

There was a good reason Sean Halliday wasn't at the high school because he was over in a corner yucking it up with two other salesmen, feet parked up on a desk. He stood when he saw us. He wore a mustard-colored dress shirt and a god awful green speckled tie, shirt sleeves rolled up to his elbows. He made sure his shirt was tucked in at the waist while he hiked up his trousers to try and conceal a bulging gut. As he walked toward us, Halliday looked bigger and more imposing than I remembered. The heels of his black patent leather shoes clicked on the tile floor, the noise echoing hollowly in the spacious showroom.

"Well now," he said looking at me, "look who's here. I see you brought the little lady, Jack." He winked at Claire, flashed a phony grin. "Let me guess, you want to keep that loaner you're driving." He laughed quietly to himself when he said this, obviously enamored with his self-proclaimed majestic status inside his kingdom. His combined scent of Polo cologne and peppermint chewing gum drifted our way. It immediately produced flashbacks of the deer accident.

Claire took a step forward when he approached us. She held up the loaner key in one hand, her own in the other. She looked him straight in the eye and didn't mix words. "I'm returning your loaner and taking my car." She pressed the loaner key in his hand, took a step back.

Halliday didn't know what to make of this, looked back and forth at the two of us. "Whoa, slow down here sweetheart," he said. "Why don't you tell me what's going on. What do you mean, 'taking your car?' We've scheduled your rig for this week, all the parts have been ordered."

Claire maintained eye contact. "Return them," she said. "The appointment is cancelled."

Claire's words bit into the air.

He straightened, snapping his chewing gum. "Am I missing something here? Is there a problem I should know about?"

Claire looked sharply at him, crossed her arms. "Yes, there's a problem. I don't do business with people like you."

Halliday blinked rapidly, shot Claire a puzzled look. "I beg your pardon?" The showroom got very quiet, a few salesmen drifted over.

Claire looked straight at him, narrowed her eyes underneath the brim of her baseball cap. "I'll make this short and sweet so that we're perfectly clear. If your son so much as touches my boy or his friend Forrest Poole again I'll personally see to it that he's arrested. Consider yourself warned."

Halliday just stood there, stunned.

Claire didn't break eye contact. "Do you understand me?"

Halliday turned both palms up, looked at me. "Jack, you want to tell me what the hell's going on here?"

I started to open my mouth, but Claire cut me off. "Jack has nothing to do with this." She added quickly, "This is between you and me."

A muscle twitched in his jaw.

My eyes swept the showroom. The salesmen behind Halliday started whispering. He turned around and silenced them with a dirty look, then edged closer to Claire.

"Look," he said in a low tone, "why don't we talk about this in my office? There's been a little misunderstanding here." He laughed softly, sucked his teeth.

Halliday stepped toward Claire and touched her elbow to show the way, but she pulled her arm back. He took a step away, raised his hands.

She glared at him. "There's been no misunderstanding, and there is no need for an office chat. This conversation's over."

He looked at the key in his hand, face darkening. He furrowed his brow, clenched his teeth. "I don't think I like your attitude, *senora.*"

I watched Claire's cheeks flush and neck muscles become taut for the second time this afternoon. "And I don't like the way you conduct your business, here or in your home."

Billy Halliday's blackened eye flashed through my mind, as well as Mrs. Halliday facing the music alone back at the school.

Claire looked at me, gestured toward the door. "Let's go, Jack."

We took several steps before Halliday snorted in derision. "What I do in my home is no goddamn business of yours or anybody else."

Claire stopped, turned. Another stare down, more silence. I watched a slow burn move across Halliday's face. He looked dangerous and I moved in closer.

Claire sent back the slightest trace of a smile. "Nobody's business? Really?

After today I wouldn't be so sure of that."

He just stood there, his face taking on a blank expression. He didn't know what to say.

Claire slung her pocketbook over her shoulder. "Send me a bill for the loaner," she said as we headed for the door. She stopped after taking a few more steps, then turned around again and walked back to Halliday. She made a show of opening up her purse and taking out a credit card. She held it in front of Halliday's face so that he could see it in plain view.

"I'll pay for it on my credit card, *pendejo*," she said, her lips curling. "I understand you've learned a lot about credit cards lately." Claire gave Halliday a crooked little smirk before she turned to join me.

As we walked away, the showroom was eerily silent. When we got to the door I held it open for her. On the way by she hissed, "Nobody fucks with my kid."

# *Twenty-one*

Sean Halliday and his band of merry men glared at us from behind the showroom window as Claire called a wrecker to have her jeep delivered to the house. Once that was done, we raced across town and got Nathan's wire reattached, barely making the last appointment of the day. We were going to stop somewhere for a bite to eat, but Nathan wasn't really hungry and just wanted to get home. We picked up some sherbet to help get him through the night.

Nathan was doing much better when I checked in on him later in his bedroom. He'd just finished showering and was under the covers talking to Forrest. I pulled up a chair and plopped down, hoisted my feet up on the bed. The swelling in his lower lip had lessened considerably, now just pea-sized.

Nathan rang off and put his phone on the night stand. He leaned back against the pillow, hooked his hands behind his head and looked at me.

"You okay?" I asked.

"I'm okay, Dad."

"Honest?"

"Really, I'm fine. You need to stop worrying."

"How 'bout Forrest?"

"He's okay, too."

Nathan tried to conceal a little smile.

"What's so funny?"

"I was just thinking about something he said."

I raised my brow.

"When he tripped in the hallway and fell to his knees, Forrest said he had Halliday right where he wanted him. He said if I hadn't jumped in it would have been a bloodbath."

We both laughed, Nathan touching his lower lip and wincing.

He got quiet, turned inward for a minute.

"This kind of stuff has happened before," I said. A statement, not a question.

He nodded.

It's one of parenthood's most painful moments, discovering your child is the one being singled out or laughed at because he's different and doesn't fit in with the crowd. You know crap like this happens, maybe experienced it yourself growing up, but never thought it would be your kid who ends up with the target on his back. Somehow you thought you could protect him, wave some kind of magic wand and make him immune from it all. The heartbreak is enormous, a hurt that defies description.

Nathan snapped me out of it. "Come on Dad, stop worrying, really. I can handle it."

Claire had silently slipped into the room and was leaning against the doorframe, and had heard what we were talking about. She came over and sat next to Nathan on the edge of the bed.

The two of them looked at each other for a long moment.

"What kinds of things do these boys do?" she asked.

He sighed. "The usual stuff. Push us around when no one's looking, laugh at us. Forrest gets teased about his weight, ya know, what he eats, what he wears." His voice tailed off. "They call him 'Gump.'"

I thought of the high school hallway, what it must have been like for Forrest in front of all those students. Run, Forrest, run.

He added: "They call me Skinny Bitch."

"Why, honey?" she frowned.

Nathan smiled weakly. "Come on Mom, I'm scrawny, but there's more to it than that. One of their games is waiting for someone to bend over a water fountain, then hitting him on the back of the head. They did that to me once and it hurt, made my eyes water. Same thing when I got roughed up in the bathroom. I guess the other guys they picked on don't cry when they get slapped around, but I did. They've called me 'Skinny Bitch' ever since."

Claire slowly nodded and bowed her head. She didn't express her sadness but wore it on her face.

I said, "Nathan, why didn't you tell us about any of this? Why didn't you tell someone at the school?" I was bothered.

"I took care of things, Dad. Besides, it would've been worse if we ratted on them."

"What do you mean, you 'took care of things?'" I asked.

"I don't drink from the fountains, don't use the bathroom."

I said nothing, tried to imagine what it would be like not using a bathroom all day even though I had to, walking past a fountain even though I was thirsty. I couldn't fathom the discomfort, the extent to which I'd avoid confrontation.

Claire stirred, slid closer to Nathan. She reached over and brushed his hair to the side with her fingers and looked at him lovingly for a few moments as only a mother can.

Finally she said, "When I was a freshman in high school, I was a pretty good softball player. I played the game a lot growing up, won all the big trophies, was expected to make some noise for the high school. I was disappointed when I got placed on the freshman team but took it in stride since our school was a powerhouse, always ranked. We'd won the state championship the previous year."

She sat there thinking for a minute, then continued. "One day the freshmen played the varsity in a scrimmage and we faced their number one pitcher, an all-state, first team selection. Loreen something, team captain. Big girl, threw very fast and had a great change. Seems like she struck everyone out that day, hardly worked up a sweat doing so. Each time she got a strikeout she'd make her index finger and thumb into the shape of a gun and shoot the batter walking back to the bench. Then she'd laugh and her teammates would whoop it up. It was very degrading and annoying."

I shifted forward in the chair, listened to Claire's mind drift.

She said, "Anyway, I was the last batter in that scrimmage, the last victim. She got two strikes on me and I don't think I even saw the ball, she was that fast. I remember stepping out of the box and watching her smirk at me, really enjoying herself out there on the mound. I knew right then and there she was going to throw me a change-up on the next pitch, wanted to throw me off stride and make me look as foolish as possible, which that pitch can do."

"Did she throw it?" Nathan asked, his fingers fidgeting with the edge of the bedcover.

"She did, and I stayed back on it like I was taught and knocked it out of the park. I knew it was gone the minute I hit it. The best part was she did too. She started kicking dirt around and glared at me as I rounded the bases, absolutely furious. When I crossed home plate I wanted in the worst way to shoot her with my own finger pistol but held back. I wasn't taught to play the game that way."

Claire pulled the covers up to Nathan's chest, smoothed them with her hand. "Anyway, that home run earned me a place on the varsity, which was quite an accomplishment for a freshman. I remember getting a fancy varsity uniform and putting it on, standing in front of a mirror, prouder than punch. The downside was that it meant not playing ball with my friends anymore. But, I reasoned it was time to move on, take my game to the next level."

I knew Claire played softball in high school and was pretty good, but I hadn't heard any of this.

She pushed a strand of hair back behind an ear, then continued. "Early on in the season, the varsity and freshman teams shared a game bus. On the way back from the game I sat with my freshmen friends in the front while the varsity sat in the back. The varsity had won big and was rowdy, which translated into taunting the freshmen and using them for entertainment purposes. Loreen along with a few of her buddies were the ringleaders, hurling objects and insults, pushing and slapping, daring the freshmen to mix it up with them, which of course no one did."

The phone rang in another part of the house but none of us moved.

Claire said, "Loreen called out for me, asked me to come to the back of the bus because she had a question about the game. She'd pitched that day and I think I got the game winning hit, so I was confident she wasn't going to pull any rough stuff. After all, we were varsity teammates."

"What happened?" Nathan asked.

"The minute I sat down the punishment began, worse than anyone else had received. Loreen began elbowing me in the ribs and punching my thighs, trying to give me charley horses. The girl in back of me kept yanking my hair, pulling it by the roots. One of the outfielders spit on me, another player stuck gum in my hair. I tried repeatedly to leave but was forced back."

Claire slowly shook her head. "I've never felt so violated and alone, so humiliated. The varsity players who weren't hurting me just sat back and enjoyed the show, and not one of my freshman friends lifted a finger to help. The coaches knew what was going on but turned their backs. I wanted to cry but knew that would only make things worse. Finally I managed to fight my way back to my seat. I stayed huddled against the window until we got back to school."

Neither Nathan nor I spoke.

"I went home that night and got myself cleaned up, didn't say a word to my parents about what happened. The next day I went to practice, handed the coach my uniform and gear, told her I was quitting. She was totally shocked and begged me to stay, said she'd talk with the team, make them all apologize. I stood firm, told her my decision was final. I didn't want these girls as teammates or as friends, didn't want them in any part of my life."

Claire looked away, fell silent for a minute. "I never played again."

After a while Claire's eyes came back to Nathan.

"I wish I could say what happened today will never happen again, but I can't. You'll find bullies everywhere, sweetheart, and they never seem to get their fill. They'll put you in difficult situations and force you to make tough choices, like today with Forrest. You'll need to look deep inside for the answers, discover what's really important to Nathan Elliot. Things like what you believe in, what you're willing to risk, what you're willing to stand up for and defend."

Claire smiled tenderly, placed her hand on his heart and held it there for a few long moments. "Trust your mother," she said, "your heart will always show you the way." She paused and smiled warmly. "It already has." She leaned over and gently kissed his cheek, then rested her head against his chest and closed her eyes for a little while.

CLAIRE AND I SAT IN THE LIVING ROOM SHARING a glass of wine, taking the edge off a rough day. We mapped out a plan for the jeep, deciding on a body shop over by the high school and arranging to get the jeep towed there in the morning. We also reserved a rental car, which would be ready and waiting for Claire when I dropped her off in the morning.

We each needed to catch up on some work before calling it a night. Claire headed off to the study to finish a feasibility study for a nearby retirement community, while I stayed where I was and tackled a new batch of writing assignments.

A few hours later, I heard Claire shutting down. She made her way back and sat sideways on the arm of a chair.

I removed my reading glasses and pinched the bridge of my nose between my thumb and forefinger. "Calling it quits?"

"Nothing makes sense anymore," she said, stifling a yawn, "too much going on today. How 'bout you?"

"The same."

"How were the papers?" she asked.

"Not bad," I said, sifting through the pile on my lap, "I wanted to read you part of one." I found the one I was looking for and said, "Remember a little while ago we were talking about how dating has changed, how it's no longer sex, drugs, and rock and roll that teenagers have to worry about?"

"Yeah, I believe that's when I told you Woodstock had come and gone, which bummed you out for days."

"Still remains a mystery to me," I said. "Anyway, this paper reminded me of the conversation we had. Listen." I slipped on my reading glasses back on and read:

*As we help teenagers find their way and make responsible choices, parents come face to face with an assortment of troubling issues, some posing stark contrast to those of yesteryear. For instance, whereas parents once worried that sneaking a brew or two would tarnish teens' budding character, the emergence of potentially lethal club drugs has produced new fears and apprehension. Along these lines, while going to a movie years ago rarely prompted anyone to question the suitability of its contents, movie ratings need to be consulted today before tickets are even purchased. And, whereas teens were once allowed to walk to and from social events because it was relatively safe to do so, this is hardly the case anymore. Indeed, in addition to arranging or approving of transportation for the evening, many parents insist that their teens carry a cell phone in their pocket and proper identification, which for some means a DNA Lifeprint card.'*

I put the paper down.

Claire said, "Yep, I totally agree. It's dangerous out there nowadays."

I nodded in agreement.

"Who wrote that, Sam Chiang?" She was familiar with Chiang's writing because I often read his work aloud. His stuff was that good.

"No," I replied, "a student named Rachel Pond."

I looked up from the paper, caught Claire's eye. I could have sworn I saw something dart across her face although I'm not sure what it was, surprise maybe, or recognition.

She frowned and sat there for a moment, folded her arms across her chest. A brief silence crept in.

"What's the matter?" I asked.

"The name, Rachel Pond," she replied. "Do I know her?"

I shrugged. "I don't know, I might've read some other stuff of hers to you."

"No, it wasn't her writing." She pursed her lips, thought a little longer. "Wait, isn't she the friend of the woman Crider picked on that day?"

I hesitated a moment. I didn't remember telling Claire about Rachel's visit, and planned to keep it that way. I went to bed that night thinking of Rachel's exposed belly and seductive smile.

"Yes, that was Rachel," I said flatly. I tried appearing nonchalant, as if Rachel were just another name in the roll book. The fact of the matter was that I was getting a little rattled talking about her, not surprising given what lurked beneath the libidinal surface. I thought of those wicked little tingles she'd been delivering, how I'd been fantasizing about her.

I looked away, pretended to busy myself with the papers.

"She's a good writer," Claire offered.

"Very talented," I replied.

Claire wasn't going to let this go. "What does she look like?"

The question took me by surprise, made me debate how to reply. "Blonde hair, blue eyes, late thirties." I chose my words carefully, didn't want to be too descriptive or sound bubbly.

"Attractive?" Her voice picked up a playful tone.

I tilted my head, pinched my eyebrows. "Why would you ask that?"

"Oh, I don't know. The day you stop looking, Elliot, is the day I start worrying."

I wondered if Claire was testing me.

"Yes," I said, "Rachel's attractive, pretty in her own way." I cleared my throat, glanced down at the papers on my lap, looked back up at her. I was getting more uncomfortable, cursed myself for reading the paper out loud.

Claire nodded, didn't take her eyes from my face.

Out of nowhere the Mohegan Sun game flashed into my mind. A few days ago I announced that I was going with Cy Rollins, hadn't bothered to ask Claire or Nathan. I knew Cy would be away at a conference all this week, a perfect alibi for the game. I'd been planning on taking Rachel all along, waited for an opportunity like today to ask her.

I felt guilty and shifted in my seat, wondered if I was wearing anything on my face.

I didn't know if Claire had somehow discovered my plans. If she did, it wouldn't have come from Cy, of that I was certain. I wondered if I'd left a trail, something making Claire suspicious. I remembered recently writing Rachel's cell number down on a post-it at work, absentmindedly sticking it in my pants pocket. I'd left the note on my bureau overnight along with a few others and some loose change, but remembered bringing it back to work the next day.

I reasoned that even if she saw the cell number, it proved nothing. It wasn't incriminating and had no connection to the game.

I told myself to calm down, that Claire was neither suspicious nor nipping at my heels. She'd asked a few simple questions and had been bantering, not baiting. I was overreacting and needed to relax.

Nathan walked down the hallway to use the bathroom, stuck his head in the living room to say goodnight on the way back.

I took the opportunity to put Rachel's paper in with the rest, straightened the pile. I looked at my watch and yawned, rubbing my eyes then my temples.

Claire came over, gave my neck and shoulders a little massage. She reached for my hand, squeezed it gently.

"You've had a rugged week so far, mister," she said. She leaned over and kissed me lightly on the cheek. "Don't stay up too late." I took a deep breath, inhaled her lilac scent.

As she was walking away I said, "Hey, you."

She stopped, turned around.

"You were terrific today."

She tilted her head.

I said, "Your son and I think you're pretty special, you know."

I caught a glimpse of a younger Claire. The innocent teenager spurred by moral conviction, the bruised kid sacrificing her love for the game in favor of her principles, the same uncompromised conscience on display today at the dealership.

She smiled again and nodded.

I muffled a laugh. "Senor Halliday challenged the wrong senora to a gunfight."

She rolled her eyes. "Pendejo," she scoffed.

"By the way," I said, "what's a 'pendejo?'"

She wagged a finger at me. "Shame on you, Dr. Elliot, you're slipping. 'Pendejo' is slang in Spanish. Its beauty is that it can be used as a noun, adjective or adverb."

"So what's it mean?"

She replied matter-of-factly, "I don't know exactly, but essentially it's a cross between a slime bucket and a scum sucking pig."

"I knew that," I said, suppressing a smile.

She rolled her eyes again and went off to bed. I watched her leave, switching lights off as she made her way to the bedroom. I put my head back against the chair and closed my eyes, drifting away with my thoughts for a little while. When I knew Claire was settled in bed, I went into the bathroom and swallowed four aspirin, then tried to decide between the gin or the vodka.

# *Twenty-two*

Simon Trask was not at all what I imagined. I'd had a while to think about him, wondering how he talked and dressed, his demeanor, anything that could provide a glimpse of the missing piece. I have to admit, I'd created exaggerated images of the guy, on one extreme a debonair Don Juan type—tall, dark and handsome—an arrogant bastard sweeping heart-struck women off their feet while shamelessly adding notches to his belt, including one bearing my wife's name. At the other end I pictured a silver haired sugar daddy, an aging fossil a stumble or two away from a nursing home, but whose pockets were loaded with riches.

Trask was standing in front of me along with an audience of about a hundred other people gathered at an evening real estate seminar in downtown New London. I'd accidentally discovered an advertisement for the program a week or so ago in a shoreline newspaper, the blood rushing through my veins when I saw that it was being sponsored by Simon Trask Properties. It was being held at a Holiday Inn and open to the public, promoted by the agency as a way to help prospective clients discover the financial potential of real estate investment.

I arrived at the seminar early, telling Claire I had to hobnob at a wine and cheese reception at the college for some visiting scholar. I waited in the parking lot watching people arrive and chose to follow a small but loud group into the hotel. They provided a perfect cover to slip past a registration table and grab a seat in the back row. I tried not to make eye contact with anyone.

Trask was about my age, lean and muscular, tallish. He was a good looking guy with dark eyes and hair, the hair flecked with gray and styled to look casual and windswept. His angular face framed a strong nose and square jaw, a two or three day old scruff creating a ruddy, rugged look. Five years ago the appearance would have been called sloppy, today it was considered chic.

Trask stood in front of the audience and introduced himself, keeping his hands in the trousers of an expensively tailored dark suit. He wore no tie, choosing instead a freshly starched white shirt open at the neck. Fifteen minutes into the program he removed the jacket and rolled his cuffs, displaying strong forearms and hands, as well as a flat stomach and slender waist. Trask was clearly a guy who took care of himself.

I listened to him while prowling for things to hate, arrogance or egotism perhaps, maybe swaggering in front of the crowd. I found none of that. On the contrary, he was laid back and engaging, a pleasing, resonant voice mixing with a warm, easy smile. You could see he had a genuine interest in people. He was playful with the audience but obviously knew his stuff, including how to convey it to a mixed audience.

The guy was neither the brazen Casanova nor the geezer looking for something tasty to gum. Trask was the real deal, good looks and a likeable demeanor matched by intelligence and financial savvy. Take away the misery he'd brought into my life and I'd probably end up liking him.

For now he was nothing but trouble.

Trask made roving eye contact with the audience, several times looking in my general direction. I lowered my head each time he did, pretending to be taking notes on a pad I'd brought along. Once he looked right at me but only for a moment, eyes darting away.

I was relieved when the lights dimmed and he launched into a power point presentation on financial goals and risks. At the bottom of each power point slide was a company logo with the words, 'Simon Trask Properties, Since 1995.' The words materialized into 'Strap95' without any effort on my part.

I'd done some homework on Trask since discovering his number on Claire's cell. His agency was a fairly large residential and commercial real estate outfit, with branches in New London, Cromwell, and several other Connecticut towns. I assumed the paths of Claire and Trask crossed at the Cromwell Pointe project, making the dots easy to connect from there. When I took a second look at our phone bills, I saw that she'd called his office on a number of occasions. I didn't question this before because I thought they were project related, same with gas fill-ups and other charges. The combination of business and pleasure had thrown me off the scent.

Whether or not the affair was still going on bugged the hell out of me. I'd spent many nights drinking myself into oblivion or thrashing in my sleep trying to figure things out. A part of me wanted to believe that it was finished, that what I found in the attic was a memory, a remnant of the past. Since the discovery I'd been watching Claire like a hawk and was reasonably certain she hadn't been seeing him.

But I had every reason to keep turning over stones. The fact that she hadn't seen him could simply mean they were cooling it for a while. Claire still deleted her email cache, leaving no trail of anything sent or received. There was also that lengthy evening phone call with Trask, sandwiched between lies about working late.

Finding Trask's phone number and finally getting to see him in the flesh were breaks in my favor, and tonight I intended to seize the opportunity. After the program I planned on getting in his face and introducing myself, warning him in no uncertain terms to stay away from my wife. I'd brought along a copy of the emails to rub under his nose if he resorted to denial. I was willing to take on the consequences of a heated exchange, in many respects welcomed it. A lot had been building up inside of me.

I felt the anger bunching the muscles of my neck, working its way into my shoulders.

As Trask moved to one side and began his presentation, I closed my eyes for a moment and drifted away with my thoughts. I had so many questions about this guy. He didn't wear a wedding band, which made me question if he was married or had children, whether he was divorced or never married. I wondered if this was his first affair, curious if he'd told anyone about it. I was interested in what kinds of deception he used to cover his tracks and avoid suspicion, if he had to continually look back over his shoulder.

While I didn't doubt that Cromwell Pointe brought him into contact with Claire, I was curious how they first met, how the sparks flew. I wondered who made the first move, how it escalated from there. I tried to picture Trask holding Claire's hand, hugging her, sharing a laugh. I wondered what they talked about when they were together, how often they connected on the phone or emailed when they couldn't meet. I wondered if Claire pined for him when she was with me, counted the days until they were together again.

I could feel tension rising in my body.

I wondered if Claire primped when she knew she was going to see him, spent extra time with her makeup or fussing in front of the mirror. I wondered if she bought new outfits to look more attractive, hoping he'd notice and feed her a compliment. I tried picturing them sitting for hours in a car, wondered if they talked first then fooled around or if it was the other way around. I wondered if Claire teased, or if she ever resisted. I wondered if they used the back seat.

Trask rattled on with real estate lingo, something about public records and title searches. I thought about Claire's emails, the anger still sharp after all this time, especially the day trip to Newport. I tried picturing the two lovebirds that day, away from it all and not having to worry about being seen. I wondered if they packed travel kits, what they brought along. I pictured the two of them satisfying their lust, sharing a shower, resting in each other's arms. I wondered if they turned down the covers, got underneath. I wondered how difficult it was for them to say goodbye when the day was over.

I was brought back from daydreaming when the lights came back on. I blinked several times and shifted in my seat, had to work on refocusing.

Trask had finished his power point presentation and was wandering back to the center of the audience while making some concluding comments, none of which I really heard. When he was finished, he fielded a few questions from the audience. When there were no more, he thanked the audience for coming and received appreciative applause. I looked at my watch and was surprised to see that the better part of two hours had been consumed.

I remained in my chair as the crowd began filing out. Trask stationed himself by a small table next to the exit door, handed out printed materials as people left. About five or six of them stopped to ask questions.

Trask's back was to me. My plan was to wait until he was down to the last person, then make a move.

While I waited I felt an adrenaline rush in my blood, heart pounding in my chest. I mentally rehearsed what I was going to say and how I was going to say it. I could feel the anger rising in my throat, knew I had to keep it at bay in order to get everything out.

Finally I got up from my seat, took a look around. The room was empty save for a man and woman talking with Trask, apparently a couple. They kept jabbering away, making me realize I should act now. Trask's back was still to me. I approached from the side, took a deep breath and steeled myself.

When I was about ten feet away, Trask's radar somehow kicked in. He shifted on his feet and turned sideways, folded his arms across his chest. I'm still not sure how he sensed my presence. He appeared to be watching me out of the corner of his eye.

And then something told me to stop, to rethink the confrontation. I'd reflect on this moment for many years, questioning if I did the right thing, wondering what would've happened if I'd gone ahead and squared off with Trask. I'd never know if I could've prevented some of the tragedy and tears that followed.

I suppose at the last minute I got fearful of what I might hear from Trask, that the affair was ongoing or the two of them were in love. Maybe it sunk in that threatening him was foolish on my part, as feeble as snooping on Claire and trying to keep her under lock and key. Maybe the futility of it all struck me right between the eyes, the bitter resignation that if Claire wanted to continue seeing Trask, she would. There was no way I could ever stop her.

I continued walking toward the door. When I passed Trask, he turned my way ever so slightly. The conversation with the couple stopped. Trask and I exchanged a glance and for a brief moment, I thought he was going to say something. Instead, he lowered his eyes. He looked clearly uncomfortable, the color rising in his cheeks.

There was no doubt in my mind he knew who I was.

I'd later learn that Trask recognized me the minute I walked into the conference room. Sooner of later he expected something like this to happen, prepared for it in fact. He knew what I looked like along with lots of other details about my life, which really blew my circuits. He'd visited Guilford College on a number of occasions, knew where I parked and the location of my office, was even familiar with my teaching schedule. He knew when I arrived on campus and when I left, the people I talked with and the ones I avoided.

I wasn't the only one playing cat and mouse. I didn't know it at the time but Simon Trask would exert a profound influence on our lives in ways I never thought possible.

BY THE TIME I GOT HOME IT WAS AFTER ten o'clock and I needed a drink, something strong to steady the ship. I got a coffee mug and went to the refrigerator, filled it halfway with orange juice and the rest vodka, and knocked it back. By the time I put my things away in the study I felt better, much more relaxed. So good in fact that I came back and poured myself another round, sending it down the chute the same way. I believe rehab programs call it gulping, I call it liquid lightning. I smacked my lips, savoring the wave of relief finding its way to my toes.

Nathan was sound asleep but I found Claire soaking in the bathtub, head resting against the back, bubbles surrounding her. Next to her was a glass of wine, some bottles of bath gel and lotion, and a pink disposable razor. I'd brought along a can of beer and had taken a few gulps, a boozer's way of masking the hard stuff and deflecting raised eyebrows.

She smiled when she saw me.

"Still up?" I asked, raising a brow. Claire usually didn't have a bath this late. I looked at the wine glass, then at her. Truth be known, she looked a little minced.

"Long day," she replied, "lots to do when I got home." She took a long swallow of wine. "First moment I've had to myself."

Our bathtub is an oversized one that juts out from a mirrored wall. It's framed in dark ceramic tile with room to sit.

Claire straightened, bubbled water swirling just below her breasts. She picked up a sponge and ran it over her arms, breasts shimmering from the bath lotion.

"How was the reception?" she asked.

"A barrel of laughs," I said sarcastically, "you know how those things are." If Trask recognized me at the seminar, I wondered if he'd called Claire and told her. If he did, she knew I was lying through my teeth.

She squeezed the sponge, held it out. "Want to do my back?"

I took the sponge and walked around to the back of the tub. Claire had some wine while I positioned myself then leaned forward, elbows tucked.

"Nathan sleeping when you came home?" Claire asked, turning her head to one side.

"Out like a light." I dipped the sponge in water, started rubbing her shoulders. She had delicate shoulder blades and a trim, narrow waist.

I wondered what Trask thought of her body.

"Everything okay here?" I asked.

"We're fine," Claire replied. "Dean Rolfe called to tell us Billy Halliday has been suspended indefinitely. Nathan says he's going to an alternative school, at least that's the rumor among the kids." She finished her glass of wine, released the tub's drain with her toe.

"That's good news," I said, pleased the hallway misfit got the boot. I could only imagine the relief Nathan and Forrest must have felt. "You haven't scheduled any more welterweight bouts with his old man, have you?"

"I hung up the gloves yesterday," she said. We both snickered.

A minute passed.

Claire said, "Nathan wanted me to tell you he got his history paper back from Mrs. Beckwith. He got an A."

"He aced it? Wonderful." I'd been helping him with a paper on the battle of Thermopylae, thought he'd done a pretty good job.

We talked some more as I rinsed soap bubbles from her back. She wore her hair clipped up, exposing her neck. I wondered if Trask knew she was ticklish there, got a little skittish when kissed in the right spot.

She leaned back, rested her elbows on the edge of the tub. I got the bottle of lotion and squeezed some in my hands, reached over her and began applying it to the top of her shoulders, then her breasts. Her breasts were sensual, very slippery and warm. I cupped them from underneath and felt their softness, lifting and massaging. I made circular motions with my fingertips around her nipples.

Claire sighed and closed her eyes.

My adrenaline rush from hunting Trask had turned into erotic arousal, lust and longing sidetracking anger and frustration. I thought of Trask touching my wife's body like I was doing, felt a stirring in my groin. As I glided my fingers over her slippery breasts, my hands became his. I started getting an erection.

This is crazy, I thought, not understanding these conflicting feelings.

Claire stopped the tub from draining when the water dropped below her thighs, and reached for the disposable razor. She lifted a leg out of the water and applied some shaving gel, rubbed it in and started shaving. She did the other. She curled her toes forward as she worked, calf muscles bunching. She then did her thighs, shaving upwards and occasionally swishing the razor back and forth in the water. When she was done she used both hands to splash water over her legs.

I got hard watching her. I was hoping she'd do more of her upper thighs, maybe some pubic hair. She usually shaves the sides, especially during swimsuit season. Sometimes she surprises me by shaving everything, something I find brazen and sexy.

Claire rinsed the razor in the water, placed it on top of a face cloth on the edge of the tub. She held up her empty wine glass. "Jack, get me a refill, will you?"

I came around to her side and took the glass. She rested her elbows on the edge of the tub and leaned back, giving me a full view of her glistening body. She parted one leg slightly, toying with me. I fantasized Trask drooling over her, wondered if Claire teased him this way too.

Claire's eyes flickered across my face, then slid their way down my body. She stopped at my erection, parted her lips slightly when she saw it straining against my trousers.

"Come back and finish shaving me," she purred, eyes never leaving the bulge. She outlined her lips with a finger.

I sucked in a breath, not needing any more prodding.

I went to the refrigerator and refilled her glass, poured one for myself. I was a little tentative and unsteady on my feet, blitzed as well as sexually wired. On the way back I made sure Nathan was still sleeping, locked the bathroom door behind me.

Claire was sitting on the edge of the tub on a folded towel, trailing a foot back and forth in the soapy water. I handed her a glass. She was pink all over and smelled of lilac. After a few sips she put her glass down and smiled coyly, playfully raised a brow. I took the hint and removed my trousers, then my underwear.

I turned to face Claire and was fully erect. I removed the rest of my clothing, threw it to the side in a heap.

She gestured with her chin toward the razor and shaving gel.

I sat down and she turned my way, straddling the tub. I used my hands to part her legs, thighs smooth and silky soft. I gathered some bath water with a cupped hand and let it trickle over her. I did this several times before I applied the shaving gel, working the area into a warm lather.

Once I softened the hair I touched the slippery wetness of her lips, gradually running my fingers along their length, then making slow circular motions. Claire moaned softly when I did this, shifting her position slightly and tilting her pelvis forward. Her whole body was warm to the touch.

I began shaving away her silky hair, small sections at a time, rinsing the blade as I went along. I pulled her skin taut with one hand and gently shaved with the other, taking my time. It was difficult focusing given the alcohol I'd consumed and the location of the worksite. I was incredibly aroused.

Claire arched back, using her arms to support herself. She closed her eyes and parted her lips, breathing deeply. A blush spread across her cheeks and down the sides of her neck. Her breasts were full, nipples hardened.

I rinsed her off when I finished, ran my fingers over the smoothness. I patted her dry with a hand towel but could tell her lips remained moist. They'd become a shade darker, swollen and warm, inviting.

I went to my knees, lowered my head and tasted her. She lifted a leg and placed it around my shoulder, pulling me towards her. I swirled my tongue around, felt her clitoris harden as I licked and nibbled. I pulled and parted the lips, probing and teasing.

At one point Claire grabbed the back of my hair and pressed my face into her wetness, holding me there. She stiffened and shuddered, then relaxed her grip.

I finally lifted my head and found her open mouth, kissed her hungrily. Claire licked her scent from my lips, circling my lips and sucking my tongue. She ran her tongue over the prickly stubble of my beard, her breath warm and sweet.

I led her to the vanity and pushed aside some hair brushes and towels. I lifted her up by the waist and set her down. She was still pink and warm, skin incredibly smooth all over. I grabbed the shaft of my penis, rubbing the head back and forth against her lips before penetrating her. She moaned softly and gripped my shoulders, wrapped her legs around my waist.

I braced my hands overhead on the vanity frame and began thrusting, slowly at first then with more intensity. Claire looked at me with heavy lids and locked her ankles behind me, pulling me into her, wanting to be forcefully taken. I drove my pelvis against hers, our bodies rhythmically slapping together. She closed her eyes and leaned back, breasts swirling with each thrust. At one point she started to moan but then clamped her mouth, fearful of waking Nathan. The clip holding her hair broke free, making her look even hungrier.

I fantasized I was Trask screwing her with reckless abandon. I thought of the madness of it all, the cuckold ravishing his wife, brought to orgasm by her betrayal and infidelity.

I shut my eyes, willing myself to forget.

LATER WE WERE IN BED, UNDER THE COVERS. I LAY with my hands behind my head, looking at the ceiling, unable to sleep. I was thinking about my encounter with Simon Trask, the journey I'd been on and where things stood. I knew a confrontation with Claire was inevitable, the pain having lingered too long. Holding back no longer served a purpose.

My thoughts were interrupted when Claire rolled my way, rested her head against my chest. I thought she'd fallen asleep. I shifted and wrapped an arm around her shoulder.

She looked up at me, traced my lips with a finger. "You okay?" she asked quietly. She slid her leg up the length of mine and draped it over my thigh.

"Just trying to fall asleep," I said. "You?"

"The same," she replied, yawning. "Counting sheep."

A few moments passed.

She put a hand on my chest. "Jack, why don't you stay home tomorrow night? You've had a long week and it's not even half over. We'll have a quiet evening together."

Her comment took me by surprise. I thought about it, images of Rachel Pond coming to mind. I really wanted to see Rachel, had been looking forward to spending time alone with her. I knew opportunities like tomorrow night would be few and far between.

"I can't disappoint Cy," I replied. "He's been looking forward to the game ever since I asked him to go."

She put her hand on top of my underwear, gave me a playful squeeze. "If you stay home, I guarantee you that I'll be more entertaining than Cy Rollins." She tapped my penis for effect. "You never know what kinds of things can happen in a bathtub."

I muffled a laugh. I gave it some more thought, debated how to reply. Finally I said, "I can't cancel at the last minute, Claire. Besides, it will do me good to get out and do something different, something fun."

I waited for her to respond but she remained silent. I took a deep breath and yawned.

Claire sighed, snuggled into my chest. We stayed quiet in the darkness. Before long she was asleep, her chest rising and falling against me.

My mind wandered back to last night and Claire's interest in Rachel, maybe a little too much. Tonight an effort to keep me home. I wondered again if she knew something I didn't, if she'd made some kind of connection.

Nonsense, I thought. I'd covered my flank and was fretting about nothing.

I untangled my arm from Claire and rolled over. I knew it was getting late and I needed some shut eye. I gave in to darkness and closed my lids, let sleep overtake me.

I'd later discover that I should've trusted my instincts and exercised more caution, kept my antenna up. Claire had been watching and waiting in the shadows for some time, and knew all along Cy wasn't going with me tomorrow night.

# *Twenty-three*

Rachel Pond and I agreed to rendezvous a little before the game at the Mohegan Sun's indoor waterfall, probably one of the most popular meeting spots in New England. It was smack in the middle of the casino's concourse area and impossible to miss. In fact, it was a literal conversation stopper, the roar from the fifty foot falls dropping jaws and drowning out words, even spraying some mist up toward the ceiling.

I'd arrived early, not sure how much traffic I'd hit and wanting to walk around a little when I arrived. The drive took about 45 minutes from Spencer Plain, roadway signs and billboards pointing me in the right direction as well as trying to lure me to Foxwoods, another Connecticut casino. I got my bearings when I spotted the Sun's imposing hotel, its futuristic glass design jutting eerily from the wooded surroundings. I thought the structure was a first class monstrosity and an eyesore to the rolling countryside, wondered what the tribal council was smoking when the architecture was approved.

I was leaning against a wall about a hundred feet from the waterfall when I spotted Rachel walking briskly from the other direction. I stood and stuck up a hand, caught her eye. She flashed a smile of recognition and headed my way.

She walked with confidence and poise, clothes tasteful and conservative. Nothing fancy or flashy, a simple white silk blouse tucked into stone washed jeans, black pumps. The only jewelry she wore was a simple wristwatch and a thin gold necklace. She wore her hair up as usual, and just a touch of makeup.

No wedding band.

Rachel surprised me with a hug, stood on her toes to reach me. Her fragrance was a woodsy, floral blend, lily of the valley maybe. It was natural and light.

"I'm not too late, am I?" she asked, straightening the shoulder strap of her purse. "I had trouble finding a spot in the parking garage." She looked at me with eyes the color of blue ice chips, their paleness still catching me off guard.

"Not to worry," I said, checking my wrist watch. "We've got plenty of time." I helped her drape a sweater she was carrying over her shoulders. "You should've done valet parking," I said, "little more money, lot less fuss."

"We should've gone in one car," she replied, poking me in the ribs. "Heaven forbid if someone spotted us walking in together."

I smiled, playfully swiping at her finger.

We walked along a stylish avenue of shops and boutiques, storefronts displaying everything from sporting goods and clothing to golf clubs and jewelry. Ahead of us we could see a portion of the casino's gambling parlors, splashed with seasonal themes. The place reflected the history and traditions of the Mohegan tribe: rocks, wolves, artwork, exposed timber. The casino was hopping, crowds everywhere.

We entered the arena and found our seats just before tip off. As expected, the seats were excellent, midcourt and close to the action. Claire and I had been here several times for concerts, but never sat this close. Same for Rachel, who followed the Connecticut Sun, a women's professional basketball team sponsored by the tribe.

The game was fun to watch, although neither the Celtics nor Nets went full throttle. Because it was an exhibition game, most of the regulars played for only limited stretches, the coaches instead choosing to focus their attention on new faces, especially draft picks. Rachel had purchased a program at the door and pointed out players being shuffled in and out of the lineup. She impressed me throughout the game with her knowledge of basketball, understanding defensive switch-offs, low posts, and the like. She knew what she was talking about.

The arena seats brought us physically close together, more so than we'd ever been before. Initially this made me uneasy and I felt like a schoolboy on a first date, nervous and giddy, and even pulled my elbow away from the armrest when we bumped a few times. During the game Rachel touched my arm or leg to make a point, sending goose bumps through me. I found myself stealing glances at her as often as I could, everything about her jumping out: woodsy scent, rosy skin, silky hair.

I felt the temperature rising.

We left the game with only a few minutes left, the Celtics having built a big third quarter cushion and putting the game out of reach. Once outside, we decided to stroll the concourse, stopping at a Ben and Jerry's and getting some ice cream, chocolate chip cookie dough for her and chunky monkey for me.

We sat down on a bench next to a skinny, disheveled guy in sunglasses who was slurping the remains of a super-sized soda. When he finished he stood up and straightened an electric blue fanny pack before heading down the concourse.

We licked our cones while eyeballing the crowd, a cultural smorgasbord if I ever saw one. All kinds of people paraded by: young and old, rich and poor, fit and feeble. Loud people, happy people, sad people. Boozy college students, smooching couples, wandering teenagers, off the bus tourists. Stylish types fresh from the salon, frumpy types just visiting the planet. Designer suits and funky jewelry, imitation fur and biker's leather.

All different yet surprisingly alike, drawn to the casino to wine and dine, watch live entertainment, or gamble the night away. The slot machines and tables beckoned around every corner, and optimistic souls were driven by the prospects of running the tables and pocketing riches. They were lured by the glitz and glamour around them, loosening their purse strings under the casino's hypnotic spell, sticking around until the well ran dry.

We finished our cones and Rachel reached over with a napkin, swiped at some chunky monkey on my chin.

"Can't take you anywhere," she teased, offering me a fresh napkin.

I used it to clean up, dabbed at the corners of my mouth. "Ready to do a little gambling?" I asked.

She recoiled a bit, arched her brows. "Gambling? You?"

I stood up and balled the napkin, tossed it in a nearby bin. "Why not? Let's give the slots a whirl, twenty buck limit for each of us, my treat."

Rachel nodded. "Lead the way, professor."

We walked to the end of the concourse and entered a large gaming parlor, taking a minute or two to get our bearings. The room seemed to stretch forever, recessed overhead lighting contrasting with the bright colors and flashing lights of the machines. Row after row of slots beckoned, the air filled with the sounds of ringing bells, sirens, whistles, and other assorted noises. Excitement was in the air. Interspersed throughout the room were separate gaming areas for baccarat, blackjack, craps, keno, and roulette. To our left a large group was immersed in pai gow poker. Attendants dressed in snappy, colorful blazers were positioned throughout the room, surveillance cameras hung from the ceiling.

We searched for some vacant slot machines, no easy chore given their popularity at the casino. We finally found two machines side by side in the middle of a row. On one side, a grinning Asian guy in vibrant orange, high-topped sneakers worked three machines at once, like some kind of whirling dervish. On the other side an elderly woman wore a glazed expression as she spun her machine, an unlit and flattened cigarette dangling from her lips. She looked like she hadn't slept in days.

Rachel and I sat down and went to work. The spin reel button on mine was still warm from the person before me. I watched the dials whirr and roll, tease and trick. A couple of times I came close to hitting a winning combination but lady luck was obviously giving me the cold shoulder. My money was gone in a about five minutes, my rags to riches fantasy evaporating right before my very eyes.

I swiveled my chair to watch Rachel, who was working her machine at a much slower pace. Almost at once the bells started clanging and colored lights began spinning on top of her machine. She'd struck a winning combination and her winning ticket popped out of the machine. Rachel squealed in delight, leaned over and gave me a big hug and smooch right on the lips. As she clutched the receipt for her winnings, people in the aisle craned their necks our way, most with pinched, sour expressions.

Behind me a booming voice rang out. "Jack Elliot!"

I knew the voice, and got a sinking sensation in my chest because it could only belong to one person: Hal Morris. Dread and apprehension rushed through me. Of all the people to spot me at the casino with another woman, this was the worst possible scenario. I could picture Morris calling Claire into his office tomorrow morning, morally willing himself to share the gut wrenching news, head bowed and eyes misty.

I fought to calm myself, and slowly turned around.

But it wasn't Hal Morris.

It was Bruce Whitbourne.

While I was relieved it wasn't Morris, the sight of Whitbourne tied a few knots in my stomach. He was a rumor monger who lived for moments like this, trying to get the goods on someone or sticking his nose into other peoples' business.

He stood there in all his glory leering at me, standing alongside a woman I didn't recognize. He held a cocktail glass in one hand, a gin and tonic from the looks of it, and took a sip.

"As I live and breathe," he said, "Jack Elliot raking in the riches." He looked at me with a smirk, bald held gleaming in the casino lighting.

"Hello, Bruce," I said, unable to muster much enthusiasm. I forced a smile, difficult to do through clenched teeth. The last time I saw this worthless stooge he and the Ice Maiden were using me as a punching bag.

Rachel was still in her chair and had her back to us, working the slot machine and hoping her luck would continue.

Whitbourne wore a fringed suede jacket that barely fit around his pot belly, jeans that rose to his ankles, some kind of civil war belt, and scuffed cowboy boots. The woman next to him was fifty-something, mousy looking with pasty skin. She wore a ridiculous looking paisley headband, a shapeless dress, clunky sandals with thick wool socks. They looked like a couple of gypsies.

"You here with Claire?" Whitbourne asked in that whiny voice of his, immediately driving the knife home. He knew Claire from faculty get-togethers, and had talked with her on a number of occasions. He knew damn well she wasn't here. He'd seen me with Rachel, and probably witnessed the lip-lock a few minutes ago. I knew he had every intention of making me squirm, tightening the screws.

"No, Claire's not here," I replied, my eyes roaming aimlessly around the gaming hall. He took another sip of his drink, kept a bead on me.

I looked at his partner, gave her one of my charming little smiles.

"My apologies, Jack," Whitbourne said, "Allow me to introduce Barbara Snelgrove, my soul mate." He looked at her with those dead eyes of his, wrapping his arm around her shoulder and pulling her close. She fluttered her eyelids, obviously enamored by this lamebrain.

I didn't know whether to throw up or just turn my back and walk away, especially when I heard reference to 'soul mate.' Whitbourne had a shady reputation with women and according to campus rumors, had gone through several divorces, the last one supposedly turning quite ugly. Rumor had it he had a mean streak, enjoyed knocking women around.

Rachel finished the last of her wagering and came over to my side. The four of us stood around in silence, the kind where everyone waits for someone else to speak up.

Whitbourne looked at Rachel. "And who might this be?"

I said quickly, "This is my friend Rachel." I made the introductions.

Whitbourne stirred his cocktail with the swizzle stick, took it out and chewed on the end. He kept his eyes on Rachel.

"Doesn't Rachel have a last name?" he asked with his usual repugnance.

I was about to answer but Rachel jumped in.

"She does ... I mean ... I do," she snickered, making a face. "Rachel Pond."

Whitbourne stood there for a few moments, let the name sink in. I saw something register, wariness perhaps. "Rachel Pond," he repeated. "Sounds familiar." He thought some more, gestured toward her with the cocktail glass. "Guilford College?"

Rachel nodded. "Yes, I'm a student there."

I felt a tug in my gut, didn't like the tone of his voice.

Whitbourne chewed some more on the swizzle stick. He looked over at me with those shifty, reptilian eyes, then back at Rachel. I could see the light bulbs going off in his head: Jack Elliot out on the town with another woman, a student no less. He smiled crookedly through sharp teeth, and I could feel the screws being tightened a little more.

Nobody spoke.

I didn't like the way this was playing out, knew it could only spell trouble for me back at the college. I'd have to keep my guard up, stay on my toes.

Barbara broke the silence. "How much did you win?" she asked Rachel, eyeing the receipt in hand.

"Fifty dollars," Rachel replied. She waived the ticket back and forth for emphasis and grinned, wrinkling her nose. You'd think she just broke the bank.

Barbara returned the smile, leaned forward and touched Rachel on the arm. "Good for you. Now you should take your winnings and walk away, especially here at the slots." Barbara's headband began slipping down her forehead, making her look like a pirate. All she needed to complete the look was a black eye patch, a knife clenched in her teeth, and a few "Argh ... avast, me hearties."

I perked up at the prospects of an escape route. "My thoughts exactly," I chimed in, "we should cash out right now. Besides, it's getting late." I stretched and yawned for effect.

Whitbourne seemed to have lost interest in Rachel, and looked down at his watch. "Night's still young. We're going to stick around, go play with the big hitters." He rubbed his hands together for emphasis.

Barbara rolled her eyes and shrugged. "As far as Whit's concerned, the only game in town is blackjack."

Whitbourne took the swizzle stick out of his mouth. He swirled the ice around in his drink a few times, drained what was left. "It's the only game where you have any kind of chance, Jack." He paused. "So long as you know what you're doing."

He proceeded to feed us a bunch of malarkey about his proven methods of beating the house, pure rubbish if I ever heard it.

When he was done blabbering, Rachel said, "Luck plays no part?"

He pulled Barbara close again and gave her a peck on the cheek. "That's why I bring along Babs," he winked, "she's my good luck charm." I fought an overpowering urge to gag. Whit and Babs, I thought, how touching. The thought of the two of them rolling in the hay and then doing the horizontal hula created a frightful mental image.

They said goodbye and headed off, the fringed military warrior leading the way, the wayward pirate from the Barbary Coast in tow.

RACHEL AND I WERE ENJOYING A NIGHTCAP at *Lucky's Lounge,* a hip, retro bar located on the casino's second level. We ended up here after Rachael had cashed out and pocketed her booty. She wanted me to take half, but I refused, instead agreeing to let her buy a round of drinks.

The place was fairly quiet and filled with a well-dressed crowd, most drinking at a circular bar in the center of the room, a few couples having dinner in a lower dining area. The place had a low ceiling accented with soft purple neon lighting, a couple of plasma TVs, walls covered with black and white Hollywood movie stars, a large cut granite fireplace.

We sat in a booth upholstered in red vinyl off to a side, separated from the bar by a polished wood divider and chrome railings. A waitress had taken our order and returned with our drinks along with cocktail napkins and some pretzels. Rachel was having a peach tree madras while I was working on a draft beer.

I'd been bellyaching about Whitbourne ever since we left the gaming parlor, bemoaning the fact that we got caught on his radar. I'd given Rachel a little background on the guy as well as my superficial and fragile relationship with him at the college.

I said, "Whitbourne likes to snoop and catch others off guard, play the moral crusader like tonight. His eyes lit up the minute he found out I was with a student from Guilford. God forbid."

"But we weren't doing anything wrong," Rachel replied. "We watched a basketball game together and played some slots, big deal. That's hardly scandalous behavior."

"Doesn't matter with this guy. In his mind he stumbled on to something juicy, something worth chewing on for a while. I could see his brain synapses firing, catching me out on the town with a mystery woman. Who knows what he'll do with that."

I took a swallow of beer. It was very cold and had ice crystals floating in the head.

I added: "You've got to remember, I'm on the hot seat already with the classroom crap."

Rachel thought about this for a moment. "Are you going to confront him about tonight?" she asked.

"I'm sure that's what he wants me to do, stew about it then come crawling to him. But I won't give him that kind of satisfaction."

A long minute passed.

She held my eyes for a moment before speaking. "Will he tell your wife?"

"I don't think so." I paused, and pursed my lips. "If he does, things could get a little complicated."

Rachel arched her eyebrows in curiosity.

I hemmed and hawed. "I didn't tell my wife I was meeting a woman tonight, one of my students. I told her I was going to the game with a buddy of mine from the faculty."

For a brief pause, we both kept quiet.

Finally Rachel said, "Why?"

I shrugged and leaned back against my seat, not sure how to reply. "I don't know, I guess I wanted to keep you to myself." I let out a long sigh. "I didn't want Claire to know about you, or have to answer questions about you."

She reached for her cocktail, shaking her head. "Really?"

I nodded, felt my blood moving faster. "Why, is that so hard to believe?"

Rachel hesitated, made a face. "No," she said, "because it's the same thing I did with my husband." She held my eyes again.

We fell silent, sipped our drinks. The alcohol was sending a tingle of warmth through me.

Time passed, difficult to say how much.

Rachel shifted in her seat. "Maybe tonight wasn't such a good idea."

I pinched my eyebrows together. "Are you serious? We've had a terrific evening, an absolutely wonderful time." I paused and leaned towards her, resting my forearms on the table. "Haven't we?"

She nodded. "It's been great." She paused, then added, "It's the best non-date I've ever been on."

We both laughed, her smile dazzling. For a second, our knees touched beneath the table.

We exchanged a look.

She sipped her cocktail, then cradled her chin in her hand. "How long have you been married, Jack?"

I had to think a minute. "Almost 18 years. You?"

"Since ninety-five." She raised her cocktail and gestured with it. "You'll have to do the math, Jack. I don't drink and try to calculate numbers."

I smiled at her.

Over at the bar a bunch of guys were watching a college football game, some southern conference match up. They cheered as a quarterback darted into the end zone and broke a tied game. Several of them stood up from their stools and swapped high-fives.

The waitress returned and we decided to have one more round before hitting the road. I was relaxed from the booze and less stressed, Whitbourne a fading memory.

After the waitress left, Rachel glanced away and seemed distracted by something.

"You okay?" I asked.

She said, "No, I'm just kicking myself. I'd planned on bringing you something tonight. I forgot it."

"Something for me?"

She nodded and put a finger to her lip, tapped it a few times, thinking. For a brief moment I saw something else register on her face, a hint of sadness maybe, but just as quickly it was gone.

Finally she said, "I'll get it to you," her voice tailing off.

I nodded silently to myself, not sure what just happened. The exchange struck me as peculiar, and I'd think about it later. I'd always wonder if I should've said something more at that point, prodded her perhaps.

The waitress returned with our order and we fell back into conversation, drinking and munching on a few pretzels.

We were loose and relaxed, enjoying each other's company. She looked at me from across the table, didn't take her eyes from my face. I studied her when she spoke, my mind registering details I'd missed from afar: twin piercings in her left ear, the soft contours of her clavicles, a small scar on her little finger. I looked at her hair, again imagining it unpinned and cascading to her shoulders.

Out of nowhere I said, "You've got great eyes." I surprised myself.

The comment hung there for a moment.

She smiled, then lowered her eyes. My first thought was that I'd offended her, that the compliment was inappropriate. But then I realized she was looking at my hands, studying them.

"Hands say so much about a person," she said.

I didn't know how to respond.

"They were the first thing I noticed about you. They're strong but gentle, full of character. I remember one day in class you handed back an assignment and our hands happened to touch. Yours were so soft, writer's hands."

She surprised me by reaching over for one of them, and ever so gently took it in hers. She lightly stroked it with her fingers, tracing first the back and then the palm. Her motion was soft and slow.

My heart quickened, and I felt myself getting hard. Was she teasing me or testing me? I didn't know.

She placed her hand over mine and squeezed it softly, then let go. "You're a good man, Jack," she murmured. "I'm glad we met."

<hr/>

WE FINISHED OUR DRINKS AND LEFT the bar, headed for the parking garage and Rachel's car. We rode an escalator down to the casino's ground level, passing alongside a bubbling stream running parallel to another artificial rock formation. The casino was still busy.

We passed by a sporting goods store, its display window filled with jackets, boots and other ski wear. Rachel paused in front of the window to look.

"Do you ski?" she asked.

"No, never tried it. You?"

"Yes, in fact I'm going this weekend with my husband, leaving tomorrow night."

I got a twinge of jealousy with the mention of her husband.

"People ski this early?" I asked.

"We go to Bretton Woods up in New Hampshire, by Mt. Washington. Their slopes open in early November, lots of snowmaking on the trails."

We resumed walking and left the main casino, picked up a long hallway to the parking garage elevators. No one else was in the hallway. Rachel surprised me by slipping her arm through mine, her breast pressing against me. More quickening of the heart.

We rounded the corner to the elevators. A half dozen people were waiting and had their backs to us. Rachel gave my arm a little squeeze and slipped hers away. She smiled at me and I smiled back. We joined the group and rode the elevator to the third level.

It was cold in the parking garage. I stood by Rachel's car as she got her overcoat from inside. She turned to face me.

"I've had a wonderful time. I really didn't want the night to end. Thank you, Jack."

"It's been great, Rachel," I said, shuffling my feet and getting that schoolboy feeling again. "Thank you for coming with me."

"Would you like me to drop you off at valet parking?"

"No, I think I'll walk. The fresh air will do me good."

Rachel looked at the ground then raised her head slowly, came over and tenderly kissed my cheek. She let her lips linger for a moment. Our faces were inches apart when I opened my arms and pulled her close, hugging her. The contact was long overdue, seemed right. I felt her chest rise and fall, warm breaths against my neck.

We stayed that way for a few moments. When we separated she stood there looking at me, studying the details of my face. We smiled, and not a word was spoken. She brought the flat of her hand to the middle of my chest and held it there, as if feeling for a heartbeat, then lifted it up and gently pressed her fingers against my lips. She smiled once more, a little sadly, before turning and getting into her car.

I watched as the car disappeared down the ramp. I stood there alone in the cold for several minutes, her woodsy scent on my shoulder, my mind in overdrive. I was saddened to see her leave, disappointed the night was over. I wanted to see her again, had no idea where she was taking me. I took a few moments to gather myself, then turned up my collar to my ears and headed for the exit door.

I had no way of knowing that as soon as I disappeared, a car parked in a far corner pulled out from its spot and left the garage. I'd eventually find out it was Rachel's husband. He'd been watching us in the parking garage and had been trailing us all night long in the casino. I'd been blindsided yet again, soon to learn that Claire's pryings were the least of my worries.

# Twenty-four

The osprey was alone in the sky, scanning the water for prey. It flew with grace and speed, swooping down for a closer look then rising soundlessly and circling back for another pass. It spotted its prey almost at once, hovering a bit before folding its wings and descending, tumbling almost instead of diving, talons extended. It splashed into the water legs first, disappearing for a few moments beneath the surface, reemerging with a fish in its grip.

I was watching the osprey from a boardwalk in Old Lyme, one that passed underneath a railroad drawbridge and straddled the coastline, offering a sweeping view of Long Island Sound and the mouth of the Connecticut River. The boardwalk jutted out into the water on stout pilings, cutting across a stretch of marshlands and ending with an elevated viewing deck.

It was an unseasonably mild Friday afternoon, a reprieve from a week of gray skies and stiff winds. Winter was knocking on our door and days like this would soon be a distant memory, replaced with drifting snow, freezing temperatures and runny noses. It didn't take any arm twisting to get me outside after running some errands in this neck of the woods. The boardwalk beckoned with an opportunity to stretch my legs and get some exercise, maybe buoy my spirits after a jagged week.

I'd spent most of the morning at Guilford in a lengthy re-accreditation meeting. The college was nearing the end of its ten-year accreditation and

212

gearing up for a visit from the New England licensing board next spring. An institutional self-study was underway, each segment of the college helping to develop a document detailing where Guilford had been over the past ten years and its vision for the future. My particular focus group consisted of faculty, administrators and staff, and we'd been working hard for the past year evaluating Guilford's various academic programs.

I attended the meeting in body but hardly in spirit. My mind was still reeling from what had happened over the past few weeks, derailed probably the more appropriate term. I found myself drifting away at regular intervals, trying to sort out my miseries and make sense of my life. This was no easy chore given what sat on my plate: my wife was screwing another guy, I'd demolished one of our cars, my job was in jeopardy, and my kid had been beaten up. For good measure, seductive images of Rachel Pond kept creeping into my head, and while tantalizing, added to the unsteady terrain.

I was leaning against a piling, shielding my eyes from the slanting November sun. The osprey had flown to a nest in the middle of the marsh, one that sat high atop a thirty foot pole. Every so often I could see it poking its head over the top and craning its neck for a better look, almost like a periscope. There were no other ospreys in sight.

I wandered over to the elevated viewing deck, where I found a slight woman standing alone peering through binoculars at the nest. I stopped a few feet from the deck and paused to enjoy the view, resting my elbows on the railing and breathing deeply, filling my lungs with fresh sea air. To the left, the water softly lapped the marshland, grasses rustling in the breeze.

The stranger broke the silence. "Hello down there."

"Hello yourself," I replied half-heartedly, flashing one of those patented New England smiles, reserved and tight.

"Beautiful day," she said.

"That it is."

I didn't feel much like talking and she apparently felt the same, continuing to look through the field glasses. She was dressed warm for the weather. She wore a light blue ski parka, the kind with the fur-lined hood, faded jeans, and rubber soled boots. She had on a white roll brim hat, and a dark blue scarf knotted loosely at the neck, and matching gloves. A field pack rested on a nearby bench, next to a large thermos.

I looked out at the water, letting the sun warm my face. Not a boat or ship was in sight. The osprey still sat alone in its nest.

I stayed for five or ten minutes, then decided it was time to leave. I had some more errands to run, none more important than a trip to the local packy. I was already running low on vodka even though I refueled on Monday. The truth be known, I had a hankering for a nip or two right now, not to get snockered mind you, just enough to wet my whistle and oil the hinges.

I pushed away from the railing.

"Wait," the woman said, "don't go. Come up here and have a look." She still held the field glasses up to her eyes.

I wanted to make tracks but didn't want to appear rude, least of all to a woman. I reasoned staying another minute or two wouldn't hurt. I fought back a sigh and climbed the short flight of wooden stairs.

She lowered the field glasses and handed them to me, smiling.

She was in her late sixties, give or take a few years. She had a kind, attractive face with soft, gently wrinkled skin. She wore red lipstick and her short hair was silver, wavy and soft. There was a perkiness about her, no doubt owing to a pair of bright, brown eyes and dimpled cheeks. Her eyes danced mischievously, giving me a moment's pause.

I took the binoculars and she gestured toward the nest. I turned the adjustment dial and brought the nest into focus. They were good field glasses and sharply defined the osprey. I'd never seen one up close. It was a handsome bird, brownish black coloring on its wings with some speckling on the breast. Its head was white with a dark crown, and further distinguished by black eye stripes. The stripes reminded me of a bandit's mask.

I lifted a foot and rested it on the middle railing, leaned forward.

"What's your name?" she asked.

"Jack Elliot," I replied, watching the osprey devouring the fish. At one point it shook its head vigorously, ruffling its feathers.

"Jack Elliot," she repeated, then paused. "Strong name."

I smiled at the expression, words from another time. "And yours?" I asked.

"Madeline Gilbert."

I lowered the binoculars and turned to her. "It's a pleasure to meet you, Madeline."

She nodded and grinned, eyes crinkling at the corners. Her knit hat gave her a jaunty, sprightly look.

I held up the field glasses. "May I look some more?"

"Please, be my guest," she replied. She had a smooth, pleasant voice.

The osprey appeared to have finished the fish and was just sitting there. I examined the nest, a patchwork of seaweed, driftwood, cornstalks and pieces of trash. It was several feet high, much larger and more elaborate than I'd imagined.

It was quite still around us, as if we were in some remote, faraway location. A few minutes passed.

After a while Madeline said, "So tell me, Jack Elliot, what do you see out there?" She'd taken a seat on the bench behind me and was rummaging through her field pack.

"An osprey enjoying his lunch."

"Besides that. Anything unusual catch your eye?"

I shrugged. "Well, he obviously ain't saving leftovers for the others."

She laughed out loud. "That's because there aren't any others. He's all alone. Been that way for a while now."

I lowered the glasses and turned to look at her, a little puzzled. "Why's that?"

She shook her head slowly, smiling at me. "A birdwatcher you're not." She lifted her hand and made flying movements with her fingers. "The others migrated south about three weeks ago. For some reason, this one's a straggler, a loner. He's not supposed to be in Connecticut, at least not now. He should be well on his way."

She'd taken a notebook from her field pack and uncapped a pen.

"You a birdwatcher?" I asked.

"Part birdwatcher, part people watcher. I come down here mostly because it's quiet and peaceful, gets me out of the house. Sometimes I report what I see to the ornithological folks. I've been keeping an eye on this one."

"So what happened to this guy?" I asked. "Is he hurt or sick?" I had to admit Madeline pegged me correctly, I knew little about birds.

She wrote something in her notebook, then looked up. "No, it looks to me like he's a young one, a later hatch. I don't think he's quite ready to migrate."

"But he will eventually?"

"Yes, I believe so."

I turned around and looked back at the nest. The osprey sat still.

"Why didn't his family stick around? I mean, aren't birds of a feather supposed to flock together?"

She shook her head. "Not ospreys. They don't travel in flocks or families like some other birds. In fact, the adults usually move out first."

I frowned for a second or two. "That's a little cold," I said with a touch of sarcasm.

"Oh, it's not as callous as it seems. Ospreys are never truly lost or abandoned. They're instinctively driven, and this one will know when it's time to get up and leave. He won't need anyone to remind him. For now he's in a good fishing area, one that's had some pretty good southerly breezes. One of these days a cold front will come down from the north and give him the push he needs to get going."

"He needs a good tail wind."

She nodded. "That, plus he'll be getting hungrier as it gets colder. Most fresh water freezes around here, so he can't stay anywhere inland. Even at mouths of rivers and coastal salt areas, the surface water gets colder faster. The fish tend to swim deeper and will become more difficult for him to catch."

"So he's got to head for warmer climates." I paused for a moment, thinking. "How far south does he flap? Florida, maybe?"

She laughed playfully. "Jack Elliot, you are a card. Weren't you ever in the Boy Scouts?"

I shook my head, feeling a little chastised. I was in the Boy Scouts for a little while but never made it past the lofty rank of Tenderfoot. I hated everything about the organization, from knot tying and compass readings to the neo-Nazi panache of the uniforms, especially those ridiculous neckerchiefs. I remember with particular disdain a poison ivy inflammation I contracted during one of those week long, idiotic jamborees. I scratched incessantly at body parts too intimate to share with my parents, and was horrified when my scrotum turned fire engine red and ballooned to a size rivaling that of an adult male baboon. What a nightmare.

Madeline kept smiling. Her cheeks were flushed from the cold air, giving her a healthy glow. "Ospreys migrate a tad further than Florida. They usually head for South and Central America."

I raised my eyebrows in surprise. "Are you serious? And they come all the way back?"

She nodded. "Every year, usually mid-March. They're like clockwork, one of the few things we can count on these days." She chuckled to herself. "I use them as my calendar. Spring hasn't really arrived until I see one or two circling in the sky."

I looked out at the osprey and then at the expanse of water, trying to imagine the journey. I was fascinated. I'd seen these birds my whole life but obviously knew nothing about them.

I looked at Madeline, who busied herself writing something else in her notebook. I was enjoying the company and believed she was too. I was glad

I stuck around. The booze store could wait. She was easy to be with, very interesting and spontaneous.

Madeline stopped writing and closed her notebook. She reached for the thermos next to her and unscrewed the top. "Would you like some tea?" She pulled an extra plastic cup from her field pack.

I hesitated for a moment.

"What's the matter, won't let an old broad buy you a drink?" She flashed a dimpled smile, those impish brown eyes sparkling. Her knit hat framed her face just so in the afternoon sun, giving me a glimpse of the young woman. She was quite attractive.

"Sure, why not," I said, sitting down on the bench next to her. She slid her field pack out of the way.

I held the cups while she poured from the thermos. Her hands were smooth and slender, red nails matching her lipstick, nicely shaped. A large diamond ring and wedding band on her left hand caught my eye. She wasn't poor, that was for sure.

We cradled the cups in our hands and sat back, relaxing and enjoying the moment. The tea was hot and tasty, some kind of raspberry flavor.

We looked out at the nest and batted the topic of ospreys back and forth some more.

"I've seen a lot of artificial platforms like that around here," I said.

She nodded. "Some osprey build natural nests but most of the population can be found on man made nest platforms like this, or something like it. The nests themselves are made by the osprey."

I pointed at the nest. "Why does part of the pole have metal wrapped around it?" A two or three foot wide sheet of metal encircled the post, about halfway up.

"Keeps raccoons from climbing up and preying on the eggs and nestlings. They can't get a grip on the metal."

I nodded, took another hit of tea. "Ospreys like to be up that high?"

She was patient with my questions. "The taller the better, especially in marshlands like this. They prefer an unobstructed view of the surrounding sky, and closeness to the water." She nodded toward the nest. "That's why there are no trees higher than the nest out there."

A couple of seagulls screeched overhead and caught our attention. We watched them swoop high in the sky.

"You know your stuff," I said. I turned to face her, hooked my arm on the back of the bench, wood creaking. "So you're a people watcher, too?"

She smiled, her face radiating charm. "Oh, that's a little hobby of mine. I like looking at people and wondering where they're going or where they've been, what kind of lives they've lead."

She unknotted her blue scarf. "I don't miss much."

She sipped some tea, gave me a sidelong glance. "In fact, I watched you working your way down the boardwalk."

I raised my eyebrows. "Really?"

"Uh-huh. You looked like an interesting sort of fellow."

I smirked. "That's the nicest compliment I've had all week." I tilted my head. "So tell me, what did you see?"

She crossed her legs and smoothed out her jeans. They were the lined kind and she had them rolled up a few inches at the ankle, red plaid flannel showing at the cuff.

"Well," she said, "we know I didn't see a birdwatcher."

We laughed.

I said, "What was your first hint, no duck boots?"

She smiled, then hesitated. "No, actually you struck me as someone out of sorts, kind of drifting along and preoccupied."

A slight breeze rustled the pages of her notebook.

She continued: "You walked like you were carrying the weight of the world on your shoulders."

Her comment hung around for a while. I nodded slowly, tentatively.

I said, "Well, you're not too far off."

I was about to say more but my cell phone rang through my overcoat, causing both of us to startle. Madeline and I looked at each other as I put my tea down and struggled to get the damn thing out of my pocket. I felt guilty that I'd left the ringer on and disturbed the silence of the surroundings. I could've been wrong, but even the osprey turned our way.

The call was from Jeanne Bannister of Thomson Publishers, the project editor for my book. She was calling to tell me that several reviews had arrived much earlier than anticipated and had been FedExed to the college yesterday. Her voice was loud and intrusive, making it impossible for Madeline not to hear. Jeanne thought I might want to take a peek at the reviews over the weekend then compare notes with her early next week. I thanked her and signed off, slipping the cell back in my pocket, ringer off this time.

I looked over at Madeline. "Sorry," I said sheepishly.

She smiled politely. "There's nothing to be sorry about." Her voice was quiet, forgiving.

She straightened, folded her hands in her lap. "So you're a writer, are you?" I detected a hint of admiration in her voice.

"I am," I said, finishing my tea and handing her the empty cup. She stacked the cup on top of hers and slipped both inside the field pack.

Her eyes brightened. "How exciting. What kind of books do you write?"

"College texts, books on creative writing."

"Books that teach students how to write, or appreciate creative works?"

"Both."

She mulled this over. "That must be interesting. Are you a college professor?"

"Yes, I teach at Guilford College. It's located down the interstate a bit."

She nodded her head, a look of recognition on her face. "Do you teach just creative writing?"

I shook my head. "Usually a literature course as well."

Out of nowhere, Madeline began chuckling, shaking her head.

"You're amused," I remarked.

"I am." She thought about this for a moment, then her hand flew to her mouth. "Oh, please forgive me, how rude of me. I wasn't laughing at you. I was thinking about my husband. He could've used a creative writing class or two."

I turned toward her, puzzled.

"After he retired he tried his hand at poetry, something he always wanted to do when he was younger but never had the time. A friend once told him he had talent."

She playfully shook her head back and forth. "He would spend hours writing, then make a big show of reading aloud what he created. I was his audience."

"Was his stuff any good?" I asked.

She rolled her eyes. "Oh God, it was dreadful, simply dreadful. It took everything in my power not to laugh, yet he'd be so serious when he read it to me. He'd pace the room, pausing for effect and furrowing his brows just so."

She giggled and had to stop for a moment and gather herself. "Everything he wrote had to have some kind of jingle-jangle."

"Doggerel," I said.

"Is that what it's called? Anyway, he'd force corny words to rhyme, like 'bloke' and 'choke.' I remember one day he was working on a poem and yelled from the study, 'Honey, can you think of any words that rhyme with osprey?'"

"Did he ever catch on to you?"

"Oh God, yes. Once I couldn't help it and just burst out laughing in the middle of a reading. I was in stitches and couldn't stop."

"Did he get mad?"

"Furious. He was absolutely appalled that I would find his writing humorous."

"What did he do?"

"At first he just stared at me, hands on his hips, not knowing what to make of my outburst. Then he broke into hysterics, laughing at himself. At that point, neither one of us could stop. I don't think we ever laughed so hard."

Madeline got quiet and clung to the memory, eyes far away.

"Does he still write?"

"No," she said, hesitation in her voice. After a while she said, "He became sick and passed away about three years ago."

It was an awkward moment, one of those times when the conversation swings in another direction and you're unprepared for the shift.

"I'm sorry, Madeline."

She gave me a grateful smile, but her eyes grew misty as she weighed the memory.

"What was his name?" I asked.

"Everett."

She turned to look at me. "Do you have a family?"

"Yes, a wife and teenage son. We live across the bridge in Spencer Plain." I held her gaze. "How 'bout you, any children?"

She nodded. "A son. He makes his home in California with his family."

We were quiet for a moment or two.

Over to the right a middle-aged couple came into view on the boardwalk and stopped at the railing, looked out at the water. She had her arm linked in his, head resting on his shoulder. They looked very much in love. Madeline watched them and her eyes got a far away look, as if she were watching scenes of her marriage playing out in her mind.

Madeline said in a soft voice, "Toward the end, Everett and I would come down here quite a bit. It was close to home and always quiet, peaceful. When he had the strength we'd walk the length of the boardwalk and watch the ospreys. They became a favorite of his, occupied his mind. Everett liked watching them fish, especially the young ones. He'd take pictures of them and even tracked their migration. We talked about going to South America someday to see where they wintered."

She paused thoughtfully. "We never got there."

I kept still, letting her drift.

"We never planned on the possibility of a fatal illness. I mean, who does?"

"Was it sudden?" I asked.

"A year or so after he retired, he just wasn't feeling himself. It seemed like he was always tired and getting run down, no energy level. For a while we thought it might be the retirement blues, but then he started losing weight and having digestive problems. We got concerned. Our family doctor wanted a second opinion so we sent him for tests at Yale-New Haven." She cast her eyes downward. "We found out he had liver cancer, pretty far along."

I took it in, nodded.

"Everett never really knew what hit him. He was diagnosed in May of that year and barely made it to September." She sighed. "It was fast, a blessing I suppose."

Some long minutes passed. She reached over and got her gloves from the other side of the bench and put them on, making sure each of the fingers were snug.

"We spread his ashes across the water here because he liked the location so much," Madeline said.

"I come and sit to be near him," she said softly. "I can sense him here, feel him." She looked out at the osprey nest. "I sometimes think he's come back in this life as an osprey. When no one's around I'll talk to him, tell him how I'm doing, how much I miss him."

The emotion rose in her throat. "Maybe he's that straggler out there, for some reason wanting to spend a little extra time."

She looked down shyly. "Now you're really going to think I'm a daffy old dame."

"Not at all," I replied. Actually, I was quite touched. I could see her getting pangs of loneliness when the ospreys left in the fall and her spirits soaring when they returned in the spring. I wondered how she fared during the months in between.

The couple on the boardwalk stirred and straightened. They hugged for a few moments, swaying a bit before turning and leaving. They leaned into each other as they walked away, arms knotted.

Madeline watched them depart and she took a deep breath, or maybe it was a sigh. I couldn't help but think another memory had been shaken loose, one of warm hugs and soft touches.

"How long were you married?"

"Forty-one years," she replied, obvious pride in her voice.

"Wow," I said, "that's a long time." I really was impressed. "You must have some secrets to share with the rest of us, right?"

She thought about it for a moment or two. "Oh, I don't know if I'd call them secrets." She pursed her lips. "Maybe some simple rules to live by."

"Like what?" I asked, leaning toward her. With the turns my life was taking lately, I was in the market for a few pointers.

"Well, we never allowed ourselves to get bogged down by unimportant things. We didn't let distractions get in the way. We saw too many people wasting time and energy worrying about things that never came to be."

Her alert eyes tracked the middle-aged couple until they disappeared from sight underneath the railroad drawbridge.

She looked at me and added, "That doesn't mean we always had smooth sailing. No one does. When we hit trouble spots we worked together, supported each other. Seemed like adversity toughened our hide, made us more resilient."

She was right. I said, "So many people are afraid to stumble or fall, to make a mistake or show weakness."

She nodded and held my eye for a long moment. "Shallow is the life that leaves no scars, Jack Elliot."

This was a very wise woman.

She continued: "We didn't hold grudges. We made a rule to never go to bed angry or leave the house fuming. We tried to fight fair, not hit below the belt. As we got older, Everett and I realized that fighting took up too much cussed energy. It simply wasn't worth it."

She spoke with such simple eloquence. "Forgiveness was the best gift we ever gave each other. We both knew that stewing or smoldering about something in the past were crimes of the heart. Forgiveness can't undo what happened yesterday, but it helped tame many a feud in our house."

She shifted her position on the bench. "We also respected each other, right from the beginning. We accepted each other's imperfections and shortcomings, the mistakes and the weaknesses. Everett wasn't perfect and neither was I."

She paused for a moment or two, smiled to herself.

"Why the smile?" I asked.

"Oh, I was just thinking," she said. "Every woman wants the perfect husband, the faultless partner. Now that Everett's gone, it seems that his imperfections are what I miss the most. These were the things that ended up making him so special: the snoring, the hissy fits, the dripping faucets he couldn't fix."

"The poetry," I added.

"How could I forget the poetry?"

We shared a smile.

I watched as she drifted through her life, sharing special moments, refreshed by what she retrieved.

She said: "We also made it a point to live each day to the fullest. We tried to make each day better than the last."

"Carpe diem," I said.

"Absolutely," Madeline replied. "Seize the moment, seize the day. We tried to take advantage of every moment we had, especially in the end." She paused, looked beyond me. "We ran out of tomorrows," she said, her voice trailing off.

I looked her way, shaking my head in admiration. "Forty-one years," I said.

"And it's over in a blink." She reached over and patted my arm. "That's why you're much too young to be walking around with the weight of the world on your shoulders."

I nodded and leaned back, hooking my hands behind my head and watching a gull fly motionless in midair. She was right, my mind was in need of an overhaul. I had too much tumbling around in the dryer.

We talked a little more after that and then we both got quiet, the gentle waves lapping the pilings beneath our feet. The afternoon sun still felt good, but it was dropping in the sky and losing its warmth. The blue was bleaching in the sky.

I looked at my watch and realized I needed to get moving. Nathan would be getting home from school and I'd decided to backtrack to the college and pick up the book reviews that had been FedExed, provided I could get there before closing time.

I announced that I had to leave and stood up, extending my hand. "It's been a pleasure talking with you, Madeline. Thank you for the tea and the company."

She took my hand, holding on to it for an extra moment. "The pleasure has been all mine, Jack. Thank you for letting an old gal ramble. I hope we talk again someday."

I put on my gloves, hiked my collar. "Are you going to be okay down here by yourself?" My protective side didn't want to leave her alone. "How about if I wait around until you're ready to leave? I could walk the boardwalk, come back and get you."

She turned her brown eyes toward mine and shook her head. "You're a gentleman, but that's not necessary. I'll be fine here."

I stuck my hands in my pockets and took a last look at the osprey, then turned and winked at Madeline. "Keep an eye on that one. Make sure he flies straight."

She nodded, a contented and peaceful look on her face.

I left the boardwalk that afternoon with my happiness restored, my spirits revitalized and replenished. While my problems were far from resolved, Madeline Gilbert was the calming influence I needed. She was a lonely, unpretentious sage and the few hours I spent with her were a welcome respite from the upheaval in my life. Her simplicity and unabashed honesty opened my eyes and encouraged me to listen to my heart, to look within and discover what was really there and important.

I'd return to the Old Lyme boardwalk several times in the weeks that followed, hoping to see her again and check on the straggler. I would find neither.

## *Twenty-five*

I backtracked to the college and arrived with plenty of time to spare. I'd called ahead from Old Lyme and as expected, the FedEx package had arrived and was waiting. I parked the Volvo facing out in a small, reserved lot not too far from the post office and a few spaces away from other vehicles. My car was only a few months old and I still babied it, washing it every week and trying to protect it from parking lot dings and dents. I realized that New England snow and salt would soon take their toll, but for now it sparkled.

As I walked to the post office I noticed a good sized gathering of students on the campus green watching an intramural football game. While Guilford had a varsity athletics program, intramurals were also popular and attracted considerable student support, the numbers this afternoon boosted by the unseasonably warm weather. In addition to hooting and hollering, someone's sound system blasted rap music, *50-Cent* I think. The late afternoon sunlight created a golden mist on the green as well as angular shadows.

I stopped for a moment to watch a play in progress. The quarterback handed off to a running back who did an end sweep and thanks to some fancy footwork and impressive downfield blocking, went the length of the sidelines and found the end zone. With the fans cheering wildly, he stuck out his chest and spiked the ball in true showboat fashion.

An air horn sounded, apparently ending of the game. The running back was mobbed by his teammates while the opposition walked dejectedly from the green, heads down and shoulders sagging. After a few minutes of high-fiving and raucous cheering, girlfriends hovering nearby, the winners began disbanding and heading for their cars, no doubt in hot pursuit of liquid refreshment and further celebration. A number of choice shoreline dives and dumps beckoned, joints where booze was cheap and proprietors were known to often turn a blind eye toward underage drinkers.

I heard someone yelling my name. I turned as a maintenance truck rumbled by, some kind of flatbed rig loaded to the hilt with landscaping equipment. I smiled when I saw Chiang standing behind the cab with another guy, holding on with one hand while waving animatedly with the other. He wore his trademark knit hat and sunglasses and was grinning ear to ear, cigarette dangling from his lips.

Inside the post office, I walked past rows of postboxes and approached the counter. The place was empty. The postal clerk was a former student of mine and came to life when she saw me. She got my package and I signed for it, all the while trying to remember her name. Although I couldn't recall it, I had no trouble remembering her appearance since she belonged to a couple of subcultures, punk and Goth my best guesses. She sported wild hairstyles and colors, had a propensity for black lipstick and nail polish, and wore bold outfits of crushed velvet, black lace and leather. Today she wore black jeans and spiked boots along with an oversized black cape. Her black hair was spiked and had lavender streaks running through it.

She was also the undisputed campus leader in body piercings, earning particular distinction for dangling hideous jewelry like black skulls and chrome lightning bolts from her ears, eyebrows, nose and lower lip. When she was taking my course, I used to wince just looking at her, my knees wobbling thinking of the metallic surprises lurking in parts unknown.

If all this weren't enough, her tongue was impaled with the largest stud I'd ever seen, one nearing ball bearing proportion that caused her mouth to list to one side. It clattered incessantly against her teeth when she spoke, complementing an Elmer Fudd lisp originating from her lopsided kisser.

She flashed a big smile at me, the Fuddian accent immediately kicking in. "How ah woo, Pwofessaw Ewiott?" Clatter, lisp, clatter.

"Fine, thank you," I said, "and you?" I almost said, 'and woo?'

I smiled at her, trying to keep my eyes from lingering too long on the metal contraptions dangling from her face, a silver crescent moon stuck in her left eyebrow and a gold corkscrew hooked on an earlobe begging attention.

She reached over and touched my arm. "Gwate. I'm having a weally gwate semester." More clatter, more lisp.

When I looked down at her hand I almost jumped out of my shoes, her mottled and blotchy skin sending shivers up and down my spine. When I came to my senses, though, I realized she was wearing black fishnet gloves, inexcusable fashion ignorance on my part.

She said, "I mith your clath, I weally do. I want to get woo again."

I smiled and thought, I bet you do, but not nearly as much as you want to get that siwwy wabbitt.

A few more customers came in and I told her I had to move along and inspect the contents of the package. She said, "Nithe theeing you again."

"My pleasure," I said. All kidding aside, students like this are genuine free spirits and should be applauded for their nonconformity. They're also the primary reason why I keep my doors locked and double bolted at night.

I TOOK THE PACKAGE OVER TO A counter by the window and opened it. I skimmed the cover letter from my editor Jeanne Bannister and began leafing through the reviews. Despite being a successful author, I still get jittery when reviews arrive, a quirk I've never been able to get under control. I've always had nightmares that some sinister professor will hatchet my manuscript and convince the editorial team to make sweeping changes, in the process ringing my bells and delaying the production schedule.

From what I could see, though, this wasn't going to happen, at least not with this batch of reviews. In fact, things looked pretty good. I spent about ten minutes skimming through the comments and suggestions, looking for common themes and proposed changes. Overall, the reviewers liked what they saw and while I needed more time analyzing their feedback, there were no crossed swords or bloodletting.

I slipped everything back into the package and headed for my car. The reviews were a shot in the arm, and I decided to stop by my office and pick up the latest version of my manuscript. I'd been plugging in minor changes at the college, but now with some reviews in hand I could do some serious tinkering at home. It would only take a minute or two to swing by my office and transfer the manuscript to jump drive.

As I walked to the parking lot, my thoughts were interrupted when an older, red pickup truck passed by at a pretty good clip and screeched to a halt in a space next to my car. The driver banged his door into mine as he started getting out, the sound kicking me in the groin and sending a wave of irritation through me. A moment later, the irritation mixed with repulsion as I got a look at the driver and passenger.

Barry Crider and Anthony Slocum stood there in all their glory. This was the first time I'd laid eyes on them since the classroom altercation. From the looks of it, they'd just come from the intramural football game and were getting something to eat, the cafeteria being just around the corner. Their voices and laughter were loud as they turned and walked away. I heard one of them belch, which produced waves of laughter and general hilarity. They never gave me a glance.

I quickened my pace and went over to my car, then kneeled down to inspect the door. The molded door guard had absorbed most of the impact, but a red streaked ding was clearly visible by the door handle. I exhaled in annoyance. While I was pretty sure the paint could be removed with rubbing compound and some elbow grease, the dimple was there to stay.

I was upset, not just because of the dent but how Crider had swung his door open with reckless abandon, not even bothering to look at what he'd done, walking away as if nothing had happened. I straightened and looked over at his pickup truck, filthy and dented, its rusted bed filled with empty beer cans, rusted tools and other crap.

I looked at the two of them walking away. "Hey!" I shouted, making no effort to conceal my anger and irritation.

They kept walking.

I shouted louder. "Crider, Slocum!"

This got their attention and they stopped, turned around. It took a second or two for them to realize I was shouting at them, a few more to recognize me. Crider smiled and nudged Slocum in the ribs. They walked my way with a mixture of punk and swagger.

I studied the two of them as they approached. Crider rolled his eyes and spread his arms, one of those, 'What do you want?' gestures.

When they got closer I said, "You just dented my car."

"What are you talking about?" Crider frowned. He wiped at his runny nose with the back of his hand.

I pointed back at the Volvo. "Come over here and look at what you just did."

Crider and Slocum looked at each other, shaking their heads in annoyance. They strolled over, taking their sweet time. Crider wore a torn flannel shirt and jeans, high top sneakers. He was sweaty and dirty, dreadlocks plastered against his forehead. Slocum wore a filthy hooded sweatshirt and one of his oversized baseball hat backwards, ears tucked inside.

The three of us stood in the narrow space between the two vehicles. I pointed to the dent.

They stared, remained silent. They both reeked of alcohol, obviously looped from the intramural game.

I looked at Crider, pointed to the damage. "You did this when you got out of your truck. I saw you do it."

Crider leaned in for a closer look, flicked his hand dismissively. "Come on, man. That's not a fucking dent, that's a scratch." His tongue was thick, eyes a little glassy.

They both stepped away. Crider stuck his hands in his pockets, then spat on the pavement. Slocum had dip in his mouth and hawked his slime not too far away, some of it dribbling down his chin. They made striking poster boys for the college, scholars at work and play.

I glared at the two of them, gestured to my car. "That's a brand new car."

"Pretty wheels," Slocum said, giving me a macho wink, a gesture along the lines of the kiss he threw me in the classroom. Like Crider, he was a little tipsy on his feet.

I barked at Crider. "That's it? That's all you've got to say about denting a forty-five thousand dollar automobile, that it's just a fucking scratch?"

Crider laughed darkly. "What do you want from me, man? Why are you busting my balls?" He pointed at the door. "Shit like that happens all the time."

Slocum nodded his head, "All da time, brother." He scratched his ass then broke the air with a belch that he pulled from deep in his throat. Put on a leash, Slocum would have made convincing evidence at the Scopes trial.

I stood there shaking my head, then glared at Crider again. "You should have been more careful," I snapped.

Crider smirked. "More careful," he mimicked, "that's a good one. Is that what this is all about? You want a fucking apology?"

His arrogance absolutely galled me. "Yeah," I said, "that would be nice. How about an apology?"

He snorted derisively. "And what if I don't give you one? You gonna cry to the cops again, have them handcuff me for scratching your door?"

It was plain to see this imbecile was enjoying himself. He playfully bumped Slocum with his shoulder and they both laughed. Slocum lost his balance, legs a little rubbery, which led to more laughter.

I felt my jaw tighten, cheeks flush. I was getting nowhere with these two losers, kicked myself for even having tried.

I turned and opened the car door, rested a hand on the top of the door, the other on the roof, and started to get in. I hesitated at the last minute, looked Crider's way. "You know, it didn't have to be this way."

A small group of students walked by, laughing and joking. They paid us no attention.

"The classroom business," I continued. "We could have worked that out, didn't need anyone else involved. I was willing to work with you." I shook my head. "That letter wasn't needed, you didn't need to go behind my back."

Crider looked over at Slocum, a confused expression on his face. Neither spoke.

I exhaled in irritation, slowly shook my head. "Don't play stupid. Both of you know what I'm talking about."

Crider smiled at me in a wasted way, then spat in front of my car.

I looked at him, expressionless. "Tough guy," I smirked. "That gangster routine doesn't cut it with me Crider. Who the hell do you think you are anyway, pushing people around, talking smack all the time?" I jutted my chin his way. "Your day's coming, and that letter isn't going to change a thing."

He glared at me, brow darkening, balling a fist at his side. Slocum stood next to him, arms crossed across his chest.

I gave them a dismissive wave. "Get out of here, both of you. You make me sick to my stomach. If you don't leave, I'll take your advice and call campus security."

I paused for effect, stared straight at Crider. "I'm sure they'd be interested in learning how you've been driving around on campus under the influence. Maybe I'll have them give you a breathalyzer right here, see how tough you are then."

Crider bristled. He opened his mouth to speak, then closed it. He knew I had him by the short hairs. I'd bet anything he had a record with alcohol infractions here at Guilford.

I looked over at Slocum. "While I'm at it, maybe it's time I gave your baseball coach a call, let him know that one of his hot shot scholarship players is walking around drunk as a skunk, lipping off to the faculty. That what you want Slocum?"

The baseball coach at Guilford was an arrogant and argumentative pipsqueak named Clyde Crenshaw. He regularly posted winning seasons and liked strutting around campus in color-coordinated sweat suits telling people how important he was. He was smug, chased anything in a skirt, and possessed an IQ rivaling that of an earthworm. Crenshaw acknowledged you only if he needed something, like academically spoon feeding one of his pea-brained thoroughbreds, and had the annoying habit of calling everyone 'sport.' Other than that I liked him a lot.

Slocum shifted on his feet, got a little pale. He began licking his lips nervously, obviously dreading a confrontation with Crenshaw.

The silence was longer this time.

I reached into my coat pocket and got my cell, then held it up so they could see it.

I was betting that Slocum would blink first and he did, throwing his hands up. "Okay, okay."

Crider wasn't far behind. He mumbled to Slocum, "Fuck this. Let's get something to eat."

They couldn't resist one-upmanship before they left, Crider flipping me the bird and Slocum grabbing his crotch.

I blew them a kiss goodbye.

I DROVE MY CAR ACROSS CAMPUS AND PARKED it in the lot next to my office. The place was pretty much deserted, people locking up their offices and making tracks for the weekend. I waved to a few faculty members pulling out of the lot and hustled up to my office. An hour or so of daylight remained and the wind had picked up, returning a chill to the November air. Our brief reprieve from winter was over.

Once in the office I switched on my desk computer and inserted my jump drive to transfer my manuscript. While I waited for the computer to do its thing, I fiddled with a few things on my desk, straightened a few papers. A post-it bearing Rachel Pond's phone number caught my attention, information I was keeping from Claire's roving eye. I picked it up and stared at the number, flicked it back and forth against the palm of my hand.

Why not, I thought. I had minutes to spare.

I closed the door, picked up the phone and pressed the number. She answered after a few rings.

"Hi Rachel," I said, "this is Jack Elliot."

There was a slight hesitation. "*The* Jack Elliot?"

"The one and only."

We both laughed.

"Are you busy, maybe in the middle of something?" I asked.

"Nothing that can't wait," she replied. Her voice was soft, like velvet.

Now that I had her on the line, I wasn't quite sure what to say. "Well," I said, clearing my throat, "I'm just calling to see how you're doing, making sure you got home okay last night. I'm here at the college."

"Jack," she said, pausing for a moment. "What on earth are you doing in your office after 4:00 on a Friday afternoon? Don't you have a life?"

I laughed, shook my head a bit. As easy as that, she'd disarmed the tension. "I had to pick something up. While I was here I saw your number. I'd written it down the other day when you left your message." I hesitated. "I hope its okay I called."

She said, "Of course it's okay. It gives me a chance to thank you again for last night. I had such a nice time."

"Me too."

"It's funny you should be calling now."

"Oh?"

"For some reason I've been thinking about *The Natural*. I wanted to share a part of it with you."

"Malamud's book?" I asked.

"Yes, I know it's a favorite of yours," she said. "After we discussed it in class I went out and purchased a copy."

I was impressed. "Did you like it?"

"Very much."

"Which scene were you thinking about?"

"It's toward the end of the novel, when Roy opened his soul to Iris. He gets talking about his missed opportunities and shattered dreams, what might've been. I thought it was such a tender moment for Roy, one that must've taken great inner strength from such a guarded man. At any rate, in this part he looked at Iris and said, 'My life turned out different than I thought, not like I wanted it to.'"

I remembered the part well but remained silent, didn't want to interrupt her flow.

Rachel cleared her voice. "Do you remember how Iris replied?"

"Tell me," I replied.

"Iris said, 'Whose does?'"

I shifted in my seat.

Rachel said, "I thought it was such a simple yet powerful statement, one that made me look at my own life. I've stumbled and made mistakes too. Things didn't turn out the way I thought."

I didn't know where she was going with this.

Rachel continued: "I liked how Iris told Roy that mistakes are what make good people better. She said to him, 'We have two lives, the life we learn with and the life we live with after that. Suffering is what brings us toward happiness.'"

I waited for the connection but was interrupted by loud knocking on my door. I excused myself and put a hand over the receiver. "Hold on a minute, I'll be right there," I said in a raised voice. I didn't want my privacy disturbed, at least for another few seconds.

"Company?" Rachel asked.

I listened for footsteps retreating down the hallway but heard none. Whoever it was had probably taken a seat outside the office. My guess was that it was Whitbourne coming to pay me a little visit, sniffing around for some dirt. I wouldn't put it past the nosy, no-good chump.

"Wouldn't you know it? Here we are on a late Friday afternoon, I finally get the courage to call you, and someone picks this very moment to pound on my door."

Rachel replied, "And here I am jabbering away." She paused. "By the way, did you have any problems with that professor we saw, Whitbourne was it?"

"Not at all. In fact, I didn't even see him today."

"That's good," she said soothingly. "Now see? All that worrying last night for nothing."

While I hadn't seen Whitbourne, I still needed to figure out what I was going to say to him if he asked about Rachel. As far as I was concerned, the suspicion on his face last night still spelled trouble.

Rachel said, "Listen, you go. I still have a little more packing to do before we leave for New Hampshire. We'll be heading out in about an hour. Call me back so I can say goodbye. Can you do that, Jack?"

"I can," I relied. "I'll get back to you."

We signed off and I hung up the phone, took a deep breath. The earlier aggravations and frustrations caused by Crider and Slocum had melted away. Rachel had that kind of effect on me.

I closed my eyes for a moment and massaged my temples, my mind jumping all over. I needed to get a handle on things. I was attracted to this woman, the energy between us unmistakable. The sparks were flying, temperatures rising. I was enjoying the ride and the attention, truly flattered that she found me attractive and desirable.

But I knew I had to be careful, not wanting the ice to crack beneath me. Fantasies were one thing, acting on them another. We were both married and she was one of my students, a sure fire recipe for disaster if things weren't kept above board. My encounter with Whitbourne last night served notice on the kinds of perils that lurked.

Beyond the risks, something else disturbed me. I was allowing myself to buy into a defenseless double standard when it came to Claire's transgressions. Just a few weeks ago, I was outraged at her infidelity, obsessed with uncovering her past while stalking her like a common criminal. Now I was fanning the flames of my own temptations. Talk about moral duplicity. I wondered if this was some kind of subconscious motivation on my part, maybe a desire to get even with Claire.

Loud knocking jolted me back to the real world. The stranger at my door had returned with vigor, shattering my thoughts and splashing cold water on my wayward libido. I got up and straightened myself, mentally fumbled with what I'd say if I found Whitbourne on the other side. I took a deep breath, then opened the door.

And there stood Malcolm Taylor, wearing his usual puzzled expression, empty briefcase at his side.

I breathed a sigh of relief.

Malcolm cocked his head to one side. "You grade my examination yet?"

No greeting or apology, no smile or small talk. Talk about a no frills conversation, cutting right to the chase.

"Hello, Malcolm," I sighed, stepping outside in the hallway for a look around. "Was that you knocking before?"

"It certainly was," he replied, apparently pleased with his persistence. He was wearing a new pair of fake eyeglasses, big black frames, olive trench coat buttoned all the way up to his chin. Rain hadn't been in the forecast for days.

I raised an eyebrow and said, "What are you doing hanging around this late on a Friday afternoon, young guy like you?"

"I saw your car in the faculty parking lot when I was walking around."

Given the day I had, finding new campus parking spots rocketed to the top of my to-do list.

"Well, to answer your question, yes, I've corrected your test." I ushered him in and sat down at my desk, beckoned him to do the same in one of the chairs.

I found his examination and handed it to him. Actually, I was quite pleased with Malcolm. He'd worked hard and turned in some quality writing. He'd earned a solid B, a significant improvement for him.

It took forever for Malcolm to process my comments on the exam. Of course, striking the proper intellectual pose fed mightily into this. Several times he'd read my feedback and put a finger to his lip, deep in thought. Other times he'd frown, tilting his head this way and that, before moving on.

He made a big show of turning the pages, making sure the creases were just so and smoothing whatever wrinkles he found. Finally he got to the last page, where I wrote some concluding comments and circled his grade. When he saw it, a look of pure astonishment swept across his face. He hunched over and began giggling and rubbing his hands together up by his chest, much like a kid appraising a long awaited toy. His glee was incredibly spontaneous and genuine, so much so that I started chuckling.

He looked over at me, repositioning his glasses. "How 'bout that," he said.

"How 'bout that," I echoed. "Take a bow, Malcolm, you did a good job. I'm proud of you." This guy was growing on me.

He closed the blue book and patted the cover, savoring the moment. He sat there for a minute or two just nodding his head, rocking a bit, quite pleased with himself. After a while he placed the exam inside his briefcase, struggling a bit I'm sure with which empty divider to activate.

"That reminds me," I said, rising from my chair and walking over to a table. "I've got something for you." I picked up a bag and handed it to him. Inside was *The Log from the Sea of Cortez,* by John Steinbeck. I got to thinking about Malcolm the other day when I was at *R. J. Julia,* a charming and quaint bookstore located in nearby Madison. I wanted to prod his reading a bit.

Malcolm held the paperback book in his hand while looking at the worn hardcover copy of *The Sea of Cortez* inside the briefcase. His eyes went back and forth between the two titles.

"It's a narrative of the bigger book, Malcolm. It's Steinbeck's recollections of the journey and the guy he sailed with, Ed Ricketts."

He raised his eyebrows. "You bought this for me?"

Malcolm didn't quite know what to make of this, but I could see he was clearly moved. He looked at me with appreciation, struggled to say something. I could see things racing through his head.

Finally he said, "You probably know I've been having some trouble finishing the big book," he said, his voice trailing off. After seeing it in his briefcase for two years, I wondered why he'd think that. "My grandfather handed it down to me and made me promise that I'd read it cover to cover. He said it would teach me a lot."

I nodded. "Your grandfather must be a wise man. It's a good book, but you need to stay with it." I thought the paperback might help you better understand Steinbeck as a person, maybe why he wrote what he did."

He put the book in his briefcase and snapped the locks shut, and stood up. He lingered at the door for few seconds, shifted back and forth. "You're the only person besides my grandfather who's ever given me a book." He stumbled, lowered his eyes. "Thank you," he said quietly.

"Don't mention it." I turned in my chair, retrieved the jump drive from the computer, and stuck it in my jacket pocket. Over my shoulder I said, "You know, it's been a while since I've read *The Sea of Cortez*. Perhaps it's time I went back and reread it. Maybe we can both read it and compare notes, start our own little book club."

"You'd do this with me?"

"Only if you're serious."

"I'm serious."

"Good, then first read the paperback and after that we'll tackle the big book." I reached over and we shook on it. "Now if we can only get you to listen to some real music instead of Big Boi and Andre, you might turn out okay after all."

Malcolm had to chew on that for a minute but then broke out in a wide grin, slapped his thigh in pantomimed laughter. He wagged a finger at me from under his nose, then gave me a high five. I returned it with one of my patented knuckle taps. It felt good.

## *Twenty-six*

After I saw Malcolm off, I shut down my computer and locked the office, anxious to get on the road. I was worn out from the day, the whole week really. At the end of the hallway I switched off the bank of ceiling lights and pulled on my coat. There was no one around.

I was about halfway down the stairs when I heard someone's car alarm system blasting outside. I cocked an ear and paused to see if it would stop, but it kept wailing. It made quite a racket, even through the walls of the building.

A few moments later, footsteps pounded up the steps toward me.

Malcolm rounded a flight of stairs, panting and holding on to the metal handrail.

"Dr. Elliot," he said, eyes as big as saucers, "that's your car." He pushed his fake glasses up against the bridge of his nose, the lenses partially fogged.

I startled. "What happened?"

"I dunno, I saw some guys near it when I came to get you."

I hurried down the last few flights, Malcolm in tow. I heard his attache case banging against the wall a few times.

When I got outside I could see the Volvo's warning lights flashing in the distance, the alarm loud and annoying. I quickened my stride while groping for the keys, hoping that I'd remember how to disable the damn alarm once I got there. I could make out two guys near the car, another in the middle of the lot with his back to me.

When I got close enough, I did a double-take when I recognized Crider and Slocum. I didn't know who the third guy was because I rushed past him, and didn't get a good look. All three were shouting, but the ear-splitting alarm made it impossible to hear what they were saying. Malcolm stayed behind me.

Once I got the alarm disabled, and eerie silence blanketed the parking lot. Not a word came from anyone, no movement.

I pressed the remote and unlocked the doors, and walked over to see what might've triggered the alarm. It didn't take long to find the answer. A deep, ugly gouge ran the length of the side panel, crisscross scratches dug into the hood.

My new car had been keyed.

For a moment I just stared at the damage, shaking my head. My breathing quickened, chest tightened. I felt my face flush with anger.

"Those guys did it," the stranger said, voice strangely familiar.

I turned around. It was Chiang. In the confusion I hadn't recognized him. He was in his work clothes and must've just finished his shift.

"I saw them do it," Chiang said flatly.

I looked over at Crider and Slocum.

"That's a fucking lie," Crider shouted. "You weren't even here. We were just walking through the lot."

I'm told hindsight is twenty-twenty, and I suppose at this point I should have just taken out my cell and called campus security, left it to the proper authorities. Our campus police had power of arrest and represented the logical intervention. But I didn't. I was hot under the collar and not thinking very clearly.

I walked over to where Crider and Slocum stood, about ten paces from my car. From the looks of them, they'd guzzled more snake juice. They must've seen me pull into the faculty lot after I left them at the post office, then followed me here.

They eyed me warily as I approached.

Slocum was pale and unsteady on his feet, a crooked smile frozen in place. Crider seemed less hammered and had his arms crossed, mouth tight and narrow. The rims of his eyes were red.

I stopped a few feet in front of Crider. I tried staying relaxed, but felt my voice tighten almost immediately. I narrowed my eyes and gestured with my thumb toward the car. "You do that?"

Crider looked at me with total contempt. "Fuck, no." he snapped, spittle flying from his mouth. He flung a dismissive wave toward Chiang. "I told you, he's fuckin' lying. He didn't see nothin'."

I let out a long breath, turned to Slocum. "I suppose you didn't have anything to do with this either."

Slocum lowered his head and started snickering. "I dunno what da fug you're talking 'bout." He wore a lopsided grin as he looked at me.

I stared back at him hard, felt my heart beating faster. Raising my voice I said, "You think this is funny, Slocum, some kind of big joke?" My jaw was clenched tight.

Slocum wiped the smile from his face.

"Answer me," I said, rage flushing my cheeks.

He raised his head slowly and sneered at me, slurring, "I got nuffin' to say to you." He burped under his breath.

Chiang cut in. "They both did it. They didn't know I was watching them." He gestured toward a spot behind my car. "I was behind that hedge collecting my tools. I saw it all."

"That's total bullshit," Crider snorted.

Slocum said, "He's a fuggin' liar, doesn't know wha da fug he's talkin' 'bout."

With daylight fading Chiang took off his sunglasses, stuck them on top of his knit cap. He looked at Crider. "It's not bullshit and you know it, man."

Crider and Slocum looked at Chiang, recognition coming across their faces. Up to now, they hadn't realized who he was.

My mind flashed back to that fateful day in the classroom, how they regarded Chiang with hostility for lending me a hand, how I worried what they might do to him.

My worst fears were playing out right in front of me. I thought of Nathan trying to take on Billy Halliday at the high school and getting swatted aside.

Crider turned to face Chiang, furrowed his brow. "You mind your own fucking business, asshole," he snarled.

Chiang looked at Crider, stole a glance at Slocum. When he finally spoke to Crider, his voice was steady and even: "Why don't you show him the screwdriver you've got in your back pocket? It's the one with the silver paint on the tip."

I could hear a sharp intake of breath from Malcolm, who I'd forgotten about. He was still behind me.

Crider was furious, eyes narrowed. He was breathing loudly through his nose.

This was getting uglier by the minute, and I could feel my heart banging against my ribs. I was upset with what Chiang was telling me about these two misfits, but much more worried about his safety. Crider was drunk and could go off at any minute, Slocum no doubt following his lead. If this turned into fisticuffs, Chiang wouldn't stand a chance.

I knew I had to defuse this, and fast. Calling campus security from my cell would take too much time and divert my attention. I took a quick look around the parking lot, saw no one around. My mind was racing.

I looked back at Malcolm, who had his briefcase clutched against his chest, as if someone were going to steal it. He looked horrified, eyes wide and mouth open.

"Malcolm," I said, measuring my words, "I want you to go call campus security. There's a call box outside our classroom building by the entrance."

Malcolm just stared at me, feet frozen.

I raised my voice a notch, tried to keep my composure. "Malcolm, listen to me. I want you to do this now. Put your briefcase down and do what I'm asking."

Malcolm's lips moved ever so slightly to each word of my directions. He looked at me and nodded, slowly at first then rapidly. He put the briefcase down on the pavement and took off running, arms flapping.

I refocused on Chiang. "I'll take it from here, Chiang. You go and we'll talk later, I know where to find you." I wanted him out of harm's way.

Chiang met my gaze and held it, shifted uncomfortably on his feet.

I shook my head reassuringly. "It's okay, I'll be fine. Don't worry."

Chiang nodded slowly and started to turn.

I began to feel better, a little less anxious. That is, until Crider opened his mouth.

"Yeah, you run along, Chink," Crider sneered. "You and I are gonna have a little talk anyway, you brown nosing scumbag."

"Sland eyed mudder fugger," Slocum slurred.

I shouted above them. "Ignore them, Chiang. Just go." My fear was that given the opportunity, Crider and Slocum would break Chiang apart like a wishbone.

"Please, Chiang," I implored, "just go."

I positioned myself between them. Crider stepped toward me and started to raise his hands, maybe to push me out of the way, but thought better of it. Instead he angrily pointed his finger at Chiang and shouted over my shoulder, "You heard him, get the fuck outta here you fish-eyed freak." He was perspiring heavily and the veins in his neck bulged.

A long minute passed and I gave Chiang a quick glance, saw that he hadn't budged. He and Crider stared at each other, neither moving. The tension was thick. Finally Chiang walked over to me and stood next to me.

Without taking his eyes off Crider and Slocum he said sideways, "I think I'll hang here with you for a little while longer, boss." His voice was calm, not a trace of fear in it.

He then locked eyes with Crider again, another stare-down. After a moment or two, he flashed Crider a confident, cocky smile and if my eyes didn't deceive me, winked in Crider's direction. I couldn't believe he was mocking Crider's tough-guy swagger, taunting him really.

Finally, Chiang broke the silence. He looked at Crider and said, "You want me out of here?" He laughed to himself, quite amused, not breaking eye contact with Crider. Finally, Chiang said, "This ain't Dodge, Crider."

It became quiet. No one spoke, the tension ratcheting up once again. In the distance I could see Malcolm making his way back from the classroom building. Campus security was no doubt on its way.

Suddenly, Crider lunged at Chiang. For a big guy, he was quick and had caught me off guard glancing away, if only for a few seconds. I tried stepping in front of Chiang to protect him, but Crider flung me out of the way, causing me to lose my footing. I fell to one knee, scraping myself on the pavement and tearing my pants. I cursed out loud.

Slocum barreled by, but I somehow managed to grab a fistful of his sweatshirt. He tried swatting my hand away but I held tight, regaining my footing behind him. He was shorter than I and muscular, but the booze had made him slow and clumsy. Using both hands I pulled his sweatshirt up over his head, then wrapped my arms around his chest. He wasn't going anywhere.

From underneath the sweatshirt he mumbled, "Wha da fug, wha da fug?"

When I looked up I saw that Chiang had somehow managed to escape Crider and they stood about ten yards apart, sizing each other up. It was a clear mismatch, Chiang giving up at least seven inches of height and probably sixty pounds. I feared the worst and knew Chiang wouldn't have a chance.

Crider lunged, but Chiang quickly backpedaled. A couple of times Crider feinted one way and then the other, just to see what Chiang would do. Chiang read the moves and kept a safe distance away, still backpedaling. Crider moved easily in his high topped sneakers, Chiang slower in his body coveralls and construction boots.

I had my hands full restraining Slocum but managed to shout, "Chiang, get out of here. Just run!"

Crider snorted laughter. "Yeah, go ahead and run you little yellow bastard. Chop, chop."

Over to the side, I noticed that Malcolm had returned and stood watching, hand covering his mouth. He still looked petrified.

Slocum renewed his struggling and tried to break free, but my hands remained locked around his arms. He tired after a minute or two and stopped, although his drunken threats continued from underneath his sweatshirt, "Gonna fuggin kill you, goddamn mudder fugger."

Campus security was still nowhere in sight.

It wasn't long before Chiang had run out of space to backpedal. With his various feints and lunges, Crider had backed him up against a chain link fence at the far end of the lot. He had nowhere left to maneuver.

Chiang didn't take his eyes off Crider, and felt the fence with the back of his hands.

Crider snarled, "End of the line, slope."

Chiang looked to the left and to the right of the parking lot.

"What's the matter, lose your fuckin' rickshaw?"

Chiang extended his arms and held his palms up. "Don't do this," he implored. "You don't want this."

"You don't want this," Crider repeated, drawing out each word mockingly. "You oriental faggot. It's pay-back time."

Crider picked up a few stones from the pavement, then began throwing them hard at Chiang. One hit Chiang in the leg, but the kid didn't flinch. Crider took another step forward and hawked up a glob of phlegm, spat it on Chiang's coveralls.

I had to do something. I pushed Slocum away and decided to take my chances alongside Chiang.

Once free, Slocum started swinging blindly from under the sweatshirt, muttering, "Take dat, mudder fugger. Dat's right, Anthony's bringin' da pain." When he finally got the sweatshirt off his head, he realized I was no longer there.

I got to the other end of the lot just as Crider made his move, and if I blinked I would have missed the entire exchange. Crider must have telegraphed the attack because Chiang was immediately up on his toes. He crouched into a fighting position, spreading his arms wide at his waist, squaring his shoulders. His eyes became tight slits.

Crider charged and let loose a nasty left hook, but Chiang easily pulled away and it missed by a wide margin. Crider's momentum carried him forward and Chiang sidestepped and darted in front of his opponent. Chiang's movements were fluid and his quickness catlike, even in work boots.

Crider turned around to discover he was the one now trapped.

I stood there mesmerized, watching Chiang prance confidently on the balls of his feet, waiting for Crider to make his next move. I now wondered if Chiang's backpedaling was an act, a tactic to get Crider right where he wanted him.

I felt a hand tapping me on my shoulder and knew without even turning it was Slocum. His face was sickly pale and soaking wet from his ten round bout with his sweatshirt.

"Yer fuggin' dead man woggin'," he slurred.

I pushed him away and he stumbled over his own feet.

What happened next in front of me will forever be etched in my mind.

Crider was furious for having the tables turned and charged forward, arms outstretched, teeth bared. This time, there would be no ducking or sidestepping from Chiang. Chiang held his ground and met Crider head on.

With lightning speed, Chiang drove the heel of his boot hard into Crider's midsection, doubling him over and knocking the wind out of him. Chiang withdrew his leg and hesitated for a fraction of a second, most likely assessing Crider's position. He then pivoted on one leg while flexing the other, swinging his entire body around in an arc and delivering another kick, this one squarely underneath Crider's unprotected jaw. The sound was not unlike that of a punted football.

Crider's head flew back and his legs crumbled, causing him to drop like a sack of grain into a sitting position, shoulders slumped forward. He was not unconscious, but likely seeing every star in the galaxy. He sat there squinting downwards, glazed and disoriented. At one point he shook his head back and forth, trying to clear it. Blood began bubbling out of his nostrils and then spilled downward, first all over his shirt and then the pavement.

Chiang stood there for a few moments staring at Crider. He then turned and walked over to where Slocum and I were standing. Slocum had gotten up from the pavement but was swaying back and forth on unsteady legs. Chiang stopped directly in front of Slocum and grabbed a fistful of his sweatshirt. "You want some of that?" Slocum bristled and cowered, a look of panic in his eyes. He shook his head from side to side, struggled to say something but couldn't.

Even though Chiang was shorter and nowhere near as muscular as Slocum, he reached over and grabbed Slocum by his right earlobe, physically separating him from me and pulling him toward Crider. Slocum cried out in pain. Chiang said, "It looks like your friend has taken a nasty little tumble. Why don't you go over there and hold his hand." He let go of Slocum's ear and pushed him in Crider's direction. Slocum wobbled over the rest of the way.

I just shook my head in astonishment at the way Chiang had handled the two of them, and had to suppress a laugh over the way he had just spoken to Slocum.

Behind us a police cruiser pulled into the lot, roof strobes flashing.

Chiang looked at me, raked a hand through his long black hair. Somewhere in the fracas his knit cap and sunglasses had gotten knocked off his head. He stared at my ripped pants, blood seeping from my scraped knee.

"You okay, boss?" he asked.

I smiled weakly and nodded through the pain.

The police officer called to the scene was Oakley, the cop who'd escorted Crider and Slocum from my classroom the day of the fracas. He was adjusting a night stick on his belt, looked up and recognized me. He grinned and gave me a little wave of the hand as he approached.

I'd forgotten how big he was, a wide body straight from a fitness center. As he approached I could see the muscles in his broad shoulders and arms. He had a somewhat ruddy complexion, wide nose offsetting a jutting, prominent jaw.

I extended my hand. "Jack Elliot."

"I remember you Dr. Elliot," he said crisply, clamping my hand. "Roger Oakley."

I gestured toward Chiang. "This is Sam Chiang. I believe you've met him too."

The two nodded.

Oakley looked over at Crider and Slocum. "What's the problem here?" Oakley asked, his brow knit with concern.

"There's been a physical assault," I said. "You might want to first check the big guy on the ground. He took a pretty good shot."

Oakley began walking towards them, then abruptly stopped and shot me a puzzled look over his shoulder. "Wait a minute, aren't these the two guys from . . ?"

I cut right in. "Yep, the classroom."

He continued walking, shaking his head.

Oakley found Crider in the same sitting position with his head in his hands, rubbing his temples. Slocum was nearby, still stumbling around.

Oakley kneeled down and huddled with Crider for a few moments, then helped him to his feet. Oakley talked with the two of them for a few minutes, then rejoined us.

Oakley said, "He refused medical treatment and seems okay, but we'll run him by the campus health center just to be sure. In the meantime, why don't you tell me what happened. We'll do a written statement once you bring me up to speed."

I took a deep breath and recounted the events, beginning with my earlier run-in with Crider and Slocum by the post office. I described how I found them near my car after the alarm system sounded, and how Chiang appeared at the scene. Chiang explained how he witnessed the two of them damage my car, Crider with a screwdriver and Slocum with a key. I described the verbal assault, including the ethnic slurs directed at Chiang, as well as the eventual physical assault.

When I described Chiang's quick work of Crider, Oakley's eyes widened. He smirked as he looked over at Crider then back at Chiang.

"You did that?" Oakley said, rubbing the corners of his mouth. I could tell he was impressed as well as amused.

Chiang nodded, shrugged modestly.

Oakley whistled softly through his teeth, shook his head. "Damn," he muttered.

We shared a few more details, including Crider's rock throwing and spitting, as well as Slocum's involvement in the entire mess.

Oakley crossed his arms, looked over at Crider and Slocum. Up to now his voice had been low and even, but anger crept into it. "I've had it with those two. They're nothing but trouble, a couple of wiseasses." He looked at me. "After your classroom episode, we told them they'd better clean up their act, especially Crider."

He hiked up his holster. "Stupid bastard," he mumbled.

Not my choice of words, but a stirring portrayal nonetheless of Crider.

Oakley asked us to stick around while he dealt with Crider and Slocum. Chiang and I talked a little before he went looking for his knit hat and sunglasses, then clocked out over at the maintenance department.

I walked around to clear my head, every so often stealing a glance at Oakley shaking down Crider and Slocum, then eyeballing my damaged car at the other end of the lot. My nerves were shot and I could've used a stiff drink or two to calm down. My whole body seemed to be either tingling or trembling, and I had a rip-snorting headache to boot. The adrenaline had worn off and I was recoiling from everything that happened, blood pounding in my eardrums. My arms and shoulders ached from restraining Slocum and I was still grimacing from the pain coming from my banged up and bloodied knee.

Other than that, it had been just another day at the office.

# *Twenty-seven*

After a while I spied Chiang leaning against the hood of my car, smoking a cigarette. He'd recovered his knit cap and had it pulled low, sun glasses back on top. I walked over and stood next to him, neither of us speaking for a little while.

I watched him take a long drag. "Those things are dangerous, you know."

"So are street fights," he shot right back.

I shook my head, had to smile. The abrasion on my knee had started to crust over but I could still feel a little blood seeping from it.

"Sorry about your car," Chiang said, running his hand along one of the deeper scratches. He took a deep pull on his cigarette.

"It can be fixed," I said, rubbing my eyes.

"Jackasses," Chiang said quietly.

I extended my hand. "Listen, I want to thank you. You really stuck your neck out for me. What you did took a lot of courage."

He reached over and clasped my hand. His soft, childlike grip offered sharp contrast to the martial arts side I'd just witnessed.

"Back there," I said, gesturing with my thumb to where Oakley's cruiser was parked, "your brother teach you that?"

He nodded, and his eyes became vacant for a moment or two. He took another drag from the cigarette, exhaling out the side of his mouth.

A little while ago I was talking with Chiang about Nathan and Billy

Halliday, and Chiang confessed that he too had been bullied as a kid growing up. He said his brother Ray told him to avoid troublemakers and the bullying would eventually let up. Walk away from it was Ray's advice.

"I thought Ray told you that almost everyone gets bullied, that it's like a rite of passage for most kids."

Chiang looked at me. "He did, but he also told me sometimes you gotta push back."

"Like today."

He let out a long breath. "I'd reached my limits with that guy."

"You and me both," I said.

He inhaled on his cigarette and held it in his lungs for a moment, then let the smoke escape through his nostrils.

I studied him in the dying light. "Your brother taught you well."

Chiang chewed on this for a minute, shrugged. "Basic street fighting rules."

"Like what?" I was curious, never knew when my next gang war or rumble would be.

He finished the cigarette and dropped it on the pavement, stubbed it out with his foot. "Oh, I don't know, Survival 101 tips." He flashed me a cynical grin. "Don't back down, take the bully out first, make sure he stays down for the count, stuff like that."

"Crider was a tall order."

Chiang slowly shook his head. "It's not the size of the dog in the fight, it's the size of the fight in the dog. Besides, he was drunk, very predictable."

"You didn't seem too worried about Slocum."

"Nope, never gave him a second thought. He was all yours." He smiled at me.

"You baited Crider, didn't you? All the dramatics by the fence."

"Don't forget the wink I gave him," Chiang said. He smiled at me, as if we'd just shared a closely guarded secret.

I added, "You had him right where you wanted him."

Chiang pulled his knit cap down lower. "You could say that."

"He never knew what hit him."

"He won't soon forget it either."

We shared another laugh.

It got quiet again. At one point I looked over and studied him, the diminutive, floppy haired kid who'd ridden to my rescue twice now.

He caught me looking.

"What?" he asked curiously.

"You could have ignored everything, you know, just walked by and let me handle things by myself."

He thought about that for a moment, then said, "Couldn't do that, boss. Ray used to tell me there are two kinds of people in the world, those who stand up for what they believe in, and those who duck for cover."

His voice had the usual undertone of pride toward his brother.

I looked over at the police cruiser. Oakley was talking earnestly to Crider and Slocum. They both stood next to the car listening and nodding gravely. Crider held a towel and what appeared to be an ice pack to his bloodied nose.

My eyes returned to Chiang. "I take it big brother never liked ducking for cover."

Chiang nodded his head. "Wasn't his style."

I could see things racing through his mind, wondered if he was going to finally open up about Ray.

I said, "He died when he was young. What was he, twenty-five?"

Chiang nodded and stuck his hands in his coveralls, let out a long breath. "He died from cancer, HIV infection. Kaposi's sarcoma."

For some reason, I never thought to connect Ray's death to AIDS. Chiang's guardedness about his brother all along now made sense. I fumbled for words. "I'm sorry. That's tough stuff."

A momentary silence passed between us.

He eventually returned my look and shook his head. "All of us were shocked with the diagnosis. He was always healthy, working out and taking care of himself. But then he started getting tired all the time, run down. Lost a lot of weight, something like thirty pounds in six weeks."

"Did your family care for him at home?"

"For as long as they could, then he had to be hospitalized."

"Were you home at the time?"

He shook his head. "I was here. It was my freshman year."

I waited a moment, then said, "Did you get to spend time with him?"

Chiang got quiet, stared down at the pavement. After a moment he slowly raised his head, looked at me. "Not as much as I should have." His voice was nearly a whisper.

"You had trouble dealing with it."

He nodded, nibbled on his lower lip. "Eventually I was able to accept it, but my parents never got over the shame and embarrassment. I don't know what was worse for them, knowing their son was gay or watching him die from

249

AIDS. They kind of tiptoed around the whole thing. Meanwhile there was Ray, stuck in the middle, alone."

"Did he have a partner?"

He shrugged. "If he did, we never knew."

Another police cruiser swung into the lot, pulled up next to the other. A female officer got out, stood next to Oakley. We watched quietly from a distance.

After a while Chiang said, "In the end he pulled away from me, didn't come visit. I stopped going home."

I kept still, let him talk.

He folded his arms across his chest, rested his chin on his hand. "I remember the last weekend I saw him at home. He'd lost a ton of weight, I mean his clothes were hanging off him. His bones looked as though they were going to poke through his skin. He had purple lesions on his body, a foul odor." His voice tapered off. "We talked a little, but it was hard for both of us. I didn't know what to say anymore, so I kind of just sat there."

He looked at me from time to time smiling, the sad kind.

I tried to picture how this played out. "So he was home in Boston and you stayed here."

Chiang nodded. "Pretty much. This is where I hid ... it was safe."

I wrinkled a brow. "Did you guys write?"

His face brightened a little. "All the time, emails and letters. Sometimes several times a week."

Chiang shifted his weight against the car. "When I went home for the funeral, I stayed a few extra days. My mother and I sorted through his belongings, you know clothes and stuff. Anyway, we were just about done when she reached under his bed and pulled out a shoebox, handed it to me. She said Ray wanted me to have it."

I listened intently, intrigued.

He coughed into his hand, scratched his chin. "Inside were all the letters and emails I'd sent him since he'd gotten sick. He'd kept every single one of them." His voice tightened. "My mother told me that sometimes she'd check in on him late at night and find him reading them. He'd have them spread out on the bed."

We traded looks.

Chiang said, "When I opened the box, I saw that he'd put all the letters in order, even the emails."

I hugged myself against the dropping temperature. The low afternoon sun cast part of the parking lot into shadow.

"That surprised you?" I asked.

"Yeah," he said, "probably because I'd done the same thing with his letters."

I slowly shook my head, thinking about how close these guys must've been growing up.

"Did you go back and reread what you wrote?"

He nodded. "Every word. When I first wrote them, I thought they were about Ray and his illness, you know, my asking how he was doing, telling him to hang in there, that kind of stuff. I'd tell him about my life here at Guilford, hoping my letters would help fill his days, give him something to do."

He stood there thinking for a moment or two.

"But it was strange when I went back and reread them."

"How so?"

He pinched the corners of his eyes with his thumb and forefinger, lowered his voice. "I realized the letters weren't about Ray, they were about me. They were filled with the sadness I was feeling, how I was coping. I didn't realize it at the time but I was writing to him about my life, my insecurities and doubts, my hopes and ambitions." His voice faded. "My fear of losing him."

There was activity over by the police cruisers. Crider and Slocum were being put into the back seat of the cruiser driven by the female officer.

Chiang continued. "When I went back and reread them, I realized how much I'd grown that year. Reading them helped me heal, helped me mend. I could see things clearer."

He looked around, pained, and said quietly, "It was like he left me with a gift."

I waited a minute. "He did. He wanted you to remember."

He looked at me and nodded.

I got the feeling he hadn't shared this part of his life with anyone, that these were memories staved off since Ray died.

Another minute went by.

I cleared my throat while crossing my arms across my chest. I sputtered for a moment before finding the words. "Look, Chiang, I don't think you were hiding at school or turning your back, nor was Ray when he chose to stay away. You need to get over that. You were a kid fresh out of high school who didn't know any better and he was a guy whose life had been turned upside down. His world changed in ways that you and I can only imagine. Who knows, maybe he thought he was protecting you by staying away. Big brothers do stuff like that."

I pushed myself away from the car, got in front of him so I could look him square in the eye. "Your letters kept you connected, strengthened an already special bond. The two of you shared a gift, one that enabled you share an incredibly difficult and painful journey. You were there for him. Ray treasured what you wrote, your letters no doubt bringing him much needed comfort. Maybe you didn't see each other as often as you wanted, but I'd be willing to bet what the two of you wrote surpassed most of the conversations you ever had."

I placed my hand on his shoulder, kept it there for a moment before giving it a gentle squeeze. "It's time to stop being so rough on yourself."

Chiang thought about it for a long moment, didn't say anything. He looked away then back at me, his eyes a bit glassy.

He nodded.

A FEW MINUTES LATER, THE POLICE cruisers headed our way, leaving the lot. The one transporting Crider and Slocum drove by first, the female officer nodding in our direction. Oakley stopped his cruiser next to where we stood, lowered the window.

"You guys okay?" he asked. He craned his neck to look up at us.

"We're okay. How 'bout them?" I asked, gesturing toward the cruiser leaving the lot.

Oakley shook his head, his mouth set in a frown. "They're both in hot water, and they know it." He reached over and grabbed a clipboard sitting on the passenger seat, some kind of printed form on top.

"I've got to get some more information from the two of you," he said.

Oakley braced the clipboard against the steering wheel and asked various questions, this time filling in various sections of the form. He was efficient and professional, pressing us when he needed more detail and listening with a trained ear to everything we had to say. I liked his style.

When we were almost done, Oakley raised his eyes in a questioning look. "Who's Malcolm Taylor?"

I cringed. In all the commotion I'd forgotten about Malcolm.

Chiang immediately cut in. "I forgot to tell you," he said looking at me. "When you were walking around I ran into him. He told me he had to go, had to catch the last commuter bus home."

I felt guilty and made a mental note to call and thank Malcolm, make sure he was okay. It then dawned on me I hadn't called Rachel back. I glanced at my watch with a sinking feeling, realizing she was well on her way to New Hampshire with her husband. I really wanted to say goodbye, the wicked tingle giving way to pangs of missing someone special. I'd have to wait and see her at our next class.

I looked at Oakley. "Malcolm was the student who made the call to your office. I instructed him to use the call box outside the classroom building."

"Was he a witness to any of this?" Oakley asked.

I said, "He was the one who came to get me when my car alarm went off and I'm pretty sure he saw most of what happened."

Oakley made a notation on the form. When he finished he capped his pen, wedged it in the top of the clipboard.

I rested a hand on the door, then leaned toward Oakley. "So what's going to happen to those two?"

He sighed, slouched a little behind the wheel. "Of course I can't tell you any of this," he said, winking. "They both failed a sobriety test, so we're gonna keep them over at the security office until the Dean of Students arrives. Crider still refuses any kind of medical treatment, and the other jackass is crocked to the gills, making no sense whatsoever, talking jibberish. Wants to know why his ear hurts so much. Goddamn, you'd swear he was the one knocked to the canvas."

Oakley scratched the back of his neck. "Anyway, I'm sure the parents or guardians are being contacted, maybe legal counsel being arranged. Those two are going to be facing some pretty serious charges."

Oakley let this sink in for a minute. He said, "We've done the preliminaries and we'll get a formal statement later. We're counting on both of you for continued cooperation."

Chiang and I nodded.

Oakley drummed his fingers on the steering wheel, exhaled a deep breath. "They're going to get the book thrown at them." He flipped through the report as well as other notes attached to the clipboard. Take your pick: intoxication, disorderly conduct, vandalism, verbal and physical assault. While Crider was the primary, Slocum was an accessory to everything, which puts him in equally deep shit."

Oakley said, "I'm sure there are also grounds for a hate crime, given the abusive language and behavior directed toward Mr. Chiang."

I would later learn that all of the charges stuck, including the hate crime, resulting in Crider's and Slocum's permanent dismissal from Guilford College, plus sentencing from the court.

I rubbed more fatigue from my eyes. It had been a long day.

"You guys can take off," Oakley said. "We'll handle this from here. I've got both your numbers should we need to talk some more over the weekend. Like I said, we're going to need your signatures on some formal documents."

We jabbered a little more before I thanked Oakley and tapped the roof of the cruiser, stepping back.

Oakley touched two fingers to his forehead in an informal salute and drove off, leaving the two of us alone in the parking lot.

Darkness had set in. I was dog-tired and starved. I fished the car keys out of my pocket, then unlocked the doors with the remote.

I turned to Chiang and said, "What do you say we get out of Dodge and get something to eat?" I hesitated for a moment. "By the way, where in God's name did you dredge up that cornball line?"

Chiang snickered. "I don't know, probably an episode of *Kung Fu*. You liked it though, admit it."

I looked at him and just shook my head.

Chiang struck a martial arts pose, making me laugh.

I gestured with my chin toward the car. "Come on, the least I can do is feed you," I said. "You look like you could use a square meal, put some meat on those bones."

"Sounds good to me," Chiang said, reaching for my keys. "I'm driving, right?"

I pulled them away. "Wong."

Chiang picked up on the humor and recoiled in mock indignation. "No need to get your knickers in a twist, boss."

He got into the passenger seat grinning.

# *Twenty-eight*

I was driving to work Monday morning in my scratched Volvo and heard on the radio that snow was heading our way. Not a big snow storm, but the first of the season, a cold front from the north bumping heads with some moisture moving up along the coast. The temperature was going to drop and clouds were expected to move in overnight, delivering the white stuff sometime tomorrow morning. Hard to believe given the warm spell we had last week.

Snow being forecast before Thanksgiving was newsworthy and consumed most of the morning news. It made me realize how quirky New Englanders can be when it comes to snow. At one time they were known for their hardiness, rugged souls able to withstand whatever Mother Nature threw their way, as unflinching as they were unflappable. Today, worry lines often sprout at the slightest mention of snow and communities don't waste any time battening down the hatches. There's storm center updates, school cancellations, platoons of idling snow plows, and panic in the grocery store aisles.

Absolutely silliness, I thought, and hardly worth a second thought. However, I wondered if we had enough milk, bread, candles, bottled water, a working radio, rock salt, toilet paper and batteries. I'd have to touch base with Claire later.

The red message light on my answering machine was blinking when I got to my office, and I wasn't surprised to learn that Evelyn Chadwick wanted me to call as soon as I got in. I called her extension and Livinia Dawson picked up.

"Mornin', Jack," she said, a bounce in that sultry voice of hers.

"Hi Liv," I replied. "Got your snow shovel out?"

"Good grief, Jack, that's not even funny. These bones of mine ain't ready for ol' man winter, not before Thanksgiving anyway."

I laughed softly to myself.

Liv said, "You doing okay?" She'd heard about the Friday fracas, I'm sure, her concern genuine.

"Hanging in there, thanks." I paused for a second or two. "Why am I not surprised hearing from your office first thing?"

"News spreads fast on this campus, you of all people should know that. Hold on, Jack, I'm going to connect you to Evelyn. She said to put you through immediately."

Chadwick came on the line momentarily, her voice crisp and cool, her usual commanding presence.

"Jack, Evelyn here."

"Hi Evelyn."

She began without ceremony, got right to the point. "I'm sitting here reading through Friday's incident report from the security office."

I decided to play everything low key, especially since my last encounter with her majesty was hardly cordial. I didn't want to gloat and remind her I was right all along about Crider and Slocum.

She said, "To say I'm shocked about what happened would be an understatement. First and foremost, I'm calling to see if you're okay and not injured."

"I'm fine." I wanted to tell her my banged up knee required intensive self-medication this weekend and put a significant dent in my booze cabinet.

I could hear her sifting through papers.

"And the student who helped you, Mr. Chung, is he okay?"

"That's Chiang," I said. "He's fine, too."

Chiang and I left the parking lot Friday night in search of food and I called Claire along the way, filled her in on the fight and invited her to meet up with us. She accepted without hesitation, having been worried about my whereabouts all afternoon, and brought Nathan and Forrest along. We ate barbequed chicken and ribs at a place not too far from the college, the guys in total awe of Chiang as I recounted his parking lot exploits.

Chadwick continued: "I'm still processing things and will be speaking with the Dean of Students and the security office later this morning, Dr.

Whitbourne as well. I assure you the two students will be prosecuted to the fullest extent of the law. They are both facing a variety of charges."

"So I've been told," I replied.

Whitbourne being roped into this didn't surprise me a bit, although the mention of his name left my insides cold. The fact that he'd seen me with Rachel last Thursday night had gnawed away at me all weekend. I didn't trust him one bit and knew it would only be a matter of time before the fringed warrior made his move, turning the thermostat up on me a notch or two. I vowed not to get caught flatfooted.

She cleared her throat. "While I have you on the line I'd like to touch base on a few things." I could hear her chair creak as she shifted in it. "First, let me make sure I have this right. All four students involved in the incident were enrolled in your course?"

I had to pause for a moment. "Did you say four?"

"That's right. There's Crider and Slocum, and then Chung, I mean Chiang." She hesitated then added, "I also see the name Malcolm Taylor."

I smiled to myself. Malcolm again managed to slip in under the radar. "Yes, that's correct. Malcolm was the student who called the security office. He's also in the same class." I reminded myself I needed to call him today.

She seemed to be taking notes as I spoke.

Chadwick said, "Another question. Other than what happened Friday afternoon, have you had any contact with Crider or Slocum?

"None since the classroom altercation."

"No interaction on campus, no phone calls or emails? No contact of any kind?"

"Absolutely none. They dropped off the face of the earth. I had no idea where they'd gone or what they were up to."

Of course, now I knew better. They were busy trying to hang me with their poison pen letter.

After a second or two, Chadwick shifted gears. "Any hesitation on your part going back to class tomorrow?"

I paused. "I'm not sure I understand the question."

"Jack, what happened last Friday has already created a campus stir, which shouldn't come as any great surprise. A police incident involving four students and a professor from the same course doesn't translate into idle chatter, at least not on this campus. If there's any discomfort on your part walking into that classroom, we can arrange coverage. Just tell me if there's anything you need."

I relaxed, realized she was looking out for me. The Ice Maiden had a heart after all. I said, "I'll be fine with the class, thanks. I should be there, and want to be there."

I paused, ran a hand through my hair. "Where do things stand with Crider and Slocum?"

"Arrests were made and we expect a hearing date to be announced sometime soon, maybe even today. In the meantime, they're not allowed to set foot on campus. What they've done is being taken very seriously."

"Good," I said, arching the small of my back and resetting myself in the chair. "I guess that pretty much takes care of the letter they sent."

"The letter?" she replied, surprised.

"The letter about me. Given the circumstances, I'm assuming it's going to be tossed."

There was a long silence.

Finally Chadwick said, "I'm afraid what happened Friday night doesn't change the letter."

I was puzzled. "Why's that?" I asked.

She replied, "Because the letter wasn't written by either one of them."

I sat there stunned, felt my heartbeat quicken. "The letter was written by another student in the class?"

"That's correct."

"Who?" I felt like I had just been punched in the gut.

"You know I can't answer that, professor, I've told you that before." An edge had crept into her voice. So much for tender mercies of the heart.

I kept quiet as I tried to take all of this in. It didn't make sense, but I knew from Chadwick's tone I'd best stay away from the topic, at least for now.

We talked a little more, although I didn't hear much. I tried keeping my voice steady, but it was difficult. I was really bothered by what I'd just heard, the information rattling around in my brain. I felt the beginnings of a headache and was thankful when the Ice Maiden finally signed off.

After I hung up, I sat there thinking for a few minutes. All along I'd assumed Crider and Slocum had sent the letter, never considered the possibility that it could have originated from someone else. It suddenly dawned on me that Chadwick had told me as much the morning I met with she and Whitbourne. *'Let's not lose sight of the fact that this is the perception of only one student.'* The comment went right by me and I never picked up on it. The fact that Crider and Slocum hadn't sent the letter now explained their confusion outside the post office Friday when I confronted them with it. They had no clue what I was talking about.

I swiveled in my chair and looked out the window. A pale sun hung in the sky and clouds were moving in. It looked like the wind had picked up.

I was confused. If Crider and Slocum hadn't sent the letter, then who had? It was difficult imagining who had the ax to grind with me, who wanted to make my life difficult. Having seen the two thugs in action all semester, I'd be willing to bet they'd bullied someone to write it. Maybe they'd pressured someone to sign a letter they'd written themselves. Of course, someone apart from Crider and Slocum could've done it, a student simply displeased with how I handled the outburst. Anything was possible. Who knows, maybe the college's baseball coach had a hand in this. Slocum was a top scholarship player, and Coach Crenshaw had a reputation for doing virtually anything to protect his baseball players.

My head was spinning and the day had just begun.

LATER THAT MORNING I WAS ABOUT TO PUSH open the faculty restroom door just as Bruce Whitbourne was walking out. I had my head down and narrowly missed bumping into him in the doorway. I startled a bit when I saw who it was.

"Hey, Jack, what's up?" he said, stopping in his tracks. He eyed me like a vulture.

"Morning," I mumbled, unable to proceed because he was blocking the way.

He didn't move. "I'm glad I ran into you, Jack. I need to see you sometime today when you get a moment. It's important."

He'd made his move and I was ready, deciding to call his bluff. "How 'bout in a few minutes, soon as I'm done here?" I looked him right in the eye and smiled big and warm, wanting as hard as I could to come across both collegial and cooperative. It was total torture.

He thought for a minute, then shook his bald head. "I was thinking more along the lines of this afternoon. Let's make it four-thirty, my office?"

He obviously wanted to twist the screw, make me stew about things all day long.

I didn't break eye contact. "I'll be there, Whit."

CY ROLLINS ATE THE LAST OF HIS PASTRAMI and rye sandwich and washed it

259

down with a swallow of beer. He wiped his mouth with a napkin and looked at me from across the table. "So what you're telling me is that neither Crider nor Slocum sent the letter to Chadwick."

I nodded. "My guess is that they put pressure on someone else to write it."

Cy and I were having lunch at a bar and grill around the corner from the college, a hole in the wall offering great sandwiches at decent prices. He'd called me earlier and wanted to get caught up after having been away at a conference most of last week. He'd missed all the fireworks, including my bombshell meeting with Chadwick and Whitbourne, the damage done to my car, and the fist fight in the parking lot. Little things.

I'd just finished telling him about Chadwick's phone call this morning.

He shook his head in disbelief. "That's some curve ball." He folded the napkin and stuck it on his empty plate, put his silverware on top.

Cy said, "I agree with you about Crider and Slocum. They probably strong armed someone to write it, maybe wanted it to look like the class was turning on you. But let's face it, the letter could have come from anyone."

I nodded while I finished my hamburger.

"Chadwick told you nothing else this morning?"

"Nope."

Cy straightened in the seat. "Well, there's not much advice I can offer. You're not going to find out who the letter writer is, at least not now. Let's face it, you don't have a whole lot to go on. Chadwick obviously isn't going to show her hand, and Whitbourne won't because he's enjoying himself too much. Plus, he's an incompetent asshole. All you really know is that Crider and Slocum are out of the picture and the spineless coward still sits in your class."

We finished our beers and got the check from the waitress.

We split the bill at the register and then walked out to our cars. We stood in the fresh air for a moment buttoning our coats. The temperature had dropped noticeably since this morning and the wind had grown some teeth.

Cy hung around, shifting his weight from one foot to the other, acting as if he had something on his mind. He looked a bit nervous.

"You okay?" I asked.

He coughed into his hand. "Listen, Jack, there's another reason why I wanted to get together today."

I nodded and waited for him to talk.

He fumbled with his words. "There's something I've been meaning to share with you, but didn't know if I should or even if it's my place." He lowered his head and muttered, "This probably isn't the best time either, with all the other crap you've got going on."

He was clearly uncomfortable.

I looked at him with eyes encouraging him to continue.

He did: "I'll just go ahead and say it. I was heading over to the fitness center two or three weeks ago, taking one of my campus shortcuts. I happened to see Claire sitting in her car in a student parking lot. She was surprised to see me, flustered actually. She said the two of you were going to have lunch or something and that she was waiting for you. Anyway, we got to talking and the conversation somehow got around to local medical schools. I guess a friend of hers has a daughter applying to colleges and Claire wanted to ask me some questions. I gave her the information I thought she needed and then had to take off."

I nodded at what he was saying but my hearing had snagged. Claire and I didn't have lunch two or three weeks ago, nor was she ever parked on campus waiting for me. In fact, it had been several years since she had even visited Guilford.

I was initially confused, but then it all made sense. Claire was keeping tabs on me.

I got a knot in my stomach and became fearful that I would lose my composure in front of Cy.

Cy wasn't finished. "This weekend Claire called me at home with a few more questions about schools." He pulled gloves from his coat pocket, fidgeted with them. "At the end of the conversation she casually asked if I enjoyed the basketball game with you at the Mohegan Sun last Thursday night."

I felt my face flush with a mixture of embarrassment and shame. I couldn't bullshit my way out of this or deny any part of it. In fact, I was speechless. I'd been caught telling a brazen lie and couldn't deny it. For my own selfish reasons, I had used a trusted and valued friend. I'd taken advantage of Cy and in the process devalued our relationship. I disgraced myself and felt horrible.

I stood there naked and defenseless, raw and vulnerable. I lowered my eyes.

He sensed my uneasiness and placed a comforting hand on my shoulder. "It's okay, Jackie," he said reassuringly. "I told her we had a great time, said we needed to get out more." He laughed too hard.

I wanted to crawl into a hole and disappear, but knew there wasn't one big enough, at least not on this planet.

Cy kept his hand on my shoulder and looked at me with compassion in his eyes. There was a long pause before he spoke again. "You needed to know these things, Jack."

I looked at him and nodded, compressed my lips. He'd done what he set out to do, whistled a warning shot over my head. He didn't mix any words, didn't pull any punches.

Just like that, the conversation was over, finished as quickly as it began. We both knew there'd be no need to revisit it.

We stood there on the sidewalk a little longer. He pulled his hand away and took a couple of steps backwards. He finally raised his chin by way of goodbye, turned and left without a word. I got in my car and sat there in silence, watching the wind swirl litter around in the street.

I WAS IN A FOUL MOOD BY THE TIME I RAPPED on Whitbourne's opened office door. I didn't wait for a response, just walked in and sat down in one of the leather chairs. Whitbourne was at his desk reading something, and didn't even look up when I entered.

He took his sweet time finishing, making me feel like an unimportant and disposable undergraduate. Eventually he removed his reading glasses and slipped them into his breast pocket, then looked over at me with his best vinegary expression.

We nodded a greeting.

Whitbourne didn't speak right away, just sat there pressing his finger tips together. Eventually he said, "Evelyn told me about the fight in the parking lot." He gave me an amused, smug smile. "You continue to make headline news, Jack. Pretty soon you're going to need an escort wherever you go." He laughed to himself.

I knew Whitbourne was going to do his best to rattle my cage. I told myself beforehand I'd have none of it, that I'd stay cool under fire. Other than wanting to grab his stupid civil war bugle from the bookcase and blasting it as loud as I could into his ear, I thought I was doing pretty well.

He hiked an eyebrow above a hooded eye. "So are you going to tell me what happened or do I have to keep hearing about it from other people?"

I didn't respond right away, then did so grudgingly. I gave him a condensed version of what happened, then answered a few questions he had along the way. He tried coming across as the understanding and caring supervisor, but

I knew he couldn't have cared less about my predicament or me. In fact, he looked pleased with my misfortunes.

He sat back and thought about everything for a minute, then began running his hands along the top of his head. He released a deep sigh.

"So you were right about those two guys," Whitbourne said.

"Surprise, surprise," I said sarcastically. "I told you from the start those two freaks were nothing but trouble. They never should've been admitted to this college or allowed to hang on for so long." I shook my head in disgust. "I'm sure their next career stop will be a real credit to Guilford, no doubt mopping floors at some fast food joint or selling used cars in a crumbling, rat-infested neighborhood. Really validates the college mission, puts such a distinctive feather in our cap."

Whitbourne didn't answer, instead he gave me a slow, crooked smile.

I returned a hard stare. "The biggest crock is that I still have to defend myself for standing up to the two of them and throwing them out of my class, something no one else around here had the courage to do. What a joke." I was getting hot under the collar. It took great effort to keep from raising my voice.

We just sat there looking at each other.

This was getting old fast, a total waste of my time. My brain was scrambled from everything that had happened today and I wasn't thinking very clearly. I was beyond tired. My fuse was short and I knew I had to get out of Whitbourne's office before I lost it.

Finally I said, "Look, are we done here? It's getting late and I've had a long day, still have lots of things to do." None more important than getting pie-faced as soon as I could wrap my hands around a bottle.

Whitbourne's response surprised me. "No, Jack, we're not done here," he snapped back. He got up and stepped around the desk, then went over to close the door. He brushed by me on the way back.

Whitbourne resettled himself behind his desk. "I wanted to see you because I've got something on my mind, something that's been really bothering me. A delicate subject, shall we say." He raised his hands and used his fingers to make parentheses around the word 'delicate.'

Here it comes, I thought, my skin tingling. I could feel my heart rate pick up, chest tightening.

Whitbourne leaned forward and spoke. "It involves that woman I saw you with at the casino last week."

I stiffened and immediately got defensive. "That woman has a name. If I'm not mistaken you were properly introduced. Her name's Rachel Pond."

"Some friendly advice is in order, Jack," he said, his eyes darting back and forth. "Be careful with her," he said in a low voice.

I couldn't believe my ears. "Be careful?"

Whitbourne narrowed his eyes. "You heard me. Be careful, very careful." I barked a laugh, shook my head. "Why? Because she isn't my wife? Or is this because she's a student?"

"Neither," he said, locking eyes with mine.

I did a double take. "Then why is this any of your business?"

Whitbourne got up from his desk and walked over to me. He stood about a foot away and his unblinking eyes bore into me. He said, "Because Rachel Pond is the student who wrote the letter."

# *Twenty-nine*

It smelled like snow. Even though flakes had yet to fall, it was only a matter of time. Dark and ominous clouds had arrived overnight as predicted and moisture hung in the morning's dense air. As I made my way from the car to my office, a peaceful lull blanketed the area, the air fresh and clean, colors soft and hushed.

I was fighting a brutal hangover, one clamping my head ever since I cracked open my eyelids this morning. Handfuls of Motrin hadn't stopped the throbbing coming from my temples or the back of my eyes. The skin across my forehead felt like it was stretched too tight and my mouth was as dry as a riverbed. I felt weak and queasy, groggy from not getting enough sleep.

I was a physical wreck but I knew I had to get to the college early and connect with Rachel as soon as I could.

Yesterday I was dazed when I left Whitbourne's office and immediately tried calling her. I figured she'd be home from New Hampshire but her cell phone rang and rang, her answering service cutting in each time. I didn't know if Rachel's husband had access to her cell so I kept the message general but with a tone of urgency: 'Rachel,' I said, 'this is Jack Elliot. I need to speak with you right away about something important. Please call me as soon as you get in, no matter the time.'

She never did.

When I got home last night it was difficult keeping my composure. At the dinner table I directed my attention to Claire and Nathan, going through the motions and putting up a smokescreen about my day. I wanted to tell Claire about Rachel's letter to Chadwick, but given the extent of my relationship with Rachel, I didn't want to open up a can of worms. I kept things to myself.

After we were done eating I excused myself on the pretense that I needed to work on my manuscript, retreating downstairs to the family room. I had much on my mind and wanted to be alone. I tossed drinks down the hatch all night trying to unravel the mess, but went to bed still baffled and confused. I thrashed all night long, slipping in and out of dark dreams.

ONCE IN THE OFFICE I PUT MY CELL PHONE on the desk and brewed some coffee, then opened the window blinds. The first snowflakes were falling, lightly at first and then in greater number, some nudged by the wind and whirling. I stuck my hands in my pocket and leaned against the wall watching them dance, soft and gentle, dusting the ground like a fine powder. It was supposed to snow for most of the morning and then clear up by noon time.

I stood at the window for what seemed like an eternity.

After a while I looked at my watch and frowned, then sat down at the desk. I knew I had to get organized and focused. Beyond my need to talk with Rachel, I recognized that today's class was important in terms of getting everyone back on track. Chadwick would be looking on from the sidelines, putting me under the microscope for the rest of the semester.

My mind, though, wasn't cooperating. I was still dragging my feet and rehashing everything that happened yesterday.

I tried understanding what I could've done to earn Rachel's disfavor. The fact that she'd written the letter contradicted everything I knew about her. I thought of the talks we'd had about the classroom altercation, the advice she'd dispensed of so freely. I thought we had a trusting relationship and I'd let my guard down, taken her into my confidence. Our night at the casino now seemed like some kind of cruel hoax. She'd deceived me all along, kept her true nature hidden.

I kept telling myself there had to be an explanation, something that didn't meet the eye.

If Rachel's letter wasn't enough to rattle my cage, Cy's revelations about Claire were. While I'd felt a twinge of suspicion from her the night before the game, her campus stakeout was a flat out mystery. If Cy's observations were correct about Claire snooping and stalking at the college, it was a time when I had nothing to hide. My contact with Rachel outside of the classroom was virtually nonexistent. For the life of me I couldn't figure out why she was sniffing around then, what she was trying to ferret out.

I massaged my temples, then the back of my neck. I closed my eyes for a moment, drifting with my thoughts. I felt like I was in a fog, shuttling between confusion and uncertainty. Nothing made sense, not even Whitbourne. In my wildest imagination I never believed the guy would tip his hand to keep me out of harm's way, a gesture risking his job and surely placing him at odds with the Ice Maiden. I had to give the dusty historian some credit, he wasn't the cowardly lion or trained seal I thought.

I was brought back from my thoughts by soft knocking at the door. Thinking it was Rachel, I quickly moved to open it, my heart thumping wildly. Finally, I thought, some answers.

When I swung open the door, though, I saw that it wasn't Rachel. It was Lois Winslow. My heart sank but I didn't let it show.

Her face was flushed and contorted. At first I thought it was from the snowy conditions, or maybe because she was out of breath from climbing the stairs.

I tilted my head and studied her, realizing then she was distraught and had been crying. "Lois," I said slowly, "are you okay?"

She stood in the hallway and lowered her eyes, shook her head slowly back and forth.

"Why don't you come sit," I offered. I put a hand on her arm and gently guided her into my office toward a chair.

She sat down, sniffling. A tear silently rolled down her cheek. She pulled a tissue from her coat pocket and swiped it away, then dabbed at her nose.

"Can I get you some coffee, maybe some bottled water?"

She shook her head.

I gave her a moment to collect herself. "Tell me what's wrong," I urged.

Lois mumbled that she wouldn't be in class today, then stopped. She started to say something else but the words caught in her throat. All I heard was 'accident.'

I pulled my chair closer to hers. "You've had an accident."

Lois shook her head vigorously. "No, no," she repeated. "Not me." Her eyes got moist and she choked back a sob.

I waited.

Finally she cleared her voice, took a deep breath. She spoke in a near-whisper. "Rachel and her husband were up north skiing and had a car accident. Last night. I just found out."

Rachel's name slapped me to attention. "What happened?" I asked.

She looked down, swallowed hard. "Their car skidded on an icy patch in New Hampshire. They collided with a big rig. The car rolled over and down an embankment." Her voice tapered off, the strain showing on her face.

I felt a chill go down my spine. Images of Rachel flashed through my mind.

"How bad?" I asked. My voice was distant and strained, like it wasn't mine.

Lois got a stricken look on her face and more tears spilled from her eyes. She buried her face in her hands.

I asked again. "Lo, how bad?" I was panicking.

Lois wiped her eye with the back of her hand and continued. "Her husband was killed. Rachel is in critical condition. She's in a hospital up there."

The room started spinning, my mind unable to digest what I was hearing.

"What do you know about Rachel?" I asked. "What kind of injuries?"

She shook her head, sniffling. She struggled to continue. "I don't know. The accident's been on the radio this morning but I haven't heard anything else." She found another tissue and blew her nose. She got up and dropped it into the trash container by my desk, and returned to her chair.

She sat there gathering herself while I ran through what I'd just heard.

"I'll know more this afternoon," she said quietly. "I called Rachel's house this morning and spoke with her sister. We're going to touch base later today." She looked away.

I felt lightheaded, my pulse beating against my ears. I looked at the cell phone on my desk, thought of the unreturned calls from Rachel last night, the fact that I'd forgotten to call and say goodbye to her Friday night. I ached inside.

A long minute passed.

Lois must have sensed my sadness. She looked at me and said softly, "I'm sorry to have done this, I really am. But I thought you'd want to know, needed to know."

I nodded, staring at the carpet wide-eyed, my mouth a tight line.

Finally I said, "When you get an update, will you call me here or at home?" I scribbled my home phone number on a piece of paper and handed it to her. "Please, Lo. I'm counting on you."

She said, "I promise," and turned for the door. "I really have to leave, my husband is parked outside waiting for me."

She stopped after taking a step. "Wait," she said turning, "I forgot something." She reached inside her purse and pulled out a folded piece of paper, handed it to me. "Rachel sent me an email just before she left for the weekend. There's something in it about you."

I knew Rachel and Lois were close friends but didn't know the kinds of things they shared, what the reference to me might be. I didn't care. I longed for any kind of connection to Rachel. I took the paper and unfolded it. The message was brief:

*Hi Lois. We'll be leaving in a little while and will be getting home Sunday night. I'll call when we get back. Maybe lunch the first part of the week? In the meantime, I hope you have a relaxing weekend. When you see Dr. Elliot, please tell him to look for a package I put in the mail this afternoon. I sent it to the college. Thanks, Lo. Rachel*

I quickly processed the email. She was sending me whatever she forgot to bring to the casino. That was simple enough. But the message wasn't what caught my eye, rather it was the screen name Rachel had used. It practically jumped off the page.

*Strap95.*

I kept staring at it, the adrenaline rushing in my blood.

"Dr. Elliot?"

I glanced up at Lois, who was looking at me with concern. "You all right?" she asked.

I looked back down at the email, tried keeping my voice level. "This screen name, *Strap95*." I pointed to it with my finger. "Does Rachel work for Simon Trask, you know the real estate guy?"

Lois stared at me for a few seconds then looked at me funny. "I suppose you could say that." She paused for a moment. "Why do you ask?"

"Doesn't the screen name, *Strap95*, stand for Simon Trask Properties, how long it's been in the area, you know, since 1995?"

She thought for a moment, pursing her lips. "I guess it could. Actually, it's Rachel's screen name, one she shares with Simon. It's a combination of their names and the year they got married. You know, Simon Trask and Rachel Anne Pond."

I did a double-take, felt my pulse accelerate once more. "Hold on," I replied. "Rachel Pond is married to Simon Trask?" My mouth went dry.

She nodded. "Yes, she's kept her maiden name."

I tried slowing my heartbeat.

Lois looked at me. "You didn't know that?"

I shook my head. She'd only spoken of her husband in sweeping generalities, just as I'd done with Claire. It seemed safer that way, easier. She never shared, I never pried.

I thought about her screen name and the combined initials. I'd misread them from the start, had no reason to believe they stood for anything else. Same with the numbers, although now I remembered snatches of the conversation at the Mohegan Sun when I asked Rachel how long she'd been married. *'Since ninety-five. You'll have to do the math, Jack.'*

Lois and I fell into another silence. I looked away, trying to calm down. I felt beads of perspiration on my forehead.

Finally I handed the email back to Lois. She put it in her purse, then reached over and touched my arm.

"Are you sure you're okay?" she asked.

I nodded absently. "Just overwhelmed by everything," I mumbled.

"Of course, we all are." She looked at her watch. "Listen, I really have to go," she broke off. "I can't keep my husband waiting." On the way out she said, "I'll call with any updates."

With that, she disappeared.

I pushed the door closed and sat down, my head spinning, body weary. I ran my hands over my face, rubbed my eyes. I was reeling from the news of the accident and Rachel's connection to Trask, a one-two punch that had truly staggered me. Shock and disbelief blurred everything. Trask was gone and Rachel lay clinging to life in a hospital hundreds of miles away. I didn't know if she'd live or die. I felt helpless and heartsick, waves of sadness and dread washing over me.

Her letter to Chadwick no longer mattered.

But then another thought crashed to the forefront, one that did matter and called me to action.

*Claire.*

I USED MY BARE HANDS TO CLEAR SNOW from my car's windshield and rear window, having forgotten to wear gloves and pack an ice scraper, causalities of this morning's four-star hangover. I wasn't a pretty sight with snow in my hair and fingers turning blue, huffing and puffing in the frigid air, my eyes stinging from the icy wind. Every so often I had to stop and blow into my hands, rubbing them together. Several inches had fallen and it was coming down at a pretty good clip. The car fish-tailed on a few icy patches as I drove away from campus.

Before I'd left the building I stuck a note on my office door, telling students that I would be away for the day. I called Claire from my car but she wasn't at work and she wasn't answering her cell. I listened to a local radio station as I made my way home, news of Trask's death and Rachel's hospitalization making the news, just as Lois had said. There were no updates.

Claire's rental car was in the garage, puddles of melted snow underneath. Her car engine pinged, an indication that she hadn't been home that long. I called out her name when I entered, but the house was still. With school canceled this morning, Nathan was staying at Forrest's until later this afternoon, Marion riding herd on them. As I walked through the house I saw that the study was empty, the computer turned off. Claire wasn't in the living room and the bedrooms were empty, same with the bathrooms. I called her name again and checked the spare bedroom. Nothing.

I was getting worried.

I was about to close the door to the spare bedroom when for no reason I walked over to the far window and looked out.

Claire stood alone deep in the backyard with her back to the house, out by the gazebo. With the woods and swirling white stuff, she looked like a hooded figurine inside a snow globe.

I was relieved and was about to join her when I stopped and returned to the window, drawn for some reason to her footprints in the snow. The gazebo was about seventy-five away from the house, the window providing me with an elevated view of the trail she'd left. Her footprints led to the gazebo and then veered to the left twenty feet or so, stopping in front of a dogwood tree. The snow was flattened in this area, suggesting she'd moved around some. Her footprints then led to a nearby dogwood where there was more flattening. She stood there now in silent vigil, head bowed.

Claire's footprints spoke to me. They connected the two flowering dogwoods she'd planted last fall, the ones she'd surprised me with after I'd been away for a weekend. Twin dogwoods planted at a time when she was seeing Simon Trask, a symbolic gift from her lover.

Trask's secret gift was no longer a mystery.

# *Thirty*

I made my way to her. It was quiet, the snow now as soft as baby powder, fluffy and feathery. It sprinkled the nearby woods, making the spidery and bare trees of autumn look fresh and untouched. I didn't see any birds but over to my right I heard some rustling from a thicket, likely a startled squirrel or hare. The blanket of snow made the sounds keener.

Claire had her back to me but turned as I approached. She had a glazed expression, one of pain and sadness. Her makeup was smudged and she had dark hollows under her weary eyes. The end of her nose was red and her lips were chafed. A layer of snow coated the hood and shoulders of her coat.

She smiled weakly and dug her hands deep into her pockets, scrunching her shoulders. Her breath made little clouds in the cold air.

A few minutes passed without either of us speaking.

She looked at the twin dogwoods and broke the silence. "He gave me those." Her breath plumed in the cold air.

"I know," I replied.

Claire looked at me with a bland face, showing neither alarm nor surprise, weary resignation if anything. She simply nodded to herself and lowered her eyes. I'll never forget how frail she looked, the cruel twist of fate leaving her pale and peaked, withered really. With Trask dead, Rachel hanging in the balance, and our marriage adrift in uncharted waters, I wasn't much better off.

Neither of us moved from our spots.

She let out a deep breath and shuddered, her breath ragged. Her eyes got moist and tears began spilling from her eyes. Her shoulders started bobbing.

"Claire, I'm sorry," I said, putting my arm around her shoulder and pulling her near. She leaned against me heavily and rested her head against my chest.

"It's okay," I said quietly, "let it out." She did just that, softly at first and then with her whole body. I rocked and shushed her as she sobbed, holding her close and stroking her back. She trembled against me, her breath warm and moist.

After a while the tears began to subside and she regained control. She pulled some tissues from her coat pocket and blew her nose. She took a couple of deep breaths and tried to blink her eyes clear.

"You all right?" I asked. I reached over and brushed a strand of hair from her forehead. The rims of her eyes were pink from crying.

She looked down and swallowed, bit her lip and nodded.

"Do you want to go inside where it's warm?"

"No," she said, "I want to stay here."

I turned to leave, thinking she wanted to be alone.

Claire surprised me by reaching over and touching my arm. She spoke in halting sentences. "Jack, don't go. Please. Stay with me." Her eyes pleaded with me.

For a moment, I debated what to do, then nodded. I pointed toward the nearby snow-cloaked gazebo, which offered a sanctuary from the falling snow. "Let's sit for a while."

She followed me.

We sat on one of the benches, Claire putting space between us. The wood was cold.

Claire removed her hood and brushed some snow off her coat. She sat on the edge of the bench and rested her hands on her lap. She stared at the floor for a long time.

She raised her head and said, "I need to tell you some things, Jack."

I looked at her, blankly.

"I don't even know where to begin." Her voice was tentative and shaky.

I raised my eyebrows. "Why don't we start with the truth."

She shifted a bit, and I watched as she chased thoughts in her mind, likely wondering where to begin. Finally she said, "I had an affair with Simon Trask. I'm not going to deny it or lie about it, and I'm not going to stand here and blame him for what happened, especially now."

Her lips began quivering and I thought she was going to lose control

273

again, but she didn't. I started moving towards her but she raised a hand, warding me off.

I stayed put.

She continued, "You need to understand something from the start. I didn't get involved with him because of you." Her voice broke.

I interrupted. "Claire, don't do this to yourself now. This isn't the time."

Claire snapped, "Don't tell me what I can or can't do, Jack," anger flashing in her eyes. She stopped in mid-sentence and took hold of herself. "I'm sorry, that wasn't supposed to come out like that." She took a breath, fluttered her hand in the air. "Forgive me, I'm not thinking clearly." Her voice was faint.

I nodded and relaxed a bit. "It's okay," I said.

Claire said, "There are some things I can't dance around any longer."

I didn't argue.

She took a deep breath. "I met him when we lived in Hadley, six years ago. We were at a fall conference in Cape Cod, one you probably don't remember. I was there representing the landscape agency and he was with his property investment firm."

The fact that she met Trask so long ago was a surprise, the first of many. But contrary to what Claire thought, I did remember the conference. That was the weekend I spent alone with Nathan and got drunk, the time he had a nightmare and couldn't find me in the house.

Claire said, "I was alone at the conference, but I wasn't there looking for someone. We happened to meet. He and I attended one of the morning sessions and got to talking afterwards. We sat together for some other programming. He was a nice guy, easy to be with and interesting. After the day was over he asked me out for a drink. He told me straight out he was married and I did the same. One drink led to a few more, and we ended up having dinner together."

She shifted on the bench and looked down, shook her head a little. "I was drinking pretty good back then, trying to blot things out." She looked over at me. "The pool accident happened that summer."

I bristled at the mention of the accident. It stirred old ghosts, made me realize Charlie Ledger was still at work altering our lives. I wondered if he was ever going to loosen his grip.

"I enjoyed the time we shared. We had a lot in common. We talked the night away, had breakfast together the next morning. He was a perfect gentleman. When the conference was over we exchanged phone numbers."

The wind picked up and swirled some snow around in the gazebo.

Claire said, "He called me at work a couple of weeks later and asked me out to lunch. I'd been thinking about him, hoping he'd call. We got together and had a nice time, picked up where we left off. We began seeing each other fairly regularly after that. Sometimes we'd have lunch or coffee, or just meet by the water and talk. We shared a lot and became close. He was someone I trusted, a person I wanted in my life."

I started to say something but decided against it. My mind was racing with a hundred questions.

Claire fell silent. Her eyes narrowed, remembering. When she spoke again her mood had changed. "As much as I liked him, deep down inside I knew things weren't kosher. The fact I never told you about him was a red flag, I should have known that from the start. The friendship lines were blurring. I was attracted to him and started feeling guilty about my feelings. I liked him too much. As much as I enjoyed being with him, I knew I was getting in over my head, knew things couldn't continue. I told him how I felt and he was crushed, said he'd do anything to salvage the friendship. He'd grown just as attached to me."

I watched as she fell into her thoughts.

"We attempted talking things through, even tried cooling our heels for a while. But I knew we were kidding ourselves, still playing with fire. In the end, we decided on a clean break. We knew any kind of contact would rekindle what we were trying to put out. We promised each other no contact, no letters or phone calls. Nothing. It was harder that way but the only realistic way. That was about the time I quit my landscaping job in Northampton and decided to stay home."

I swallowed hard and looked away. I knew none of this at the time, thought the only reason for her quitting was to spend more time with Nathan. Of course, what did I know? I was shrink-wrapped in my own little world of booze and oblivion.

Claire and I sat there for a little while watching the snowflakes. It had started to let up, the sky not nearly as dark. The flakes were getting larger.

She continued: "When we moved to Spencer Plain I never expected to see him again. The years passed and we honored our promise. I always wondered what happened to him. As fate would have it, we were thrown together at Cromwell Pointe last year. He had property up there and I was involved with the landscaping project. I was totally shocked to see him and tried avoiding him. He did the same. It worked for a while, but it wasn't a long term solution. We started talking one day and the gates flew open. I realized how much I'd missed his company. He told me he'd never stopped thinking about me."

My stomach soured and I could feel my jaw tighten with anger.

She chewed her lip while absently tugging at her coat sleeve. "We broke our promise and began spending time together last fall. We both knew from the beginning we couldn't keep our feelings at arm's length, didn't even try." Her voice tapered off. "We slept together."

The piece of the puzzle leading up to the hidden emails locked into place. I was no longer in the dark about how things started.

Her eyes moved away from mine. "Don't ask me why I did it. I've asked myself the same question over and over, why I was willing to risk everything." She paused and looked beyond me. "I had a wonderful husband and son, a great job, a beautiful home. The things most people dream about. Maybe that was the problem, everything too perfect and predictable. Maybe I needed a break from taking care of everyone else, maybe I was being devoured by the monster of habit. I don't know. What I do know is that Simon came along and ruffled my hair, lifted me up and away. He put passion and excitement in my life. It was crazily stimulating."

My head was swirling. I was trying my hardest to absorb everything and keep still, but I was running out of patience, jealousy and irritation climbing in my throat. I didn't want to hear this. My steamy, lustful fantasies of Claire screwing another guy vaporized, replaced by sizzling jealousy and anger.

"We spent a lot of time together in Cromwell, sometimes just talking for hours. He never got tired of listening." She let out a long sigh. "One day we went away to Rhode Island and talked nonstop the whole time."

And just like that I lost it. I raised my voice and cut her off. "Do me a favor and can the rest, will you? I know all about your escapades in Newport."

Claire stiffened. "How?"

"I found your emails. The ones you hid in the attic, the ones you thought you'd recovered." I stared at her for a long while, could see the surprise on her face. She looked away, then nodded solemnly.

The minutes passed.

I regretted coming on so strong almost as soon as the words left my mouth. I realized she was under immense strain and torn up inside.

I did some backpedaling and softened my demeanor. "Claire, I know you've been through a lot. I feel terrible about what happened. That's why I came home in the first place and why I'm out here with you."

I took a deep breath and let it out slowly. "I just can't handle hearing any more about the two of you, at least not now. I'm sorry. I don't need to know the rest."

I stood up and walked to the other side of the gazebo, my back turned to her.

"That's where you're wrong, Jack," she said. You do need to know the rest."

I turned around, my eyes giving her a searching look. "Why?"

She spoke in a thin, reedy voice. "Because Rachel Pond caught us."

EVERYTHING SLIPPED INTO SLOW MOTION. I STOOD THERE staring at her, not knowing what to say. I folded my arms, shoulders drooping. I stared at her in disbelief. "You've got to be kidding."

Her face grew taut and her mouth tightened. "There's nothing to kid about here, Jack."

It took me a moment to calm down. "Tell me what happened," I said.

"One of Rachel's friends spotted us when we were in Newport and couldn't tell her fast enough. Rachel followed Simon to Cromwell a few days later and saw us together. She waited until he got home that night and confronted him. Basically told him to break it off or pack his bags."

I slowly sat down on a bench opposite Claire, felt like I was in a trance.

She took a deep breath. "He came to see me the next day and delivered the news. We ended it, and that was the last time I saw him."

I couldn't think straight.

Claire looked at me and said softly, "I'm sorry, Jack. About everything."

I held her eyes for a moment then glanced away.

Finally I said, "Why didn't you tell me his wife was taking my course?" My voice climbed the ladder. "Claire, how could you do this to me? The three of you knew what was going on and left me in the dark. When were you planning on letting me know?"

"I didn't know she was in your course, Simon didn't know either. Honest. He found out by accident two or three weeks ago when he came across a paper from your class. She'd left it out on a desk. He gave me a heads-up that day." As an afterthought she said, "He never told Rachel he saw the paper."

"He called you?"

She nodded. "At the agency. It was the first contact we've had in a year. I was uncomfortable talking with him at my desk so I had him call my cell when I left the office. I didn't want Rachel seeing my number on his cell so I called him from a pay phone when I was heading home."

My mind jumped and dredged up the night I followed her home. *The phone call by the water.*

I said, "How could Trask not know his wife was at Guilford?

Claire looked at me and said, "Simple, she's financially independent and takes care of her own bills. She's quite wealthy. All Simon knew was that she was taking a couple of classes, something she'd been doing for the last five years at several other colleges in the area. The two of them lead very independent lives, always heading in different directions."

She continued. "Rachel knew you were a professor at Guilford, Simon told her that a while ago. Why she chose to take a course with you now is anyone's guess. He thought it might be to spite him, get even with me or just toy with you."

"So she's been sitting in my class with a hidden agenda, an axe to grind."

Claire nodded. "Something like that."

"Bullshit," I spat. "I don't believe it."

Claire looked away. "She has a nasty side, Jack. She's an angry woman."

I shook my head, amused. "She has a right to be."

Claire started jiggling her foot again. "I know that. She was nonstop with ugly emails to me, calling me every name in the book and threatening me should I ever have contact with her husband again. They used to pile up in my computer mailbox. After a while I wouldn't even open them, I'd just hit the delete key.

And later delete your cache, I thought.

I shifted on the bench. I could understand Rachel's anger toward Claire and Trask, but had difficulty seeing the piece directed at me. I refused to believe Rachel's relationship with me was driven by twisted motives, that she was trying to draw me into some kind of crossfire. This was not the Rachel Pond I knew. Call me naïve or thick-headed, but I even believed an explanation existed for the letter sent to Chadwick. All I needed was some time with her once she recovered and got back on her feet. I felt certain she could explain everything.

This prompted me to reach in my pocket, feel for my cell. I realized I still hadn't heard from Lois, didn't know how Rachel was doing. I made sure the ringer was switched on.

I looked at Claire. "All right, so you found out she's attending Guilford. What did you and Trask do about it?"

She turned both palms up. "Realistically, what could we do? What could anyone do? We obviously couldn't stop her. Since she didn't know we were on to her we decided to play possum. Simon followed her around, trailed her on campus a couple of times."

She added sheepishly, "I did the same."

So that's how Cy found Claire in the parking lot, I thought. No wonder I couldn't figure out why she was there. *She was snooping on Rachel, not me.*

I stood up again and shook my head, spread my arms. "Damn it, Claire, why didn't you just come out and tell me?"

She looked me square in the eye, then smirked. "And when was I going to do that, Jack? Before you asked Rachel out on your secret little date at the Mohegan Sun or after?"

I shifted uncomfortably on my feet, lowered my eyes. A wave of guilt washed over me, nourished by a defenseless double standard.

Claire said, "I like Cy, but tell him he's a lousy liar. I knew you weren't going with him anyway, could feel it in my gut. My intuition kicked in when we were talking about Rachel the other night."

"I was that obvious?"

She shook her head. "No, you were that blasé. Too cool and laid back."

"I suppose Trask knew we were going, too."

She nodded. "He was there all night at the casino, followed her home."

Claire looked at me with a crooked smile on her face.

"What?" I said.

"I didn't want you taking her, Jack. The night before the game, I did everything I could think of to keep you home, from the bathtub to the bedroom." She sighed. "All I had to show for it the next day was a four-star hangover and a razor rash the size of Hartford."

We both smiled weakly.

More silence. We watched a bright red cardinal fly past the gazebo and perch on one of the dogwoods. Behind us a muffled clump of snow fell from a tree. The air had warmed and the snow had stopped, just as predicted. It would probably melt by the end of the day.

Claire drew her legs up to her chest and wrapped her arms around them, resting her head on her knees. She sniffed a few times and her eyes got moist. I watched as a single tear worked its way from the corner of her eye and down the length of her nose, suspending itself for a few seconds before dropping to the floor. I felt a chord of sadness for her.

I went over and reached for her hand. She took it and I drew her into my arms, holding her tight. She stiffened at first, then hung her arms around my waist. Her body seemed so small and fragile.

We left the gazebo and headed for the house, leaving behind a fresh set of footprints. We stopped for a moment when the sun broke through the clouds, making the woods around us shimmer and the snow brilliant. It looked like a painting.

I turned toward Claire, who was shielding her eyes from the glare. In the bright sunlight her face looked even more tired and worn.

I studied her, letting out a long breath. "Tell me one thing."

She tilted her chin upwards, found my eyes, and waited.

"Why?" I asked.

She held my eyes, pained, and said, "Because I was foolish, because I made a mistake."

"No," I replied, "why didn't you just take off with him?"

"Because I never stopped loving you," she said, almost in a whisper.

WE STOOD JUST INSIDE THE DOORWAY KICKING snow from our shoes when my cell phone rang. When I glanced down I saw an unfamiliar number on the display. It was Lois, keeping her promise and giving me an update on Rachel. It seemed like ages ago that Lois sat in my office, delivering the news.

I spoke with Lois, Claire standing with her head half turned away, looking at me sideways. It was a short conversation, no more than a minute or two. I thanked her and pressed off, placing the cell on a nearby table.

Claire came over and stood by me.

"That was about Rachel," I said, my voice sounding distant and hollow.

Claire grew very still.

"She died from her injuries about an hour ago."

I left the room, wanting to be alone.

# *Thirty-one*

The package Rachel mailed before leaving for New Hampshire was waiting at the campus post office the next afternoon. It was one of those white, custom shipping boxes, the kind you buy at specialty mailing stores. The package was a little larger than book size and addressed to me in Rachel's handwriting, which I'd grown to recognize. The package wasn't very heavy and when I shook it, nothing moved around inside.

As eager as I was to discover what it was, I didn't want to open it at the college. Instead, I decided to head for Stony Creek, a small and peaceful shoreline village not too far from the college. I needed to gather my wits and wanted no distractions, particularly since I didn't know what I'd find inside the box. I knew I had to brace for the possibility of something connected to Claire and Trask, maybe some photographs or a videotape.

I hoped a letter accompanied whatever was sent.

The day was cold with a light rain falling, a return to a raw, silver November in Connecticut. Traffic moved along at a pretty good clip. As I drove south, my mind wandered to yesterday. At our request, Forrest's mother agreed to keep Nathan overnight so that Claire and I could be together. We spent the day stunned and disturbed, speaking in unsteady voices, listening and comforting as best we could.

I was really frazzled. There was only so much I could say or do for Claire, the exposed betrayals and secrets leaving me tentative and distant. I was staggered by Rachel's death and could only imagine Claire's pain. As the day wore on she retreated more and more into herself.

It was difficult watching Claire because I knew she suffered alone. It struck me how most survivors of a clandestine relationship are at best, an afterthought. Their tears are silent and their respects go unpaid, their presence neither welcome nor wanted. Some are shunned and others scorned, painful reminders that they never belonged and their feelings don't much matter. Forbidden passion can have a cruel, final twist.

Yesterday dragged. By late afternoon we were emotionally exhausted and mentally spent. We tried walking around the block but the exercise and fresh air did little to clear our heads. We reheated a casserole for dinner but only picked at it. Claire went to bed early and I drank away the evening. I thought about Rachel and got sad all over again. I relived our night together at the Mohegan Sun, and I regretted not calling her back on Friday and saying goodbye. She died leaving so many loose ends.

Claire and I slept poorly, both of us getting up at the first gray light of day. We were in no better spirits and made half-hearted attempts at breakfast conversation. Claire still had a faraway look in her eye and I struggled with another nasty headache. I felt restless and agitated, my patience paper thin with everything. We agreed going to work was better than the alternative. I was glad to get out of the house.

Grieving was going to take a while. I could only hope that the pain would lessen and life in the Elliot household would return to normal.

I CAME TO A STOP SIGN JUST ABOVE Stony Creek and saw a small liquor store across the street. Motrin hadn't put a dent in my headache and I thought about snagging a bracer to take to the village, maybe a couple of beers or wine coolers. I looked at the store then at Rachel's package sitting on the passenger's seat, then back at the store. I did this a few more times, back and forth. I pulled away from the stop sign and continued driving.

I needed to be clear headed.

The wooded road looped its way into the village and Long Island Sound opened before me, big and captivating, even on an overcast day. The main street was narrow and cramped, a few small restaurants and shops mingling with New England clapboards, lots of boats in dry dock. Several wooden docks extended into the water, a few guys working out there in yellow foul weather gear. Parking is next to impossible during the summer but I had my pick today, the village desolate but peaceful. I pulled into a spot looking out at the Sound and the Thimble Islands.

Hundreds of rocks make up the Thimble Islands, many pink granite, reminding me of the Maine coastline. Most of the islands are small, but stately summer homes have been built on the larger ones, most without heating, electricity, or running water. The homes are largely from the Victorian era, complete with gingerbread trimmings, widow walks, and gazebos on postage stamp size lawns, creating a sort of doll house illusion. During the summer, commercial launches connect the islands, ferrying people, groceries and other supplies. The whole scene is a throwback to another era. Legend has it the pirate Captain Kidd's treasures remain buried somewhere out there.

For a little while I just sat there staring out at the water. The rain had stopped and a light mist blanketed the harbor. The houses I could see were dark and quiet, asleep for the winter and bled dry of color. A fog horn sounded somewhere in the distance.

The surrounding lull and calmness were worth the drive, I decided.

I reached over for the package and put it on my lap. I got a Swiss army knife from the glove compartment and sliced open the sealing tape. Once I removed the bubble wrap, I saw an envelope with 'Jack" handwritten across the front. I felt my heart skip. Underneath the envelope was something bundled and sealed in more bubble wrap, the contents obscured. I removed the letter and left the bundle where it was, putting the box back on the passenger's seat.

I found my reading glasses from an inside pocket and removed the letter from the envelope. It was rather thick, blue ink on ivory parchment stationery. The paper was embossed with Rachel's monogram at the top. I unfolded the letter and stared at it for a few moments, admiring her strong, flowing script. Rachel had beautiful, expressive handwriting, characters perfectly formed.

The fact that she'd never write again was unsettling, the letter representing a solemn, spiritual connection to the other side. I touched the letter with my fingers and traced some of the words. I wanted to be where her hand had been. I brought the letter to my nose searching for a scent but found none.

The date and time in the upper right hand corner indicated she'd written the letter Friday, the day after we went to the casino and before she left for New Hampshire. She'd begun writing the letter early in the morning. I began reading slowly, wanting to take my time.

*Dear Jack,*

*This is a difficult letter to write and one I've been postponing for a while now.*

*I've been less than honest with you and can no longer live behind a veil of dishonesty and deception. The intent of this letter is neither vindictive nor malevolent. Rather, its purpose is to explain how our lives came to intersect over the past few months.*

*The truth is rarely simple and must be told from the beginning. I am Simon Trask's wife and about a year ago I discovered his involvement with your wife, Claire. I am not sure how much you know about their relationship, but do know it is not my place to share. Such matters rest with the two of you and under your roof.*

*I will share, though, how much the discovery devastated me. Of all the things that can go wrong in a marriage, I never thought my husband would be dishonest and unfaithful. I trusted him and never had any reason to doubt his word. Our marriage was a happy one, full of vibrancy and warmth, or at least that's what I thought.*

*My world was turned upside down and I fell into a deep, black hole. I was miserable and depressed. My ego and self-worth were shattered. I was full of self-criticism and embarrassed that everyone would know. I didn't want to see my friends and became a recluse. I stayed home all day. I lost interest in everything.*

*I became an angry, sullen woman. I'd start fights with Simon and nitpicked everything he did. When I wasn't snarling at him it seemed like I was storming out of a room or giving him the cold shoulder. Of course he was into playing the 'perfect husband,' which only angered me more. He couldn't do enough for me. He was constantly at my beck and call, telling me over and over how much he loved me.*

*Forgiveness wasn't a word in my vocabulary.*

*When I wasn't angry at Simon I was upset at Claire for stealing my husband and throwing our marriage into a tailspin. I sent her venomous emails and even threatened her. I made it a point to find out what she looked like and where she worked. I followed her several times in my car.*

*I got caught up in the victim role. I felt betrayed as well as powerless. I didn't think the two of them had any idea how much they'd hurt me. I believed they got off way too easy, that their suffering was nothing compared to mine. I harbored a grudge and wanted to get back at both of them.*

*That's how you fit in, Jack. I'm ashamed to say I devised a twisted plan to use you to get at them. I knew you taught at Guilford so I signed up for your course. You didn't know who I was, and my husband was too busy being on his best behavior to pay any attention to my doings.*

*I had every intention of seducing my way into your life and creating friction. I figured if Simon had screwed around, so could I. In the process, Claire would find out what it was like feeling helpless and hurt. If you didn't take the sexual bait, I was determined to rock the boat any way I could to make life difficult for you and your family.*

*I was as nasty as I was spiteful.*

*The first part of my plan was getting you to notice me. I made sure I submitted quality work and spoke up in class. I knew the readings inside and out. I tittered at your humor, stuck around after class. When I knew I had your attention I began flirting. I'd use a coy smile here, some schoolgirl blushing and giggling there. I knew you liked me right from the beginning.*

*The classroom altercation with Crider was unexpected. I couldn't have staged it any better. When Crider screamed in class that you'd threatened him, I saw my chance. I showed up in your office later that day with coffee and a sympathetic ear, or so it must've seemed to you. In truth I was there only to discover what you'd said to Crider, what set him off. I got what I wanted and left, although I made sure I flirted and bared some flesh on my way out of your office. That night I wrote a letter of complaint to Chadwick with a copy to Whitbourne and mailed it the next day. I wanted to rock your career.*

*I'm not proud of what I did, and you have every right to be upset and disappointed. I take full responsibility for my actions and accept the consequences. I was as deceptive as I was manipulative and will regret writing that letter for the rest of my life. I'm ashamed of myself and can only hope that someday you'll accept my apologies.*

*I've tried making amends. I recently spoke with Dr. Evelyn Chadwick and formally retracted my letter. I told her I was misinformed and guilty of not having any facts to support my claims. I expressed my regret for sending the letter and sent her a written apology. I shared how Crider was a nuisance in other classes and intimidated other faculty members, that you were the only one who had the courage to stand up to him. Lois also sent a letter singing your praises.*

*There were other stirrings beyond the letter to Chadwick, and I must make another confession. Beyond the fakery and ulterior motives, deep down inside I realized I liked you. I was drawn to you, found myself thinking about you all the time. Fitting punishment for the vengeful woman, yes? I could feel a chemistry developing between us, which only added to my confusion and uncertainty about everything. I was a lost soul and realized I was dragging you down with me.*

*I wanted to tell you all of this last night at the casino. I had a speech rehearsed in my head, but for some reason couldn't find the right words or moment. Maybe the moral high ground was steeper than I thought, or maybe I was just too ashamed and embarrassed. Maybe I was flustered and tongue-tied in your company, having you all to myself for an entire evening. Or maybe it was because I knew I'd never see you again.*

I paused, looked up from the letter. It took the last sentence for everything to click. She'd written the letter to bare the truth and clear her conscience, then to say goodbye. I shifted in my seat, sat slightly forward.

*I must leave, Jack. Our paths converged for all the wrong reasons, and my letter of rebuke to Chadwick further complicated matters and spun everything out of control. Bumping into professor Whitbourne last night makes the footing that much more unsteady. I can't do this to you, Jack. I refuse to make your life any more difficult and must find mine. I withdrew from your course today and will not return.*

I looked out at the water and thought of that night, details drifting back. The glimpse of sorrow on her face while we were having a drink, how closely she studied me in the parking garage. Fingers pressed against my heart, then my lips. We would never see each other again.

*I believe things happen in this world for a purpose. Despite the hurtful intent of my letter to Chadwick, it served to bring me to my senses. It was like a symbolic awakening. I remember reading a copy of it not too long after I put it in the mail. I couldn't believe the things I'd written or the course of action I'd chosen. It made me realize how hurtful and vindictive I'd become since my discovery of the affair, even to kind and innocent people like you.*

*The letter made me realize how anger was poisoning me.*

*I knew I needed to start making changes in my life. I had to stop blaming myself for what happened. Simon was the one choosing to involve himself with another partner, not me. While we needed to explore what was happening in our marriage that might have led to the affair, I was shouldering way too much fault.*

*I also needed to forgive him for what he did. If I didn't, I recognized I'd never be able to move past the anger and resentment. I'd remain in the same rut, a woman leading a miserable life.*

*I don't know the role forgiveness plays in your life, Jack. I used to see it as a sign of weakness, giving in or letting someone off the hook. But it's not that at all. Simon isn't getting away with anything. I don't condone what he did nor do I excuse him. But we needed to focus on the healing, not the hurt. Forgiveness is something I needed to do for my own sanity.*

I remembered my boardwalk encounter with Madeline Gilbert and her reminiscences of her marriage. She and her late husband Everett were cut from the same cloth, not holding grudges or ignoring unhealed wounds.

*Of course, forgiveness takes time and requires commitment. As much as Simon hurt me, I realize deep down I still loved him and recognize he feels the same towards me. I know he's remorseful and upset with himself over what happened.*

*We're both committed to preserving our marriage and restoring it the center of our lives. Healing will not be easy, but my hope is that we'll be stronger because of it.*

I looked away for a little while, scanning the dull horizon. She'd found peace in her life before it was taken away. How poetic, I thought. She also had the moral courage to sort out her feelings about us and walked away, protecting two damaged souls from further harm. I read on:

*Fittingly, I draw this letter to a close asking for your forgiveness and understanding. I ask not to be judged too harshly. I am not an evil person, Jack. Rather, I was wounded and confused on so many different levels, trying only to find my way back. With your help, I got pointed in the right direction.*

*I'll miss you and your classes, that special knack you have of weaving creative writing with ordinary life, the special relationships you forge with students. I'll long remember how you took Chiang and Malcolm under your wing and gave Willie the incentive to finish his degree, how you rode to Lo's rescue and became her real life knight in shining armor.*

*Your teaching and writing are rare gifts, your passion for learning contagious. I hope the classroom always remains your home and that you'll use those beautiful hands of yours to craft many more books. You touch so many lives in so many different ways.*

*Take good care of yourself, Jack Elliot. I'll never forget you and the piece of time we shared. Gratitude is the memory of the heart.*

*Fondly,*

*Rachel Pond*

I STARED AT THE LAST PAGE, NOT WANTING the letter to end. I looked back out at the water, drifting away with images of Rachel. The way she tilted her head when she spoke in class, the pale freckles that ran across the bridge of her nose, the soft, honey voice. I thought of the closure captured by the letter, the abrupt finality of the accident. The sorrow of never seeing her again was immense.

I straightened the pages, folded them neatly along the crease and slipped the letter back in the envelope. I tapped the letter against the palm of my hand, my mind miles and miles away.

I don't know how long I sat, not that it mattered. I watched a fishing boat chug into the harbor, six or seven seagulls swooping in its wake. Some seagulls soared high in the sky, floating on wind currents, others dropped down low and skimmed the water's surface. The boat's motor left behind a trail of smoke and soot.

I put the letter back in the box and took up the package.

The bubble wrap was layered and sealed with packing tape. I used the knife to cut through it, unwound the layers. I found a gift wrapped package inside, fancy silver foil paper with blue ribbon and a flattened bow. For some reason I straightened and fluffed the bow before unwrapping everything. Inside was a plain white box containing a book.

I lifted the book from the box and my breath was literally swept away.

It was a first edition copy of Bernard Malamud's *The Natural*, published in 1952. It looked brand new, complete with the original dust jacket. I held it delicately in my hands for a few minutes, absorbing its importance and beauty. I sucked in a breath when I opened the cover, for there in the upper right was Malamud's signature in bold, black ink. I was holding a rare book, easily worth hundreds if not thousands of dollars. I'd later discover my initial appraisal was slightly off. The book was valued at over twelve thousand dollars.

Rachel never bothered to mention the gift in her letter.

A wave of emotion washed over me. The connection of Malamud's book to Rachel and me, as well as to our creative writing course was as tender as it was touching. Bittersweet, in fact. I was overwhelmed by her thoughtfulness and generosity. When she told me on Friday she'd purchased a copy of the book I never in my wildest imagination thought she meant an original, signed edition.

I sat there spellbound, in total awe of what I held in my hands.

I was brought back by a scent I detected in the car. Not an old book smell, which was quite apparent, but something fresh and distinct.

I tilted my head and lightly sniffed the air. It was a woodsy fragrance, lily of the valley if I wasn't mistaken.

It was Rachel.

I sniffed the gift wrap and the ribbon, then the tissue paper. The scent wasn't there. I again brought the envelope and letter to my nose. Nothing there.

Was I imagining her presence? I've been told that pining for a scent often accompanies grieving. A minute went by and I detected it again. This time I was certain of it.

It had to be coming from inside the book; there were no other possibilities. I checked under the dust jacket, inside the end pages. Nothing. I carefully fanned the pages with my thumb. More nothing.

288

I was frustrated and about to give up when I decided to fan the pages one more time.

This time I was rewarded.

A ribbon bookmark was tucked inside a page. I brought the book closer and inhaled the scent on the ribbon. It was unmistakenly her fragrance, dizzying me for a second.

It was if she had reached out and touched me.

I rested the book against the steering wheel and studied the opened pages.

The ribbon was cut shorter than the trim size of the book so that it lay hidden when closed. No wonder I couldn't see it. She'd placed the ribbon sideways so that it was positioned directly underneath a quote:

*'We have two lives ... the life we learn with and the life we live with after that. Suffering is what brings us toward happiness.'*

I smiled sadly and slowly traced my fingertip back and forth along the ribbon. I should've known where to look. Rachel had of course shared that quote with me just before she left.

She wanted me to remember.

My eyes began to well, not just from the quote but the ribbon she chose. It was pale blue, the same shade as her eyes. Eyes like blue ice chips. Eyes that sparkled and danced, eyes that held the truth and bore forgiveness.

I kept the ribbon in place and slowly closed the book. I rested both of my hands on it for a few seconds.

After a few moments I turned in the seat and put the book back in the box, then placed Rachel's letter on top. I started the car and pushed the defroster switch to defog the windows. When the windshield cleared I stared straight ahead at the harbor fog making its way toward me.

My eyes misted. I brought my forefinger and thumb together and followed the contours of both lower eyelids to the bridge of my nose, swiping the moisture away and clearing my vision. I straightened and fastened my seatbelt.

It was time to go home.

# *Thirty-two*

The snowstorm that struck the Connecticut shoreline before Thanksgiving was a warning of things to come. New Englanders were forced to brave a winter that roared in like a lion and left untamed. Old-timers said it was a humdinger, the snow and teeth-chattering temperatures rivaling winters of bygone eras. Even on relatively calm days, the sun made it a habit of hiding behind clouds in the steely-gray skies, creating strings of depressing, gloomy days. People were cooped up and moody, the dreariness of the weather mirroring their darkness.

We got smacked by two especially nasty storms, both creating states of emergency and shutting down airports, industries and schools for days. The first was an ice storm that struck just after Christmas, freezing power lines, major highways and bridges. Thousands were left without heat, unable to venture from their homes because the roads were too treacherous. The second was a 'classic Nor'easter' in January, a blizzard that dumped three feet of snow over a two-day period. High winds combined with the snowfall to create drifting and dangerous conditions, including flooding when the stuff finally melted.

I'm not a big fan of winter, less so as I've gotten older. I'm not the hardy, outdoorsy type who enjoys snapping on the cross country skies at the first sign of snow, stacking firewood or frolicking in waist-high snow banks with my dog. Snow may be great for kids but I consider it as much a nuisance as an annoyance. I get depressed when I receive my heating bills, curse potholes with a vengeance and want to reach for a shotgun whenever I hear the incessant beeping of snowplows. I hate eggnog and cuddling under goose down, and as far as I'm concerned, Jack Frost nips in all the wrong places.

Spring couldn't come fast enough for me. It wouldn't be long before the days got longer and warmer, and gentle, cleansing rains would be turning everything green. I could feel Spencer Plain yawning and beginning to stretch from its long winter nap. Purple crocus would soon crack open the ground, daffodils not far behind, and flowers would be budding on pussy willows and forsythia. Robins would be pulling at worms, woodpeckers drumming the trees, peep frogs serenading the night. Nurseries and greenhouses would be setting out Easter lilies and hydrangeas, tulips and pansies. Coffee chatter at the office would shift from politics to the Sox, Frisbees would fly in the air, skateboards would rule the sidewalks, and ice cream trucks would be coming out of hibernation.

I could smell spring in the air. Bone chilling days would soon be a memory, dingy skies and dirty slush put on hold for at least for another year. Puffy clouds and blue skies were making a comeback, the air fresh and crisp. It seemed like everyone's spirits were rising with the mercury.

IN A PERFECT WORLD, HUSBAND AND wife ride off into the sunset and live happily ever after. Loyalty is unflinching, partners steadfast and true. No problem is insurmountable, no issue too difficult. When storm clouds gather, love provides sweethearts with the spiritual strength and guiding light necessary to triumph.

If only it were true. People aren't perfect and neither are relationships. Most marriages come with blemishes and flaws and aren't manufactured in heaven. For every prosperous marriage there's one tumbling to earth with a resounding thud, partners beating a hasty retreat in opposite directions. Even those looking normal can be wobbly, husband and wife having learned to ignore what ails them and live an empty shell existence.

Relationships are not maintenance free nor designed to run on cruise control. Every so often, it pays to look under the hood and see how things are running. When damage has been ignored or hidden, repairs don't come cheap, especially when trust has fizzled. There are no universal parts for betrayals of the heart, no push button solutions. Those couples wanting a second chance must be willing to hunker down for the long haul, roll up their sleeves and face the music.

Couples like us.

Claire and I knew we were in trouble and couldn't tackle things alone. We asked around and got the name of a therapist, Dr. Emily Winterberry, supposedly a hot shot marriage counselor practicing in Niantic, a small seashore town not too far away. It took a few weeks to get in and see her because of a waiting list, but she was worth the wait, a no nonsense clinician who cut right through the baloney. Winterberry was in her fifties and had a kind face with dark green eyes, dimpled cheeks and chin. She wore her thick silver hair pulled back in a bun, dressed on the casual side, and had one of those warm, therapeutic smiles. Her office overlooked a large bay and was tastefully decorated with stylish Ikea furniture. It had a fresh, sage and citrus scent. Between the prime office location and sleek furniture, not to mention a waiting list of clients, it looked like Winterberry was chipping out a nice living.

Nathan wasn't part of the therapy, at least not in the early going. While he knew we were having difficulty coping with the loss of friends, that's all we shared. His knowledge of Trask and Rachel was nonexistent and we chose not to complicate his life any more than necessary.

In the beginning Claire and I spent time exploring how things came undone. Such was a complicated tale to tell, causing Winterberry to hoist her eyebrows and widen her eyes more than once. Let's face it, our problem wasn't that of your typical unfaithful spouse. Claire had been involved with Trask not once but twice, but hadn't seen him for a year. I'd snooped and played private investigator, seizing opportunities to trail both Claire and Trask. Rachel was added to the mix and her whereabouts were in turn monitored by Claire and Trask. Throw in my misguided longings for the bottle as well as for Rachel and that pretty much covered everything, with the exception of Rachel and her husband perishing in a tragic car crash.

'Fascinating dynamics,' Winterberry said repeatedly in a clinical voice, softly clucking her tongue and occasionally jotting notes in a worn spiral pad. I often wondered what she was really thinking behind the professional facade. Even my hair was curling once we got everything out on the table, convinced that our marriage was a burning vessel and we were candidates for the loony bin.

We saw Winterberry on a weekly basis. Under her watchful eye we dug in and went to task, lowering our shields and baring our souls. As we gathered steam we griped and growled, sparred and sulked. It wasn't always pretty.

Sometimes Claire would cut in on me, other times I shouted over her. Once in a while she hissed and I snorted. Winterberry prodded and channeled, summarized and crystallized. When we weren't expressing annoyance we looked at each other with empty eyes, sometimes swapping refrigerator smiles. More than once we skipped a beat and just stared out the window, watching dust particles float in the slanting winter sun.

Spilling your guts is hard work. I'd often come home hollow and spent, wondering if we had the resources to survive, the resiliency to ever turn the corner. There was an underlying sadness to it all, a recognition that things couldn't go back to the way they were before. Winterberry pointed out we were grieving the loss of old ways, innocence more than anything. Betrayals are costly mistakes, she said, ruffling partners' routines and comfort zones, leaving behind guardedness and skepticism, caution and suspicion. Such protective walls do not get torn down overnight.

We spent lots of time talking about Claire's relationship with Trask. While Claire blamed herself for the affair and downplayed my role, Winterberry wasn't so quick to pass me over. After all, she pointed out, Claire had been willing to give up her relationship with me to be with him. We talked about infidelity's pushes and pulls, how Trask likely supplied Claire with what was running in short supply at home. I remembered the things Claire had shared about Trask, his sympathetic ear and appreciative eye for example. It was difficult sitting there and learning about the romance and spontaneity they shared.

I thought of the rust we'd gathered over the years, the comfort of routine and habit making our marriage predictable and bland. Claire was right, we had the things most people dreamed about but our marriage had gone flat, the two of us slowly drifting apart. It reminded me of the anecdote of the middle-aged couple sitting at the breakfast table. They were sipping coffee, reading the morning newspaper. The husband, out of the blue, lowered his paper, and with a puzzled expression on his face asked, 'When did you get reading glasses?' The wife looked at him and replied, 'About five years ago.' 'By the way,' she asked, 'when did you go bald?'

We'd drifted and gotten lazy, lost the old spark. We both wanted it back.

To her credit, Claire never dodged or ducked. She expressed regret and remorse for what she'd done, took full ownership of the deception and lies she'd spun. She knew her choices disappointed me and that it would take time for me to trust her again. She could've easily pinned the blame or whatever else she wanted to on Trask, and I never would've known the difference, but she didn't. She'd chosen to be truthful ever since that fateful, snowy day in the gazebo.

She even confessed why the emails were hidden in the attic. From the very beginning I never understood why she'd hang on to something so incriminating, why she'd be willing to put herself at risk. When Winterberry asked about it one snowy afternoon in January Claire's face reddened, then fell. She admitted getting sentimental and stashing the emails away like a diary, perhaps wanting to reread them in years to come. Winterberry said this was not an uncommon practice among women especially, clinging to romantic keepsakes. She added some women never let go of anything attached to a meaningful relationship.

And if it weren't for a hungry mouse, I probably never would've known.

In the end, it was Rachel who showed us the way. I shared her letter with Claire and we chose to discuss it in therapy. It was eerie and a bit unnerving sharing a letter that connected four lives, especially since she and Trask were gone, but her words were like a beacon. Rachel was right, mending was not possible without forgiveness. I realized that if we were ever going to regain control we had to move past the damage and focus on the future. The fact that Rachel had forgiven her husband was the nudge I needed.

But that didn't mean our work was finished. Other issues needed to be addressed.

We realized the road to recovery and forgiveness stretched back to the swimming pool tragedy. Our tailspin began with the death of Charlie Ledger and we never got things squared away like we should have. Rather than locking arms and digging in our heels when our world came crashing down, Claire and I ducked for cover and chose separate escape routes. I began my descent into a bottle trapped in my own private nightmares while Claire was driven--or drawn--into Trask's arms. We became strangers under the same roof, two lost souls suffering alone. Although we received some family therapy before moving to Connecticut, darkness still prowled below. We knew we needed to catch up with all our demons, past and present, and put them to rest once and for all.

And that included Nathan, who had kept his pain so deeply shuttered that it went undetected for years. But the past would find him, fittingly, where it all began.

IN FEBRUARY THE FAMILY WAS IN HADLEY AT A Mexican restaurant called

*Fiddlers*, munching on nacho chips and dip along with some baked jalapeno poppers. *Fiddlers* was where Claire and I met a number of years ago when we were students at UMass. The same Aztec murals covered white stucco walls, with sombreros, serape blankets and wooden art stuck in between. The charbroiled aroma of chiles, peppery sauces and tortillas wafting from the kitchen was intoxicating, just as we remembered it.

We were here more or less spur of the moment. It was President's Day and I'd been scheduled to attend a morning writer's symposium at UMass. At the last minute, Claire and Nathan decided to tag along. They were off for the holiday and didn't want to stay holed up in the house all day, the winter blahs getting to them like everyone else. I was delighted to have the company.

We decided to make a day out of it. Claire dropped me off at the university for the morning and went shopping with Nathan in a nearby mall, stopping first at *Field of Dreams* to say hello to some old landscaping buddies. Afterwards the three of us had lunch in downtown Amherst before strolling through the town's shops and boutiques. We spent the rest of the afternoon driving around nearby Hadley. We hadn't been back to our old neighborhood since moving to Connecticut.

We revisited our old stomping grounds: Nathan's elementary school and playgrounds, a public park where we attended summer concerts, a pond where we liked to picnic and feed the ducks. Not much had changed, maybe an occasional new road or housing development, a few new stores here and there. Lots of farm land and wooded acres remained, keeping Hadley rustic and peaceful.

We decided to swing by and see our old house. As we approached, I slowed the car and we gawked like the out-of-towners we'd become. The place looked neat and tidy, although it was hard to tell with all the snow they'd gotten up here. Icicles hung from the gutter and smoke curled from the chimney, a couple of toboggans were leaning against the side of the garage. Two large snowmen stood side by side on the front lawn and waved to us with tree limb arms. A warm memory of years gone by raced through my mind, the three of us bundled in mittens and scarves playing in the snow, red-cheeked and happy.

As we drove by the house, the swimming pool peeked at us from the backyard. We looked but didn't speak. Another memory caught up to me, this one not so warm, one of EMT vehicles and police cruisers jammed crazily in the driveway, panic and confusion out by the pool. I looked in the rearview mirror at Nathan, who had turned away from the window and straightened in his seat. He caught my glance but slid his eyes away from mine. I nudged the accelerator, looping around the neighborhood before making our way back into town.

THE WAITRESS BROUGHT OUR DINNERS to the booth, big platters of enchiladas, tostadas and fajitas. We ordered another round of drinks before she left, soda for Nathan and me, and ice water for Claire. I was drinking non-alcoholic beverages these days, having stayed away from the sauce close to three months. I was not missing the booze nearly as much as I thought I would. I certainly didn't miss the brutal hangovers and cloudy thinking the next day.

The food was delicious and there was plenty of it. For a while we got quiet and tended to the business of feeding our faces, every so often stealing from each other's plates. The waitress returned with our drinks, leaving cans of soda and glasses while taking away the empties. Nathan and I drank straight from the can.

I looked at the two of them sitting across from me, Nathan on the inside. "You two glad you tagged along?"

Both nodded, chewing their food.

After a moment Claire said, "It's been a great day, a nice break. Thanks for bringing us."

I looked at Nathan. "Were things like you remembered?"

He thought about it. "Different," he said, "for some reason smaller."

I smiled. "Childhood has a way of doing that. Reminds me of what a Russian novelist once said, Paustovsky I believe. When we were kids everything somehow seemed more vivid. The sun seemed brighter, the thunder louder, the grass taller."

Nathan nodded and lowered his head, took a big bite from his chicken fajita. I stole a glance at him when he wasn't looking. He was turning into a handsome kid, especially since his braces had been removed last month. He'd put some weight on this winter and was also starting to fill out, no doubt helped by Chiang's fitness program and martial arts training. Chiang had taken both he and Forrest under his wing, meeting with them on a weekly basis in a local fitness center and teaching them self-defense skills. Bullies no longer existed in any of our lives, and Chiang became something of a celebrity in the Elliot family.

When he visited, Chiang was always welcomed with open arms, but Claire insisted that he not smoke cigarettes in the house. When he snuck one or two outside, Claire always chided him—good naturedly of course--for setting a bad example for Nathan and Forrest. She eventually convinced him to protect his own health and ditch the cancer sticks for good.

Our eating slowed down. We gabbed about the day, places we saw, people we remembered. The conversation was light and upbeat.

At one point Claire said, "I'm glad we got to drive by the house and see the old neighborhood."

"Me too," I replied. "We spent some good years up here."

I darted a look at some people being seated a few tables away from us, two younger couples, attractive and well dressed. The place had gotten quite busy since we arrived.

Out of nowhere Claire said, "I noticed we all got quiet when we went by the swimming pool."

I nodded my head. Nathan looked away, said nothing.

We stopped picking at our food.

The comment surprised me, and I debated how to reply. "It's hard not thinking about what happened, even after all these years," I finally said.

Nathan looked at me.

"Right?" I said, meeting his eyes.

He seemed surprised that the focus had shifted his way. He shrugged, ignoring the question.

My eyes shifted to Claire. "What happened will never go away, you know that."

"I know," she replied. "I just thought it would get easier over time."

I let out a sigh. "So did I, Claire. Somehow I thought today would be different, that all our good memories up here would overshadow the bad."

Nathan nodded but remained silent, head slumped.

The waitress came and began clearing the table. We passed on dessert but Claire and I ordered coffee. We had a long drive ahead of us.

I would always think about where I went next with the conversation, wondering if I should've opened my mouth or bitten my tongue. I chose the former, thinking I'd been presented with an opportunity to clear my conscience, get things out in the open.

I started tentatively. "After all this time I thought the guilt would lessen." I looked back and forth at the two of them. "To this day, I think I could've done more for Charlie."

Claire tilted her head and studied me. A few moments passed.

She said soothingly, "Jack, it was an accident. It wasn't anyone's fault, you know that. We talked about this after it happened. You did all you could, we all did."

I took a deep breath and let it out slowly, leaned my arms on the table. "There's something the two of you don't know about the drowning, something I need to get off my chest." I paused for a minute, thinking. "I'm not sure why I've never told you."

Nathan's eyes widened. He stared at my mouth, watching me form the words.

I cleared my voice. "When Charlie fell into the pool that day I dove in to get him and brought him to the surface. That's when I told Nathan to go into the house for help."

Nathan nodded while reaching for the soda can in front of him. He started fiddling with it, and I noticed his fingers were trembling.

"After Nathan left I tried getting Charlie to the shallow end of the pool. When I turned I somehow lost my grip and he sank back down to the bottom. I had to dive down and pull him up all over again." My voice tapered off. "Who knows how things would've turned out if that hadn't happened."

For a little while no one said anything, the words just hanging in the air. Conversations from other tables drifted our way.

Claire finally broke the ice. "Oh, sweetheart," she said, her voice soft and gentle. She reached for my hand, squeezed it. "You can't do this to yourself. There's no way of knowing what might've happened."

She was about to say more when Nathan cut in, spoke over her.

"What do you mean you lost your grip? How could that happen?" He stiffened in his seat and talked rapidly, his voice louder than usual.

I flinched at the outburst, taken back by his questions and tone.

"I don't know," I said.

He must have seen the surprise on my face. "You don't know?" His face darkened and his voice quavered. "You were in charge. None of that was supposed to happen."

I cringed, his words bringing back a sharp sense of helplessness and failure. My stomach started churning.

Claire placed her hand on his arm. "That's enough, Nathan."

He looked at her sharply then slouched back against the seat, again fidgeting with the soda can on his lap.

The silence was longer this time.

I shifted in my seat. "Nathan, I don't know what happened today any more than I did back then. I was scared, I know that much. I probably panicked. Maybe I lost my grip because I was exhausted, or maybe he did something to slip out of my arms."

Nathan looked up, glassy-eyed. He nodded numbly.

I paused a beat then said, "You're right, I was in charge that day." I lowered my voice. "I did the best I could."

I looked over at Claire and shot her a quizzical look, not knowing what else to say. She gave me a quick head shake, one of those 'drop it, we'll talk later,' faces. Hadley had obviously stirred some unpleasant, unresolved memories. We were also tired and touchy.

We skipped the coffee and asked the waitress for our check.

Claire excused herself to use the restroom while I paid at the table with a credit card. I slid out of the booth and waited for Nathan to pull on his jacket. When he stood, something shiny fell from his lap to the floor. I reached down and picked it up, stuck it in his hand.

The metal tab from his soda can.

We both looked at it sitting in the flat of his hand, neither of us saying a word. I watched his fingers tremble. He lifted his head and his eyes slowly met mine, a flicker of recognition passing between us. I looked back down at the metal tab, felt my scalp tingle. Suddenly everything made sense, Nathan's outburst at the table as well as what he'd kept to himself all these years.

My breathing picked up a notch and the walls of the restaurant seemed to shrink around me. Everything stood still. I began recalling details from the swimming pool accident, things I hadn't thought about in years. I saw images of Charlie and Nathan before the drowning. I was watching the two of them from outside the pool fence. I saw Charlie's horseplay off the diving board, the sounds of cannonball splashes mixing with Nathan's squeals of delight and belly laughter. Nathan was holding a can of soda in his hand, unable to contain his excitement. He played with it while watching Charlie's antics, bending the pull tab back and forth, giving his hands something to do. As Charlie approached the diving board for his last dive, he swiped the can from Nathan's hands, unaware of the loosened tab. I watched as Charlie ignored Nathan's protests and raced to the diving board for the fatal plunge, not realizing until now that Nathan had been shouting a warning.

A warning no one heard, including me.

The revelation staggered me. My eyes remained fixed on the soda tab. All this time my son had been waging a private war, an innocent and frightened child held hostage by his own terrifying secret. He'd suffered alone, like me, convinced the drowning was his fault. I ached for him, couldn't help but wonder how this translated into his shyness and anxiety, his loss of interest in sports.

Nathan shifted on his feet. It appeared as if he wanted to say something but caught himself at the last moment, eyes darting away. I wanted to comfort him in the worst way, but was fearful the wrong words would come out of my mouth.

I reached over and took the soda tab from his hand and placed it on the table behind us, then placed my hand on his shoulder. We looked at each other without speaking for several long moments. I pulled him toward me and we hugged, his head briefly resting on my shoulder. We rocked ever so gently.

We pulled away and I gently squeezed his forearm. His eyes never left mine. "Leave it here, Nathan," I said almost in a whisper, "it's okay."

We took a step away from the table. "We'll all be okay," I said reassuringly, a lump gathering in my throat.

Nathan's eyes searched mine for a moment. He nodded.

I felt at that moment a bond of understanding had been forged between us, an alliance based as much on relief as it was on moral absolution.

We'd both set ourselves free.

# Thirty-three

For as long as I've been teaching, I've told myself that if I can make it to spring break, I'll survive the rest of the academic year. I've always viewed the vacation as a watering hole, a chance to catch a breather and recharge my batteries when I need it the most. Not only do I get a respite from lectures but I'm given a chance to catch up on tests or papers that have been hanging over my head, maybe even fiddle with some of my own writing. Since Nathan and Claire's schedules don't jibe with mine, I usually have the house to myself and enjoy the peace and quiet.

A few days ago a letter arrived from the college informing me that I had been granted tenure. The letter contained glowing comments from Bruce Whitbourne and other faculty members, including Cy Rollins. Given the tumultuous events of last fall, I was quite pleased with the news. Whitbourne's academic endorsement and his totally unexpected support regarding my personal predicament prompted me to see him in a different, more favorable light, and Chadwick's stamp of approval on my nomination produced a warm glow and hope for future cooperative academic partnerships. My friendship with Cy, tested under fire, was none the worse for wear. Regarding the dashing, mischievous scamp, no finer friend ever existed in my life.

I learned years ago that college students also can't wait for spring break, but for entirely different reasons. They apparently need a breather from football games, concerts, keg parties, and clubbing so that they can decompress and unwind. While I'm sure there are lots of students doing community service projects and other constructive activities, growing hordes are hopping planes in search of warm climates, sandy beaches, and altered states. Spring break has become a social institution, popularized by shoddy and sleazy television shows like MTV's Spring Break, where rock and rap stars work beach crowds into a frenzy with lascivious antics and borderline talent.

Spring break gives college students a chance to demonstrate the merits of higher education and the knowledge they've gained. They rarely disappoint. Many go on a week-long bender, laying in the sun all day and roaming the streets at night. Mix raging hormones, distilled spirits and a perceived cloak of invulnerability and you've got a freak show worthy of the big top. There's something for everyone, from bared breasts and shucked skivvies to smashed furniture and drunken arrests.

The funny thing is those footing the bill often don't know where their kids are staying, let alone what they're doing, or even worse, with whom. I suppose it's easier for some parents to stick their heads in the sand and pretend everything's peachy. Shame on me for grumbling and being such an old stick in the mud. After all, we're talking about good clean fun during an important college holiday, higher education's pilgrimage to party.

WEDNESDAY ROLLED AROUND AND I'D BEEN proofreading galleys from my latest book all morning. In spite of all the household disruption last fall, the manuscript went into production as scheduled and so far we hadn't hit any glitches. It was a new edition of an existing title, which made the work a little easier, although proofreading galleys is a curse no matter what the book.

I got up and stretched, rolled my shoulders to work out some kinks. Sunlight was streaming through the window and I could hear birds chirping. I went to the front door and stuck my nose outside, realized I was missing out on a beautiful spring day. All work and no play was making Jack a dull boy, especially today. I needed to brush out the cobwebs and enjoy some fresh air, get a little sun on my face. The galleys could wait.

Since it was around noon, I picked up some coffee and a turkey sandwich at a local deli and decided to drive to the boardwalk in Old Lyme. I had returned to the boardwalk several times in the fall after meeting Madeline Gilbert, hoping to bump into her again, but to no avail. Along the way I called Claire on my cell and told her where I'd be, asking her to meet me there with Nathan after school was over. She was working at a site by the school and the three of us had a therapy appointment with Dr. Winterberry later in the afternoon.

Nathan had become part of our therapy shortly after the visit to Hadley. We talked that night on the way home and a few other times before suggesting the prospects of Winterberry lending a hand. Both Claire and I emphasized the merits of consulting a therapist, someone who could listen objectively to each of us and provide feedback and direction. There was no arm twisting on our part to get him to go, nor any adolescent bull headedness from him. I think Nathan found comfort in the fact that he and I were in the same boat, both of us having shaken loose troubling secrets.

Letting yourself off the hook and asking for personal forgiveness are not easy chores, especially when so much time has been allowed to pass. Both Nathan and I felt to a certain degree we were responsible for Charlie's death. Nathan felt if he hadn't wiggled the soda tab free Charlie never would have swallowed it, and I had similar guilt about letting him slip from my arms.

Winterberry listened very carefully to the details we provided. She empathized with our suffering and pain, but was quick to disarm our ownership of the responsibility. She reminded us that it was Charlie, not us, who made poor choices that day. Furthermore, neither of us had deliberately set out to hurt him or force him to take the soda can into the pool.

While we talked about survivor's guilt years ago, Winterberry gave the topic a different spin. She pointed out that in the wake of accidents or tragedies, many of us won't rest easy until we attach some kind of blame or fault. Such is faulty thinking, she said, because many things happen in the world without cause or reason. All of us are vulnerable to such circumstances, even those living absolutely perfect lives. Life is seldom fair and plays cruel tricks, she said.

We also spent a good deal of time talking about secret keeping. I remembered one day in therapy looking around the office, realizing we were a family of secret keepers. The swimming pool tragedy set us in motion, each of us reacting differently and covering our tracks. Claire waltzed off with Trask, Nathan sealed his lips and pulled away, and I did the same while diving for the bottle. On the surface it looked like we'd recovered, but underneath we were a family in pain.

I was right with my assessment last fall: we were the broken bone that healed crooked, functional but impaired.

While our circumstances were unique, Winterberry shared that we were not alone in secret keeping. She told us most families keep secrets. Secrets are normal and sometimes serve important functions, like strengthening the bond between two siblings. However, shockers like ours rumble the very foundation of family life. This is because family members assume they know pretty much everything there is to know about each other, especially with regard to serious matters, and also believe they have a right to know. Anything less is viewed as a betrayal, a breakdown in trust creating distance and suspicion. The more deeply rooted the revelation, the more complex the emotions and the longer healing will take.

The Elliots were learning that first hand.

THE ENTRANCE TO THE OLD LYME BOARDWALK is located at the end of a short, winding road, one canopied by old, high shade trees and graced by handsome colonial homes. Once I got down by the water I steered my car into a small lot at the end of the road. I got out and stretched, drawing the fresh sea air into my lungs. My head cleared almost immediately. I pulled on a blue, lined nylon jacket and slipped a pair of new binoculars around my neck, a Christmas present from Claire.

I locked the car and walked across the lot, deciding to eat lunch before walking. I found an empty bench next to an elderly gent who looked like he was working a crossword puzzle in a folded newspaper. He wore a plaid flannel jacket, baggy trousers and a faded duckbill cap, angled to the side the way old-timers often do. He wore thick eyeglasses that slid down a large, bumpy nose.

We nodded hello to each other as I sat down.

The sun was bright and it took me a minute or two to get used to its reflection off the water. The Connecticut River stretched before me, its current swift and strong. To my left the railroad drawbridge was up, allowing a barge and some fishing boats to pass through. Up river I could see the tall Baldwin Bridge, steady traffic streaming across.

I took my time and ate my sandwich while sipping coffee, enjoying the warm sun on my face. When I was done I collected my litter and stuffed it in a nearby trash container. I headed for the boardwalk but stopped for a minute, taking the plastic protective caps off the binoculars and putting them in my pocket. I brought the binoculars to my eyes and zeroed in on some nearby fishing boats.

From behind I felt a firm hand touch my shoulder. I almost jumped through my skin, then spun around.

It was the old codger from the nearby bench. He'd apparently gotten up to leave right after me and crept up from behind. I hadn't heard him.

He stood there grinning, measuring me up. "Little jumpy today, skipper," he said.

"You shouldn't scare people like that," I blurted, my heart still pounding. "You could give someone a heart attack."

He didn't respond, just kept smiling. He was a little guy, oversized ears matching his nose. He hadn't shaved in a few days.

A mother pushing a stroller approached and I stepped out of the way to let her pass. I turned my attention back to him.

"Did you want something?" I asked.

He furrowed his brows. "You seen any ospreys with those fancy spyglasses of yours?" He reached over and touched the binoculars for effect. I hadn't heard anyone call them spyglasses since my childhood days.

"I haven't," I said.

"Me neither," he said. "Course, I ain't been looking for 'em like you." He laughed out loud—a sputter more than a laugh—sounding as if it had gravel in it. He took off his hat and scratched the top of his head, gesturing with a whiskered chin toward the boardwalk. "Birdwatchers," he said with a smirk. "They're working up a lather because the ospreys are running late." He returned the hat to his head, angled it just so.

I raised my eyebrows at him, amused.

"You'd think the world was coming to an end," he scoffed, shaking his head and sticking his folded newspaper in my hand, for whatever reason. He shuffled away in the direction of the parking lot.

I held the paper and muffled a laugh, watched him leave.

He must've known I was watching because he gave me a little dismissive wave from behind. "They'll get here when they're good and ready," he said over a shoulder. "They'll find their way home."

He kept walking, not waiting for a response.

IT WAS COOLER ON THE BOARDWALK, THE SEA breeze ruffling my hair as I made my way underneath the railroad drawbridge and out into the open. The sun was high in the sky and wispy clouds looked like they'd been brushed across the blue sky. A small, single prop plane floated by, inching its way across

Long Island Sound. The sunlight danced on the water, soft and hypnotic.

Some people were walking along the boardwalk, a few sitting on benches. I stopped for a moment to take in the peacefulness. I really liked this place. The sea grass rustled and whispered in the breeze, seagulls crying and wheeling overhead. The people weren't loud and in a hurry, which added to the serenity of the surroundings.

I worked my way toward the end of the boardwalk and the elevated viewing deck overlooking the marshes and nearby osprey platform. I had hoped to see Madeline, but the viewing deck was empty. Maybe she would come later, I thought, as I stood by the railing and looked out at the water. I raised my binoculars and studied the osprey platform in front of me. The nest was intact but empty. I looked overhead from all directions. Seagulls circled the drawbridge and to my left a small flock of geese honked by. No sign of anything else.

I climbed the wooden staircase to the viewing deck, deciding to stay for a little while. I looked around and saw that the seating was different, a new bench added to one side. When I took a closer look I saw that an engraved rectangular brass plate had been fastened to its back. I hunched over and read:

*Ospreys*
*"They leave us each autumn, a sadness they bring, but buoy our spirits by delivering spring."*

*In memory of Everett and Madeline Gilbert*
*Winter, 2012*

I wouldn't be seeing Madeline Gilbert again. I'd later visit a public library and find her obituary, a small piece in a local newspaper. She contracted pneumonia in December and never recovered, dying soon after from respiratory complications. The obituary said she'd enjoyed a long and successful career as an elementary school teacher in various Connecticut schools before she retired. She and Everett had made their home in Old Cornfield Point, just around the corner from Old Saybrook. The Gilberts were survived by a son, Mason, an architect who made his home in San Diego.

I wasn't sure why her death saddened me so much. I slumped down on the new bench. I used a finger to trace the poetry inscribed on the brass plate, no doubt the work of Everett. I reread the verse, made a small and tired smile. Madeline would've called it jingle-jangle, absolutely dreadful poetry.

I found it tender.

Winterberry was right, life was seldom fair. I really wanted to see this woman again, in fact had expected to sooner or later. I touched my binoculars, thinking of the pair Madeline owned and how I described them to Claire when she asked me for Christmas gift ideas. I wanted to show them off to Madeline like a schoolboy, tell her that I'd been reading up on ospreys because of the interest she sparked. I wanted her to know that I wasn't carrying around the weight of the world any more, that the wind was back in my sails. I wanted to tell her how much our chance encounter meant last fall, how her words rang true about so many things.

*Shallow is the life that leaves no scars, Jack Elliot.*

I'd never get the chance. I stood and walked over to the railing, looked out at the water. The obituary would tell me Madeline's ashes were scattered here during a sunrise ceremony. She was with her husband now, I thought, where she wanted to be. I remembered how she pined for Everett, sitting alone here and feeling his spirit among the ospreys. She'd found her peace. For all I knew the straggler showed her the way when he finally flew away and became a distant speck in the sky.

The gentle waves lapped the marshes behind me.

Madeline's death and the spreading of her ashes made me think of Simon Trask and Rachel Pond. Their deaths had been so abrupt and difficult for us. While therapy had enabled Claire and me to resolve many issues, the grieving piece remained jagged. Neither one of us got the chance to say goodbye, the lack of closure magnified by not attending the funeral services and having any correspondence with the family.

I didn't know it at the time but we would achieve closure in late spring.

I would be sleeping in late one Sunday morning, Claire's side of the bed empty when I got up. When I padded into the kitchen to get some coffee I happened to see her standing near a window in the dining room. She had her arms folded and was staring out at the dogwoods with one of those faraway looks in her eyes. The dogwoods were bathed in morning sunlight and in full blossom, one pink the other white. I didn't want to disturb her so I backed quietly away. I announced my entry a few moments later with a cough or two in the hallway.

Much to my surprise, the next afternoon when I got home from work the two dogwoods were gone. They'd been dug up and taken away, the holes filled in and smoothed over. When asked about it later, Claire got tight-lipped and simply replied it was something she needed to do. I let it go at that. The truth be known, the dogwoods had made me uncomfortable ever since I learned of their origin.

The removal of the dogwoods spurred me into action with Rachel's book. As much as I treasured *The Natural*, I knew in my heart I couldn't keep it. Accepting gifts from students is morally thorny, especially one as extravagant as this. Claire was initially stunned when she learned of the book's value, but reminded me of Rachel's financial independence and wealth. We talked about various options and I eventually decided to place the book on permanent loan to Guilford's special collections library. The college's head librarian was overjoyed with the acquisition and agreed to my conditions, donor anonymity and the right of Rachel's family to retrieve the book at any time.

A final part of the story would unfold a few weeks later.

I was home alone on a Saturday morning doing some spring cleanup in the backyard, including raking, gathering broken branches and tidying the gazebo. While working by the gazebo I noticed the topsoil had sunk where the dogwoods once stood. I decided to redig the holes and place a few large rocks inside, preventing future sinkholes.

When I dug down a few feet, my shovel grazed against something solid, a small block of wood I thought. I put the shovel aside and knelt down, removing the object from the ground. It was a small wooden box. After brushing its surface clean I realized it was a hinged jewelry box, one Claire had kept on her bedroom bureau. It hadn't been in the ground very long.

I stared at the box for what seemed like an eternity. I felt like a trespasser who had no right unearthing the box and holding it, let alone viewing its contents. I told myself to put it back where I found it, fill in the hole and walk away. If the contents had anything to do with Trask I was accomplishing nothing but reopening old wounds, undoing all the healing that had taken place.

But I couldn't walk away. While I'd forgiven Claire for what she'd done, the shock of finding the hidden emails in the attic last fall still left me guarded and cautious. Claire knew it would take time for me to trust her again and finding something like this wasn't helping matters. For all I knew, the box contained more love letters or other romantic keepsakes from Trask, more secrets kept from my prying eyes.

I lifted the lid and looked inside, and realized in an instant I couldn't have been more wrong. The box was empty save for two faded dogwood blossoms, one pink the other white. I got a vision of her staring at the trees from the dining room a few Sundays ago. I realized now she'd been taking in the blossoms for the last time, just before the trees were removed.

She'd found her closure, made her peace.

I closed the lid and returned the wooden box to the hole, making sure it was positioned just as I found it. I straightened and took a deep breath, stood there for a few minutes leaning on the shovel. It didn't take long to figure out what I wanted to do. I refilled the hole but not before placing a ribbon inside the box, a pale blue one.

HOW LONG I DRIFTED AWAY I COULDN'T be sure, but the afternoon peace was shattered by the sound of a fast approaching Amtrak train. I could hear it from far away, rumbling and clattering down the tracks. I turned around on the deck and watched a line of dingy passenger cars roll by, shaking the earth and lumbering across the drawbridge.

The train scattered a flock of seagulls at the far end of the boardwalk. Once it disappeared, though, they flew back and prowled the shoreline for food. With nothing better to do I tracked them with the binoculars. One swooped down and landed on a boardwalk bench and began pecking at some bread crust someone had left behind. It separated a piece and shook its head as if in spasm, then went after more. Several other seagulls landed nearby, perching themselves on the railing.

In a little while I saw Claire and Nathan making their way from underneath the drawbridge. By now, the boardwalk had emptied. I looked at my wristwatch, surprised that several hours had passed so quickly. I waved to them but they didn't see me, their attention focused instead on the seagulls by the bench. The seagulls startled at the movement and sound of approaching footsteps, flapping away in different directions.

I was watching the seagulls scatter when I first saw the two of them, high in the sky.

They were soaring effortlessly on wind currents, their wing beats unhurried and gentle. At first I thought they were eagles but when I looked through the binoculars I could see they weren't. They each had that distinctive crook in the elbows of their wings, their undersides mostly white. They were adults, probably mates, their wingspans easily approaching five feet, probably more. They were graceful, magnificent creatures, their beauty enhanced by the backdrop of the deep blue sky.

My eyes widened and I could feel my heart thumping against my ribs.

I waved excitedly and got Claire's attention, pointed upwards. At first she thought I was directing her attention toward a seagull, one that had flown away from the others with a small fish in its mouth. She turned and shot me a puzzled expression. I shook my head and stuck my hand higher in the sky. She shielded her eyes from the sun and saw the ospreys this time, pulled on Nathan's sleeve to show him. They both craned their necks and watched them circle.

A few minutes later, one of the ospreys peeled away and swooped down toward the nest. It was a little larger than its partner. Its wing beats were slow and steady, enabling it to glide down and scout the inlet before soaring upwards again. As it did so it passed right over me. I could clearly see its white head and dark crown, the stripe extending through the eye down the cheek.

The two called out to each other with rising, shrill whistles, a sharp contrast to the monotonous screeching of seagulls. Together they descended toward the nest, their large wings spread full and wide. One approached the nest and hovered above, using rapid wing beats to stabilize its motion before settling inside. The beats from the great wings were loud—a resounding *flap-flap-flap-flap-flap*—the sound cutting across the marshland in the quiet afternoon air. A few minutes later its mate did the same.

I must admit I got carried away with all of this, found it strangely exhilarating. I experienced a rush when I first spotted them in the sky, their arrival providing a sense of beauty and wonder. Whatever else I had on my mind didn't matter, the power of nature as invigorating as it was cleansing. For reasons I can't describe, the rhythm of what I saw instilled a sense of purpose and hope. It was a renewal of sorts, an appreciation of a simple joy.

I turned from the nest toward Claire and Nathan. They'd watched the ospreys but now pushed off from the railing, deciding to have a foot race along a length of the boardwalk toward me. When they stopped, out of breath, Claire playfully hooked an arm through Nathan's and waved to me with the other. They had a look of mischief and delight on their faces, both energized and happy.

I descended the deck's staircase and moved to join them, craning my neck for one last look at the ospreys. A smile settled in the corner of my mouth as my eyes skirted back and forth from the ospreys to Claire and Nathan.

They'd found their way home.

# About the Author

Jeff Turner is a Waterford, Connecticut born author.

As a lifelong academic and Professor of Human Development and Family Relations, Turner is no stranger to publishing. The textbooks on which he has worked have been used in over three hundred colleges, both nationally and in translation internationally.

However, after devoting many years to creating these college-level textbooks, Turner could not resist the urge to turn away from the pedagogical, and to devote himself to the craft of fiction. Using his free time over the course of several years, Turner made this yearning a reality.

*The Way Back* is his debut novel.